The School Run

About the author

Ali Lowe has been a journalist for twenty years.
She has written for bridal magazines, parenting
titles, websites and newspapers in London and then
Australia, after she moved to Sydney seventeen
years ago on a trip that was meant to last a year. She
was Features Editor at *OK!* in London, where she
memorably stalked celebrities in Elton John's garden
at his annual White Tie and Tiara ball.

Ali lives on the northern beaches of Sydney
with her husband and three young children.
The School Run is her third novel.

Also by Ali Lowe

The Running Club
The Trivia Night

ALI LOWE

The School Run

HODDER &
STOUGHTON

First published in Great Britain in 2024 by Hodder & Stoughton
An Hachette UK company

1

Copyright © Ali Lowe 2024

A CIP catalogue record for this title is available from the British Library

Hardback ISBN 978 1 399 71780 9
Trade Paperback ISBN 978 1 399 71781 6
ebook ISBN 978 1 399 71782 3

Typeset in Plantin by Manipal Technologies Limited

Printed and bound in Great Britain by Clays Ltd, Elcograf S.p.A.

Hodder & Stoughton policy is to use papers that are natural, renewable
and recyclable products and made from wood grown in sustainable forests.
The logging and manufacturing processes are expected to conform to the
environmental regulations of the country of origin.

Hodder & Stoughton Ltd
Carmelite House
50 Victoria Embankment
London EC4Y 0DZ

www.hodder.co.uk

For Rafferty, Savannah and Atticus

Prologue

A figure treads the winding pavement that hugs the rugged coastline between St Ignatius' Boys' Grammar School and the heart of Pacific Pines. The path itself is small, and next to it runs the main highway, abuzz in rush hour with black or blue or silver cars full of boys: one, two or sometimes three. Boys in straw boaters and smart woollen blazers with green lapels and a motif on the breast pocket featuring two lions, stately on their back legs and haloed by a Latin motto felix quia fortis (happiness through strength). Boys with angry red spots and braces and furry top lips, with squeaky voices, deep voices, quiet voices. Boys who are tall, short, chubby, lithe.

It is ten o'clock at night and the road is shrouded in blackness, save for the sporadic bursts of dull orange lamplight. The School Run, the name given to this busy thoroughfare by the locals, is strangely quiet this evening. It will clutter later, this main passage into town, when St Ignatius' – or Iggy's, as they call it – closes its doors and ejects the throng of prospective parents who are inside the Great Hall with their eleven-year-old sons quaffing cheese and wine, praying their blessed boy has done enough to get him over the line and inside Iggy's hallowed inner sanctum! That a door will open for him, which in itself will open a lifetime of doors.

Most parents have already put in the groundwork: obtained referral letters from external sports coaches and piano teachers, written lengthy, platitude-laden letters to the board of governors, made sizeable 'donations' to the school's charitable foundation. Perhaps they've even joined the principal's tennis club. The lengths these 'perfect' parents will go to in order to showboat their 'perfect' families on Gala Day is a joke. All of it is a joke – the ludicrously pricey uniforms, the shiny pews, the erect backs singing from dog-eared hymn sheets, the pristine white painted lines on the shamrock-green sports field with the sign that warns, Do not walk on the grass!

The walker presses an earbud deep into the canal of their ear and jabs at the lit-up screen of a phone. The noise drowns out the roar of the ocean as it smashes against the cliffs below, leaving behind pristine white spray that slides off the moss on the rocks. There is nothing special about the sea when you live beside it – it becomes as generic, as unremarkable, as stirring milk into tea or pulling on a rugby boot. The water is not afforded so much as a blink as it sucks back out, dramatically, building up its strength to smash the rocks again. Nor is the vague rumble of thunder out over the ocean, or the slow grumble of the approaching car. Why would it be? This is just a road after all, nothing new. In fact, so tuned out is this human being to their sinister surrounds that there is barely a flinch at the screech of the brakes as the bonnet performs a scoop and a toss, throwing everything – the body, the phone and the earbuds – like papers in the wind, up, up into the air.

It is a sliding-doors moment: a stroke of misfortune, made by choice. If only the earbuds had been left at home! If only the advice of a mother, offered years ago, had actually sunk in: 'Listen out for cars!' However, there is no time to contemplate any of this, no time for any kind of rational thought. It happens too fast for that. But for those few seconds, as momentum renders the walker completely weightless, before skull meets concrete and the hapless pedestrian notes the venom in the eyes of the driver below, a memory of an old Latin tutor will play loud and clear in the mid-section of the brain, sped-up and on loop.

Memento vivere. Remember to live.

SATURDAY

I

Kaya

Kaya Sterling does not dislike Estella Munro. The fact her new neighbour appears aloof and self-satisfied does not faze her. As far as Kaya is concerned, encountering someone like Estella Munro is a bit like drinking a flat white with bitter froth. The first acrid taste cannot be all there is to her – there has to be something pleasant beneath.

Kaya and Ollie have only lived in their new home for four days. Palm Cottage, which is not really a cottage at all by virtue of two spacious floors and four bedrooms, sits on the cliffside looking proudly out to sea, the first in a row of five houses a little along from the winding bend that leads from the heart of Pacific Pines to St Ignatius' Grammar. Four bedrooms is far more than they need for just the two of them and Kaya feels they rattle around in the big house, but Paul had insisted they move to his childhood neighbourhood and to the house he had always cycled past as a boy. He had loved the way it sits clad in a jacket of snowy white slats along the cliff face, with an overgrown, oval backyard fenced off to the perilous headland beyond; and how the beauty of the house can only be appreciated from the water, sitting atop the cliff face as it does, or as a steering wheel is twisted round that perilous turn, leaving the heart of Pacific Pines far behind in the rear-view mirror.

One day, Kaya will charter a boat so she and Ollie can see their new home from its best vantage point, bobbing together on the very waves they hear caressing the cliff face as they fall asleep each night. She has added it to her never-ending to-do list stuck to the imposing chrome double-doored fridge, which is also way too big for their requirements: 'paint shed', 'make new friends', 'charter boat'.

Estella has been standing on Kaya's new driveway for less than a minute, both of them under the hot October sun, with Bandit weaving through their legs as retrievers do. Kaya has already watched her neighbour take in the front yard up close, her pursed lips suggesting disapproval. The previous owners of Palm Cottage had introduced a variety of species of plant in both the front and back gardens, the effect being an unruly, almost English feel, wild and overgrown, unlike the landscaped affair next door with its perfectly clipped hedge and slick, pruned palms.

Pacific Pines, Kaya is swiftly learning, is a suburb that is vastly different from its neighbours. It sits neatly at the bottom of the headland that is one of the ancient arms to the Pacific Ocean, providing a gateway for cruise liners and cargo ships to Tasmania, New Zealand, Fiji and the United States. Ocean View Parade, to all intents and purposes a winding cliff road, is the main thoroughfare connecting Pacific Pines to nearby Lawton Sands with St Ignatius' Grammar standing statuesque at the highest point of the headland before the cliff road descends into the outskirts of the next town.

Kaya has heard the School Run can be arduous when there is traffic, this single route out of town, which is why many of the kids take the cliff steps when they get to the bends. The steps descend steeply down to a picturesque, white-sanded beach, which itself leads to the coffee shops and main street of Pacific Pines, a suburb bustling with wealth and entitlement.

And here is Kaya's new neighbour, the embodiment of privilege. She is shorter than Kaya, with a shiny bob that bounces lightly on her square shoulders, indicative of a salon blow-dry. She is dressed in a simple, knee-length linen shift dress. So far she has only said, 'Munro, number six. Here is your post. Damn postman always gets us mixed up,' and has held out a bejewelled hand to shake the very ends of Kaya's fingers, and Kaya has felt the frostiness of the other woman's touch despite the beat of the spring sun. But in these fleeting moments, Kaya has already made an assessment of her new neighbour, and it is that she is icy and devoid of softness. She makes this assumption in one part of her brain and immediately berates herself with another, because people have bad days, don't they? Not everyone is as good at small talk as she is.

Estella looks Kaya briefly in the eye before her gaze snaps to Ollie as he dribbles his soccer ball on the tiled deck outside their new front door: bounce, bounce, bounce. For Kaya the sound is as familiar as birdsong, and as comforting (if she can hear the bounce, she knows Ollie is near) but Estella squints dramatically each time plastic meets ceramic.

'Ollie!' Kaya is suddenly conscious of the noise. 'Please stop the bouncing until the lady has—'

'Munro,' the woman snaps, as though she thinks Kaya has forgotten her name already, as if she has pegged Kaya as one of those women who cannot process basic information. She looks over Kaya's shoulder and into the house beyond, down the hall, possibly in search of another human, for proof of life. She will not find any.

'Munro with a "U", *not* an "O" like Marilyn,' she says.

'That pesky "O".' Kaya smiles. 'Some like it *not*.'

Estella's lips move stiffly upward and Kaya feels the heat rise up her neck. Perhaps Estella just didn't get the joke! A bottle is thrust into her hands. 'This is for you and your husband,' Estella says. 'A 2017 Châteauneuf-du-Pape.'

'Oh,' Kaya stutters, taken aback. The thrusting of the bottle had felt more perfunctory than welcoming, suggesting that a gift from the cellar to one's neighbours is just the 'done' thing in these parts, but Kaya realises that even if the sentiment is not necessarily there, it is a kind gesture, nonetheless, and she appreciates it.

'Thank you so much, Estella,' Kaya says. 'This looks lovely. It really is kind of you. But, just so you're aware, my husband is . . .'

The words trail off, as they always do when Kaya delivers The News.

'Oh,' Estella says. 'Is your husband . . . *dry?*'

'Dry?' Kaya does not compute.

'Does he not *drink*?' Estella pulls her jacket closed.

'Oh no, Paul's not dry,' Kaya tells her. 'He's dead.'

She doesn't mean to say it quite like that, so abruptly, the word 'dead' fired like a bullet from a gun, but she has learned it is sometimes easier to simply rip off the Band-Aid. She has also learned it is best to use the word 'dead', however confronting it may be, instead of a less jarring turn of phrase that could be open to interpretation, such as 'gone' or 'left us'. These might suggest divorce, adultery even, and neither of these things apply to her marriage to Paul, or the way he was taken from her.

'Good Lord!' Estella's palm spans the breadth of her collarbone. '*Dead?*'

'Yes. As in deceased.' *No longer here. Gone. Left us.*

Ollie resumes his bouncing.

'Right,' says Estella, stumped.

'I'm so sorry,' Kaya tells her. 'To come out with it like that, I mean.'

'When?'

'Well, just now . . .'

'No, no. I mean, when did your husband . . . *pass?*'

'Oh!' Kaya touches her forehead, an underwhelming face palm. 'Paul died a year ago.'

Estella rubs her chest in a circular motion, as if she is trying to massage the stress away. Kaya waits silently as her neighbour processes her own grief.

'How?'

'Cancer,' Kaya chirps. It is force of habit. A way to try and soften the blow for others, to trivialise the last nineteen months of hell so that the recipient of The News does not feel awkward.

'I see.' Estella twists her wedding ring on her finger. 'My deepest condolences.'

'I just . . . I find it easier to tell people straight out, because then they're not wondering what I've done with Paul,' Kaya says. 'You know, if I've got him stashed in a cupboard upstairs!'

Estella's left eyebrow raises a fraction.

'I mean, I did have him in the cupboard for a while back in Perth.' Kaya hates herself for being so glib. 'But then when we arrived here in Pacific Pines, we scattered the ashes. Paul now currently resides partly at his old school, partly in the ocean . . .'

'Quite!' Estella turns her head towards Ollie, whip-lash-fast. Kaya has seen movies in which the baddie breaks someone's neck with less force. 'Do you work?'

'Me?' Kaya is thrown. 'Yes, I'm a physio . . . I'm hoping to rent a room at Total Physio in Lawton Sands, once Ollie and I have settled a little.'

'I see. And how old is Ollie?'

'He's twelve today.' Kaya turns to Ollie. 'Ollie, say hello to Mrs Munro.'

Ollie looks up. 'Hello, Mrs Munro,' he says in the mono-tone voice kids reserve for greeting teachers in assembly. Kaya waits for her new neighbour to baulk at the formality and say, 'Happy birthday! Call me Estella, *please*,' like other friendly street dwellers might, but she doesn't. She merely stares intently at Ollie before looking to her hands to study her own fingernails.

It is always the same when Kaya tells people The News – they forget how to use their hands. Fingers drum on surfaces, ears are scratched until they glow red. She understands it, of course. How could a person know how to respond if they haven't experienced this kind of loss themselves? She'd been like that, before Paul. She hadn't understood the intricacies of grief or the politics of discussing it, so she does not begrudge the awkward hands, or the blinking eyes and the 'Um, well, anyway . . .'s. People are just people after all.

The mums at Pacific Pines Primary School had been the same. She hadn't meant to tell any of them, not on Ollie's first day, but they had all fussed around her in the school yard yesterday, cooing over Ollie and asking where Mr Sterling was. Was he at work? Were they *divorced*? (And if so, she was in good company! All the *cool* mums in Pacific Pines community were divorced. Take Tammy O'Farrell – she was a riot! Always on the margaritas and swiping right on Tinder! They were secretly jealous of her, they said, because their husbands were all like overgrown children. Oh, to be single again – although the sex part, *good Lord no*! They didn't have the energy for *that*!)

And so Kaya told them about Paul, about how she'd lost him to cancer, and she had watched as they tried not to let their eyes widen and hands fidget and their speech begin to fail them. Kaya knows that each of them fears, deep down, that if they get close to her story, it might happen to them, as if death is catching somehow, like a promiscuous strain of flu.

As she stands on the driveway talking to Estella, Kaya feels a flash of gratitude for Bec Lloyd, the kindly woman who left a box of cupcakes on the doorstep at Palm

Cottage the previous morning with a note that read: *Welcome to Pacific Pines! Please enjoy! Bec x.* Kaya had been so touched, and the cupcakes had been delicious – rich, red velvet slathered in sweet cream-coloured fondant, with 'welcome' written in blue icing on each and every one. Kaya had put the business card, printed with the words *Cakes by Bec* and a sketch of what looked like Cupid, the Roman god of love, eating a giant cupcake, up on the fridge next to the to-do list as a reminder of how kind Bec had been.

Estella turns away from Ollie and fixes her gaze back on Kaya. 'Is Oliver a sporty child?' she asks.

'Very.'

'Tall, isn't he?'

'Yes. He takes after his—'

'Rugby?'

'Yes, he does enjoy—'

'Union? League? League would be my guess.'

'Gosh,' laughs Kaya. 'This feels a little like speed dating!'

'Oh dear, does it?' Estella's brow furrows. 'I wouldn't know!'

Kaya cringes. Does Estella think she is on the dating scene so soon after losing Paul? Should she clarify that she is not? Or that, even if she *was*, she is most definitely not the type to speed date? She hates the idea of someone judging her in so short a time, just like Estella is doing now. The woman probably thinks Kaya is some sex-hungry widow, in town to land herself a wealthy, married man. *Oh, the shame . . .*

'Kaya?' Estella all but snaps her fingers. 'I asked if Ollie played rugby league?'

Kaya blinks. 'Union, actually. But really, it's all about rowing for Ollie.'

Estella regards her suspiciously. 'Rowing,' she mutters to herself. 'That *is* unusual. Who does he row for?'

'Klara Bay Rowing Club in Perth,' says Kaya. 'Ollie was the youngest oarsman they've ever had, actually. He recently won the—'

'I see,' says Estella. 'And are you Catholic?'

'I'm sorry, are we . . .?'

Another sigh. '*Catholic?*'

Kaya is thrown by the rapid segue. She thought they were talking about sport!

'No.' She shakes her head. 'We're not really religious.'

The truth is, Kaya did go to a Catholic school, but she has never been a woman of faith. Except when Paul was dying. Then she had prayed like they told her to at school, at church on her knees, and yet nothing happened and Paul had died anyway, and now she feels positively hard done by. So no, she isn't religious. After all, what has God ever done for Kaya?

'A non-believer, then?'

'Well, I suppose if you have to categorise me, then yes.'

Estella's shoulders drop a little, as though a weight has been lifted. 'And Oliver is currently in Year Six at Pines Primary?'

'It's just Ollie. And yes.'

'So he'll be going to Pacific Pines High School this coming January, I presume?'

'We've applied to St Ignatius' Grammar, actually,' Kaya says and she is sure she sees the other woman flinch. 'My husband Paul wanted him to go. It was his last wish.'

It is true. The only reason she and Ollie upped sticks from the comfort of Klara Bay and now reside in this wealthy school community four thousand kilometres away is because Kaya had promised Paul, on his deathbed, she would do it, that she would uproot herself and Ollie and move to Pacific Pines to get him in to Iggy's.

'So, you are an atheist, but you'd like your son to have a Catholic education?' Estella asks, her head tilted to the side in faux confusion.

Kaya shrugs. She knows it sounds sacrilegious, but Paul had been raised in the Catholic faith, and he'd turned out OK, and so Kaya had agreed to it. Paul had considered it a school of opportunities and so why wouldn't she also want that for Ollie?

'Anyway, it's only really worth the effort if the boy is baptised,' Estella chirps. 'You know, Kaya, you wouldn't be the first person to move to Pacific Pines to try and get their child into St Ignatius' Grammar. I mean, the competition for places is *insane*. Two hundred students for one hundred and twenty places! Of course, in the past, you would simply put your child's name down at birth and he'd be guaranteed a place, but Ursula Deacon changed the policy when she came in as principal two years ago, so this will be the third annual Gala Day. It's not a bad thing, I suppose because it does weed out the wheat from the chaff. Not that it will be a challenge for *my* boys.'

Kaya must look confused or overwhelmed or both because Estella leans in and says, 'You *do* know about Gala Day, Kaya?'

Kaya nods. Ollie is registered for it. In three days' time, he will join those two hundred other pre-teens vying for a place at Iggy's in one long day of assessment – first on the sporting field and then in an interview – followed by a parents' cheese and wine party afterwards. Pretty gruelling for an eleven-year-old boy (so far as Kaya knows, St Ignatius' Grammar is the only school in the country that has such an elite and brutal selection process and offers places so close to the start date), but Ollie seems OK with it – and if Ollie doesn't mind, neither does she.

'Gala Day is being run by Ursula Deacon's son Sam this year,' says Estella. 'Have you heard of him?'

'No, I don't think so.'

'He's the head of sport.' Estella looks out across Kaya's garden, pensive. 'He was away playing rugby for Saracens in England and moved back to Australia a few months ago. He's the one you need to impress. But, like I said, you do have a much higher chance of entry if your son is baptised. Fortunately, we are a Catholic family,' muses Estella. 'The twins were baptised a few years ago, and will be confirmed next year.'

'You have twins? How lovely.'

'Archie and Jonty. Identical. Both academic and *very* sporty – in fact they're off somewhere playing cricket right now. Definitely Iggy's-bound.'

'Oh! They have places already?'

'Well, no.' Estella straightens her back. 'But they will. On their own merit, of course, but it helps to have friends in high places, and I am very good friends with Martha Weaver, Felix Weaver's mother.'

'I'm afraid I don't know who Felix is,' says Kaya, feeling like she has failed yet another test. Should she know Felix Weaver as *well* as Sam Deacon, the sports master?

Estella feigns shock. 'Felix is the outgoing school captain at Iggy's! Delightful boy. Martha and I are very close.' She crosses her index and middle fingers and holds them up to denote just *how* tight she is with the school captain's mother.

'Naturally, Martha has put in a good word with Ursula Deacon for the twins already,' Estella continues. 'In fact, Felix will also be helping to spot the talent at Gala Day – it's been the departing school captain's role for the last two years – so I'd be surprised if my boys are not hand-picked.'

Kaya wonders if Estella has not contradicted herself. First she said her boys will get into the school on their own merit, and now she's saying she thinks they'll get a leg-up because of their mother's connections. Perhaps natural talent just isn't enough at this elite college.

'How wonderful.' Kaya hopes Estella does not sense the weariness in her voice. 'I'm sure your boys will be an asset to the school. Am I right in thinking you have a daughter too?' Kaya already knows the answer to this, because she has heard the two of them arguing in the garden: yelling and hissing and snarling. Yesterday she heard the teen shout, 'You're so old, *Estella*. What would *you* even know?'

and then Estella's clipped reply, 'Now, now, mind those pesky hormones, Felicity!'

Estella's pupils are pin dots. Her skin, flushed and alive when she was speaking about her twins, has turned dull, the glow extinguished like the blowing-out of a candle.

'I do,' she says. 'Felicity is seventeen. She's off to university in January – she has just finished her exams at Asher's Girls' School. Asher's is the sister school to St Ignatius' in case you don't know. I went there as a girl, actually. We both did, my husband and I. What I mean is Conrad – *Dr Conrad Munro* – is an Iggy's old boy, although he was three years ahead of me. He was school captain, in fact.'

'That's interesting. So was Paul!'

Estella folds her arms. 'Well, why didn't you mention that? The sons of old boys definitely get preferential treatment when it comes to school admission.'

'I didn't get the chance . . .'

'And your surname?'

The quick-fire question round is back.

'Sterling. Kaya and Ollie Sterling.'

Estella pauses. She bites indelicately on the lacquered red tip of her thumbnail. 'Nope,' she says after a moment. 'I don't recall him. Conrad may, he's better with names than me.'

Kaya opens her mouth to offer more details about Paul, but Estella beats her to it.

'Well,' she says, 'I must get going. My trainer is arriving at twelve. Carlos is the best in Pacific Pines. Do let me know if you'd like his number.' She looks at Kaya's hips. 'Anyway, welcome Kaya. I hope you and *Ollie* will be very happy here.'

'Thank you,' says Kaya, slightly bemused by it all.

'Oh, and what kind of car do you drive? A Holden?'

'No, a—'

'Good. As you know, Holdens have gone out of production, so there's been a spate of thefts recently – parts are astronomical on the black market! Doesn't apply to us of course – our cars are all relatively new.'

All? thinks Kaya. *How many does the woman have?*

Estella turns back down the driveway, her quilted designer bag swinging about her hips at the end of a gold chain-mail strap. Kaya watches her go, wondering why her neighbour has brought her expensive bag with her from next door. Has she done it to make Kaya, in her denim shorts and a vest top and covered in plant mulch from moving pots around all morning, feel bad about herself? Kaya blinks the thought away, annoyed at her own attitude. She does not want to dislike Estella – after all, wasn't the purpose of the woman's visit to welcome her, with wine?

When Estella reaches the front gate, she turns around. 'Pacific Pines High School really isn't a bad alternative, Kaya,' she says. 'I'm sure Ollie will fit in perfectly there if he doesn't get a place at Iggy's.' Then she unlatches her own fence and disappears from view.

Kaya feels her shoulders slump in defeat because she realises she has lost a competition she didn't know she was a part of.

Ollie sidles up beside her. 'She is *awful*,' he says, his top lip pulled up to his nose.

'She isn't that bad,' Kaya laughs. 'I'm sure she's nice deep down. Some people just don't make a good first impression. Anyway, let's get cleaned up and go and get some birthday ice cream!'

Ollie bounds off to change his muddy shorts, and as she stands watching the closed gate in front of her, Kaya wonders what Paul would have made of Estella. She is pretty sure he would have been disappointed. Women like her always got his goat: the pushy, self-important types. Women who carry an air of superiority inside their extravagant designer handbags. But really, it is no use wondering what he might have thought because he is not here, and this means he can no longer influence Kaya with his amusing character assessments. And even if she does hear his voice everywhere and his sardonic one-liners in the strangest of places, she understands that now he has been gone a year, it is time to make her own mind up about things and start afresh here in Pacific Pines. So she decides that even though Estella does not radiate the warmth of, say, a plug-in heater, she is not downright hideous, either, and at this point in time, before she gets to know the *real* Estella Munro, Kaya is prepared to take any form of friendship she can get.

2

Estella

'Not a hope in hell, my dear,' is what Estella says to Conrad when she enters number six Ocean View Parade after visiting her new neighbour. She shuts the front door with a flourish, flaps her arms about under the air-conditioning vent to dry her perspiring armpits and moves her large Jo Malone lime-and-mandarin candle a little to the left. Felicity is in the habit of taking it upstairs to mask the smell of the cannabis she doesn't know Estella knows she smokes. But Estella isn't stupid. She can detect a waft of weed at twenty paces!

The previous week she found a ready-rolled joint in Felicity's jewellery box and she had taken it and smoked it on the stone bench at the end of the garden while the rest of the family was at Pizza the Action at Pacific Pines Mall. Well, it wasn't as if Felicity could ask Estella if she'd seen it, was it? Imagine it: 'Mum, where's my spliff?' Oh, how that had amused Estella later, as she devoured the leftover cheese supreme Conrad had brought home with him during a rather fervent attack of the munchies. To get one over on Felicity when Felicity thought she was getting one over on *her*!

'Not a hope in hell of what, my darling?' Conrad looks up from his newspaper. Estella believes he is the only man left on planet Earth who doesn't read the news on his iPhone. He flips the broadsheet in half with ease and picks up his espresso.

'Boy next door,' Estella clarifies. 'He won't be going to Iggy's.'

'Oh?'

'Well, they're not Catholic for starters.'

'Heavens above!' Conrad does the sign of the cross.

'Her husband passed away a year ago.'

Conrad looks up. 'A widow?'

'Yes, and she seemed quite nonchalant about it. Cracking jokes and so on.'

'You mean she wasn't weeping beneath a mourning veil?'

'She certainly was not.'

'Now, now, Estella! How did he die? The husband?'

'Cancer, she said.'

'Of the . . .?'

'I don't know. I'm hardly going to ask her what kind of cancer it was on the driveway, am I? That's *your* remit.' Estella looks out of the window and sees Jonty kick a green-and-gold rugby ball high from a tee set on the ground. It flies through the air and bounces against the fence where the end of the garden meets the cliff edge. If she had a dollar for every ball they've lost over that cliff! 'But the boy's sporty, apparently,' she muses. 'He *rows* of all things. Good at it, she said.'

'Rows? I'd think rowing would be very appealing to the school,' Conrad says.

'Rubbish!' Estella snapped. 'Iggy's wants rugby players, not someone to enter the Oxford and Cambridge boat race.'

'It's a prestigious sport,' Conrad says. 'And it is well known Iggy's are trying to widen their sporting pool, as it were. I'd say they'd be *very* impressed with a rower.'

'Rowing is obsolete. And anyway, we're hardly overrun by lakes on the coast, are we? Where's he going to row in Pacific Pines? The duck pond? Anyway, rower or not, I just don't think they have the credentials.'

Estella looks out of the window again. She has nothing against Kaya or Ollie personally, and she doesn't want to deny the boy a good education, but the competition is tough. The fact is, Iggy's offers their boys certain essential things no other school within miles does: prestige, sporting excellence, a university place in the bag, and of course the International Baccalaureate, which guarantees a boy's acceptance to universities around the world and not just Australia. Iggy's boys go to Yale, to Cambridge – not to mention the co-curricular travel. Estella wants these opportunities for Jonty and Archie – to see them travel to Fiji to play rugby and Whistler to ski and Paris to hone their languages and eat croissants and broaden their view of the world. She *aches* for it: for the prestige and status it will bring them and gird them with through life. For the status it will give *her*.

And the closure. The fact is, Estella needs to get her boys into that damn school with the cast-iron gates and the Latin motto and the shamrock green rugby fields so she can finally bury the demons of her past, put to bed the thing that happened to her on the sacred turf of Iggy's all those years ago. The thing that broke her and shattered her into a thousand pieces and took away any semblance of her once-owned softness needs to be redressed, to be made better, to be absolved, to be *closed*. And she can only do this – she can only bolt the door on the shadows that haunt her – if she gets her darling boys inside the inner sanctum of St Ignatius' Grammar.

'They'll get in.' Conrad's voice is weary. 'We've been at Mass every Sunday for the last two years for this precise reason. The twins are incredibly sporty . . .'

'Jonty is sporty.'

'Come on, darling. Archie isn't hopeless.'

'Oh, he is, Conny.' Estella opens the window to the garden.

'Give him some credit, my dear.'

'Archie couldn't catch a fucking cold,' she says to the fence that divides her place from Kaya Sterling's. She doesn't mean to be quite so brutal, but the fact is, Archie is terrible at sport, and Estella doesn't know how the actual hell she is going to get him through the Gala Day. 'You know it and I know it.'

She hears a rustle behind next-door's fence and hopes the woman and the little rower boy didn't hear her slander her own child. She quickly shuts the window and closes the blind.

'Well,' continues Conrad. 'Archie will get in on his academic ability in a flash. He's a straight-A child.'

'Yes, but they're not looking for academic excellence, are they? If they were, then Jonty would be screwed. It's the sports stars of the future they're looking for, and that is why I am worried about Archie.' She rolls her head on her shoulders. 'It's so stressful. I can't see a way around it.'

'Sweetheart, please stop worrying. We've done everything we can. I'll see if I can put another word in with Ursula Deacon, but then we have to leave it.'

'So you *are* treating her?'

'I can't say. Patient confidentiality.'

'Oh please. Lawton Hospital is hardly MI6, is it?'

'It is more than my job's worth, darling, and you know it. But what I *will* say is that I'm sure it will all be fine. If the worst happens, the twins will just go to Pacific Pines High.'

'Nope.' Estella sweeps her hair up into a low ponytail, as if she is tidying up the conversation, halting it. She pulls the hairband tight. 'That is not happening.'

'Anyway,' Conrad continues. 'Don't you have a referral letter from the mother of the school captain or something?'

'You know I do. I had to sign up for a whole term of those godawful craft classes to get it.'

Conrad's eyes flicker with amusement. 'At least we got a macramé owl out of it.'

Estella smiles. 'Anyway, it won't make a bit of difference because *everyone's* getting referral letters now. As soon as I told Bec I had a letter from Martha Weaver, she downed her oven gloves and trotted straight off to get one for Cooper.'

Estella swears Bec can only think for herself when it comes to sodding cakes!

'Yes, but *Bec's* letter wasn't from the school captain's family, was it?' Conrad says.

Estella nods reluctantly and plucks a notebook from the coffee table. She will put Ollie on her list and cross him off. This is something she loves to do – add things to her to-do list that she's already done. Sometimes, she will write things like 'Pay gas bill' and then score straight through it. It pleases her no end.

'What are you doing?'

'Adding Ollie to the competition list!'

Conrad has seen her adding to the list before. 'Estella, you *are* joking?'

'What?' She double-clicks the end of her pen, obstinate. 'I'm only keeping track. No harm in sizing up the opposition. It's not like I'm publishing it.'

Conrad shakes his head with an indulgent smile. 'Come on then! How many innocent Year Six boys have you got on there?'

'A few.' She studies her nailbeds. There are twenty in the running of which Estella is aware. She knows for a *fact* that Ursula Deacon prefers to enrol local Pacific Pines boys so that families can be hands-on with activities before and after school. Word has it she's had a nightmare in the past with boys who live out of town missing important matches because they can't get to the grounds in time; matches have even had to be forfeited. Local boys don't miss weekend sporting fixtures because of roadworks or tailbacks, or because a bridge is up.

'So, the boys on your list . . . Are you going to start picking them off, like in an Agatha Christie novel? Is this the Pacific Pines equivalent of *And Then There Were None*?'

She smiles. Conrad can be an awful dick sometimes, but Estella does love him.

'Right then,' he says. 'Who have we got?'

'No!' She closes the book with a pout.

'Come on, darling!' He is enjoying this, she can tell.

She sighs and opens the book again, like she was always going to. 'Cooper Lloyd.'

'Cooper?' Conrad laughs and coughs at the same time and bangs on his chest with his fist. 'You can't put your best friend's son at the top of your school hit list, you're Sage's godmother! Poor Bec and Tom.'

'Oh Conny, don't be so naïve!' Estella smiles. 'Bec may act all sweet and innocent, but she's far from it. Don't be blinded by the big blue eyes and the size eight arse, and the "Would you like a tray of red velvet cupcakes?" She's not as sweet as she looks!'

She sighs. 'Look Conny. I love Bec and Tom like family, you know that, but when it comes to Iggy's, I'm prepared to fight dirty.'

'Clearly!'

Estella chews on her cheek. 'Well, *great*,' she snaps and scores though Cooper's name. 'Now you've made me feel bad about it . . .'

They sit in silence for a moment. Estella picks irritably at the mohair blanket on the right arm of the sofa, folded into four. She stares at Ollie Sterling's name crossed out on the list and feels a growing sense of unease. She doesn't recall the name Sterling at all. As an Asher's old girl herself, she remembers all of the school captains at Iggy's from her years there, plus a few either side. She would remember the name Sterling, she is sure of it. Something about what Kaya has told her just doesn't add up.

'Do you remember a Paul Sterling from Iggy's?' she asks Conrad, her minor strop forgotten.

'Sterling, you say?' Conrad briefly closes his eyes and Estella watches his lids flicker in thought. 'No. I don't recall the name.'

'Me neither,' she says. 'I think our new neighbour is lying.'

'About what?'

'About her husband being an old boy,' says Estella. 'And he is not here to deny it, either, is he?'

Conrad sighs. 'You're like a very glamorous pig on a truffle hunt, my dear.'

Husband and wife are silent for a moment, until Estella speaks. 'I must give her credit where credit's due, because it is a very good tactic, I suppose,' she says as she inspects the irritating chip in her pillar-box-red nail polish that's been bothering her all morning. 'Unless you get found out.'

SUNDAY

3

Bec

Bec has three cakes to make by the afternoon. The first is a *Frozen*-themed cake for Melody Mason's fifth birthday, the second a three-tiered chocolate mud affair for Grace Adams' fourth wedding celebration at the yacht club (what was that phrase about husbands and hot dinners?) and the third, a traditional white fondant-covered sponge for Mal and Elaine Christie's silver wedding anniversary. She usually bakes the sponges the night before each party and decorates in the morning, allowing them time to cool overnight on a wire rack. And so here she is on a Sunday morning with an array of colourful sponges in front of her: eight twenty-inch layers in rainbow colours for Melody, four chocolate sponges for the tiers of Grace's wedding cake, and three red velvet sponges for the Christies.

It is quiet in the kitchen aside from the faint hum of the TV from the living room where Tom and the kids are finishing off a movie from the night before – something about a lost dog. Bec smiles. She adores her job and considers her time in the kitchen time away from life. Time that is just for her. Therapy, almost. The baking of a cake and the subsequent decorating (and this only applies to cakes because Bec is very reluctant and unqualified when it comes to baking savoury goods) is like meditation: the rhythmic mixing, the slathering, the smoothing, takes her away to a higher plane where she doesn't actually have to think about anything particularly taxing such as washing Cooper's rugby kit, or hassling Willow to tidy her room, or cleaning up after Sage's painting sessions. Today she has two hours of precious baking time before she leaves for Mass with the kids, and Bec intends to savour every last second.

Even when she worked full time at the busy Roman Room at the Australian Museum when Willow was small, she would bake at the weekend. That was how Cakes by Bec started, with the odd movie-themed cake for a child's party here and a silver anniversary cake there. She had loved teaching little kids about gladiators and Pompeii and life under the Caesars during the week, but when Cooper was born the long commute into the city proved too unworkable for her and she turned to full-time baking.

Sometimes the two worlds serendipitously collide. A few months back, she was commissioned to make a giant mud cake in the shape of the Roman Colosseum for an esteemed Latin professor's seventieth birthday and the experience had brought her infinite joy. The man himself had been a rather grumpy, self-important type (a flourless sponge?) and far too serious an academic to appreciate the trickiness of fashioning travertine limestone and volcanic rock out of coloured fondant, not to mention the bust of the emperor Vespasian, founder of the Flavian dynasty, in marzipan and wrapped in gold leaf. But he had offered a generous nod of approval nonetheless, and his wife (an effervescent lemon drizzle) had been ecstatic. It had been such a thrill for Bec to combine her two eclectic passions in one, and she had worked on the cake for way longer than she should have for just four hundred dollars. It had worked out at about twenty dollars an hour when you factored in baking and creating time, the cost of ingredients and the half-tank of petrol it took to drive it out west.

But for Bec it is not about the money, it is about the satisfaction. It's about doing a good job. She hasn't had any complaints in over a decade of baking cakes (and she must have made close to a thousand) and she doesn't want one now. Well, there had been that *one* complaint, right at the start. At the time she had considered it most unfortunate, but it had actually been quite fortuitous as it turned out. It had all been because of her engagement ring. She'd been wiping cake mix off her fingers and back into the bowl when the emerald-cut diamond centre stone, which unbeknownst to her was loose in its claw setting, dropped into the batter of a seventh birthday cake and chipped the tooth of the little child's elderly grandfather. Estella Munro (a sharp-tasting lemon curd) had been livid that little Felicity's party had ended with her father (*definitely* a sour coffee sponge) being rushed to the emergency dentist in Lawton Sands at a devastating cost to his pocket *and* his emotional wellbeing. The family had threatened to sue, but Bec had arrived on Estella Munro's doorstep the following day clutching her own seven-year-old daughter Willow's hand, and baby Cooper bouncing on her hip in a sort of, 'Look! I'm a mum too! Please don't be too hard on me!' way. She had promised to bake Estella's next occasion cake, and the one after that, for free. And so there, on the threshold of Estella's home, the other woman's icy stare had eventually melted because she was also a new mother to sleepless twin boys and she was in the trenches, too. And as the two women chatted, Willow and Felicity declared themselves best friends, demanding a play date the following week.

That was, and is to date, Bec's one and only baking cock-up, and, as it happens, she gained a best friend out of it. Yes, Estella can be caustic – she can be downright offensive sometimes. But when the chips are down, she is dependable, she is safe. When Bec's mum had been sick, Estella had rallied – no softness, no hugs, but practical help: babysitting, lifts to the hospital, frozen-meal deliveries. These were the things that had sustained Bec during that time. They had shared secrets over the years as they drained bottles of Pinot Noir. Their friendship had grown in depth and respect. It had celebrated ups and plenty of downs – and it had all started thanks to the fortuitous mis-placement of an emerald-cut jewel between the lilac and yellow layers of a vanilla-flavoured rainbow cake.

Bec has had the largest slice of the Pacific Pines cake-making pie ever since, and it is a roaring trade. Not many mothers she knows in this seaside community have time to make their own children's birthday cakes – they are all so busy with work, or exercise classes, or running their homes. Bec once asked Estella why she didn't make birthday cakes for Flick or the twins, and Estella had cack-led. 'Firstly,' she'd said, 'I don't want to walk around with food dye in my cuticles for weeks on end like you do, and secondly, I'm not having Tanya Carter-Cohen arrive at my house to pick up Anais and feast her eyes on some shit show of a cake. That's why I get *you* to do it, and Tanya is none the wiser.'

Bec has been baking for her own children since Willow's first birthday, and she is now eighteen. She could probably recall every single one if she were given a pen and paper, but she has her favourites: the chocolate mud Care Bear cake for Willow's sixth birthday, the rainbow My Little Pony cake aged eight, the caramel Barbie cake for the big one-o, and most recently, the iPhone cake. Willow still hasn't outgrown this annual tradition, although Bec suspects it may change now she is on the cusp of leaving home. The whole idea of this, of Willow packing up for university in a few short months, is almost too much to bear, but Bec tells herself that she will at least still have two of her babies in the nest.

Cooper's departure to high school in the new year is almost unfathomable to her. At the moment he is still hers, her special boy, but Bec knows she may not have him for long, not once he starts at high school and she becomes cloyingly uncool. Not once the hair comes, and the sticky bed sheets, and the voice begins to crack. She's heard that is what happens with boys – even the St Ignatius' Grammar ones who all seem to ooze manners and look like the kind of kids who unstack the dishwasher without even having to be asked.

The uncertainty of where Cooper will be schooled is a real worry for Bec. She and Tom are desperate for him to go to Iggy's because the fact is, Iggy's boys go far, they thrive. They can just about afford it now Willow has officially finished at Asher's Girls' School – provided Tom keeps on designing big buildings in the city and Bec continues making cakes a few times a week at a few hundred dollars a pop. It's not that they have anything against going down the public route – it's just that Pacific Pines High is not right for Cooper. Bec has heard time and time again that academically gifted boys rise to the top like the cream in milk at the local public school, but the middling kids, the academically average ones, the *shy* ones, like Cooper, get lost in the crowds. And while Cooper isn't at the bottom of the class by any means, neither is he at the top, and she doesn't want him to languish in the lower-middle unseen, with hundreds of others, splashing his little legs to keep up like he is swimming through buttercream. Her boy needs a smaller school that will nurture him, with smaller classes, a smaller teacher–student ratio, and moreover, somewhere where his sporting talent will shine.

She is plagued with worry that Iggy's might be too stuffy, or too entitled, but she has to weigh up the pros and the cons, and in her and Tom's eyes, the pros have won by a decent margin. Now they just have to hope, to pray to the God that Bec genuinely believes in, that being a gifted sportsman from a Catholic family will be enough to get Cooper over the line and through the gates of Iggy's. Well, they will know soon enough since there are only forty-eight hours until Gala Day and a further four days until the offer letters go out.

As Cooper starts high school, Sage will start kindergarten and Bec will no longer have cartoons as the soundtrack to her afternoons, or make sandcastles on the beach in the mornings, followed by cupcakes at the various coffee shops in Pacific Pines and Lawton. She is savouring Sage's last weeks as a pre-schooler, because having watched Willow blossom and grow so damn fast, Bec knows not to wish away those last precious moments with her third child. Sage's teenage years will arrive in the blink of an eye and so she is determined to enjoy every single minute. At five, Sage is half Cooper's age, and she sometimes wonders if people think her children have different fathers because of the large age discrepancy between her first and third children. Sometimes she offers up the information anyway, telling even virtual strangers that Sage was a happy accident. She wishes she didn't feel the need to explain herself, but that's just who she is: always open and honest, over-explanatory.

The fact is, Sage wasn't exactly a *happy* accident, which is something Tom has, thankfully, forgotten now he's deeply in love with his baby girl. Bec remembers the day he found out she was pregnant – how he'd walked in through the door with his wetsuit rolled down to his waist and his towel around his neck; the way he put his hands around her waist from behind, like he has always done, nestled his head into her neck and said, 'Dinner smells amazing,' and she'd said, 'You'd better get dressed, the Munros will be here soon!' How Tom had smiled and said, 'One second,' and opened the fridge and pulled out a cold beer and flipped it open, his eyes closing dreamily for the first sip followed by a long, contented sigh. Then the bottle opener, teetering on the edge of the countertop, had dropped deep into the kitchen bin and Tom had been forced to put his entire arm in to retrieve it and pulled out the positive pregnancy test Bec had physically stuffed to the bottom to buy some time. She recalls the look on his face – the shock, the terror, the *disgust*. The strangled sound in his voice as he said, 'No. This is not happening, Bec!' The way the words and phrases tripped off his tongue: *This isn't what we agreed! I can't go through it all again!* While Bec desperately tried to shush him so that Cooper and Willow wouldn't hear him from upstairs.

Even today, Bec can still see a faint trace of spaghetti sauce on the walls that are painted in Dulux Lexicon Quarter, and picture her mild-mannered husband sweeping his hand across the bench and smashing the ceramic bowl into which she'd decanted the fresh crab meat moments before. She recalls the way the red sauce and the slippery spaghetti flew in slow motion out of the bowl and landed on the wall before the ceramic bowl hit the wooden floor and smashed cleanly into three pieces.

She can almost hear Estella calling, 'Hello? Anybody home?' and 'Christ, it smells like downtown Naples in here,' before arriving in the kitchen to see her and Conrad's dinner splashed across the walls and the parquetry flooring and Bec leaning over the bench in tears as Tom stood next to her, his hands running through his hair.

Bec remembers the following days. How Tom had stomped around the house breaking her heart with his scowl and his brooding eyes and his involuntary sighs. But then, quicker than the anger had come, it had receded, and she had caught him watching her belly in bed one morning and then the next day leaning and placing his head on the little bump that was popping out already. He had softened like a marshmallow over a flame.

This all amuses Bec now because Tom adores Sage more than anything. Even more than his other two children, she is convinced of it. Not that he would ever admit it to anyone, even her. Sometimes Bec thinks that if the house was on fire and Tom could only save one of their offspring, he would pick Sage. And this is a biological anomaly, points out Estella occasionally, since, out of the three children, Sage is the *least* like Tom. She is a dead ringer for the Roche side of the family, Bec's side, particularly Bec's late mother Pamela, with her blonde curls and plump, square face, and the dimple in her chin. Yet Tom bonded with Sage the quickest, the fastest, the strongest.

So yes, their children *are* spread out, but that is the way their family works. Estella once asked her, 'Don't you get bored with life being so . . . *samey*?' and Bec had laughed and said, 'No, of course I don't!' She hadn't been offended at the time, only when she'd thought about it later. What she wished she'd replied was, 'Don't you ever get bored of always wanting *more*?'

The fact is, Bec has never wanted more than exactly what she has. Well, mostly never. Maybe once or twice she's been greedy, like the time she wanted Sage, but otherwise, no. She loves the familiar routine of her life; it makes her feel safe. She is a creature of habit, a player-by-the-rules. She doesn't particularly like to take risks (why bother?) or do things that make her feel uncomfortable. She sometimes gets nervous when she is more than an hour away from home. And like most mothers, she does find it hard watching her children grow and change even though she understands it is the inevitable progression of human life.

She hears a loud giggle from the living room at the front of the house.

It's followed by a plea from Cooper. 'Sagey, shhhh! I can't hear!'

She smiles and picks up her phone and Googles 'Silver wedding cake' for some inspiration. She will roll the fondant tonight and store it in the cupboard, so it is easy to dress the cake quickly tomorrow – she'll be pressed for time after Mass. It is her favourite part of the whole process: rolling out the fondant and draping it over the sponge, tucking it in at the bottom, hospital corners! Or slathering on the sweet buttercream with a flat spatula as the cake slides around on the rotating cake wheel. These are just two of the tools of her trade that line the pantry, from floor to ceiling. Spoons and whisks, metal moulds and cake tins, baking paper and piping bags, not to mention the creative kit. A rainbow box of food dyes, cupcake holders and the sheets of edible gold leaf fight for space amid Tom's protein powders, tinned goods and children's healthy snack bars. These items are what take a basic sponge from moist (and no, she doesn't have a problem with that word) to marvellous.

There's an email in her inbox and she knows before she even clicks on the icon that it's from the spammer again, call it a sort of sixth sense. She's had a few from the same address in the last couple of weeks and each time they bring goose bumps and a sense of dread.

The sender's name sits in bold at the top of her inbox: Lucki_Texta.

Bec braces herself. *I know what you did, Rebecca,* the message reads.

She feels dirty, violated. *Ugh,* she thinks. *Who* are *these vile trolls who sit behind their screens and make threats to normal, God-fearing people?* She's sure it is just some random pervert sitting behind a computer in Belarus or somewhere techy, but it's still unnerving the way they use her name. *I know what you did, Rebecca.* No one she knows calls her that, aside from Estella when she's trying to make a point. She hasn't been called by her full name on anything other than official forms or by, say, medics, since about 1980.

She clicks on the upper right corner of her phone and the screen blackens.

It's nothing, she tells herself. She had a few similar messages last year that said stuff like: *We know your password and if you don't pay us in Bitcoins we'll release all of your pornographic home videos.* Well, Bec had known *that* was spam because she is definitely not the type to make pornographic videos. Her and Tom's sex life still rocks her world (vanilla sponge is not boring for everyone, thank you very much. It can be very sweet and yes, moist) and they are still very much in unison, like the prongs of an electric whisk, when it comes to that. But sexy home videos with three children in the house? Just no.

Bec unwraps a large block of fondant and pulls a lump from the end. She pours a few drops of silver colouring into the centre. The colour that emerges as she kneads the sugary dough is delightful. It complements the top of Bec's kitchen bench with the large vase of white lilies and the large jasmine-scented candle and the giant clam shell overflowing with pert yellow lemons. There isn't a jot of mess, there never is! The only hint of anything amiss in the kitchen is a black stream of smoke coming from the burning wick of the candle.

She watches it twist into the air, sinister and wily, and thinks how even beautiful and innocent things can be deceptive, how secrets and darkness can fester on the inside of even the most pleasant of things, of people.

She dusts off her hands, picks up her phone and opens her inbox.

I know what you did, Rebecca, she reads again.

She presses delete with a firm, decisive finger and glances towards the closed doors of the living room. Then she places her phone face-down on the bench.

4

Estella

Estella emerges from the front door and sees Kaya climbing into her car wearing a bright floral summer dress that looks like it belongs on a rack at the Salvation Army, which was most likely its very provenance. Her son wears an oversized suit and tie.

Estella nods a perfunctory hello over the fence because she would never want to be *rude* and steps into Conrad's Range Rover, filling it with a waft of her signature Bulgari Pour Femme. Jonty pretends to have a coughing fit and Felicity mutters 'At last,' under her breath and opens the window dramatically, as if she's being suffocated by the smell, which is ironic really, since Estella would sometimes like to suffocate Felicity. Only temporarily, of course – for the duration of an argument, for example, or perhaps for an entire weekend.

'Ugh, turn up the aircon,' says Felicity.

'That'll just circulate it,' mumbles Jonty.

'Where are they going?' Estella asks Conrad.

'Who?' Archie's head whips up from his coding book.

'The neighbours.'

'They have names!' Felicity chews her gum noisily.

'Do they?' Estella flicks the overhead mirror down and draws fuchsia on her lips. 'I didn't know that. Thank you for the clarification, Felicity. And my, what a delightfully ladylike sound you're making.'

Felicity makes an exaggerated 'clack-clack' as she chews. 'Talking of names, mine is Flick, not Felicity. And do I really have to come to Mass?'

'Not according to your birth certificate, *Felicity*.' Estella ignores the second part of the question.

'I think you'll find it's my basic human right to choose what people call me.'

'Does that mean it's my basic right to call you Shithead?' asks Jonty.

'Call me what you like, dick weasel.'

'Now, now, kids,' says Conrad in that faux-annoyed voice Estella finds rather irritating. She wishes he'd just tell them all to shut the fuck up.

Estella can detect the faintest waft of cannabis and Impulse body spray inside the car. God, what she wouldn't give for a spliff at the end of the garden.

'Ollie's in my scripture class.' It is Archie. 'He doesn't know anything about God. He keeps asking all these weird questions.'

Estella chews on this for a moment. She wonders why Kaya hasn't put her son in with the unruly gaggle of atheist kids at Pacific Pines Primary, with their weekly musings about whether or not it's ethically right to steal a loaf of bread from a large supermarket corporation if it helps someone in need. Nauseating to the extreme! Unless she is being tactical, of course . . .

'He's got some good soccer tricks,' says Jonty. 'I saw him out the window.'

'Not as good as yours,' says Estella. She reaches round the back of her seat and squeezes Jonty's knee. Knobbly and thin, like Conrad's.

'No one's as good as Jonty-wonty-woo,' purrs Felicity. '*Gag!*'

'You're right.' Jonty grins. 'I'm glad you finally realised it.'

Estella barely registers the sibling merriment. 'Where *are* they going?' She watches Kaya slowly reverse out of her driveway and narrowly miss her own postbox.

'Would you like me to get out and ask?' says Conrad. 'I'll ask what type of cancer her husband had too if you like, see if I can sneak it into the same sentence!'

Estella peers into the wing mirror as Conrad turns on to Ocean View Parade and towards the bend that leads to the centre of Pacific Pines.

'Good God,' she says. 'She's following us!'

She sees Felicity roll her eyes dramatically in the overhead mirror as she chews on her spearmint Extra.

'I'm telling you, Felicity, *she is following us*! She waited until we were out of our driveway before she reversed out of theirs!'

'Oh puh-lease,' drawls Felicity. 'Driving behind us on the only road out of town is hardly following us. She's probably popping out for groceries.'

'Dressed like the Amish?'

'That's classy, Mother. The woman's only gone and lost her husband and you're assessing her sartorial offerings,' says Felicity.

'Pre-menstrual, are you darling?' chirps Estella.

'Gross,' says Jonty.

Felicity coughs the word 'menopause' and Conrad fixes his eyes straight ahead.

St Martin's Catholic Church is bustling with families, all of whom seem to have high-school entry-age children and, sure enough, Kaya Sterling pulls up right next to the Munros in the car park. Kaya gives Felicity a butter-wouldn't-melt smile as the two emerge from their doors concurrently and Estella feels her top molars connect with the bottom ones.

'Hello,' says Kaya, beaming. 'You must be Felicity!'

'It's Flick,' says Felicity. 'Kaya, isn't it?'

'Yes, and this is Ollie.'

Ollie says, 'Hi,' to Felicity and the twins. Estella nods another hello to Kaya.

'How lovely to see you, Estella,' Kaya chirps. 'What a wonderful dress you have on!'

'Zimmermann,' Estella informs her. 'Where is yours from?'

'Oh, it's not designer,' says Kaya. 'It's an old one, but a favourite.'

Bingo, thinks Estella.

'I thought you said you and Ollie were non-believers,' she says through thin lips.

Kaya smiles. 'Oh, I was having a bad day! We do dip in occasionally, don't we Ollie?' The boy's obedient nod reminds Estella of a dog on a dashboard.

'In fact, we've just signed up Ollie for baptism classes,' says Kaya.

Estella narrows her eyes and feels the heat flush to her face. Kaya doesn't meet her eyes, but instead reaches out towards Felicity.

'Gosh, aren't you *gorgeous*?' she says, touching Felicity's shoulder and Felicity offers up the kind of genuine smile of which Estella has not been the beneficiary for a long while, because motherhood of girls breeds contempt in the Munro family, apparently.

And anyway, calling Felicity 'gorgeous' is complete tosh and Estella *knows* it is, because Felicity has a hangover the size of Russia and Estella had to drag her out of bed pretty much by her hair, and so she knows *for a fact* that Felicity is not remotely 'gorgeous' today and actually looks like a vagrant. Estella wants to slow-clap Kaya and say, 'Well, well, well! What do we have here? You're a churchgoer now? A perfect Catholic! Isn't *that* rather convenient?' But she understands this would not be appropriate within three square metres of Father Francis. It would be sacrilegious, in fact, which is exactly what Kaya Sterling is being by rocking up to St Martin's in her floral smock. The woman *explicitly* said on her own driveway she was agnostic, or atheist, or whatever she said she was, and now here she is, in her Sunday best, pretending to be a good Catholic. It truly beggars belief!

To further annoy Estella on this particularly stifling morning, Kaya and Ollie manage to get seats near the front of the church, next to Bec, Willow and Cooper. They are a couple of spots along from the school principal, Ursula Deacon, and someone Estella presumes to be Ursula's son, Sam. Estella sits up tall, trying to get a better look at the new sports master, whom she is desperate to meet and impress, but she cannot see anything apart from a neat sandy haircut and a thick, rugby-player's neck. But the fact Kaya is so close to him is like petrol to a flame for Estella as she sits at the back in the cheap seats, and only serves to ignite her dislike for her neighbour even further. It very briefly occurs to her it might be her own fault for changing her outfit three times before leaving the house, but she shoves that thought out of her head, pronto, because you have to look presentable at Mass, don't you, for the love of God? The only saving grace about her pew at the back, Estella supposes as the anger wanes slightly, is that at least she has a good vantage point of everybody from where she is sitting. Besides, Kaya Sterling isn't close enough to Sam Deacon to engage him in any kind of conversation! However she does watch with pique as Kaya leans in and whispers to Bec during the Benediction and Bec grins inanely back as if they are sharing some kind of hilarious in-joke. She hears herself tut out loud and masks it with a cough.

Later, Estella observes her neighbour as she takes the sacrament like a pro (it's amazing what you can learn on YouTube these days) and swears she can even hear her as she prays, because apparently, Kaya knows all the words to Hail Mary off by heart! Estella grinds her molars again throughout the service, despite what Dr Chen has warned her about the significant erosion of her enamel, and when she sees Kaya kneel before her pew for the Lord's Prayer, she leans closer to Conrad and hisses in his ear, 'Who the *hell* does she think she is? She's behaving like Mother Teresa!'

Conrad feigns shock. 'Bless you my child, for you have sinned,' he whispers and Felicity snorts with laughter.

When Mass is over, Estella looks around for the Deacons – because there would be no better time to introduce herself than when she is in her Sunday best – but they have gone already. She is disappointed, of course, but she is a patient woman and will bide her time. Over at the vestibule, she sees Ollie Sterling shaking the elderly priest's hand, and Kaya looking on proudly in her cheap, special-occasion dress. Kaya is holding up her hands in prayer, rocking them back and forth gratefully, like the old man has just offered to pay off her mortgage or something. Estella would laugh at the scene if she wasn't so outraged at Kaya's blatant duplicity and disregard for the sanctity of religion.

So irked is Estella that she makes her own point of cornering Father Francis after the service to remind him of the generous donation she and Conrad made to the church roof fund at the beginning of the month (it can't hurt to jog his memory!) and express to him just how much Archie and Jonty are looking forward to offering themselves up as altar boys at the school chapel if they are so lucky as to get a place at St Ignatius' Boys' Grammar. They are incredibly reliable, both of them, she tells Father Francis, and very keen to get in touch with their Catholic roots, which of course go way back through generations.

'Bless you, Father Francis,' Estella adds, for the hell of it. 'The way you manage both St Martin's *and* the school chapel is just incredible.'

'Thank you, Arabella,' he says, and Estella grins and bears it. He been giving her the sacrament since she was a child, the old fool, and has known her most of her life. She can't compute that he cannot remember her name! This kind of forgetfulness enrages Estella, because it's something she's always been good at – she never forgets a name or a face. But as Kaya and Ollie walk past and bid their goodbyes to Father Francis, the old man calls, clear as day, 'Goodbye, Kaya,' and then turns to Estella and says, 'Lovely family! The boy has just signed up for baptism classes,' and Estella feels something that's a combination of anger and rejection, and she acknowledges, silently, that she would quite like to punch someone, hard, in the face. And that person is Kaya Sterling.

At this very point, Estella feels very urgently that she should casually mention to Father the rather suspect number of families who are opting to baptise their school-aged children and ask him if he is aware that some of them are – *how shall she put it?* – disingenuous. So she does just that, right there, by the doors of the church. It just doesn't sit well with her, she explains to him, this blatant abuse of the beautiful religion they all adore. It is, when you break it down, impiety of the highest kind. Estella doesn't mention any names to Father, of course. Or does she? She can't quite remember afterwards. Well, no matter, she has said her piece, and what's important is that she has said it ahead of Tuesday's all-important Gala Day. She couldn't sit idly by and watch a bunch of fakers wheedle their way into Iggy's.

Estella is pleased with herself and remains so as she stands outside the large wooden doors of the church and waits for Bec. She sees her friend prattling on to someone by the altar and she sighs, annoyed. It is too hot for loitering! Over by the graveyard, Felicity and Willow giggle over a phone screen – TikTok, Estella assumes. And in the car park, Kaya ruffles her son's hair before getting into the driver's seat of her car. And is that . . . is that *smugness* on her face when she catches Estella's eye?

What had Kaya said her husband's name was? Paul Sterling. She takes out her mobile phone, pulls up the St Ignatius' website and taps in 'old boys 1990–2005', just in case Paul Sterling was a good deal younger and went through the school way after her time. She wouldn't put it past Kaya to have an unsuitably young husband, even though she isn't sure why she has come to this conclusion; she just *looks* the sort. The woman's already speed dating a year after burying her husband, for pity's sake!

'Goodbye Estella, God bless,' says a warbling elderly voice.

Estella barely looks up. 'Yes, yes, you too.'

There are several Pauls on the honours list – after all, it is a good Catholic name. Paul Addison, Paul Davis, Paul Wheeler, but no Paul Sterling. A Google search yields nothing.

'Hello!' Bec coos and Estella jumps a foot in the air.

'Christ,' yells Estella, and the elderly woman turns back and scowls. 'You made me jump!'

Bec leans in for a hug. 'Isn't it a beautiful day?'

'Not really,' snips Estella. 'Now listen, we have something important to discuss.' She drags Bec by the arm to the side of the building, right under a stained-glass depiction of Judas and Jesus at the Last Supper.

'Where are we going? What are you up to, Estella?'

Estella leans in. 'She,' she jabs a finger at the tail end of Kaya's retreating Toyota Kluger, 'is not who she says she is.'

'What are you talking about?'

'Kaya Sterling,' Estella snaps as Judas looks down on her, open-mouthed. 'The woman's a fraud and I'm going to prove it.'

5

Bec

Bec pulls her sunglasses out of her bag, the blinding sun a warning of the heat that's been forecast for later in the day. She fans herself with the paper hymn sheet she's forgotten to leave on her pew.

Estella wears that self-satisfied look she has when she's about to impart one of her theories on someone, and way too much Bulgari. 'He was never school captain at Iggy's like she said he was,' she says, triumphant.

'Who wasn't?'

'Oh do keep up, Bec! Kaya's *husband*. Paul Sterling.'

'How do you know?'

'Only the fact there's no Paul Sterling in the school records.'

'They might have missed one off. Why don't you ask Father Francis? He's been around forever.'

'He won't remember, he's half doolally. And listen to this . . .' Estella readies herself with her trump card. 'She's signed her boy up for baptism classes when she's a goddamn atheist.'

'I don't think you're meant to say that word . . .' Bec looks up apologetically at Jesus on the stained glass and sighs.

'Atheist?'

'No, goddamn . . .'

Estella shrugs. 'I've said worse.'

'Maybe we should just let her get on with it,' Bec muses. 'I mean the poor woman's just been widowed. And anyway, it's not really any of our business, is it?'

'Ahh, but it *is* our business, don't you see?' Estella's hands are on her hips. 'She is trying to get a place for Ollie at Iggy's which means she is potentially taking a place from one of us! What if Ollie takes the place that's meant for Cooper? Will you consider it your business then? I'm serious, Bec. We need to pull out the stops, do something that gets our boys noticed. To use Felicity's favourite phrase, we need to be "extra".'

'Well, thank you for the advice,' says Bec. In some small way it's rather nice of Estella to extend this advice to her and, in a secondary way, to Cooper. 'I'm glad you don't see me as competition.'

'Don't be ridiculous,' says Estella, air-kissing Bec on the cheek. 'I wouldn't think twice about trampling over you to get the last spot, best friend or not.'

Bec sighs and shakes her head. 'Bye, Estella.'

Inside the car, she thinks about Kaya Sterling. She had chatted to the woman in church and she'd seemed lovely. Bec had been sitting in her pew with Cooper and had spied her walking up the aisle with her son and waved at them. She knew the woman was Kaya because when she dropped the welcome cupcakes off the other day, they'd said an awkward hello through their car windows on the drive. Bec had said something like, 'I just dropped off something for you,' and Kaya had said, 'Oh, that's very kind,' and that had been it.

Kaya had nodded keenly at Bec's invitation to sit with her inside the church and had been heading towards her when she'd been intercepted by Father Francis, all kitted out in his robes. She had watched Kaya nod earnestly while Father pointed out various areas of the church, and she'd wondered if the woman was a genuine churchgoer, or had a fair-weather faith. Not that she really cared. Live and let live and all that. And Kaya was so nice, and she'd told Bec how grateful she'd been for the cupcakes on her doorstep when she'd finally slid into the pew beside her. And all the while Estella had been giving them such *evils* from the back of the church.

'What are you thinking about, Mum?' Willow asks.

'Oh, just about Estella. She's got a bee in her bonnet about her new neighbour. I think she's worried her son Ollie is going to steal a place meant for one of the twins.'

'She's mental,' says Cooper.

'*Coops!*'

'It's true,' says Willow. 'And she's so hard on Flick. It's hard to believe you guys are such good friends, sometimes.'

Bec keeps her eyes on the road. 'Well, believe it or not she is a good person deep down,' she says. 'She's been there for me when I've needed her.'

And there are deep-rooted secrets we share, is what she doesn't say.

At home, Bec returns to the kitchen bench and sets out her cake-decorating tools alongside the ready-rolled fondant – no rest for *her* on the Sabbath day! She will decorate the Christie silver-wedding cake first by delicately rolling out a block of pure white fondant and draping it over the red sponge, then tucking the sheeted icing under the base of the cakes. Next she will add thick strips of the silver fondant she rolled last night and neatly finish it off with the large golden '25' from Cakes R Us in Lawton.

The Adams creation will be much the same, only three cakes this time, on golden tiers (of which she has an infinite supply on the top shelf of the pantry), the top one featuring marzipan figurines, which she whipped up last week using moulding paste and has had stored in an airtight Tupperware. Melody's will have to be decorated last, since the blue dye required for Elsa from *Frozen*'s turquoise dress is an absolute bastard in terms of getting everywhere: bench tops, clothes and so on. She cannot risk so much as a blue fingerprint on one of the other adult occasion cakes.

She thinks now about what Estella had said by the doors. The stuff about the mystery husband hadn't fazed her, it was just Estella being dramatic, but it had been this: 'What if Ollie gets a place that's meant for Cooper? You have to be "extra".'

Bec lifts up the silver anniversary cake and places it carefully in a Cakes by Bec box, with the Cupid logo on the front. She feels a strong wave of anxiety about the whole uncertainty of Cooper's schooling (and the latest of those damn emails). She stops for a moment and takes a series of breaths and tells herself, *What will be will be*, even though she doesn't really believe it. What if Ollie Sterling *does* get a place meant for Cooper? For all of Estella's pushiness, perhaps she is right. Perhaps Bec *does* need to do something drastic! She cannot control her email spam anxiety, but she can control this, and she can be proactive because there isn't anything she wouldn't do for Cooper.

Tom walks into the kitchen, fresh from a run. He tries to avoid Mass when he can, taking it as his time to exercise. He puts his arms around her waist, kisses her neck and then turns to fill the kettle. She's so preoccupied she doesn't flinch from the salty sweat he has left on her arms.

'The Cake Boss strikes again.' He grins. 'Tea?'

'Huh?'

'A cup of tea. Do you want one?'

'I'm OK, thanks.'

'How was Mass?' he asks, setting down kettle and flicking it on. 'Did you confess your sins?'

'It was fine. Although something Estella said is playing on my mind.'

He sighs. 'What's she said this time?'

'Just that we need to pull out all the stops to get Cooper a place at Iggy's. You know, to go above and beyond. Estella's new neighbour is getting her son baptised to get him in, even though she's an atheist!'

Tom picks up a whisk from beside the sink and licks it. 'Well in lieu of offering them a bribe, there's not much we can do. Our kids are already children of the cloth.'

Bec spreads buttercream between the top two layers of the wedding cake.

'What would sway you if you were the school registrar?' she asks.

'A good report card?'

'Cooper has that already.'

'A letter of recommendation from a sports coach?'

'Done.' Getting a note from Cooper's coach at the Pines Rugby Club to accompany his Iggy's application was the *first* thing Bec had done, followed by a letter from the mother of one of his former teammates, who was a current Iggy's boy. Bec was so grateful the boy's mother had taken the time to do it, and it had been such a lovely letter, too.

Tom's tongue navigates the twists of the whisk. Bec watches his eyes close. 'Becs, this is delicious . . .'

'That's your bedroom voice.'

As she laughs the idea takes hold. Cakes! *That* is the thing she does well. She surveys the bench in front of her. *Yes, that's it!* She will make a giant, criminally good cake and present it to Ursula Deacon and the Iggy's admissions team. Why on earth has she not thought of it before?

'Well, that's settled,' she says, pleased with her little old self. 'I'm going to bake them a cake.'

'Who's "them"?'

'Ursula Deacon and Father Francis, of course.'

Tom grins. 'It's a lovely idea, but I'm not sure your sponge, as delightful and moist as it will undoubtedly be, will be enough to seal the deal.'

'Oh Tom, you underestimate my talents as a craftsperson.'

He laughs and shakes his head. 'I redact that statement. You are completely right. It worked with my mother . . .'

It is quite true. Any trace of British upper-crust prickliness from Melissa Lloyd had been swiftly dissipated by the slice of Bec's millefeuille on the side of the spiky woman's early-nineteenth-century chinoiserie plate. 'This puff pastry is simply exquisite,' Melissa had said. 'Marry this woman, please, Tom!'

'Well, my pastry *is* exquisite,' muses Bec. 'But it needs to be something better than that. Man cannot live on bread alone. It needs to be artistic, too.'

Tom opens the bin and drops in his tea bag. 'What are you thinking?'

Bec twitches her nose and smiles. 'An edible model of the school!'

'You've got to be kidding? How long's that going to take?'

'Shhh,' she says and shoos him out of the kitchen with her hands. 'Master at work.'

The pantry yields a Tupperware box full of food colourings in different hues of brown and green and beige, as well as fondant, modelling paste, marzipan and gold leaf. She has everything she needs. Bec stares out of the window and thinks. She decides she will craft a vanilla sponge in the shape of the school chapel, and she will drive it up to Iggy's tomorrow and present it to Ursula Deacon. She will use her most syrupy voice as she explains to the principal that she will be there for Iggy's, come rain or shine, for all of their baking needs: she will bake sponges for anniversaries, cupcakes for Mother's Day, lemon meringue pies for raffles, chocolate eclairs for parents' evenings, shortbread for band camp, biscuits for P&C committee meetings! This cake will just be the start.

She opens the kitchen window. 'Coops?' she calls into the garden.

She will have to do a rush job on the *Frozen* cake if she wants to get her Iggy's masterpiece underway in time to take it to the school tomorrow, and it has to be tomorrow because Gala Day is the day after – on a Tuesday of all days.

Cooper looks up. 'Yeah?'

'Come and help me mix some blue food dye for an Elsa cake, quick! I've got another job to do!'

'Sure.' Cooper traipses in, bringing mud in with him. He puts his hands round Bec's waist like Tom did before him and buries his head into her sides. She buries her head in his hair and breathes in the sawdusty smell before ruffling it with her forearm because her hands are coated with buttercream.

'Wash your hands,' she instructs, 'and then just keep adding *tiny* amounts of blue to the buttercream, and then a drop or two of green, until you have *this* colour.' She scrolls through her phone to find a photo of Elsa in her big turquoise dress. Cooper must have watched her do this cake a hundred times – this, and various forms of *Minions* cakes in banana yellow – so she knows it will be a cinch for him with her here to oversee it.

'Thank you, buddy,' she says. 'Let me know when you're done. And no dye on the worktop, please.'

'Got it,' Cooper says. Bec watches him position the phone in front of him, against a bag of flour. She is about to turn away to begin her St Ignatius' masterpiece when an email notification flashes up on screen. She grabs the phone and turns away from Cooper, clicking on the notification.

Don't ignore me, Bec, the message reads. *I know what you did.*

She feels the heat rise up her chest and presses the rubbish-bin icon, watching as the message is sucked into the virtual trash with the sound of crunching paper. *Bec*, she thinks, *they called me Bec this time. How would they know?*

'Who was that from?' Cooper asks.

'Just spam. Someone nasty trying to con me for some reason. I've sent it to the phishing folder.'

Cooper holds up the wooden spoon. 'Can I lick it after?' he asks.

'What?'

'The spoon. Can I lick it afterwards?'

'Yes, yes.' She is flustered by the sinister undertones of the email, but she doesn't have time to be. She has a marvellous, jaw-dropping cake to make and so she must file the contents of the email in the trash bin in her head, too – the place where she stores all the things she doesn't want to think about.

She rolls her shoulders, and pulls out a mixing bowl. She throws eggs, butter, flour and vanilla essence inside and gets out the electric beaters and holds them with her left hand as they do their job. With her right hand she grabs her sketch pad and Googles 'St Ignatius' school chapel' and finds the perfect image to replicate: a side-on photograph of the gorgeous, flower-lined, traditional, English-style chapel with its sandstone walls and slatted roof. She plucks out the yellow and brown food dyes for the sandstone and the roof and greens for the surrounds from her box of food colouring, plus her cutting tools and a large bag of white fondant, and she sets to work, stopping for an hour and a half only to ice the wedding and the *Frozen* cakes and load them into Tom's car with Cooper for delivery. And she does not think about Lucki_Texta in all that time.

It is one o'clock in the morning when Bec finishes the chapel cake (in the midst of it all her family has eaten, argued, relaxed, gone to bed) and it is, she believes, her finest work. It has been a marathon effort, so many stages. The mixing of the food dye into the fondant and the marzipan to get the exact colour of the church roof, the brick joins of the sandstone and the wooden doors, the scalloping of the roof and the fashioning of the steeple, the gold-leaf crucifix on top – and all this even before the gravel pathway and the native greenery that lead up to the door.

The colour palette, thinks Bec now as she stands back and observes, is spectacular. The flora lends itself to several different shades of green: the bottle-green jasmine that creeps up the front walls, the mint-hued blue chalk sticks, the silver eucalyptus. Then there is the red of the native bottlebrush and the bright yellow of the spotted emu bush at the back of the building, offset by the white and red and blue of the mini stained-glass windows.

Bec's fingers are sore from fashioning plants, her eyes ache from studying, up close, the scalloping of the roof and the intricacies of the stained glass. The balls of her feet sting from standing on them for hours at the kitchen bench on the hardy wooden floor. But she is happy, so happy! This creation is on a par with the professor's birthday Colosseum, if not better.

She sits down on the sofa with a cup of chamomile tea and sighs, long and deep. It is almost like finishing a marathon, completing a cake like this one – exhausting, gruelling and intense, but always satisfying. Exhilarating, even. She sinks into the sofa, leans her head to the side and closes her eyes, just for a second, ignoring the small clump of white icing she can see clinging to her eyelashes as she closes them.

When she wakes, it is seven o'clock on Monday morning and, despite having a half-full cup of cold tea in her hands with a significant chunk of her hair dangling in it, she realises, to her satisfaction, that she hasn't spilled a single drop.

MONDAY

6

Kaya

Kaya feels the throb in her knees. She doesn't like it down here, on the cold stones of the chapel floor. What she is doing feels so wrong. She looks up to see Father Francis gazing down at her, a satisfied smile on his face.

'Good job,' he says.

Kaya gets up, pushes her hair off her forehead.

'Bless you!' Father's palm rests on the top of her head. He is somewhere in his seventies, his face deeply lined and covered in unkempt stubble, although he has missed patches under his chin and at the sides, as if he'd shaved in the semi-light. His eyes droop to expose the raw red of his sockets, like a basset hound.

Kaya feels a pang of shame, but then she thinks back to Estella's advice and she swallows it back like an unpalatably large vitamin pill. Head back, down the hatch! Besides, isn't she doing the old man a service?

'The floor is sparkling!' he says, arms wide. 'Thank you, Kaya.'

'Oh, it's my pleasure.' Kaya smiles. She stands up and attaches the brush to the copper dustpan, which is as shiny and reflective as everything else in the place: the gilded crucifix on the wall of the vestibule, the plaques on the side of the pews.

She likes it here, inside the church. She'd forgotten the pomp of Catholic churches, with their opulence and their burning frankincense and their gilded, flickering candles. She can see Ollie has been enraptured by it, too. The way he looked around St Martin's when she'd taken him to meet Father following that encounter with Estella on the driveway; the way she casually mentioned to him, 'How about we get you baptised, little bud, like we talked about the other night? A lot of the Iggy's boys have done it. It might help you get a spot?' And he'd said, 'Sure. I don't mind.'

He'd done the first class straight after Mass, and he'd taken to it, said Father, like a duck to (holy) water. He'd been genuinely interested in the big picture. This morning, in the car on the way to school, he'd asked her why there was so much controversy about God making the world, but she didn't really know enough about the big bang theory to give him a satisfactory answer. That kind of thing had been Paul's job. He would answer those pesky questions – the ones like, 'What does the moon have to do with tides?' and 'How exactly does a plane stay in the air?' In his absence, Kaya turned to Dr Google instead, and consequently Ollie had cut short his garden soccer practice for the last few nights to study the conflict between the story of Adam and Eve and what Kaya saw as the rather more believable scenario: that a cataclysmic geographical phenomenon forced us all into being.

Kaya had felt a trickle of concern as she'd watched him. Baptism was one thing, but actually *believing* any of it was quite another. Still, she'd shaken her head, safe in the knowledge Ollie would most likely forget everything straight after he got his baptism certificate. He tended to forget where he'd left his trainers most days, so she wasn't under the illusion he was actually going to retain any of this indoctrination.

But they'd made the decision now, or rather she had, using the slightest bit of coercive control and flowery language, and they had to stick to it. It was a gateway to the school after all. *'I mean, the competition for places is* insane,' Estella had warned her. *'It's only really worth the effort if the boy is baptised.'*

A grey-haired woman in a too-tight black pencil skirt and a cream-coloured silk blouse bursts through the door. She clip-clops down the aisle in a pair of black court shoes.

'Sparkling, quite!' Her voice is nasal, like a clarinet. 'One could very easily slip over in here, Father. Be very careful, won't you?' She speaks to him as if she is addressing a person in the last stages of dementia. 'We don't want any boys, or any priests for that matter, with broken ankles now, do we?

'Hello.' Ursula Deacon extends her hand and encloses Kaya's with a strong grip. 'You must be Mrs Sterling. I'm Ursula Deacon, school principal.'

'Oh,' Kaya says. 'Hello. Thank you so much for allowing me to help in the chapel – it is such an honour. It is such a beautiful place of worship.'

'Yes,' says the older woman. 'It is. But we should be thanking *you*.' There seems to be something rather suspicious about her tone, and Kaya feels the suspicion is falling altogether on her. Perhaps Ursula Deacon has a nose for atheists. Kaya thinks the woman isn't unlike

Estella Munro, really, with her haltingly abrupt manner. She sincerely hopes this isn't what everyone associated with Iggy's is like – aloof and slightly cold. And if they are, why on earth would Paul have been so desperate for Ollie to be educated here? She closes her eyes for a second and reminds herself, once more, not to go by first impressions.

'Don't judge Estella,' she'd instructed Ollie. So they didn't judge, but they had taken to some healthy spying. On their first night in the house they'd stood together and peered out of the top window into the Munros' garden and Kaya had seen Estella on the bench at the end of her garden smoking what looked to be a spliff. Estella had sat down, opened up the Rizla paper, crumbled something on top and then added the tobacco. Then she'd twisted the end and sparked it up! She hadn't pegged Estella as the weed-smoking sort, but she probably needed it, she was that highly strung.

Now it has become a bit of a habit, her and Ollie's peering (because 'snooping' suggests a somewhat darker pastime) into the Munros' garden from the landing window. Ollie will go upstairs to change out of his school uniform and Kaya will follow him up to gather the washing and turn back his sheets ahead of bedtime and somehow they will always end up convening on the landing at the oval window with the epic sea views, Ollie's head on her shoulder. Most nights the twins are in the garden, one of them kicking a ball or doing backflips on the trampoline and the other in a book or with the violin wedged under his shoulder, the bow dancing back and forth melodiously, bouncing merrily off the strings.

It annoys Kaya that she cannot yet tell them apart with their sandy blond hair and their mother's pointed features; there isn't so much as a facial blemish or freckle to distinguish them. Although she has noticed that one is lithe, the other sluggish. One always catches and the other always drops. But Kaya would not place money on her ability to determine which is the catcher as opposed to the dropper.

The Munros-with-a-U have not bothered to check in on Kaya and Ollie since that first meeting. Kaya has only seen Estella fleetingly at Mass, where Estella stared at her a bit like some kind of stalker. It is disappointing, she won't lie. It is not as if Kaya wants to be Estella's new best friend or anything, but since losing Paul she finds herself feeling lonely a lot of the time. She craves a friendly face really, someone to call if disaster befalls in the dead of night – if she is faced with a catastrophe she cannot manage to fix on her own, like a fuse blowing, or a gas leak or a flooding tap. She thinks, perhaps, that the other woman might at least have said, 'Well, if you need anything, please call,' or popped round with a dish of lasagne, but Estella hasn't done that, and Kaya feels let down. Let down by someone she doesn't know. Oh well, not everyone can be like Bec Lloyd, she supposes. Not everyone has such an innate ability to be thoughtful. She feels a sudden burning need to pursue her friendship with Bec, so there's at least someone there to shoot the breeze with, whose husband she might be able to 'borrow', so to speak, if something needs mending. It's terribly sexist of her to think this way, and she knows it, to assume that only a man can change a fuse or repair a leak, but the fact is, Paul had done all of the 'fixing' in their marriage.

In those last months before he died, he had made her lists, given her basic how-to instructions: emailed links to YouTube about plugging a tap and changing a tyre, listed the bank accounts and the passwords and the available funds, told her where to find the car registration forms, who to call about house insurance and reminding her to transfer it from the house in Klara Bay to Palm Cottage. That was the kind of man he had been: type A. Cautious and careful about everything, so meticulous about finances. A pot for this, a pot for that. Paul had always planned for a rainy day, just in case the worst happened. And then the worst had happened, and quickly. It hadn't rained, but poured. From terminal diagnosis to death had been eight months. Eight months for a lifetime of goodbyes. She'd had to learn how to manage it all: the funeral, the house move, the high-school application, but she finds it is the little things that overwhelm her.

'Mrs Sterling?' Ursula Deacon is addressing her. 'Father Francis tells me your family is taking Catholic classes and will be baptised up at St Martin's. Is that correct?'

'Yes, we're taking classes at the moment,' Kaya replies, willing herself not to mess this up. 'But, actually, it's not the whole family. It's just myself and my son Ollie.'

The day after meeting Estella Munro, Kaya had called up Father Francis at St Martin's and had a lovely chat with him about Ollie and how she felt now was the time to get him back in touch with his father's Catholic roots.

Then she'd called St Iggy's and asked the sweet ladies at the front desk to amend Ollie's application form to note that he was a soon-to-be card-carrying Catholic, pending his completion of baptism classes. The women in the office had been delighted.

'What about your husband?' Ursula Deacon's tone is cool. 'Is there a reason why he has chosen not to participate in the family baptism?'

'Paul passed away a year ago,' she says, looking instinctively towards Ursula Deacon's hands.

'Oh, I am sorry,' the other woman replies, her fingers tinkering with the ornate gilded crucifix that hangs against her ribcage on a thin gold chain. Bingo!

'Thank you,' Kaya says. 'It's OK. I mean, *we're* OK. I mean, if I'm honest, it was while I was making sense of this loss that I made the decision to come back to the fold, as it were, and to bring my little lamb with me.'

She is proud of this because she knows the church enjoys a sheep metaphor, although she can't help but feel she is offering up Ollie as a lamb to the slaughter. And now she's lied about Paul's death making her want to reconnect with the Lord. But really, why should she feel guilty? It was Paul who put her in this goddamn predicament! He had been the one who had begged her on his deathbed to send Ollie to his old school. She'd been so worried about the money, and she wasn't even a Catholic.

'You can do it, Kaya,' he had said, reading her thoughts as he always did. 'Promise me you will.'

'But I don't know anything about Iggy's,' she'd protested. 'It would mean us moving across the country!'

He'd looked in her face then, his eyes steely. 'Listen,' he'd said. 'This is important. If you do anything for me after I'm gone, do this.'

She'd seen the desperation in his eyes, it seemed to be seeping from his skin. He coughed, a deathly, painful cough.

'I will,' she'd said, taking his face in her hands, trying, trying to make a dying man happy, to make him better. 'I'll do it. I'll try and get Ollie into St Ignatius'.'

'Good,' he'd said, with a deep exhale. 'Because there's something else you need to know . . .'

Ursula Deacon's head tilts to the side. 'What exactly do you mean by "Come back to the fold"? You were raised a Catholic?'

'I went to a Catholic high school in Perth,' Kaya says. 'But then I'm afraid I lapsed a little, until now. But no, I wasn't actually *born* a Catholic.'

Father Francis sighs and reaches out for Kaya's hands. 'You are welcome here, Kaya,' he says. 'We don't mean to pry about your motives.'

Ursula Deacon rolls her eyes. 'What Father is trying to say is that there have been rumours that some of the parents in our current baptism class may be somewhat disingenuous about wanting to convert to Catholicism . . .'

Kaya feels a little warm. Is it hot in here? 'Did somebody suggest that Ollie and I . . .?' she begins.

'No, of course not,' Ursula Deacon snaps.

Kaya's face flushes pink and she fights the words inside her head that sing like a Christmas jingle: *You're going to hell! You're going to hell! You're going to hell!*

The older woman studies her face, and it unnerves Kaya enough to press on in her bid to persuade the priest and the principal in front of her that she is not faking the very thing she is, in fact, faking. 'My husband was an altar boy here,' she says. 'He was school captain too. A long time ago. I think around the mid-1990s.'

Ursula Deacon looks across to the stained-glass window with the mother and the baby on it in blue-and-white glass, and squints, as if she is trying to marry the name of a former school captain with the woman standing in front of her.

'We have had a few Pauls, I'm sure,' she says. 'I don't actually know as I only took up this role a couple of years ago. But look on the pews. The previous school captains are all listed.'

'Was your son an old boy? He's the head of sports now, isn't he?'

'Sam? No, he didn't come to this school.'

'I've heard wonderful things about him,' Kaya enthuses. It's true, she has, even if it is only from Estella on her doorstep.

'Yes. He is very talented.'

'I'm sure he is,' says Kaya. She seizes her chance. 'Ollie is a fabulous sportsman,' she says. 'That's why I feel he would be a wonderful fit here at St Ignatius', given the school's sporting prowess. He's a champion rower, actually, but he's an all-rounder really. You probably saw the photos I submitted with his application.'

'I'm sure I will see them when I go through the list of applicants,' says Ursula Deacon in an infuriatingly non-committal manner.

'Ollie is actually the youngest junior rower in Western Australia . . .'

'Rowing? That is interesting. But boys are assessed on more than sport.'

'Of course,' says Kaya. She is mildly annoyed that the headteacher does not seem to realise the effort she and Ollie are putting in – that she does not seem to realise their suitability, their *potential*. But on the other hand, at least she has been granted an audience with the gatekeeper.

'Well then,' Ursula Deacon says, bringing the conversation to an abrupt close. 'Good luck, Mrs Sterling. I'll see you at the Gala Day tomorrow.'

She nods and turns away, her heels rasping again at the shiny floor. Kaya watches her leave and thinks to herself that even if she has achieved nothing else on this chapel-cleaning mission, at least Principal Deacon knows Ollie's name and those stunning photos of her son in his rowing boat and holding the Under Twelve's state trophy will get another look.

'Kaya?' Father Francis holds out a can of Brasso. 'Shall we move on to the pews?'

Kaya takes the rag and the polish and nods enthusiastically. At the door to the church, Ursula Deacon calls out, 'Father!' and beckons him with a nod of the head.

'I'll just be a moment.' Father smiles and shuffles down the aisle towards her.

The pews are already shiny, but the brass plaques on each end are covered in fingerprints – the legacy of bored students sitting through Mass, poking and prodding anything that's more interesting than a wooden pew. Kaya starts to polish, skimming the list of school captains: Scott Birch – 1990; Anton Beckley – 1991; Mitchell Moore – 1992; Conrad Munro – 1995. Then, all the Pauls – five in a row! She closes her eyes and tries to imagine her husband at this school in grey shorts, white shirt and bottle-green blazer, gazing up at the stained-glass windows in primary colours, wondering how long Mass would last, and what kind of sandwich he might have for lunch, fingering his own name on this very plaque, she knew it. She closes her eyes for a moment and tries to imagine it, lets the warmth of the feeling enshroud her.

The plaque on the second-row pew lists the more recent captains. Robin Fraser – 2012, Richard Wise – 2013, Bryan Murphy – 2014; Simon Lincoln – 2015; Mitchell Pogson – 2016 . . . all the way to 2023. On the fourth pew, there is a single name, the current captain Felix Weaver. Estella had mentioned Felix Weaver on that first day in Pacific Pines, and then, literally five minutes later, Kaya had gone back into the house and picked up a stack of copies of the school magazine, *St Ignatius' Publica*. Paul had paid a small fortune to subscribe after he got sick and would read from his bed, regaling her with the ins and outs of life at his alma mater, even though she didn't care how much money the Year Seven boys had raised for *Médecins Sans Frontières* with their 'How many items can you fit in a matchbox?' initiative. And she had flicked open one of the copies and there was Felix Weaver in the centre spread. She remembered reading the same article a couple of months after Paul died. The photo of Felix had piqued her interest then because it was so . . . perfect. It was as if the school had hired some kind of wholesome teenage model for the shoot. His nose was Roman, the cut of his jaw square. Not so much as a hint of downy hair under his nose, or an angry red zit, or an unsightly row of metal protruding from his top lip. His dark-brown hair was cut neatly over the ears, his shirt collar starched and his green-and-red striped tie perfectly knotted. In fact, the only things Kaya hadn't considered aesthetically pleasing were Felix Weaver's eyes. They were so dark. So *intense* as they stared mockingly out of the page.

Underneath his face was the headline: *School Captain Wins Top Latin Prize* and a paragraph about how Felix Weaver had won five hundred dollars for writing an essay in the ancient language about life in Rome under the Emperor Augustus. Kaya had thought to herself how unusual it was for a boy of that age to want to enter a competition in a dead language, especially a boy who did not look remotely like a classics nerd and who seemed to her more a bantering rugby sort. But then he could be both, Kaya supposed, couldn't he? Wasn't she always telling Ollie it was OK to be good at soccer *and* academia and that he shouldn't pigeonhole himself into a single identity: a soccer player, a science expert, a clarinet player, when he could be all of them? And it looked as though at Iggy's, nerdy was accepted as a personality trait. Or maybe it was just that you could get away with a sideshow of nerdiness when you were as good-looking, and likely as popular, as Felix Weaver.

Kaya looks up to the sound of whispered speech coming from the door like a hiss. She leans her head towards the piping of the window frame that travels all the way along the stained-glass windows of the chapel to the doors, making the perfect ear trumpet, and she listens as Ursula Deacon says, 'For God's sake, Father, please do not invite any more hopeful mothers on to the cleaning rota or I won't be held accountable for what I'll do.'

She feels the burn of embarrassment as Father Francis nods at the principal in a 'bless you my child' manner before turning back around and heading up to the front pews again. He has barely taken a step when the echo of another pair of heels bounces around the quad and a shrill voice slices the quiet in the air.

'Mrs Deacon?' screeches a young redheaded woman in a red floral dress 'Excuse me, Mrs Deacon?'

Ursula Deacon's sigh, followed by a deep, throaty cough, is loud enough to catch at the front of the chapel.

'What is so important, Eloise, that you have to scream like that across the quad?' the older woman snaps, nodding her head towards the building on her immediate left. 'The WI has hired out the gym for yoga until eleven, and I don't think they'll appreciate your dulcet tones right in the middle of their *savasana*. Do you, Father?'

Father Francis looks at his feet.

'I'm really sorry,' says Eloise. 'But there's a woman at reception for you.'

'Well, can't you take a message?'

'Um,' Eloise stammers. 'I *would*, but I don't think she'll take no for an answer. You see, she's brought you a *gift* . . .'

'A gift?'

'Yes. She's, um . . . she's carrying a rather large cake in the shape of the chapel.'

Ursula Deacon turns and marches angrily across the quadrangle at lightning speed, letting out yet another world-weary sigh.

Kaya bids her goodbyes to Father Francis and sets off past the administration building towards the car park. She looks in through the window and sees the women at reception huddled around, not unlike a church group singing 'Kumbaya, My Lord' round a fire. And there is Bec Lloyd in the centre, her glossy, caramel hair falling down her back and her tiny, pert bottom squished into a pair of Lorna Jane yoga pants.

At the very moment Kaya passes the window, Bec happens to step aside – completely coincidentally – to allow a view of the chapel cake. It is stunning. A perfect replica of the quaint little building Kaya has just been cleaning. Everything is minute, yet perfectly reproduced, expertly crafted – from the colours of the stained glass to the abundant greenery surrounding it. And the detail of Christ on the crucifix in gold leaf is just . . . well, incredible. Kaya wishes she could get closer to inspect it, to touch it, to eat it.

'Oh, I'm so glad you like it,' chirps Bec. 'I understand how *trying* this time of year must be for all of you in the front office, what with all the paperwork you must be doing for admissions, so this is just a little treat to say how marvellous you all are!'

Kaya smiles. She sees what Bec is doing. Bec is lovely by nature, of course, but this supersedes the boundaries of mere affability.

'Spectacular,' says Ursula Deacon, who may or may not be salivating.

'My son Cooper helped with the sponge.' Kaya watches as Bec hands a slice to Ursula Deacon on a spotty melamine plate. 'Anything to get him inside and away from the rugby ball! He *adores* the sport. But then his father did coach the Wallabies in his youth . . .'

'Well, it tastes *heavenly*,' enthuses the principal, whose steely façade seems to have melted quicker than the buttercream clinging to her plastic fork. 'We must get Father Francis in here for a bite. He'll be thrilled by this ecclesiastical creation!'

Bec flicks her hair off her shoulders and beams.

Kaya realises she is grinning too. It certainly seems as though edible treats are looked upon more favourably by the admissions team at St Ignatius' than scrubbing the chapel floor. She wishes she'd known! Not that Kaya would ever be able to out-bake Bec Lloyd – nor would she want to, since Bec has quite literally been the only person in Pacific Pines to reach out to her and show her genuine kindness.

'It's my pleasure,' chirps the master baker. 'And if you'd like me to make any cupcakes for the children tomorrow, or a chocolate torte or individual puff pastries for the parents' cheese and wine session afterwards, I'd be happy to oblige.'

'Oh no, Mrs Lloyd . . .' Ursula Deacon closes her eyes as she pops the last piece of cake on her tongue.

'Call me Bec, please.'

'No thank you, *Bec*,' says Mrs Deacon with a smile that is caramel-coloured on account of the mock-sandstone fondant she has just consumed. 'There's really no need to help cater for Gala Day. The canteen staff have everything covered.'

'Nonsense.' Bec holds up a green-stained palm and makes the stop signal. 'I'll bring a little something along tomorrow. It would be my pleasure. I mean, baking is my absolute favourite thing in the world, so it is never a chore. I actually make all of the cakes for the Asher's Girls, too. My daughter Willow just finished there and is off to university in January. I've been baking all of their occasion cakes for years: their bicentenary, the Father's Day fetes and so on.'

Mrs Deacon, mouth full, nods again. 'Well, if you absolutely insist . . .'

Kaya bites on her smile and tiptoes past the second window towards the school gate and finds she is still smiling when she opens it and steps into the car park. Smiling, and shaking her head – partly in admiration, and partly in amazement, at the lengths these mothers (herself included) will go to in order to win places at St Ignatius' for their boys. *Nice work, Bec*, she whispers to herself as she approaches the car. *Nice work indeed.*

She pulls her phone out of her bag and checks it as she walks. The messages from Klara Bay are drying up – there are only so many times her friends can send the same morale-boosting *We miss you!* message or inquire about the status of Ollie's St Ignatius' application. She sighs and looks up, and that's when she sees him. Felix Weaver. The very same boy of school magazine and Iggy's chapel pew fame. He is dressed in blue shorts and a fawn T-shirt, which Kaya realises is because he has finished his exams now and will therefore have no more official lessons at Iggy's.

He leans against the oak tree at the far end of the car park, obscured from the eyes of anyone inside the school. The way his tall body connects with the tree trunk seems to Kaya to be bordering on arrogant, as if he is providing an audience with the ancient oak, and not the other way around. He speaks animatedly to a girl, a girl with long brown hair and a willowy frame, who Kaya cannot identify, since his bulky, rugby-player's body is obscuring her from view. His head nods enthusiastically and Kaya smiles briefly at the clandestine nature of young love. Felix reminds her of the type of boy she might have been in love with at sixteen or seventeen, when she didn't possess enough self-confidence to realise the arrogant boys with the overweening sense of self-worth were not the only option. Back when she didn't realise humour and empathy and kindness were the most important qualities of all.

Kaya thinks how wholesome this encounter is, between boy and girl, and she smiles wistfully, remembering what it is like to be in love. But the more Kaya looks, the more she realises that is not what this is. The way Felix Weaver's body almost looms over this girl, how she shrinks in his shadow as he jabs at his own temple with his forefinger, his other fist in a ball. As Kaya opens the driver's side door, she hears a muffled sob and a male's voice shouting, 'It's over. I'm *done*.'

She hovers outside the car. Should she stay? Ask the girl if everything is all right? But then she tells herself no, that would embarrass them both. Kids in love, or lust, or whatever you feel at this age, she can't quite remember, are prone to arguing. Anger and passion and lust and all those things all merge together. Isn't the drama of it, the *histrionics*, all part of the allure of first love?

She is sitting down before she realises she has left her phone on the roof of the car. She gets out again and looks out towards the old oak. That's when she sees Felix Weaver walking towards her, his left hand clenching and unclenching like he's having a blood test and they're searching for a vein. His face is rigid with fury. His eyes meet Kaya's and he looks almost stunned.

'Good afternoon,' he says, composing himself.

'Oh, hello,' Kaya forces a smile and pulls her denim jacket closed across her chest. 'It's a stunning day, isn't it?'

'Beautiful,' he responds with a smile that does not reach his eyes, and Kaya suspects no smile ever has, because from the brief moment her pale blue eyes meet his almost black ones, she realises they are utterly devoid of emotion. The pupils are so wide, so dark, that they consume all of the brown. It gives her a shiver, a fleeting feeling of something akin to anxiety, this boy's malignant countenance.

'Well, I'll be off,' Kaya mutters and slides back inside the car, watching this nearly-man stride arrogantly, angrily, into the school quad, his T-shirt hanging out of his shorts at the back. When he has gone, she looks to see if the girl is there, if she does indeed need a comforting word, but no one remains near the old oak. All she sees as she squints ahead are branches swaying in the breeze, and all she hears from her open window is the rustle of leaves and the trill of birdsong that sounds not unlike the strains of a stifled sob.

7

Estella

'You've been through my stuff?' Felicity's face burns puce. 'How dare you!'

Estella isn't particularly fazed because Felicity takes after her: quick to anger, slow to repent. But she will usually repent, after a fashion. She may hold a grudge for a while (Estella knows *she* does, Conrad has told her this enough times throughout their marriage) but then she will begin to talk again, a way of hinting at an apology without actually offering one. It is a sensibility of all the Wickham women, Estella's own mother had been the same, and not a Munro trait – but it is evidently something that is deeply woven into Felicity's DNA.

She shrugs at her daughter. 'You are still legally a child, Felicity, and I am your parent. And while you're a *child* living in my house, I can and will enter your bedroom whenever I like.'

Felicity's nostrils flare. 'I think you'll find it's illegal to rummage through someone's stuff,' she says through her front teeth.

Jonty's head pops up over his copy of Eddie Woo's *Simple Maths*, or 'Maths for Simples' as Felicity likes to call it. 'It's not illegal at all,' he says. 'Mum's actually right.'

'Shut up, dickwad,' Felicity spits. She turns back to Estella. 'Reading someone's diary is *ethically* wrong.'

'I didn't read your diary,' Estella lies. 'Why on earth would I want to?'

'Because you always have to know *everything*!' Felicity throws her hands up in the air. 'You're a big fat control freak.'

Estella sighs, trying not to cling on to the words 'big' and 'fat' because she knows Felicity is just using them metaphorically. Size twelve is by no means fat, although Estella does feel it when she stands next to Bec with her skinny legs and her Pilates-toned abs. Bec hasn't yet felt the tight-panted, soft-gutted rage of perimenopause, but she will. Oh, she will! And Estella is rather looking forward to it, even though she suspects Bec will wear a hot flush as effortlessly as she wears everything else. This is a cross Estella must bear.

'Believe me, darling, I have no interest in your teenage angst,' Estella lies. 'I've got enough to worry about with the boys and their school admissions at the moment without wanting to read about which brand of tampons you're currently sampling . . .'

She knows it is wrong to be so childish, so *cruel*, but Felicity *made* her say it. God, she angers Estella with her bitter tongue and her aloof manner and her bitchy way of calling her 'Estella' when she should be Mum. This is what they do to one another, mother and daughter, this is how they always end up, in this state of combat. It is their schtick. It is Felicity's safe place in a world where you have to be polite to everyone else. Estella knows that as the adult she should know better, but she cannot help but bite back. Yet if anyone else spoke to Felicity in this manner, Estella would skin them alive.

Conrad appears in the kitchen. 'Hello, ladies,' he says.

Felicity ignores him. 'That's because you don't need tampons when you're a dried-up, menopausal old hag!' she says. *Ouch!* 'Bet you don't touch the boys' stuff, do you? Not the precious twins. I just don't matter to you!'

And here it is again, Felicity's assumption that Estella prefers the twins, that somehow she doesn't measure up to them. It is rubbish, of course. The problem is, Estella sees too much of herself in Felicity – the bits of herself she doesn't necessarily like.

Conrad retreats through the door he's just come through.

'Like I said, Felicity . . .' Estella studies the white fleck on the nailbed of her left forefinger (because she's picked off all her shellac, damn it) which her kinesiologist, Annabel Carter, says is her body's way of informing her she has a mild zinc deficiency. 'I have zero interest in your diary.'

Except Estella *does* have an interest, which is why she had opened the red, leather-bound notebook when she'd found it in Felicity's top drawer behind all of her padded Bonds bras and the coloured G-strings that could double as children's PPE masks.

Estella had gone looking for more weed and reasoned that, like all teenagers, Felicity probably wasn't particularly imaginative when it came to hiding her stash, especially given the last bag had been so easy to find. And hell, did Estella need a toke at that precise moment, what with her ongoing worry about the boys and about wooing Ursula Deacon and her son Sam. But she'd found the diary instead, with the silver pen with the big pink pom-pom thing on the end, which had made Estella feel a sudden and deep flash of affection, remembering that Felicity was still just a girl, albeit a nearly-woman, of seventeen, and it had made her realise she was really too hard on her. She'd try and do better, try and bite her tongue when Felicity's was caustic.

She picked up the book and lifted it to her nose, sniffed it, as if it might smell of something intriguing, of secrets perhaps, but all she got was a whiff of leather and the scent of the soap Felicity kept in her drawer to make her underwear smell nice. She smiled wistfully, the memories of her own teenage diary held tight in her hands – the way she'd written in it every night before she went to sleep, rain or shine, happy or sad, and given herself the therapy she didn't get from her parents. She still had the books somewhere because there were memories inside she couldn't bear to part with, although she didn't know exactly where she'd put them, just that they were somewhere in the attic with her old Asher's textbooks and her hockey medals and various other memorabilia. Signs of another life: a small white rabbit, a blue-and-pink-checked blanket, a small wristband with her name on it, stashed away for years, confined to the tucked-away in the memory box.

She gently closed the bedroom door and sat herself on the edge of Felicity's double bed with the lilac Sheridan linen and the cushion with the reversible sequins that said 'Happy AF' in gold, and 'Sad AF' on the flipside in black, and opened the book to the current week. She'd had to squint to read Felicity's loopy, public-school writing with its calligraphic bent, and she hadn't had to skim much to find out that her daughter hated her (well, she knew that already). But it was the entry from a few days ago that had really bothered Estella.

Hello hello, Diario!

So, my news is . . . I'm gonna do it with BOY. I'm scared out of my mind but I'm ready. The thing is, I think I love him. No, I don't think, I KNOW! I LOVE HIM!! There, I said it (in fact I wrote it, which is even more official) and God it feels so weird to write it in INK, but it is true! He told me he has feelings for me and I'm so happy – I'd been so worried about him liking Willow. A few weeks ago she told me he was into her and that he'd cornered her outside Asher's and begged her to go out with him, but she said she told him she wasn't interested. She actually said she found him creepy?!! But I think she was bigging herself up, exaggerating it and stuff. When I asked him about it he laughed and said, 'She's so full of herself!' He says it's ME he likes which makes me feel pretty good, especially because Willow always gets the best of everything. She got vice-captain at Asher's, she always gets her pick of boys (well, usually!!) and she even got the best mum. She and Bec are so close and what do I get? Stupid Estella with her lectures about teen pregnancy and her smug side-smiles. She literally kills my life. I hope I don't grow up to be like her.

Love, Flick xoxo

The words had made Estella's stomach flip inside out, like a plastic popper toy, her breath heave in almost painfully. She'd flipped the page, desperate to read on, but then she'd heard the front door click shut and Felicity's voice call in to the hall, 'Hello? Anyone home?' and she'd slammed the book shut and opened up the drawer and shoved it to the

very back. But she couldn't remember whether the diary
had been at the back *left* or the back *right* of the knicker
drawer when she had taken it out, and so she'd just shut
the damn thing and called, 'Upstairs! Down in a minute!'
so she didn't get caught with her hand in the cookie jar, so
to speak. And she'd walked downstairs knotted with angst
for her daughter, her precious Felicity, and down in the
kitchen she had stolen surreptitious glances at her almost-
not-a-virgin girl as she buttered her toast in her school
uniform, her skirt rolled up almost to her buttocks and her
eyeliner sculpted into a feisty point.

It wasn't the I-hate-my-mother stuff she'd written that
made Estella baulk, or even the planning-to-lose-my-
virginity part, because that could be halted. What had
broken Estella's heart was the inferiority complex, the
Willow effect – the thing Felicity had been dealing with
her whole life. In terms of appearance, Felicity is utterly
striking with her skinny legs, and thick brown hair that
hangs at her waist – but so is Willow. The two girls could
be sisters with their large eyes and tanned skin. Even as
little girls, if either Estella or Bec took them both out on
a play date without the other parent, people would ask if
they were twins, even though Willow was ten months older
(now over the age of consent, unlike Felicity).

'You're so lucky,' various women would sigh, wistfully,
particularly those of grandparenting age. 'I always wanted
twins.' Once, an older woman, who hadn't realised the
girls were with her, remarked how unfortunate it was that
one of the 'twins' was so much prettier than the other.
'That one is just so *striking*,' she'd said, pointing directly at

Willow, and Estella had been livid. Willow Lloyd *is* pretty, Estella has never denied that, but in such an *obvious* way. It is Felicity's angular, slightly pointed features that make her so much more striking: like Stella Tennant to Kate Moss. She hates the idea of Felicity feeling inferior, of her believing Willow gets the lion's share not only of looks but of everything. In her opinion, Felicity outstrips Willow Lloyd in most ways, but, unlike Felicity, she doesn't feel the need to sit in a family circle over a slice of rainbow cake and tell her.

And now here are Felicity and Willow, both about to take the ultimate step into womanhood – a step that cannot be reversed, and, from what Estella can see, Felicity views it more as one-upmanship than a considered foot forward. Bec has told her, without so much as a sniff of concern, that she and Willow have had 'the talk' and that she has bought Willow a packet of Durex for when the moment comes, so to speak. Conrad argues that Bec's contraceptive chat has merit in today's society, but Estella always batters the chatter down like a fairground vole in a hole. Of course Bec is not right! Her parenting is way too liberal, way too 'Yeah, whatever. *You* decide.' It is woke parenting at its worst. And Estella wants more for her only daughter, damn it! At the very least, true love, like Estella herself felt all those years ago, even if *that* boy (of whom she still dreams after twenty-five years with the same sense of teenage longing) had broken her heart into a million pieces. But she knows it isn't like this for Felicity. Felicity isn't in real love, even if she thinks she is: she is infatuated, and she is grateful that this boy wants her over Willow. It is not love she is in – it is a race.

Estella lets her mind wander for a moment to a place she would rather it does not go. What if there is a pregnancy? What will Felicity do about university then? What effect will it have on the twins, on their standing at school? The goose bumps that chase down her arms are unwelcome and as she watches her daughter's innocent rosebud lips open and her brace-straightened white teeth bite angrily into a slice of Vegemite-slathered toast, Estella vows Felicity will give away her virginity over her dead body! She will find this individual Felicity has nicknamed 'BOY' and have a stern word with him – and if not with him, then with his mother. And she doesn't care if she is despised by Felicity for embarrassing her because she is glad she is a graduate of the hard-knocks school of parenting, and not the liberal free-for-all academy that spews out the likes of Bec.

'Well, someone's been nosing around in my underwear drawer, because my diary has been moved.' Felicity's voice is slow and measured.

She turns to the twins. 'Was it one of you two?'

'No,' says Archie, alarm paralysing his face. 'I would never . . .'

Felicity softens, her shoulders drop. 'I know, Arch,' she sighs. 'I know you wouldn't.' She smiles at him, her head cocked apologetically to the side. Archie's features relax again.

She turns to Jonty. 'Was it *you*?' she snaps.

'Eww, like I'd ever go anywhere near your gross knickers.' Jonty puts his index finger in his mouth and pretends to vomit. 'I don't know where they've been. Great hiding place, by the way. Because no one *ever* hides anything in their underwear drawer, do they? It's like hiding cash under the mattress. Hashtag: *obvious*.'

Felicity lifts her hand and goes to swipe Jonty's head but he ducks like the pro-sportsman he is and laughs as her hand collects nothing but air.

'Ooooooh!' He does jazz hands. 'I'm scared!'

'Ugh, just go away and die,' Felicity yells. 'You know what? I cannot wait to get out of this hellhole in January. At least I'll finally get some privacy! Willow never has to deal with this shit from her family!' She looks at Estella, and Estella can see her daughter's eyes are hot with tears. 'Why can't you be more like Bec?'

She closes her eyes and takes the hit. She feels a momentary flash of anger at Bec that deflects back to Felicity, where Estella suspects it should have been directed all along.

'You'd like me to be more like Bec, would you?' She pulls open the top drawer and yanks out a whisk and a wooden spoon and waves them dramatically. 'Fine, well let's bake a nice *moist* sponge cake together then and talk about our problems! And then you can go out and pierce every orifice you like and get pregnant by some pre-pubescent limp dick . . .'

'Technically, if you're pre-pubescent, it's biologically impossible . . .' Archie begins.

'And if you're a limp dick . . .' says Jonty.

'I *knew* you'd read my diary!' Felicity kicks her school bag across the floor. 'I hate you,' she screams. 'I hate the lot of you! You can all drop dead!'

She storms up the stairs, stomps along the landing and slams her bedroom door so violently that Archie's head retreats into his shoulders like a turtle's. Then she opens her door a crack and yells, 'Except you, Archie!' before slamming it again. Archie bites down on his smile and covers his face with his advanced maths book.

Estella sighs. She is done for the day. Done with recalcitrant teenagers. Done with Conrad retreating to the basement to tinker in his man cave, leaving every single jot of disciplining to her. Done with trying to explain the nine times table on her fingers to Jonty, who just stares at her vacantly like a guppy. He can summon the intelligence to be sarcastic to his sister, it seems, but cannot identify the irony in an English set text.

She walks into the garden and calls Bec, disregarding her disdain for her friend's woke parenting because right now she needs a sympathetic voice and despair trumps annoyance, and tells her in one long hushed monologue that Felicity is planning to go all the way with a teenager she has nicknamed BOY.

'You read her diary?' Bec asks, incredulous. 'You can't do that!'

'Everyone does it.'

'I don't.'

'Well give yourself a medal then, St Rebecca . . .'

Bec sighs. 'Would you like my advice or not?'

'For fuck's sake, Bec! Felicity's about to lose her virginity and I'm losing my *mind*!' Estella turns around in a circle, the fingers of her left hand pressed to her temple.

'Calm down. She hasn't done it yet, has she?'

'No, but she will, even if it's just to annoy me!'

Estella think she hears another sigh. 'Are you holding the phone between your head and your neck?'

'Yes, why?'

'What on earth are you doing?'

'Cracking eggs. Anyway, I don't think this is about you, Estella. Just sit down with her.' There it is, the hypnotic sound, the reasoning. 'Talk to her about it. Try and be her friend. Flick needs you right now. She needs friendship and direction.'

But Estella can't do that, it does not come naturally to her. She has tried and tried but it wasn't the way she was brought up. Her strict Catholic parents had no time for friendship, just rules and indoctrination, and however hard she tries she cannot shake off what nurture ultimately taught her. Apart from the bit about drugs being bad, because right now she could murder a joint.

'Well thank you, I'll consider it,' she says snippily to Bec as if Bec had called *her* for a favour, and hangs up. She imagines Bec rolling her eyes and switching the food processor back on, dialling up the volume on some warbling Mariah Carey track.

Estella walks towards the end of the garden where the stone bench overlooks the ocean. She fingers the plastic sandwich bag in her pocket containing the weed she located inside one of Felicity's white sports socks. On the bench, out of sight from the house and overlooked only by Kaya Sterling's landing window, she pulls out the Rizlas and cannabis and rolls a spliff worthy of Bob Marley. She sparks it up and sucks in hard and exhales out to sea and feels the weight come off her like the hit from a dram of whisky. She closes her eyes and thinks about her own mother, the way they would scream at one another when she was seventeen, when Estella thought she knew everything about love and life and was about to experience the very depth of loss. She sits, now, on the same bench where she sat when she was pregnant, each time, and cradled her babies in her open hands, just inches beneath the surface of her skin, felt their limbs push against her palms. Felicity had kicked the most, proved the most irksome and outspoken even inside the womb and she smiles now, remembers what Felicity was like as a child, angelic until the age of six when her brothers came along and then somehow angry, feeling as though Estella didn't have time for her any more, when really all Estella didn't have time for was histrionics.

She takes out her phone to lose herself in Instagram for a few precious moments. There is a post from Kaya, showing Ollie nursing a rugby ball. Underneath Kaya has written: *Future Wallaby!* with an emoji of a rugby ball and tagged *#iggys* and *#stignatiusgrammar*.

'Future Wallaby my arse,' Estella mutters. She clicks on to Kaya's grid, which is full of photos of Ollie doing various sports, but strangely none of him rowing.

She takes another toke on the spliff, feels her shoulders unfurl and returns to her feed. Next is Nicole Drayton and a photo of her irritating kelpie Rocket, who always sniffs Estella's crotch whenever she has the misfortune to bump into the other woman outside Pacific Pines Primary. The damn dog never goes for Estella's hands or feet but always for the groin, as though Estella has a bag of puppy treats stuffed up there. *Most* unsavoury. Estella sighs and 'loves' the photo anyway, reasoning that, when they all leave the school in a matter of weeks, she will unfollow the insipid woman. Further down her feed, she sees the @st_ignatius_school handle and the photo of the school crest with its Latin motto *felix quia fortis,* which means 'happiness through strength', and she feels the familiar pang of yearning.

Then comes the photo underneath. Estella stares at it for a moment, confused. The woman looks familiar, the pose so recognisable. It takes her a second to work it out and then the mist clears. It is Bec. Bec beaming out from St Ignatius' Grammar's Instagram grid, next to a cake. And not just a normal, bog-standard sponge like the one she had 'whipped up' for Conrad's forty-eighth birthday last month with a token marzipan stethoscope on the top, but some bloody massive *Great Australian Bake Off* winner, shaped like St Ignatius' very own chapel. A cake with a steeple and a wooden door and intricate sandstone brickwork and a tiny little Christ on a tiny little gold-leaf crucifix. And some miniature silver eucalyptus too, fashioned out of some kind of edible icing and a goddamn kookaburra of all things perched on the roof! Estella wonders if the spliff she is smoking is a little too strong and so she takes another puff to reassess. She clicks off Instagram and on to the app again, typing in the school's handle to check she wasn't seeing things. But the same photo comes up, the first little square on the little patchwork of the Iggy's home page. And yes, the cake in the photo is still a church, and the woman grinning inanely next to it is still Bec.

The caption below reads, *This work of art was gifted to St Ignatius' by prospective Iggy's parent Bec Lloyd. Thank you so very much for your thoughtful gift @Cakes_By_Bec and good luck to your talented son Cooper at Gala Day tomorrow!*

And there is Bec, all caramel highlights and Bondi Sands tan, and she has written underneath: *Such a pleasure Ursula and @st_ignatius_boys_grammar. I sincerely hope you enjoy it. It was a thrill to make it for you and your hardworking staff! #cake #cakeart #buttercream #fondant #passion #dowhatyoulove #school #stignatius #bestschoolever #wellroundedboys #sweettreats #iheartbaking*

Estella feels a range of emotions in quick succession. The first is amusement at the use of the words '*work of art*' in the initial caption, because, after all, it is hardly a Gauguin or a Matisse they're discussing, is it? Then comes confusion. Why didn't Bec tell her what she was up to? Estella herself had encouraged the idea of doing something 'extra' – although perhaps not this extra! Had Bec asked for Estella's input, she might have suggested that it looked a little *desperate* to go to so much effort . . .

Estella lets the situation percolate. There is a sensation of discomfort, and then, with a final suck on the soggy end of the spliff, comes irritation. Bec, on the official St Ignatius' Instagram page? Bec, calling the principal *Ursula* and not Mrs Deacon? What the actual . . . ?

The resentment consumes her rapidly, like fire. She feels her back teeth clench and she lets out a groan from between them – a low growl that seems to turn into a roar the longer it lasts. Loud enough to make the rainbow lorikeet on the branch beside her fly off in alarm, anyway. She looks at the bird. 'Oh fuck off,' she says, flicking the glowing end of the spliff in the bird's general direction. She just cannot deal with it all: an almost sexually active daughter, discombobulated twins – one son who couldn't kick a ball between two posts if they were a kilometre apart, and another who struggles with his times tables – and now a conniving best friend. She cannot cope with *any* of it. Especially not with Gala Day tomorrow, when Jonty and Archie's entire futures will be mapped out for them, completely out of her control.

She taps her foot as she types a snippy text to Bec.

Strange you didn't mention your little PR stunt just now. Well done.

She watches as the three grey dots fall over themselves.

You didn't give me a chance, Bec writes. *You hung up on me. Are you OK? U sound annoyed.*

Why would I be annoyed?

Dot . . . dot . . . dot. *I really don't know, Estella.*

Estella bites her cheek to the point of drawing blood. 'Damn it,' she says, tasting metal. She feels foolish for opening up to Bec when Bec has been trying to race ahead of her. Her best friend is playing a game, and it has paid off. And now Estella must do the same – it is every mother for herself. What is the expression? Go big, or go home? She said as much to Bec and Kaya, and now both of them have turned over their best cards before she has even studied hers. Is this *her* fault? She has been far too generous with her advice – next time she will keep her helpful suggestions to herself.

Estella realises she doesn't have anything specific to offer the school, aside from the prestige of Conrad's job at the hospital maybe – but even that isn't enough to sway a headteacher when faced with a pair of twins who are strong in opposing skill sets, but entirely weak in others. What can she possibly do to give the twins, her beloved *boys*, the advantage? How can she ensure a two-for-one deal at St Ignatius'? To guarantee her boys do not fail where Cooper Lloyd, and perhaps even Ollie Sterling, both look set to flourish?

Estella looks to the ocean for answers, and when they don't come, she closes her eyes and listens to the hiss of the ocean spray as it thrashes the rocks below. Almost every time she sits on this bench and closes her eyes she feels it – that deep sense of longing, of loss. It is the same sensation that comes to her every time she is here. She can taste it, along with the sea salt and the heady aftertaste of weed. But conversely, she needs to come here to remember because she cannot have the comfort without the agony.

But now she must look forward. Archie and Jonty, Jonty and Archie. So different, yet so startlingly alike. She clicks on to her camera roll and looks at them, her boys. Two minutes apart by birth and not a mark to distinguish them, yet with personalities so utterly contrary. She opens her eyes and returns to the present. If only there was a way she could make Archie better at sport and Jonty more academic, just for one day! Just for Gala Day. Just until they have secured their places at Iggy's, until they are welcomed into the sacred fold. After that, it won't matter where they flourish or where they fail, because they will be insiders. They will be card-carrying, uniform-wearing Iggy's boys.

The idea hits her like a sharp slap to the cheek. She chews on it for a moment or two, lets it simmer in her brain. It is risky, of course it is. Conrad will say it is reckless, ill-advised. But it might just work. And they don't have many other options in the grand scheme of things, do they?

She stands up and cups her hands.

'Boys!' she cat-calls so loudly that Kaya Sterling appears at her upstairs window, eager to find the source of the noise. Estella glares up at her and sees the woman raise a limp, embarrassed hand and then retreat behind the curtain again. It isn't the first time she has seen the merry widow spying on her from that intrusive little window. Estella thinks that perhaps Kaya will not do it any more, now she knows she has been caught out and Estella has given her a warning stare.

'What's up, Mum?' Jonty jogs across the grass in his baggy Adidas shorts and singlet. Archie follows behind in a brisk walk, his always-on-the-cold-side body wrapped up in a jumper and jeans, his finger holding his place between the pages of his textbook.

'Sit down,' Estella tells the boys, patting the stone bench alternately on either side of her. Archie sits on the left, as he always does, and Jonty on the right. It is a force of habit so people can tell them apart. They have done it since they were tiny boys, and only when they purposely want to confuse do they swap positions, although this is rare. These days they have less interest in pretending they are not themselves. Jonty is far too embarrassed by Archie's lack of skill on the rugby pitch to want people to think he is him, and Archie finds it irritating when the teachers at Pacific Pines Primary School think it is *he* who is perpetually confusing acute angles with obtuse. The boys are close by virtue of sharing a womb, but they like being individuals, and Estella believes that is the way it should stay.

By the time the boys are seated, Estella's shoulders have dropped significantly and the equilibrium inside her brain has been restored, although she is peckish as anything. She could *murder* a plate of hot chips. She ruffles Jonty's hair, then Archie's. If she closes her eyes, there is nothing to distinguish the feeling of silk sliding between her fingers at that moment to tell her which boy is which. Weird as it is, the boys smell identical too – their skin, their scalp, their musty bedrooms – and Estella sometimes wonders if she would be able to tell them apart if she were blindfolded, on a game show or after some amount of time apart. If the primal bloodhound-worthy instinct of motherhood would allow her to distinguish her boys, sightless. She would fail at it, she is convinced. *That's* how alike they are.

Her boys look at her, their interest mirrored.

'I need your help with something.'

Estella knows now this was what she must do. It is her only course of action, and, even if it *is* a resolution made on a whim on the stone bench where she has made many a rash decision in the past, she will stick with it, because when Estella Munro (née Wickham) makes up her mind about something, she rarely changes it. She is notorious for it. It is one of her mainstays, her strengths.

And it is exactly what worries her about Felicity.

TUESDAY: THE GALA DAY

8

Bec

Bec wakes feeling anxious. She is a little sleep-deprived on account of staying up late to make sixty-four chocolate tortes for the Gala Day cheese and wine soirée, and then spending a little too much time staring at the bright, flashing screen of her iPhone before she turned out the light. She knows she shouldn't stare at her phone screen before bed, but looking at cake pages on Instagram is sometimes the only way she can shake off the mania of the day. There is something utterly hypnotic about watching another hand slather on buttercream with a square spatula on a cake as it rotates majestically on a wheel. The turning, the layering, is almost hypnotic to her.

She flicks on the kettle, then takes out three large Tupperware containers that house the delicate miniature tortes and touches the top of a couple of them lightly with the pad of her index finger. They are perfectly set, their surfaces smooth and reflective, and she smiles to herself as she sprinkles cacao powder lightly over the top using a small, handheld sieve. She knows she didn't *have* to do it, spend her Monday night baking, but the competitive spirit seems to have ignited in her after Estella's post-Mass warning to be extra. And besides, what else was she going to do? Netflix and chill? Hardly. Not the night before Gala Day.

Bec takes a good first sip of sweet tea and leans against the kitchen bench as she waits for the family to stir. She picks up her phone and clicks open her email, hoping for a moment's peace from her thumping heart – she just wants today to be over. Only twelve hours and she'll be home again and Cooper's fate will be in the hands of Ursula Deacon and her son Sam. Immediately she sees the name Lucki_Texta she realises she shouldn't have clicked on the blue email icon. This time the subject is *A sage situation* and even though the use of the word 'sage' can be nothing but coincidental (besides, wouldn't it have a capital letter otherwise?) Bec feels a stab of anxiety, as if the composer knows something of her family, besides her own name. She clicks on the body of the email.

Don't ignore me, Bec, it reads. *I know ALL about you.*

She looks around the kitchen in a panic, as if someone is about to jump out at her. Who is doing this to her? She takes out a chocolate torte and bites into it, closes her eyes. *It's OK,* she tells herself as the sweetness takes hold and the rich taste floods her whole endocrine system. *You know it's just spam.* She clicks the box next to the message and banishes the sender to her list of junk accounts along with the rest of the spam: the Bitcoin cons, the dozen fake emails about packages being delivered, the *Grow Your Penis by 80 per cent* offers. *Go phish!* She will not bother telling Tom about these latest messages, because if she tells him, it almost makes it sound like they are something to worry about. And they are not. They really aren't!

'Nolite te bastardes carborundorum,' she mutters to herself with a sigh. *Don't let the bastards grind you down.*

'Talking to yourself again, Mum?' It is Cooper.

'Just counting the tortes, kiddo,' she lies. 'Did you sleep OK?'

'Yeah, sort of.' He wraps his arms around her and she buries her face in his hair.

'How are you feeling?' she asks.

'Bit nervous I guess.'

Bec stands back and looks him in the eye. 'You can only try your best, Coops,' she says. 'You'll be fine whatever happens today, so don't fret. Just enjoy it.'

He pulls away, conversation over. Cooper, as a general rule, doesn't like to get too close to the source of his discomfort. He has Bec to thank for that. 'What's for breakfast?'

Bec holds up a frying pan. 'Eggs and bacon?'

'Yes!'

Bec drains her mug of coffee and sighs. Cooper's nerves have ramped up her own jitters. She rolls her head on her neck, puts her mug into the butler's sink and heads upstairs to wake Willow.

Willow is sitting up in bed, scrolling on her phone in the dark.

'Oh, you're awake.'

'Hey Mum.'

'Are you coming today?' Bec asks. 'To support Cooper?'

Bec realises she should probably *tell* Willow she is coming to support Cooper and not offer her the choice, but she has always found it hard to be that kind of mum.

'Yeah, course!' Willow's phone pings in her hand and she smiles. 'I'll be there.'

'You look happy,' says Bec as she opens the blinds. 'Who's the text from?'

'Chris Hemsworth.'

'Again?' Bec accepts Willow's deflection of the question. She won't ask again – her daughter is entitled to her privacy.

Willow brings the large brown stuffed dog she's had since she was a baby up to her chest and breathes in its scent and Bec takes in the scene: her daughter, an adult now at eighteen but still a child in so many ways. Texting a boy while she cuddles her dog.

'I'm glad you're coming,' says Bec. 'Cooper will be so pleased.' She knows this isn't strictly true. Cooper won't care if Willow is there today or not, but Bec likes to encourage harmony between her eldest children, even if it doesn't always exist organically.

Willow picks up a make-up remover wipe and slowly strokes her lashes from the root to the tip. Tom's long, dark eyelashes, with Bec's big blue eyes: a pleasing combination, she is often told by those types of people who love to look at a child's face and work out which parent they favour. This is no criticism, because Bec herself is one of those people, although she cannot see it in her own children, because biology seems to forbid it.

'I'm going to take my car and pick up Flick,' Willow says. 'She won't even get in the same car as Estella at the moment. They've been arguing again.'

'Oh?'

'Yeah, no surprise,' says Willow. 'Estella's being a right cow as usual. She read Flick's diary and *totally* denied it, but Flick knows she did because Estella put it back in the wrong place. Can you believe it?'

Bec doesn't answer. She knows full well what Estella has been up to.

'And it definitely wasn't one of the boys because Jonty can't even read a street sign, let alone joined-up handwriting, and Archie wouldn't do that to Flick because they're super-close . . .'

'I'm sure there's a reason for it,' Bec says diplomatically. 'Estella really isn't all bad, she's just—'

'*And*,' Willow is gathering steam. 'She only went and dobbed in Kaya Sterling for being a fake Catholic, which Flick is seriously upset about because the poor woman is, like, a grieving widow and everything. She watched her poor husband die of cancer and then Estella comes in and starts making her life hell for no reason . . .'

'Estella did that?' Bec feels a rush of irritation. She barely knows Kaya Sterling, but from first impressions the woman is lovely. Who is Estella to judge Kaya's motives? Perhaps there is a serious reason she wants Ollie in the school. And isn't Kaya only doing what Estella is also doing, and Bec is doing too? Nudging, pushing, giving their boys a helping hand? Bec sees now that Estella is like a swan on a lake, paddling wildly underneath the surface of the water, and that she is likely hatching a plan that will trump everyone else's efforts in the run-up to Gala Day – although what that might be is anyone's guess. Bec is not annoyed about this in itself because she wants Estella's boys to get a place at Iggy's; she knows more than anyone how much this means to Estella, why she's so desperate for it and how it will give her closure on the secrets of her past if she can get her boys over the line. But really, attacking Kaya? It's a step too far.

Willow slicks a nude gloss on her lips. 'Anyway, I'll meet you there, yeah? At Iggy's?' She gestures to the keys to her grey Holden Captiva – a hand-me-down from Bec.

'Ah, you're taking the rust bucket?' she laughs.

'It's no laughing matter, Mum. Haven't you seen the news? People are going about nicking hubcaps and head-light covers and tail-lights now it's out of production. My little car's worth a fortune with all the parts. I could literally pull it apart and make heaps on eBay. I could get a hundred and fifty dollars for one tail-light! Not that I would . . .'

'You're *holden* on to it, right?'

'Mum, that was so bad.'

Bec smiles. She suspects Willow really wants to go to Gala Day because her boyfriend will be there. She knows little about the mysterious boy her eldest is dating, only that he was at Iggy's. She hopes, or rather, she *knows*, that Willow will tell her in good time. They are incredibly close and it is a relationship on which Bec prides herself. She knows she is lucky. Too many mothers she knows have fractious, eggshell relationships with their children, yet she and Willow barely disagree on anything. Even during the early teen years, when hormones raged, angry and fear-some like the ocean's swell, she and Willow managed to ride the storm and emerge upright, intact. Estella might make the odd passive-aggressive comment to Bec, such as 'Personally I don't *want* to be best friends with my own offspring,' but Bec knows, deep down, it is jealousy talk-ing. She genuinely feels for Estella and wishes her friend had with Flick what she herself has with Willow. Every mother deserves that, surely?

'Fine by me,' she says. 'Just make sure you check in on Coops at some point, won't you? To wish him luck.'

'I'll tell him to break a leg.'

'Oh God, please do *not* tell him to break a leg!'

'I'll say it to Jonty Munro instead,' Willow says with a wink.

Bec makes to leave but turns and hovers by the door. 'Do you think it's too much?'

'What?'

'All the baking I'm doing for Iggy's? Estella thinks so.'

Willow's back straightens. 'Well Estella can get stuffed,' she snaps. 'Seriously, Mum. Estella is just jealous because you work with chocolate all day and you still look like a supermodel. You've done an epic job, and who cares if it's a little over-the-top? And anyway, your chocolate tortes are *literally* insane. The principal is legit going to *die*!'

The gravel crunches underneath the wheels of the car as it turns in through the wrought-iron gates with the giant school crest, *felix quia fortis*, surrounded by green and red twirly filigree, and proceeds down a wide, tree-lined gravel drive. The sprawling grounds ahead of them look to Bec like something from a British period drama, all stone and gravel and landscaped gardens blocked off from the public with rope bunting that demands, at periodic intervals, that visitors keep off the grass. Bendy trees intertwine overhead, throwing a dappled orange light over the sculpted pathway.

At the far end of the driveway is the main schoolhouse, a magnificent sandstone building with tall, domed windows and a large, carved wooden door. Beside it sits a rather more modern two-storey red-brick facility that backs on to the sports fields beyond – a rugby pitch and cricket oval – as well as tennis and basketball courts, and an indoor pool. The juxtaposition between the two buildings is almost laughable. Like a demure, yet elaborate, Victorian courtier standing beside a self-assured Gen Z teen in a crop top and bare legs. In the middle of the two is the chapel with a clock tower that says the correct time: twelve forty-five p.m. They have fifteen minutes before the official commencement of Gala Day.

'Have you got the brochure there, Coops?' Bec looks in the rear-view mirror. 'Give us some history.' It can't hurt to get Cooper well acquainted with the school's past ahead of his interview later in the day. He takes the brochure out of Sage's hands and Bec gets a strong waft of the thick, lacquered pages as he opens it. He takes a breath, like he is already being interviewed, and Bec's heart aches for him.

'"St Ignatius' was built by the first group of monks to arrive in the area in the late 1800s,"' he reads. '"The order of St Ignatius ordered tons of Welsh sandstone to be shipped to their picture . . . picturesque forty-acre domicile beside the ocean in the quaint fishing village of Pacific Pines, where they built the grand Main House. Main House was home to as many as eighty monks throughout both the First and Second World Wars, until the early 1920s. When the enclave's infra . . . infra . . ."'

'Infrastructure,' says Tom.

'"*When the enclave's infrastructure . . .*"'Cooper sighs and hands over the glossy magazine. 'Can you read it, Dad?'

'Sure.'Tom reaches back for the brochure.

'"When the enclave's infrastructure began to appear along the cliffside and Pacific Pines became a desirable residence for second-generation Australians, the monks decided to turn the building into a school,"' he reads. '"In 1991, the B-wing science block, swimming pool and cricket oval were added at the right-hand side of the building. The main schoolhouse remains the same as it was when the monks first opened their doors to the first boys.

'"Five years ago, we celebrated our centenary as the country's most elite school, priding ourselves in both sporting prowess and academia,"' he continues. '"Our current head, Ursula Deacon, has been in her role for two years after relocating to the Pacific Pines area with her son Sam, after a long stint as head at Arlingford Ladies' College in Esperance."'

'It's certainly a beautiful school,' says Bec. But she already knows this. She was here yesterday, cake in hand.

'Over there,' says Cooper. 'It says, "Gala Day Parents & Students This Way"!'

The long drive is streaming with parents heading right, towards the rugby pitch. Mothers clutch the hands of terrified boys, leaning in to deliver last whispers of advice before their sons face their greatest test. Mothers who walk with upright self-assuredness and well-put-togetherness reeking of desperation. Smart designer sundresses, or light pants with smart blouses and minimal-looking make-up, just as Bec has chosen for herself. She sees Estella a few feet in front, walking between the twins, Archie on the left clutching a Rubik's Cube and Jonty on the right.

Tom goes to beep the horn, but Bec pushes his hand away. 'No!' she shrieks.

'Why not?'

'I can't face her right now.'

'Why?'

'She's annoyed about the cake.'

'What cake?'

'The chapel cake.'

'Why? Didn't you offer her a slice? She looks like she's stacked on a couple of kilos.'

'Stop it,' Bec giggles. 'It's her thyroid.'

'It's not her thyroid,' says Tom. 'It's her arse.'

Sage says 'arse' and Cooper sniggers.

Bec looks in the wing mirror as they pass the Munros and sees Estella glance up at the car with a scowl, but frankly she doesn't care any more. Willow is right. Why *should* she be ashamed of using her talent to help Cooper? She doesn't need Estella's permission!

'Why is everyone walking?' asks Cooper.

'Because they had the good sense to realise the car park would be rammed,' Tom sighs. 'I didn't know it was right next to the playing field. I'll text Willow and tell her to park on the road.'

'Shall I do a uey?' Bec's eyes dart up to the overhead mirror.

'You can't, not with all these people wandering about,' Tom says. 'Let's try the car park now we're here.'

Sage unbuckles her booster seat. 'I need a poo,' she announces.

'Oh Sagey! *Now?*'

'I don't decide when a poo comes,' says Sage. 'My bum decides.'

The car park is, as predicted, full. 'Oh for . . . *fuck's sake,*' Tom sighs.

'*For fuck's sake,*' Sage announces.

'Tom!' says Bec.

'*Tom!*' giggles Sage.

Bec feels her blood pressure rise a fraction.

'Look, there's one!' Cooper points ahead to the far end of the car park.

Sure enough, there is an empty space parallel to the tiny white picket fence that lines the far end of the rugby field. It is partially obscured by the shade of a large weeping willow, which explains why no one has parked there yet.

'Nothing wrong with your eyes, my boy,' remarks Tom in a tone that sounds remarkably like his elderly father's. 'Talking of which, I spy a sausage sizzle!'

'Yes!' Cooper fist pumps. 'Can I get one, Mum?' Evidently, the eggs and bacon he demolished at breakfast haven't even touched the sides.

'Let's do it,' says Tom. 'Drop us here and I'll take Coop to the registration tent. Sage, can you help Mummy with her parking?'

Bec is mildly annoyed as they get out of the car. Tom always does the same thing at sporting events, jumps out to let Bec navigate the parking as if he's worried he's going to miss the action. 'Fine,' she says.

'Look,' says Sage as they edge into the spot. 'It's Auntie 'Stella.'

Bec turns to her right to see Estella peering at her through the car window.

'Fuck!' she gasps. 'You scared the life out of me.'

'Lovely language to use in front of Sage,' drawls Estella. She waves at Sage through the window. 'Hello, Sage darling!'

'Is everything OK, Estella, because I'm just parking . . .' Bec smiles through a clenched jaw. 'Can I catch up with you in a little while?'

'Of course,' snips Estella. 'I just thought I should let you know that Ursula Deacon has been unwell for the last couple of days and rumour has it she ate something that disagreed with her. I mean, I'm not suggesting for one moment it was your beautiful cake, Bec darling, but I just didn't want you to hear it from someone else and worry that—'

'Thank you, Estella.' Bec's finger hovers on the window's 'up' button. 'But I sincerely doubt a baked combination of butter, eggs, sugar and flour would have caused a stomach upset.'

'OK.' She holds her hands up. 'Don't shoot the messenger!'

'Well, thanks for letting me know.' The window rises and Estella's hand goes with it. 'I'll see you on the pitch.' She puts her foot a little heavily on the gas and watches the look of feigned shock on Estella's face in the rear-view mirror as her back wheel skids a little on the gravel. *Let it go*, she tells herself. *Let it go.*

Let it go is precisely what Sage has decided to do in the back seat.

'My poo is coming out *right now*,' she says, matter-of-fact.

'Oh Sagey, just hold on one more minute, please . . .' Bec turns off the engine, steps out of the car and rushes round to Sage's side, her thumbs fumbling on the stiff red release button in the middle of Sage's car seat. That's when she notices a vehicle in her peripheral vision – a navy, open-topped affair - trying to squeeze into the minuscule gap between her own car and a large tree stump.

'What on earth . . .?' she mutters. She pulls the rear door tight into her body to avoid colliding with the other car as she attempts to haul Sage out and through the gap. She can feel her neck burning red. The driver of the other car, a BMW, opens the door slightly, lightly knocking against the passenger-seat door of Bec's Kia.

Bec feels her shoulders tense. 'Come on Sagey, squeeze through if you can!'

'I can't get out and I need to poo.'

'Well breathe in and squeeze!'

'Excuse me?' says a voice, and Bec doesn't turn around to look at the driver because she is trapped, wrangling Sage out of her chair. 'I don't suppose I could ask you to reverse back in a little and move across so I can squeeze in?'

And that's when Bec feels it. Hot blood shoots up through her chest and settles in her face. Tom calls it The Rage, when Bec's anger levels tip her from sweet, softly spoken and back-bendingly tolerant to a petite ball of molten fury.

She yanks Sage's feet out of the car a little roughly and Sage winces.

'Really?' she snaps. 'And where exactly do you propose that I go?'

'Perhaps reverse and nudge over a bit to the right? I'm running so late.'

'*We all are!*' Bec slams the door with as much force as she can when there is only an inch of space with which to pull it back. She cannot bring herself to look at him.

'Well, I can't actually *get out* of my car at this point in time.'

'Can't you climb out of the top?' Bec shrieks, deranged. 'You seem to have lost your roof.'

'I would, but I don't want to damage the bonnet. It's not my car.' His voice is familiar somehow, like the voiceover on a commercial she's seen a couple of times. Maybe he *is* from a commercial, thinks Bec. A commercial selling something irritating, like insect repellent.

'Fine,' Bec snaps. She squeezes Sage through the tiny gap between the cars, lifts her over the white picket fence, and dumps her roughly on the grass of the sporting fields. She barks 'Stay,' like she might to a dog and puts two Tupperware boxes of carefully-stacked chocolate tortes by her feet. She knows that later she will hate herself for taking it out on sweet little Sage, but right now, in the grip of her frustration, she feels entitled to yell. She slams the car door and reverses out of the space haphazardly, while still managing to keep a watchful eye on Sage, who is clutching her backside as if she might somehow be able to reverse what's about to happen. She drives back into the space, perilously close to the tree trunk, and angrily pulls up the brake. Then she steps over the picket fence, grabs Sage's hand and leads her across the field towards the sausage sizzle and what looks like the clubhouse.

'I warned you, Mummy,' says Sage. 'My poo is mostly out.'

'Really Sagey? *Here?*'

Bec feels her stress levels hit overdrive. She doesn't have a change of underpants and there's no time to go home for a change of clothes.

She hears the sound of jogging feet behind her.

'Thanks for that,' the driver says, apparently oblivious to the smell wafting up from Sage's leggings. Bec turns to look at him and sees he is incredibly handsome, with a square jaw and sandy blond hair. He looks oddly famil-iar, like someone Bec knows, but cannot quite place. She guesses he must be about twenty-five.

'It's fine.' She has lost her courage now she has seen his face, as so often happens in the aftermath of an exchange between angry drivers – the safety of a car window screen providing the same sense of entitlement and bravado as a computer screen. 'But I think we *both* know there isn't enough room for two cars in that space!'

'Well, *I* don't mean to be rude,' he says with a grin, 'but if you look at the little plaque in front of us, you'll find it says "Reserved."'

'I don't think so,' she laughs, slightly overcome with hysteria. 'I would have seen it.'

The man's eyes widen and Bec sees a crinkle at the sides. 'It also says "Staff only".'

Bec follows the man's finger and sees the sign. She feels the colour drain from her face as realisation sets in.

'I won't tell if you don't!' He holds out his hand. 'Sam Deacon,' he tells her. 'Sports master here at Iggy's.'

'Oh God!' Bec stammers. 'I mean, oh *goodness* . . .'

He laughs. 'Please don't worry about it,' he says. 'It's a bloody stupid car space really. It's intended for the groundsman and his van, but he never uses it, and the sign *is* pretty small. It's my mother's car and I would have climbed out of the roof, as you suggested, if it wasn't her pride and joy.'

His mother, Ursula Deacon! Bec's skin burns puce. She remembers the woman's face as she bit into the cake. Now she is suddenly conscious of her fingers, the stains on her cuticles from the food dye.

'Sorry, I didn't introduce myself,' she says, the panic coming for her so that she barely knows what she's saying. 'I'm . . . I'm . . . Estella. Estella Munro.' She doesn't know why she has said it, but once it is out, she can't take it back. She can hardly say, 'Oops, I meant Bec Lloyd!'

'You're Estella Munro?' the sports master asks, confused.

Sage's face snaps up and Bec tugs on her hand. 'Yes. I'm . . . Archie and Jonty Munro's mother,' she says, finding conviction from somewhere. 'Archie is friends with Cooper Lloyd, the winger everyone talks about from the Pacific Pines Rugby Club. His dad Tom used to coach the Wallabies a few years back. I mean, he doesn't any more . . .'

'Right.' Sam Deacon nods.

'Cooper's my big—' Sage begins.

'Shh! Mummy's *talking*,' Bec tugs on Sage's hand.

Sam Deacon seems to find it all quite amusing. He bends down to Sage's level. 'And what's your name?' he asks.

Sage studies the stranger's face. 'Sage. My poo is all out now,' she says, and Bec would quite like the ground to open so she can fall through a large crack in the turf.

Sam Deacon bites down on his smile.

'I'm so sorry,' Bec shrugs. 'She's just turned five . . .'

He grins and waves her protests away with his hand. 'Can I help with the box? They look delicious.'

'Chocolate tortes!' Bec pulls on Sage's hand again. 'For the cheese and wine event. And thanks, but I can manage. Well, bye then! I'm sorry about the . . . um . . . car spot.'

'Forgotten already, *Estella*,' he says, in a way that makes Bec think he has seen straight through her little fib. He reaches forward and takes the Tupperware. 'You have your hands full. I'll take them to the Great Hall for you.'

Bec has no choice but to hand over the baked goods, which Sam Deacon now thinks were made by Estella. She thanks him and scurries off, and when she turns around a second or two later, he is still standing there with a smile on his face.

After an epic toilet break that involves Bec using handfuls of damp tissue and disposing of Sage's pink unicorn knickers in the ladies' sanitary-towel bin, Bec and Sage emerge from the bathrooms and into a fog of smoke from the sausage sizzle. The air smells of grease and fried onions. Tom and Cooper are by the registration tent, Cooper clutching a bright yellow ribbon.

'Here's my girl,' Tom says and sweeps Sage into his arms. 'Where were you two?'

'Shit happened,' Bec sighs. 'Tell me you didn't register whilst eating a sausage?'

'Why not?'

'Oh my God, Tom! This isn't a Sunday afternoon at the bowling club! You can't register with a sausage in your hand!'

'I don't think it's the *wurst* thing I've ever done,' says Tom and Cooper grins.

They bite down on their hot dogs simultaneously, and Sage takes a bite of Cooper's, immediately squirting ketchup down her front. Bec closes her eyes and does a deep yoga breath before opening them again.

'The Munros are over there if you want to stand with them.' Tom nods to the right.

'Sure.' Bec's annoyance at Estella has switched to guilt now she has fraudulently assumed her friend's identity. She sets up Sage's camp chair a couple of metres along from where Estella stands with Conrad and her boys, and waves at Estella. 'I'll be over in a bit,' she mouths as she clicks open a bottle of sunscreen and rubs it over Sage's face.

Estella nods. She is wearing a floral midi dress with a bolero-style jacket and large round sunglasses. Bec watches as she snaps her fingers in front of one of the twins' faces. 'Mouthguard!' she sings. 'Where is it? Come on, snap to it.' Archie (and Bec knows it is Archie because Estella wouldn't need to remind Jonty to pop in his mouthguard) presses the orange plastic onto his front teeth and it takes him a few goes to get it comfortable.

The principal, who certainly looks sickly enough, stands in the middle of the pitch alongside Sam Deacon and a tall, dark-haired boy with deep-set eyes. The megaphone squeaks.

'Hello everyone,' Ursula Deacon says. 'Welcome to St Ignatius' Grammar's third Gala Day! It is absolutely wonderful to see you all here and I would like to take this opportunity to thank you for your interest in our beautiful school.'

She gives a chesty cough and then clears her throat. 'My apologies,' she says. 'Yes, today this is indeed an assessment, but we would like to ask every boy to *enjoy* today as well as try their best. It is not meant to be gruelling.' She stops to cough three times more – deep, chesty barks that seem to make her chest rattle.

'Please do excuse me – I appear to have a frog in my throat! Just a little housekeeping first. Interviews, as you will know from your letters of invitation, will take place between two and five p.m., and will be conducted in my office. If you are unsure about your allocated time, please see Rachel in the front office. Before then, you are invited to tour the school grounds in family groups, accompanied by our current Year Ten cohort. At five thirty, our cheese and wine evening will begin. We encourage you to hang around for the whole day. The art department will be offering boys the chance to throw their own pottery and the science team will be showing boys how to make robotic cars from cardboard. Younger siblings are invited to enjoy supervised play at the gymnasium.'

Sage looks up at Bec and grins.

'What I would like to stress,' says Principal Deacon, 'is that we are a friendly bunch and we wish every boy the best of luck.' She glances at her watch. 'It is now almost one o'clock and so, without further ado, I would like to introduce you to the coordinators of the sporting element of today, our sports master Sam Deacon and our school captain Felix Weaver.'

As she claps, Bec looks at the boy who is almost as tall as Sam Deacon, the famous Felix Weaver. She looks over at Willow, who is standing under a tree beside Flick, and observes her as she gazes ahead at the trio in the middle of the pitch, a look of pure adoration on her face. Felix Weaver looks over in Willow's direction and smiles. Is *he* the mystery boy? It wouldn't be so bad, would it? Willow could do worse than the outgoing school captain at St Ignatius'.

'*Mr* Deacon, would you like to say a few words?'

Sam Deacon takes the speaker from his mother and says, 'Thank you, Mrs Deacon,' which sends a faint ripple of laughter filtering through the crowd.

'Boys, you will have been given a ribbon when you registered,' the sports master says. 'This will be the colour of your team for today. Please proceed to the clubhouse where the current Year Nine boys will be handing out player bibs in your allocated colour.

'Some of you have travelled a long way to be here today, and we appreciate it,' continues Sam. 'I'd also like to apologise for the hectic parking scenario.' He looks directly at Bec. 'Thank you all for your patience.'

Bec feels her skin burn red.

'Oh and lastly, a little heads-up,' says Sam. 'It's not *just* me you need to impress today. Felix here will be referee for all of the matches, so please remember to be courteous to the ref. His decision is final.'

Felix raises an eyebrow and looks out into the crowd, evidently enjoying his moment in the spotlight. Bec studies the dark eyes of the boy who may very well take her daughter's virginity (because eighteen is when *she* had first done it) and watches them squint and scan the crowd. She isn't expecting them to settle on her, but they do. For a moment too long, and Bec swears there is a look of recognition in them, maybe even the slightest quiver of a smirk. She feels uncomfortable, as though *she* is being assessed and not Cooper. She looks up at Tom beside her, but he is oblivious, relishing the atmosphere on the sidelines.

'Lastly,' says Sam Deacon, 'I'd like to wish you all the best of luck today and I look forward to chatting with you all over the course of the day.'

Ursula Deacon steps forward. 'Thank you, Sam,' she says. 'Well, without further ado, let the games begin!'

Tom leans in. 'And may the odds be ever in our favour.'

9

Kaya

'Hello!' As soon as she says it, Kaya feels a touch awkward, because she realises Bec and her husband are having a tender moment. Tom has one hand on Bec's lower back, his head close to her ear. Bec smiles in response and pushes him away as if he is saying something usually reserved for the bedroom. God, how Kaya misses this: the grip of a hand around her waist, the heat of breath in her ear, suggestive comments to make her blush in the most inappropriate of places. She remembers one time, before Paul got sick, when he'd pulled her into the walk-in wardrobe while Ollie was watching TV.

'Not now,' she'd said, grinning, trying to peel his hands off her hips. 'Ollie!'

'He hasn't looked up from the TV in an hour, he's not going to in the next five minutes!'

'Are you planning to be that quick?'

And it had been that quick! A *quickie* – but it had been just what the doctor ordered before the doctor ordered bed rest a few weeks later.

Memories of Paul seem to flash up left, right and centre today, and Kaya understands it's because of Paul's role in all of this, how much he wanted it for Ollie. She tries to imagine Paul here, on this very field, twenty-odd years ago, legs caked in mud, sweat dripping down his forehead. Him an old boy and Ollie a new one.

'Kaya, hello!' Bec's skin flushes pink. 'Tom, meet Kaya. Kaya, meet Tom, my husband.'

Bec seems to cringe slightly after she has said the word 'husband', in the same way people cringe when they say the word 'cancer'. It is as if her new friend feels somehow guilty that Tom is still alive and still participating in the act of husbandry when Paul is not. It happens often, and as usual Kaya feels she should overcompensate – that she should show Bec how fine it is to mention husbands, dead or otherwise.

'Tom, how lovely to meet you,' she coos. 'And what a lovely husband you are!'

She regrets immediately how creepy the words sound when they're out in the ether, but Bec laughs (with relief, Kaya thinks), her pretty face earnest and open and genuine.

Tom doesn't seem to mind, either. 'I try.' He grins. 'It's good to meet you, Kaya. Are you enjoying *The Hunger Games*?' He nods to the field.

'It is a bit like that, isn't it?' Kaya laughs. 'It's such an unusual set-up. I mean, I've never heard of a school doing a Gala Day to select kids before.'

'I know,' says Bec. 'It is bizarre when you think about it. But the private schools can do what they want. If they wanted us to fight it out with an egg and spoon race, they could.'

Kaya laughs. She appreciates Bec's flippancy. 'I'd like to see that,' she says.

'I'd ace it,' deadpans Bec. 'I spend my life trying to stop eggs from breaking. I'm a whizz.'

'A whizz?' Tom grins. 'Some might say you are *egg-ceptional*, darling!'

He scoops up his little girl Sage and blows a raspberry on her belly to make her giggle. Kaya feels the familiar pang of longing again, but forces herself to stop it in its tracks as she always does in public, and sometimes in private, too. She has to, otherwise it hurts too much.

'I'm going to leave you ladies to chat while I take Sage for a wander.' He kisses Bec on her forehead and turns away.

'You two are cute,' Kaya says.

'Oh, we have our moments,' Bec replies as if to say to Kaya, 'Husbands are so overrated, you're not missing much!'

But Kaya *is* missing much. She feels it keenly and constantly. But these are matters that must be dwelled upon at another time, and not here on the rugby pitch at Gala Day.

'How's Cooper feeling about today?' she asks.

'OK-*ish*. Cooper's more comfortable on the pitch than off it, so the interview might challenge him. He's pretty shy.'

'I'm sure he'll be fine,' says Kaya. 'He seems like a lovely kid.'

'Thanks. We think so, but unfortunately that doesn't guarantee a place.'

'Well, I'm sure he'll make a good impression.'

'What about Ollie?' Bec asks. 'Is he comfortable with all of this?'

'He's terrified!' Kaya finds it easy to be honest with Bec, disarmingly so. 'I've told him he can only do his best. I mean, what else can you ask of them? They're only twelve.'

What else can she ask of Ollie beyond giving it his best? She is already making him do baptism classes. Although strangely, whenever she tells him it is time to go to St Martin's, he jumps up without having to be asked, and then all the way home he will pummel Kaya with theological questions she will struggle to answer, like 'Who created God?' and 'If God made everyone in His image, why are some people so mean?' and 'Why does God let earthquakes happen?' In some ways, Kaya is glad Ollie is asking her more thought-provoking questions than, 'How much money do YouTubers make?' and at least he is not questioning her incessantly about death like he used to. Last summer it had been all about decomposition rates and mortuary refrigerators and the types of wood used in coffins, and for obvious reasons Kaya had found these questions altogether confronting.

Across the field, Ollie and Cooper play catch to warm up.

'I'm glad Ollie and Cooper are making friends,' Bec says to the air in front of her, allowing Kaya a view of her profile, a petite ski-slope nose and high-set cheekbones. She turns back to Kaya. 'Cooper tells me they've bonded at school. He said he really hopes they both get into Iggy's.'

'Ollie said the same and I'm so glad. It hasn't been easy for him, you know, with Paul.' It hasn't been easy at all, and Kaya feels a little too protective of Ollie as a result.

She would not appreciate anyone else pointing it out to her, but in her heart of hearts, she knows it's true.

'I can imagine,' says Bec and then checks herself. 'I mean, obviously I *can't* imagine. Oh gosh, you know what I mean! I'm so sorry, Kaya, I'm not articulating this very well, am I? The fact is I can't imagine what either of you have been through, frankly. Yet you're both so vibrant, so together!'

Kaya looks at the grass beneath her feet. Two months ago she might have cried in the face of such kindness, but not now. She is beginning to accept her life without Paul and to see the hope in it. It is all about a fresh start for her and her boy, this move, although the irony isn't lost on her that as she stands making divots in the turf with her ankle boots at her husband's former school, she feels his presence everywhere.

'Thank you,' she says to Bec. 'It's been horrible, I'm not going to lie, but we're getting there. Ollie doesn't talk about his dad every day any more, which I honestly think is a good thing. Of course, we don't want to *forget* Paul, but we do need to start looking forward more than we look back, if that makes sense. And I think it's finally starting to happen.'

'And what about you?' asks Bec.

'I'm getting there. I wasn't expecting to lose my husband so early in life, but I had a long while to prepare for it and . . . oh God, I'm sorry,' Kaya lets out a laugh. 'This is all a little morose, isn't it?'

Bec reaches out and squeezes Kaya's hand. 'No,' she says. 'It isn't. It is your *life*. Talk to me about Paul anytime. I'd love to know more about him.'

This is what Kaya has been craving, this warmth, this human connection. 'You really are kind,' she says. 'And those *cupcakes*!'

Bec laughs. 'Like I said on Sunday, it was a total pleasure.'

'I saw your chapel cake on the St Ignatius' Instagram page, too. It was amazing. I wouldn't know where to even start with something like that!'

'The things you do for your kids, right?'

'Like baptism classes,' Kaya says, and shrugs. 'When you're an atheist.' She realises what she has said as soon as it is out. Perhaps she shouldn't be suggesting to Bec, or to anyone she barely knows, that her reconnection to Christianity has ulterior motives. But Bec is so genuine it would be strangely easy to tell her anything. 'That makes me awful, doesn't it?'

Bec smiles. 'No! You're not doing anything that half of the parents here haven't already done. I could point out at least twelve boys to my left alone who've taken baptism classes so they can say on their Iggy's application form that they're certificate-wielding Catholics. It's just one of the things people do, and Father Francis is fine with it.'

'That many?'

'That many!'

'What about you? Did you and Tom do it for Cooper and Willow? Asher's Girls' School is Catholic too, isn't it?'

Bec grimaces. 'I'd love to tell you we did it for our kids, because that would put us in the majority, but actually, Tom and I were both raised in Catholic families, even though we're not practising, so Cooper was baptised when he was much younger. We did it for Tom's mother, really.'

'Fair enough.' Kaya smiles. She casts her eye down the sideline to where Estella Munro stands, arms folded, staring contemplatively at the rugby pitch. Her neighbour is so different to Bec and yet she knows the two women are firm friends. She cannot understand it, unless it is a yin and yang thing, a case of opposites attract. Perhaps Estella has a gentle side and Bec a contrary one, who knows?

Bec leans in. 'Don't fret about the Catholic stuff,' she says. 'The fact is, they *do* bear this stuff in mind when they're selecting boys and like I said, Father Francis doesn't mind. He just wants bums on seats, or rather bums on pews. I mean, if it wasn't for the ton of parents trying to get their sons into Iggy's, St Martin's would be like tumbleweed on a Sunday.'

'But I *do* think they mind,' Kaya says. 'Iggy's, I mean. Or at least they've been alerted to it. Ursula Deacon has already questioned my reasons. She said Ollie's baptism class had been flagged by a certain parent for . . . for not being entirely genuine.'

'Oh, don't mind Estella.' Bec bats a hand in the air. 'She didn't mean anything by it.'

'Estella?' Kaya feels a flash of anger. So it was Estella who had dobbed her in. What is wrong with the woman? She is making it impossible for Kaya to like her, and Kaya *wants* to like her, damn it! She desperately wants to see the good in her.

Bec looks mortified. 'Oh,' she says. 'The way you said "certain parent" . . . I thought you knew who it was.'

Kaya shrugs. 'I didn't, but I'm not entirely surprised. She hasn't been nice to me since day one, but she's even worse since she found out Ollie was taking baptism classes.'

'She doesn't mean it, Kaya,' says Bec, and Kaya realises by the way Bec has said her name that she must tread carefully. It is almost like a warning, a closing-off. Bec and Estella have history, she has heard, and Bec has picked her side.

Kaya nods. 'Well, if you say so,' she says.

'Look,' says Bec. 'Her bark is worse than her bite, I promise you. You might actually find you *enjoy* having her as a neighbour. She is a loyal friend once you have her onside. She's like a meringue – hard exterior, soft centre.'

Her voice softens. 'If it's any consolation, Estella has rubbed me up the wrong way a thousand times over the years, today included as it happens, but every time, I give myself a firm reminder that she hasn't always had it easy. I mean Felicity is an absolute nightmare and I seriously wonder—'

She stops, collects her thoughts. 'I shouldn't be speaking out of turn like this, because Estella is a very good friend of mine, but I'm just saying that there is a legitimate reason why she behaves the way she does. She has been through a lot in her life.'

Kaya looks over at Estella, takes her in with her smug smile, her pointed nose, her square Furla tote bag, and tries to imagine her being vulnerable, having a life that wasn't easy. She wants to know what it is that Bec knows about Estella's past, but she cannot ask – not here, not on the rugby field at Gala Day when the rest

of the world is at work and most other children are at
school. Perhaps on another day, over a crisp glass of
rosé on the deck overlooking the ocean, they will both
share their secrets, but for now she must hold back on
the questioning, as hard as it is. She will not confront
Estella while she is feeling angry and yes, she'll admit
it, bullied.

'Thanks,' she says instead. 'I'll bear it in mind.'

Bec sighs. 'Gosh, I really shouldn't have said anything.
Forget I did, OK?'

'Of course,' Kaya tells her.

They are silent for a moment and both seem to stare
off in the direction of Estella. She seems to be making a beeline for Sam Deacon across the grass. Oddly,
Kaya sees something in her neighbour's mannerisms
that divulge a certain . . . insecurity. Something about
the way Estella tucks her hair behind her ear nervously,
the way her face is flushed pink and her hand shaking
slightly as it reaches to smooth the hair at the nape of
her neck.

Bec appears to bristle at the sight of her friend advanc-
ing towards the sports master, and Kaya notes what looks
like relief on her face when she realises Sam Deacon has
not seen Estella and has turned to jog to the centre of the
main pitch, blowing his whistle and calling for the teams
to group into colours.

'I wonder what she was going to talk to him about,'
Kaya whispers.

'Wanting to put a good word in for the twins, I suppose,'
Bec mutters.

In the centre of the pitch, Sam Deacon hands out spare bibs to boys who have not yet had colours allocated. One of Estella's twins hands back his yellow bib and takes a red one from the sports master's outstretched hands.

Bec gets up on tiptoes. 'I wonder what's going on?'

'He's swapping bibs,' says Kaya. 'Doesn't Estella want him playing in the yellow team with his brother?'

'She does like to separate them when she can,' says Bec. 'To give them their own identities.'

'Are they both good?' Kaya asks. She knows the answer because she's heard Estella herself say it, that time she was potting the jasmine plant against the side fence, through the open window. Estella had distinctly said Archie couldn't catch so much as a cold.

Bec doesn't meet her eyes. 'The twins? Good? Um, yes, yes they are. I mean, Jonty is a little stronger, but . . .'

Kaya feels a pang of sadness that Bec hasn't told her the truth, but she cannot expect it, can she? Estella is one of Bec's closest friends after all, and Kaya is still only an acquaintance. She cannot count on disloyalty or expect to share secrets over cake and soy lattes *quite* yet.

'Look . . .' Bec points to the clubhouse, ending the discussion about Archie and Jonty and filling Kaya with a mild sense of disappointment. 'The fixtures are up!'

To the left of them, the giant state-of-the-art electronic scoreboard by the canteen area becomes swamped with boys in blue, green, yellow and red vests craning their necks to see what times their matches are and who they will play. Estella's red twin hangs a little behind.

'Which one's that?' asks Kaya. 'In the red?'

'Search me. I can only tell close up. If I had to guess, I'd say the red one is Archie, but I wouldn't bet more than five bucks on it, and I've known them since they were babies.'

The boys arrive, breathless, Ollie in red and Cooper in yellow. 'I'm up first!' Cooper pants, looking towards the central pitch with its pristine white lines and rubber-clad goalposts. 'Yellows versus blues.'

'Oh my goodness,' says Bec in a sing-song voice. 'Good luck, darling. I love you.' She pulls him in for a hug.

'You too, Mum,' Cooper says.

'Hey, Coops. Before you go,' Bec says and Cooper turns. 'What happened with Jonty and Archie? Why did they swap?'

'Estella was worried the teachers wouldn't be able to tell them apart so she got them split up,' Cooper says.

'So who's playing with you?' Bec asks.

'Archie,' says Cooper. 'He's yellow now.'

Bec's eyes light up like she's really happy with that answer, and Kaya is confused momentarily. Surely, Bec wouldn't want Archie on Cooper's team if Jonty is the star player? Or does she want him on the yellow team for that exact reason, to make Cooper look even better? Kaya wonders what that means for Ollie, to share a red bib with Jonty. Still, she cannot worry about it now – she will have to cling to the belief that having Jonty onside will make the whole red team look strong.

'There you go!' Bec throws her hands up in the air. 'I got it wrong. Red isn't Archie! Some friend I am. I can't even tell my oldest friend's offspring apart. Anyway, good luck, sweetheart!'

'Thanks,' Cooper calls over his shoulder.

'Good luck, Cooper,' shouts Ollie as he folds himself under Kaya's arm, his red bib like a shield across his chest.

Tom arrives back with Sage. 'You got this, buddy,' he shouts to Cooper.

All along the sidelines, the yellow and blue team parents are all doing the same – giving their last words of encouragement before their boys take to the field in games that will determine their futures. Down the line, Estella's face is fixed in an intense glare. She holds the yellow-bibbed Archie by the shoulders, pretty much shaking him, hissing in his ear.

Kaya feels for him. In her limited observations she realises the poor child would so much rather be at band camp or at maths club, but Estella has him here, trying out for a school that has the potential to both nourish him academically and defeat him physically. A place where he would be labelled a nerd by the cooler contingent of boys unless he got an exemption by warrant of his brother's likely popularity as a sporting star. These are assumptions, of course, but they seem obvious to her. She truly hopes she is proven wrong.

'Good luck, Coopie,' Willow yells from the sidelines. 'Go get 'em.'

Cooper grins and does a thumbs-up.

This is when Kaya realises Ollie has gone very quiet in his spot sitting cross-legged at her feet. She wonders if his nerves are getting the better of him.

'Ol?' she says, bending down to him and placing her hand on his forehead. Kaya's instinct, as it has been since

Ollie was a baby, is to put her palm to his skin to check he is not too hot. But he isn't. So she sits down beside him and kisses his forehead instead, her lips a secondary thermometer. He is still cool, but she keeps her lips there for a second anyway, just to double-check. And that's when she realises Ollie is talking to himself – a chant of some kind. She sits back on her heels and looks at him. *Is he having a fit?* She feels her heart thump underneath her dress as her brain chews over the idea. But then she hears what he is saying.

'Please Lord,' he says, palms pressed together tightly in front of his groin and eyes screwed shut. 'Please let Cooper win his match. And please let me win mine too, while you're at it. Thank you and Amen.'

10

Bec

Bec's hand settles on her chest bone as she watches Cooper jog on to the field. Everything rides on this match, everything. Cooper's future, his pride, his adult life! She wants this so badly for *all* the boys she knows here today, but of course mainly for Cooper.

She can bake all of the cakes for all of the admissions staff in the world, but it means nothing if Cooper can't prove himself worthy of a spot at the school. It all comes down to a twenty-minute stint on the pitch at the end of the day, and even professional sportsmen have bad matches. So all Bec can do at this point in time, as helpless as she is, is to trust in Cooper and in Sam Deacon's ability to spot potential.

Down the sideline, Estella's raspy voice cuts the air like a knife. 'Go!' she hisses to Archie. She stands tall, her hands on her hips, towering over him as he turns and runs on to the pitch. Bec watches him jog on the spot, shake off his hands, roll his neck, squat a couple of times. Estella has certainly schooled Archie in how to appear confident with her epic pre-match pep talk, even if his play is about to unravel him. Poor Archie! Bec cannot shake the uncomfortable feeling she is watching a drunk person, in a car, heading for a lamppost.

Once the boys are all lined up, Felix blows the whistle and Bec feels her chest constrict. Her lungs empty with the deep-bellied screams she hears herself unleash. She didn't know she could yell this loud! In all the excitement, she finds she has unwittingly crept up to Estella like a magnet, and together they shout, '*Come on*, yellows! Go!' They are all doing it – Tom, Willow, Conrad, Jonty and even Flick, although Flick is more reserved in her hysteria, like she feels jumping up and down shouting is cloyingly uncool.

'Come on, Archie!' Estella yells. '*Run with it! RUN WITH IT!!*'

Bec's palms are filmed with sweat, as they often are when she sees Cooper play. She watches the ball fly effortlessly between the rows of yellow bibs and wills him to catch it over and over until he does. He holds it to his chest and sprints down the line like a rocket.

'Come on!' Tom yells. '*Come on*, Cooper!'

'Go Coopie!' screams Sage, looking up dutifully from her iPad.

Cooper runs, but a stocky blue prop blocks his path. He needs to pass, he *has* to pass, but the only person he can pass to is Archie. Bec feels sick. The yellows have to win!

'Pass,' yells Tom, who has evidently forgotten that not only is he not the team coach, but that Archie cannot catch for toffee. 'Cooper, *pass!*'

Cooper looks momentarily panicked, but comes to at the hit of Tom's voice. He lifts his arms and does what he's been told to do. He throws the ball to Archie. Archie's arms reach out and the moment between the throw and its landing seemed to last a lifetime. The screaming has stopped, and the silence from the sidelines is palpable.

The ball began to fall, and Archie's hands shoot out and grab it low, pull it in.

'Yeeeessssss!' calls Estella, shrill.

Archie crouches down low, makes himself small, ducks to the left and then to the right and sprints through the hole in the opposition's front row. Then he runs across the line, waiting for a long, long second before he touches the ball down on the grass and motions blowing steam off his fingers.

Estella jumps up and down and punches the air. 'Yes!' she cries. '*That's* my boy! Come *on*, Archie!'

Tom looks at Bec and shrugs. 'What the . . .?' he says, eyes wide. 'That was superb!'

Bec shrugs and laughs. 'I know,' she says, bemused. She thinks that whoever's been coaching Archie deserves an Olympic gold. Sam Deacon nods approvingly and writes something on his notepad.

'So lucky!' says Tom.

The word slaps Bec around the face. No, not here! She doesn't want to think about the spam emails from Lucki_ Texta *here*. Not while Cooper is playing. Her hands fish in the pocket of her linen pants for her phone.

'Look, Cooper's converting,' says Tom, jabbing Bec in the ribs.

She fumbles with her phone and clicks on to the camera with a shaking hand, pressing record as Cooper places the ball on the fluoro green tee. He stands back, blows on his hands and kicks.

Time stands still for Bec as she watches the ball, airborne, spin through the air. It sails gracefully between the posts and the yellow parents erupt. Felix Weaver blows the whistle. 'Yellow win, six–ten,' he calls through the megaphone and Bec feels she could die with pride.

Cooper runs off the pitch euphoric, handing Bec his drool-covered mouthguard. Bec pulls him in for a hug. 'OK, Mum,' he laughs and pulls away. He turns to Archie, 'Nice work, Archie,' he says and pats him on the back.

Archie grins. 'Thanks,' he says as he turns and heads for the bathrooms.

'Can I get a Coke now?' asks Cooper.

'Sure. Come on, I'll get you all one,' says Tom, leading all three of their sugar-addicted children off to the refreshment stand.

Bec sits herself down in Sage's camping chair and closes her eyes. She hears a voice in her ear and she jumps up with a start. Sam Deacon stands in front of her with his clipboard and a smile on his face. 'It was nice to meet you earlier, *Mrs Lloyd.*'

She looks up and sighs. 'You found me out.' She grimaces. 'I realised immediately afterwards that it was a stupid thing to do. I'm so sorry.'

He nods. 'It was. Especially since I make it my business to know all the parents – especially the pretty ones.'

Bec's eyes snap up. *Say what? Is he talking about me or Estella? And did he say 'petty' or 'pretty'?*

'Oh my.' Sam looks alarmed. 'I'm so sorry. That was terribly unprofessional of me. I'm just a little bit overexcited about today.'

He *did* say 'pretty'!

'Yes it was,' Bec ventures, her hand on her cheek, hiding the rosy hue beneath. 'You're lucky I'm one of the nice ones.'

Sam Deacon shakes his head, as if to flick away his impudence. 'My apologies, Mrs Lloyd.'

'It's fine, honestly. It's flattering actually . . .'

She glances over at Estella, who is watching the exchange.

'How did you know I wasn't Estella?'

'I knew exactly who you were the moment I saw you, because your face is on the Iggy's Instagram page.' He smiles broadly. 'You're the master baker. Plus, you had a box of chocolate tortes . . .'

'Ah yes, the Instagram page.' Bec rolls her eyes. 'I'd forgotten about that. Please forgive me.'

'May I ask *why* you were you impersonating Estella Munro?'

Bec sighs. 'I was just so embarrassed about my outburst about the parking space and I'm afraid it just slipped out.'

Sam smiles again. He nods down the sideline to his right. 'That's her, isn't it? The lady with the twins?'

'Yes,' says Bec. 'Archie and Jonty.'

'They seem like exceptional players. Are they?'

Bec looks at the grass in front of her feet. She could tell Sam Deacon right now that Archie is a terrible player. She could say his try for the yellows was the biggest fluke since Maradona's Hand of God in 1986. But she cannot do it. She cannot do that to Estella, even though she knows Estella would happily push her in front of a bus to get her boys a spot over Cooper.

'Yes,' she says. 'They're both brilliant players.'

Sam nods. 'Thanks. And just so you know, I thought Cooper was exceptional too. You were right earlier, by the car, he *is* well worth a watch. You must be proud.'

Bec smiles. 'Thank you. I am.'

Sam begins to walk away and then stops and turns. 'Before I go, are there any other sporting siblings in the Lloyd family I should know about?'

'Just Cooper. He and Sage have an older sister who's at Asher's. She's eighteen, but she doesn't really fit the remit for Iggy's.'

Sam Deacon laughs. 'No, I have enough teenage boys to deal with, without throwing teenage girls into the mix as well. I'm not sure I could handle a teenage girl very well.'

'They're definitely a different species.'

'Eighteen? Are you sure? I mean, I don't want to sound cheesy or anything, but you really don't look old enough to have an eighteen-year-old daughter.'

Bec feels her hand reach up to her hair instinctively. She smooths it down. 'Believe me, I am,' she says. 'I mean, I had Willow when I was fairly young, but I'm definitely old enough!'

He studies Bec's face for a moment that seems to linger. 'Well, goodbye Mrs Lloyd – see you again shortly, no doubt.'

'Bec, please!' Bec replies. 'Mrs Lloyd sounds so matronly!'

'Bec, then.' He smiles, in the same way his mother had done in the reception when she had presented her with the cake.

Sam walks away, whistling to himself as he weaves through the thick line of spectators. As he passes Tom, he holds out his hand. The two men shake and speak for a minute, which makes Bec feel decidedly awkward, although she can't pinpoint exactly why. The chat appears to be highly animated and at one point Tom makes a low throwing motion and Deacon laughs and pretends to catch it. I bet he isn't telling Tom *he* is pretty or that he doesn't look old enough to have an eighteen year old.

Tom arrives back a minute later.

'Where's Coops?' asks Bec.

'Having a kick about with the new kid, Ollie,' Tom tells her. 'Nice bloke, Deacon. He's young to be the head of sports. Must only be in his twenties.'

'It's not what you know . . .' she quips. 'It's who your mother is.'

'He knows his sport though, I'll give him that,' says Tom. 'Conrad tells me he did a sports science degree in the UK and he got picked up there to play pro. He did a couple of years for Saracens, and only got back here a few months ago.'

'Doesn't he play any more?'

'Nah. Tendon.'

'Shame.'

'I told him I'm available to help coach,' Tom says. 'If your cake doesn't seal the deal. I said I might be able to get the Wallabies in for a visit, you know, use my contacts . . .'

'I'm sure he'd love to be able to show off to his mates about that.'

'Why do you say that?'

'Oh, no reason,' Bec replies. 'He was just a bit . . .'

'A bit what?'

'A bit . . . flirty.'

Tom laughs. 'What? No way!'

'He said I was pretty . . .'

'Really? I'm sure he was being polite.'

'. . . and that I was too young to have an adult daughter.'

'Come off it!'

'He *said* it.'

'I don't doubt that.'

'Then what do you mean by "come off it", then?'

'Nothing.'

'So you do think I look old enough to have an eighteen year old?'

Tom sighs. 'Bec, you *do* have an eighteen year old. Look, darling. I'm not saying you're not a knockout because you absolutely are. What I *am* saying is that I highly doubt the head of sport at St Ignatius' would be trying to pick up a bit of crumpet on the sideline at Gala Day, especially when his mother, who happens to be the school principal, is across the field manning the sausage stand.'

'I'm telling you, he was flirting with me.' Bec sticks out her bottom lip, partly because she knows Tom thinks it's cute.

'OK, so suppose he *was*, it wouldn't be a bad thing, would it?'

'What do you mean?'

'Well, if he fancies you, he might want to see more of you during term time . . .'

Bec laughs. 'Always thinking strategically, aren't you, Tom darling?'

Tom bends down and kisses Bec's head. 'I think you're pretty *and* sexy and all of the above. Now let's watch the reds and see if Jonty can do better than Archie, which is something I never thought I'd say at any point in my life.'

The queue for the ladies' bathrooms is about a dozen long, and so Bec gets out her phone and clicks on her email while she waits. She opens her junk folder and reads the email from Lucki_Texta again, the one that came this morning. *I know ALL about you*, it had said. Bec stares at the yellow clubhouse ahead of her, where she cleaned up Sage's soiled clothes just an hour ago. *Sage*. There are only two people in the entire world who know what she did. One is her kinesiologist Annabel – who Tom describes as a kind of 'woo-woo therapist' on account of their Neuro Emotional Therapy sessions in which Bec finds herself divulging all sorts of thoughts and emotions that on a daily basis she keeps hidden. The other is Estella. She feels the burn of overwhelm, as if her brain is a Ferris wheel and every single carriage is full of worry – about Cooper, about Sage, about the emails, about Willow and her mystery boyfriend. She sits down heavily on the seat and closes her eyes. Estella wouldn't have told anyone, would she?

She watches her friend as she walks back to the sidelines. Estella stands in front of Jonty, her hands resting on his shoulders giving him encouragement ahead of his match, just like she'd done with his brother a quarter of an hour before. She speaks animatedly in his ear, giving instruction, fighting talk, and Jonty nods his head in response. Then he turns confidently towards the pitch and nods at Ollie.

She passes Kaya, who has her arm firmly around Ollie's shoulder. He pulls away gently and jogs on the spot. 'Remember,' Kaya tells him. 'It's only a game.'

'Good luck,' Bec stops and tells Ollie. 'I'm sure you'll be amazing.'

Ollie smiles. 'Thank you, Mrs Lloyd,' he says.

'Oh goodness, call me Bec, please.'

Ollie smiles awkwardly and runs onto the pitch, casting a final glance at Kaya.

'It's terrifying, isn't it?' Kaya says with a deep sigh. 'You just don't want them to be disappointed.'

'No,' Bec says. 'You really don't.'

Both women look down the line at Estella, who is rubbing her hands together in anticipation. She is watching Sam Deacon to see if Sam Deacon is watching her boys. Beside Estella stands Archie, in his yellow bib, holding a completed Rubik's Cube, twisting the coloured sides over and over as Jonty slides in his mouthguard effortlessly and turns towards the pitch.

I I

Estella

Outside Ursula Deacon's office, Estella is finding the fidgeting an unwelcome distraction from her general angst. Archie is being grilled inside and she cannot bear the tension or the incessant jigging of Conrad's left foot. She looks at her watch. It is four fifteen p.m. – he should be out by now.

'For God's sake, clean your knees,' she says to Jonty, pulling a pack of wet wipes from her bag. Her euphoria at his triumph for the red team a couple of hours ago is forgotten – each of his four tries had been sensational, all converted expertly, making Jonty the star of the show – but now he needs to play his part for the interview. She thrusts the wipes at him.

'Knees!' she says again as if instructing a toddler (because, let's face it, he often behaves like one). 'Clean them.'

Jonty pulls a handful of wipes out of the packet and scrubs at his right knee.

'Estella darling, please calm down,' says Conrad.

'Just what every woman likes to be told,' hisses Estella. 'To calm down.' She crosses and uncrosses her legs and the swift move makes a squeaky fart sound.

Jonty giggles. 'Better out than in.'

'Give me *strength*.'

The door opens and Archie comes out wearing a wide grin.

'Thank you very much, Archie,' says the principal. She looks from Jonty to Archie and back again, her face awash with confusion.

'Gosh,' she says to Estella. 'How on earth do you tell your boys apart?'

'With difficulty!' Estella emits a nervous laugh.

Ursula Deacon thanks Archie and closes the door to her office. A couple of minutes later, which seems more like four hours ('What the hell is she even doing in there, Conny?') the principal opens it again. 'Jonty,' she says. 'Would you like to come in now?'

'Good luck,' Estella says, pulling her boy in close. 'Remember what I told you.'

You're captain of the cricket team at Pines Primary. Rugby First XV. Soccer superstar, bus monitor. You're the perfect fit for Iggy's. They'd be lucky to have you!

Estella looks at her watch again. Four thirty-five p.m. Only an hour until the cheese and wine event and she can drink a large glass of wine. She takes out her lipstick and reapplies it using a small compact mirror while Archie plays Minecraft on her phone. Conrad gets out his cross-word book. It feels like forever until Jonty comes out of the room, but when he does, he wears a look of triumph.

'Thank you, Jonty,' says Ursula Deacon. 'And Mrs Munro, I must say you have two delightful boys.'

Estella beams. 'That's very kind of you.'

'I'll see you shortly in the Great Hall.'

'Wonderful.'

'Thank God,' says Estella as they round the corner. 'Let's see if they'll let us into the hall early. I'm gagging for a drink.'

Fifteen minutes later, Estella feels a warm glow of satisfaction as she sips a rather spicy Malbec from a *glass* and not a plastic tumbler, which is one of the touches that sets this school apart. She's rather glad Conrad was called to the hospital the moment they got to the hall because she will be able to unashamedly schmooze the teaching staff without the soundtrack of his delightful sarcasm.

She watches the twins chatting and laughing with Cooper Lloyd and Ollie Sterling, and she muses on their triumph: brilliant sportsmanship followed by two successful interviews. Then she turns her attention to the hall. The Great Hall is indeed great, with its regal domed roof and green velvet curtains hanging from a West-End-worthy stage. It is a hall she knows so well from her own teenage years as an Asher's girl when they would visit for dances and plays, and how she wants it to be her domain once more. How she wants again to be queen of it, just like she was when she was seventeen and dating her own Iggy's boy.

On the far side of the room, she spies Bec and Willow, laughing like best friends rather than parent and sibling, and Estella rolls her eyes. Bec's senses must be tingling because she glances up and waves. Estella returns the greeting with a perfunctory nod and does a rudimentary scan of the rapidly filling room for Felicity, but there is no sign of her. She takes out her phone from her handbag and rings Felicity's number, but realises that the vibrating is coming from her own pocket.

'Shit,' she mutters, realising that they've picked up each other's coats and she has two mobile phones in her pocket. Felicity hates the fact Estella has the same All Saints leather jacket as her because apparently it's embarrassing ('You're, like, forty-five, Estella. You should be wearing Boden!').

She mingles for an hour with some primary-school parents before she finally catches sight of Felicity in the corner of the room, talking to a boy. Estella can't quite see who it is, but she thinks it is the boy on the rugby pitch . . . the outgoing school captain, Martha Weaver's boy. She squints and then retracts her head, satisfied. It is! It is Felix Weaver! Estella feels a flush of delight that her daughter is associating with the most recent school captain, but also a wave of fear that Felix might be the famous 'BOY' of Felicity's diary fame. She chews over her dilemma – should she go over under the guise of handing back Felicity's phone and introduce herself? Or should she leave them alone? She takes a sip of red. No, she will leave it. They can't exactly have sex here in the Great Hall after all, can they? And besides, Felix might not even *be* BOY – she can't go getting ahead of herself.

She is watching so intensely she doesn't notice Kaya Sterling appear in front of her. Kaya is dressed in another long boho-style dress with strappy sandals and a denim jacket – a little slovenly for an interview situation, in Estella's humble view.

'Estella,' she says snippily. 'May I have a word?'

Estella is irritated about being pulled away from her Felicity-watching, but she will not be rude. She straightens her shoulders a little so she feels taller. 'Of course. What is it?'

'I was just wondering why you felt the need to tell Father Francis that you believe I am only converting Ollie to Catholicism to get a place at the school?'

Estella is a little thrown. 'I don't know what you mean,' she says haughtily. 'I simply suggested to Father that he should be wary of people taking advantage of his kindness.'

'People like me?' Kaya's eyeballs seem excessively large.

'For your information, *Kaya*, I did not name names,' she says.

'No, *Estella*, I think you did.' Kaya is calm, not angry, and it is a tad alarming. Isn't this the kind of behaviour psychopaths exhibit?

'And how exactly do you purport to know what my conversation with Father Francis entailed?' she asks, fighting fire with fire.

'I was told by a very reliable source.'

'Hmm, that does sound reliable,' says Estella. '"A source says . . ."'

'Did you, or didn't you, speak to Father Francis, Estella?'

'Why does it matter? You *are* rorting the system, Kaya, are you not?'

'I'm *not* rorting anything!'

'Oh come now,' Estella laughs, hearty and insincere. 'You wouldn't be the first to fake an interest in religion to get a spot at Iggy's and you certainly won't be the last.' She swills the wine in her glass. 'Please don't take it out on me, just because I found you out. You were an atheist a week ago!'

'Take it out on you?' laughs Kaya. 'That's a bit of a pot and kettle situation, isn't it? You've been a massive bitch to me from the get-go. It wouldn't hurt you to be kind, would it? To see what a situation we're in, Ollie and I, without Paul?'

Estella feels an emotion she's long forgotten and it reminds her a little of guilt. She looks away, barely seeing Felicity turn abruptly from Felix and run out of the room. It does not quite register.

'Anyway,' continues Kaya, 'if we're taking the moral high ground, then perhaps you should tell Father in your next confession that you swapped your twins in the matches today.'

Estella's head snaps back around and her eyes lock on Kaya's. 'Excuse me?'

Kaya smiles sweetly. 'You heard me, Estella. Jonty and Archie? In the rugby matches? Made sure the boys were on separate teams and then got Jonty to play both matches because he's the better player?'

Estella feels an icy cold blast of something on her spine. 'Don't be ridiculous!' She laughs, a little too loudly. 'Why on earth would I do that?'

'Because,' Kaya makes quote marks with her fingers. '"Archie couldn't catch a fucking cold!"'

So she *had* been listening that day in the garden! A stalker too!

'How insulting,' Estella laughs, taking a slug of her wine. 'I never said that. How did you come to such a ridiculous conclusion?'

'Their knees.'

'I'm sorry?'

'First of all, Jonty had dirty knees after the first match and Archie didn't, yet "Archie" was the one who dived over the touch line in the first match. And also, Jonty has Osgood–Schlatter disease, does he not?'

'I'm sorry, Osgood *what*?'

'Osgood–Schlatter disease, Estella. Don't deny it. That's what I do,' says Kaya. 'Knees. I'm a physio, remember? I noticed the swelling on Jonty's knee below the joint. It's very common in active boys of the twins' age – especially very sporty ones.'

The two women stare at one another. Estella wonders if Kaya sees her lower eyelid quiver, ever so slightly. She can't let her resolve weaken. She cannot admit what she is being accused of. And anyway, how could Kaya ever prove it? It would be her word against Estella's, and Estella has been in this community for a lot longer than Kaya has.

She turns to Kaya, her game face firmly pasted on. 'Prove it.'

'Prove I signed up for Catholic classes just to get into Iggy's!'

Estella chews on the inside of her cheek. *She's playing dirty, is she? Well, we'll see about that!*

'While we're on the subject of things that didn't happen,' Estella says, 'what *is* the deal with your husband?' She fingers the rim of her wine glass and looks up at Kaya. 'He wasn't even a St Ignatius' old boy, was he? There is no record of a Paul Sterling here at St Ignatius'. No record at all. I checked the website *and* called the office and I scoured every line on those shiny brass plaques on the church pews. And guess what? No Paul Sterling! How do you explain *that?*'

Kaya closes her eyes and Estella sees it as a sign of triumph, an admission of guilt.

'Did "Paul" ever exist?' she asks. 'Or is he still alive and hiding until after the admission process to make his grand appearance. Like a sort of "Ta-da, I'm alive!"'

Estella knows what she has said is wrong as soon as it rolls off her tongue and she sees the hurt in Kaya's eyes. 'I didn't mean . . . I apologise, I . . .' she bumbles.

'He wasn't called Paul Sterling then.' Kaya looks deep into Estella's eyes, and there is something in the stare that sparks recognition. Estella knows what is coming – she knows it before Kaya's brain has formulated the sentence. She has always known it, really, in her heart of hearts, because she sees him in Ollie. She sees him in the boy's smile, his fingers, his shoulders, his forehead. She sees him in the way Ollie shakes the curls of his fringe from his eyes with an effortless flick of the head. The way he smiles, slightly lopsided, from cupid's-bow lips.

'I'm a Sterling,' says Kaya. 'I kept my name. You'd already know this if you hadn't talked over me on my driveway last week. My husband's surname was Palmer. John-Paul Palmer, but I believe you knew him as JP.'

Estella closes her eyes and there, behind her eyelids, she sees him in his Iggy's uniform, laughing at her and beckoning her towards him in the school quad. She giggles and shakes her head. She sees the green grass under the gum tree where they first kissed at fifteen. She sees the shiny rock surface, where they made love for the first time a few months later, her clothes strewn to the side, JP's body over hers. She hears the warm rush of his breath in her ear as he moves on top of her. 'I love you so much,' he says. 'God, I love you.' She feels the single tear of happiness fall from the corner of her eye socket and down her cheek, a tear of joy as she hears those words and feels his body inside hers. She sees it all in the space of just a second, everything he meant to her, everything they shared.

She opens her eyes.

'I know you loved him once,' says Kaya. 'He loved you too, although I'm buggered if I know why. I can't see why he could ever have loved someone so . . .' She chokes on her words. '. . . so dead inside!'

Estella feels the hotness in her eyes, but she blinks it away, stays firm, inches up her chin. She pulls her leather jacket, Felicity's leather jacket, across her chest and she turns and walks away. She does not hear Kaya call after her: 'Estella, wait! You owe it to me to *wait*!' She does not notice the touch of another hand on hers, a familiar touch, or the soft sound of Bec's voice asking, 'Estella? Are you OK? *Estella?*'

Nor does she register the incessant ping-ping-ping of Felicity's phone in her pocket with the photos coming through that she will not want to see. She does not notice any of it, because she has closed her ears and all of her senses, and instead she marches forward blindly, unsteady on her feet, searching for a doorway, for a way out.

12

Bec

Bec watches Estella all but stumble out of the room.

'Is she OK?' she asks Kaya.

'I think so.' Kaya glances at the door. 'We were just talking about a friend we have in common.'

Bec is confused. 'But you called to her, asked her to wait . . .'

'Oh.' Kaya smiles. 'I was just letting her know she'd forgotten her drink.' She gestures to the side table, where Estella's rouge lipstick stains the rim of the wine glass.

Bec isn't sure she believes this explanation, especially since the glass is more or less empty, but she's not particularly interested in refereeing a domestic between Estella and her neighbour over jasmine climbing up the fence or weeds on the nature strip or whatever is Estella's current beef. And Kaya clearly feels the same, because she has already changed the subject.

'Where's Sage?' she asks, breezy as anything. 'She's usually right there!' She points to Bec's hip.

'Oh!' Bec smiles. 'Tom has taken her home, he's on the water tonight. He's meeting the babysitter there. We booked her for seven o'clock so he should be back any minute. Unfortunately she's managed to lose a sock somewhere during the course of the day so it's my mission to find it.'

'Tried the gym?'

'Not yet, but I will.'

Sage being tucked up in bed is another reason Bec has allowed herself to loosen up a little more tonight – it hasn't always been easy being the only one of her friends to have the youngest child. For the last six-odd years, Bec has always been the one to leave a night out early and she has always felt like the world's biggest party pooper scurrying off to bath and bed her smallest babe. But now Sage is older, she has the courage to leave her without the existential terror something bad will happen to her if she isn't home to pre-empt it.

'Is Willow still here?' Kaya's caramel hair is free of its bun and tumbling over the shoulders of her floral dress, and seems to Bec at this very moment like a frangipane tart decorated with edible purple pansies and violas, all florally sweetness.

'Yes. I didn't think she'd want to be here this evening, but Flick is here and they wanted to hang out. Plus there's a boy she likes somewhere.'

'Young love?'

'Something like that!'

'Anyway, speaking of Willow, I'd better go and find her – and that damn sock. She's heading off to the cinema later and I promised I'd give her some cash. That's the other thing about teenagers – they're financial leeches!'

'I'll look forward to that,' laughs Kaya. 'See you later, no doubt.'

Bec leaves the Great Hall and walks a little further up the corridor. She stops for a moment to look at the Year Nine self-portraits, plastered all over the large pinboards on the sage-green walls, varying in their styles and level of detail. She continues alongside rows of green lockers towards the gymnasium where she suspects Sage has left her sock. It is just past seven and dark outside, the late Spring sunshine of October having given up its attempt to hang out past six fifty p.m., and she realises she likes the darkness of this isolated corridor, a part of the school that was humming with life three hours ago as the younger siblings of prospective boys swung from ropes and shimmied along beams.

She puts her flat palm up against the swing doors of the gym and steps inside. It is dark inside here, too, and Bec tiptoes across the wooden floor, negotiating the shadows of running machines and exercise bikes and dumbbells lined up in order of weight on a metal shelving unit. A sliver of moon throws a sharp angle of light across the last in the row of exercise bikes and she leans against it, taking out her phone to turn on the torch. It smells of sweaty socks and rubber. She scans the room. No sock. She could switch the light on, of course, but she doesn't want to alert anyone to her presence particularly – especially as she's not technically meant to be in here. So she texts Willow instead.

Hi darling, she writes. *Come and find me if you want that $50. Mum x.*

She likes the solitude of the darkness, the quiet outside of the Great Hall. She clicks on her email icon. Five new messages. One is a phishing scam: *Bec Lloyd, the government of Nigeria would like to award you $5,000,0000 . . .* There's also a message from her phone company, a school notification, a cake order for three weeks' time. There is nothing from Lucki_Texta and Bec gives a knowing nod, as if to confirm to herself that the emails she has been getting really *are* from a chancer and not from someone who knows what she did. How could they? It is impossible!

She puts her phone away and turns to leave, and that's when she hears a sound, a sort of clicking sound, the sound of kissing, of tongue against tongue. She is immediately embarrassed – she does not want to have stumbled on some clandestine teenage make-out session! She retreats backwards, slowly, and feels for the doors she has just stepped through, but as she puts her left foot cautiously behind her, she strikes something and stumbles. She reaches out to steady herself and hits the wall, a switch of some kind, and light floods the room. Bec squints.

The two figures in front of her spring apart, but not before Bec has seen the body of a young woman with long dark hair pressed up against the toned torso of the sports master. Her slender arms hang from his neck, her pelvis tilts forward.

'Willow?'

Sam Deacon turns around, mutters, 'Shit,' under his breath.

'Mum! It isn't what it looks like, I promise. I can explain, I . . .' She falters.

Bec feels utterly speechless for the first time in her life. She looks at Willow and then at Sam.

'This is who you've been seeing?' she manages. '*Him?*'

'Mum, it's really new. I wasn't dating him when I was at Asher's. I'm eighteen. Sam's only twenty-five. We're not doing anything illegal!'

Bec's heart beats out of control. It takes a further few more beats for her brain to compute that Sam Deacon is the boyfriend Willow plans to sleep with and not Felix Weaver, the soon-to-be ex-school captain. Moreover that Bec has facilitated this highly inappropriate union by buying a packet of condoms which surely Sam Deacon, as the head of the sports department at St Ignatius' Grammar, can afford to buy himself. She has half a mind to ask him for the money back! She looks between Sam Deacon and her daughter. Willow looks between Sam and Bec. It's like a triumvirate of stares.

'This is not happening,' Bec says. Hadn't the sports master been flirting with her just a couple of hours ago and telling her she was pretty? Is this what she wants for her daughter, a man who has an eye out for something better? Not that she classifies herself in that category, of course.

'Sam's my boyfriend, Mum!' Willow says. 'We really . . . *like* one another.'

Sam stares awkwardly at the rubber mat beneath his feet, next to which Bec can see a child's pink unicorn sock. She swoops in and picks it up – force of habit. Sam takes an alarmed step back.

'But he's . . . he's an *adult*,' Bec snaps.

'He's only seven years older than me.'

'Cooper's seven years older than Sage. Would he date someone her age?'

'Mum . . .'

'Mrs Lloyd—' begins Sam.

'Don't speak!' shrieks Bec, waving Sage's pink sock in his face. Sam holds his hands up and takes another step back. 'And he's a *teacher*!' Never mind one who knew she was his supposed girlfriend's mother when he was flirting with her!

'We're serious, Mum.'

Oh dear God.

Sam shifts from one foot to another. He can't meet Bec's eye.

'Go back to the hall, please,' says Bec in a voice she rarely uses with Willow. 'We'll talk about this later.'

Willow recognises the tone and nods. She turns to Sam with the pained look of a star-crossed lover, as if he is Romeo and she is Juliet and this BO-ridden gym is some version of the Verona balcony, and then she leaves.

Bec waits until the door of the gym is closed.

'Please,' says Sam, as if he is about to plead his case to her, beg for the right to court her daughter. 'Please don't tell my mother.'

Tell his mother? What is he, twelve?

'How long has this been going on?' she demands.

'A month or so. It was after her HSC, after Willow turned eighteen.' He runs a hand through his hair. 'I'm not a pervert. I care about her!'

Bec feels the beginnings of The Rage. 'Stay away from her,' she warns. 'Or I will report you not only to your mother but to the board of governors. Do you understand? Whether Willow is eighteen or not is completely irrelevant – she is still a former pupil of Asher's and you are still a teacher at Iggy's. It is highly inappropriate!'

Yes, Bec considers herself woke and understanding, *yes* she will allow her daughter a fair amount of freedom,

but this takes the cake. How dare he? Is he some kind
of paedophile? He has been to university and lived overseas! He's played for a British rugby club for pity's sake,
and Bec knows from Tom what they're all like! Willow has
never been away from home longer than three nights and
that was on a school camp!

'I'm sorry, Bec, I . . .' Sam whispers.

'It's Mrs Lloyd to you,' Bec says evenly. 'Mrs Tom
Lloyd.'

'Of course!' He nods. 'I'm sorry, Mrs Lloyd. If it helps,
I want to you to know I was super-impressed with Cooper
today. He . . . he has a high chance of getting into the
school.'

Bec shakes her head. She looks at the shrunken twenty-
something barely-man who now sits on the edge of the
balance beam, his head bowed, having been told off by a
prospective school parent.

'I hope so,' she says and she turns to leave.

Although does she? Does she really when . . . *this* is
what's on offer?

Willow is waiting for her outside the Great Hall. She
twirls a section of hair in her fingers, just like she did as a
child when she was worried about being told off.

'Are you going to tell Dad?' she asks.

'I can't keep it from him.'

'No, Mum! He'll stop me seeing him.' There are tears in
her eyes and Bec has always been a sucker when it comes
to Willow's tears. She softens, of course.

'Willow, you are eighteen,' she sighs. 'Dad and I can't
stop you from doing anything you want to do now you're

an adult, but nothing can take away from the fact that Sam Deacon is an older man who is probably more . . . *experienced* than you.'

'He wouldn't take advantage of me,' she says. 'He cares about me.'

'I'm sure he does, darling, but it's just . . . it's not right.' *Sick. An abuse of power.* 'The point is, he is in a position of responsibility and he should not be acting like this with an Asher's girl. He could be struck off.'

'But I'm not at the school any more.'

'He could be if it was proven anything happened before you finished your exams, and that was only a month ago.' She sighs. 'Willow, you do know this can't go anywhere, don't you? And besides, you're going to university in January!'

Willow stares at her feet and Bec thinks that at least she's not threatening to defer or anything. Then she would have trouble on her hands.

'Are you disappointed?' Willow says instead.

'In you? No. In Sam? Yes. Yes, I am.'

Willow's shoulders drop and Bec sees only the face of a sweet child. Not a woman on the cusp of being sexually active, but a little girl, saddened to have disappointed her mum.

She sighs and takes her daughter's hand. 'Let's talk about it tomorrow, hey? Tonight is about Cooper.'

Willow nods. 'Am I . . . am I still OK to go to the cinema with Flick later on? We're catching the late session at Pines Mall. We thought we'd get an Uber in case we want to have a beer. I'll pick the car up tomorrow.'

Beer and boyfriends, boyfriends and beer. What can Bec say? Willow is eighteen and an adult in the eyes of the law, even if Flick is not. She can't forbid either girl from going to the cinema just because Willow has an inappropriate boyfriend.

'Just with Flick?'

Willow looks to the floor again. 'Yes, just with Flick.'

'OK then. But text me when you're on your way home.'

'Thanks Mum. I love you.'

'I love you too.'

Then Willow turns and walks away.

13

Estella

Estella sits under the giant oak tree at the top right corner of the cricket oval, the same one she and JP sat under when they were sixteen. She watches the lights in the school hall, from the darkness, hears the buzz, the white noise. She hadn't wanted to miss a minute of the cheese and wine soirée lest she lose an opportunity to introduce herself to Sam Deacon, but Kaya has shocked her, jolted her and she needs time to recompose. She pulls the jacket tight around her and sees the skin of her wrists dotted with goose bumps.

This was their place. Their place for after class, before school, at weekends. It is still the same, this old tree, its boughs hanging low and carefree. It is where they first touched one another's bodies, felt that hot flame of desire, legs and arms entwined like the exposed roots above the earth that weave like giant veins through the surrounding soil. The tree seems no bigger or more imposing than it was twenty-five years before, but Estella knows how time distorts and dilutes things. Its boughs have had a quarter of a century of growth since they sheltered her and JP as young, ill-fated lovers. Estella wonders how many other lovestruck teenagers have sat underneath its branches over the years.

Time, of course, has diluted the strength of her feelings for JP (it has to do this, doesn't it, or no one would ever get over their first love?) but now she knows he is dead, the pain seems to have resurfaced, fresh, a virus lying dormant inside her cells. She'd always wondered if she would ever see him again and now she knows for sure that she will not.

Estella closes her eyes. She remembers being under this tree days before her seventeenth birthday, wrapped in his arms. She can remember the outline of his nose, the light tan of his skin, the way his mouth turned a little downwards when he smiled. The faint aroma of Calvin Klein's Eternity for Men on his skin. The way their fingers fitted perfectly together, hers slender, slim-knuckled, and his wide and strong and possessive. It was puppy love, really, she knows that. A beautiful, innocent infatuation that somehow turned adult, and cruel. It left her with a hole in her heart and a scorched soul.

Estella opens her eyes and wills herself not to think about it any more. She slides her fingers into the inside breast pocket of Felicity's leather jacket and touches the end of something papery and something else that's plastic. She pulls out the ready-rolled spliff and the lighter and puts them end to end, paper to flame. She looks up after a moment and sees Kaya heading towards her across the field, but she doesn't move, just takes a long, indulgent drag and stares ahead to the woods that line the oval. She doesn't react as Kaya sits down beside her, close enough that anyone might think they were good friends. Together they stare ahead towards the lit windows of the Great Hall, but they do not speak. Estella hands the spliff to Kaya who puts it to her lips and inhales deeply, puffing out the smoke in rings.

'He told me about this tree,' says Kaya eventually.

'We spent a lot of time under it.'

'He said that too.'

Estella accepts the joint back and inhales, feels the weed warm her blood.

'So he finally rid himself of the double-barrelled Christian name, then?'

Kaya nods. 'He hated it. People always thought he was—'

'French!' Estella smiles. 'Boys used to say his name with an accent to annoy him.'

Kaya smiles back.

'How long were you married?' Estella asks.

'Fifteen years. We met when we were twenty-five.'

'That's young,' says Estella.

'Yes.'

'How did you meet?'

Kaya is almost ready to go home. Her friend Sarah has not turned up. She didn't bring her Nokia because it is too bulky to fit in her tiny clutch bag, and so she has had to wait here, in this dingy bar full of medics at some random stranger's leaving do, for someone who may or may not show up. She'll get one more drink, she decides, and then go home and watch a DVD. She'd rather that anyway – it had been a drag to get showered and dolled up after a long day in the knee clinic.

She sees him at the bar. He is tall and slender and wears khaki shorts and a T-shirt, casual among the suits. He turns to her and smiles. 'Hey,' he says.

'Hey,' she says back. His eyes are dark brown.

'Are you here for Peter's leaving do?' he asks.

'Yeah, but I don't know him.'

He grins. 'So you're a party crasher?'

'Something like that. No, I'm waiting for a friend.'

'A friend?'

'A girlfriend. Sarah Soames.'

'Yeah, I know Sarah. Are you a medic, too?'

'Physiotherapist. I don't do the blood and the needles and stuff.'

He nods. 'You know, nine out of ten injections are in vein?'

Kaya laughs and shakes her head. 'That was terrible.' But he has piqued her interest with his goofy smile and his awful pun. 'What about you?'

He can't be a medic, not dressed like that!

'I'm in my third year of postgrad,' he says and Kaya stands corrected. 'The aim is to go into clinical practice here in Sydney next year. Or maybe Perth.'

Kaya nods. 'Congrats,' she says. Then, 'Hey, did you hear about the guy whose whole left side was cut off?'

Brown eyes shakes his head. 'No?'

'He's all right now.'

He lets out a boom of laughter. 'Truly awful.'

She smiles.

'Paul,' he says, holding out his hand.

'Kaya,' she replies, taking it.

Estella inspects her fingernails, picks at the flaking polish. 'He talked about being a surgeon when we were young.'

'It was one of his great loves. Like you were. He told me all about you, Estella. He didn't mention a word about any of it until right before he died and then he told me all of it, about how they separated you.'

Estella pulls Felicity's jacket tighter around her.

'It must have been so . . . so hard,' Kaya says. 'That's why he wanted me to find you. It was one of his last wishes that I send Ollie to Iggy's. He wanted me to make contact with you and tell you how sorry he was about everything.' She smiles sadly. 'There really is nothing like terminal cancer to make someone reflect on the wrongs they've done.'

'It wasn't his fault,' says Estella. *It was theirs.*

'Did you . . . did you ever try to find him?' Kaya asks.

'JP? No.' A suck on the spliff. 'I looked on Facebook out of curiosity a few years back, but he wasn't there. It was like he vanished. But then I suppose he would have done with a different name.'

'He didn't do social media.'

'Too many loony patients wanting to befriend him after they'd experienced his charming bedside manner?'

Kaya smiles. 'Something like that. Now I think about it, I wonder if he just didn't want the past to catch up with him at that stage in his life.' She looks at Estella. 'It was just the kind of man he was. He looked forward, not back.'

Estella feels a pang of longing. She knew what kind of a teenage boy JP was, but it is Kaya who knew what kind of man he was. She wishes she had contacted him, that she'd told him she forgave him, that she never blamed him for any of it, for what happened next. But it is too late now and that is the bitter pill. She drags hard and hands the smoke over once more.

'What's done is done,' she says. 'It can't be changed.'

She does not know why it is affecting her like this after so long, but the emotion suddenly threatens to engulf her, like she's trapped in the roots of these trees and is being pulled deep, deep down into the earth where she cannot breathe. She is aware of all of it: the smell of the bark and the grass, the chatter dancing on the breeze from the Great Hall, the way the branches sway in the breeze. It conjures up a whirl of memories. She closes her eyes.

'I'd like you to feel you can talk to me about Paul,' Kaya says. 'He was very open with me about . . . about all of it.'

'No need,' Estella snaps. 'It was young love, that is all.'

'I meant what happened afterwards . . .'

Estella looks at Kaya, eyes swimming with steel. 'You're not to speak about that with anyone, Kaya. Do you hear me?'

Kaya nods. 'You have my word, Estella,' she says. 'I wouldn't talk about it out of respect for Paul.'

'I hope he had a good life,' Estella says.

'I know he did.' Kaya touches her hand and Estella flinches. 'You should know that Paul was a good man, a good dad to Ollie.'

'I always thought he would make a good father,' Estella agrees.

Estella and Kaya pass the smoke between them a couple of times more while they stare at the sky in silence. Estella imagines they are both thinking the same as they gaze upwards at the unusually clear night. *Is he up there? Can he see us? What does he think of this scenario: his wife and his first love together on the exposed roots of the ancient oak tree?*

Estella hears a shrill cry from the quad, followed by a high-pitched giggle, and it brings her back into the present.

'Well, I'd better go,' she says, pulling herself up to standing.

'Estella, let's talk some more. I'd like it if—'

'No,' says Estella and Kaya nods.

'I . . . I should go and see what the twins are up to.'

'Playing swapsies again?' Kaya shrugs.

Estella smiles, despite herself. 'I hope those knees aren't my downfall,' she says.

'They won't be. I only noticed because I work with knees day in, day out and I'd recognise Osgood–Schlatter anywhere because I see so much of it. I don't think your average person goes around looking at children's knees.'

'Fucking Osgood–Schlatter.'

'Fucking Osgood *and* Schlatter,' says Kaya. 'Robert Osgood and Carl Schlatter, two surgeons.'

'Well, they can both get stuffed.'

Kaya touches Estella's arm. 'I'm good at keeping secrets,' she says. 'If you give me a chance, you'll find I can be a very loyal friend.'

Estella turns away, uncomfortable. She isn't sure she wants to be Kaya Sterling's friend just yet. Friends are something she does not have in abundance. She does not like to get too close to other people, she never has – not after JP. Only Bec knows her inside out, understands her idiosyncrasies, puts up with them. One friend has always been enough for her, just plenty. 'I'll bear that in mind,' she says.

Kaya shrugs. 'I hope it works out for you. I really do,' she says, and Estella feels a reluctant pang of warmth towards her new, and rather annoying, neighbour.

Inside Estella's right-hand pocket, a phone vibrates for the umpteenth time.

'Ugh!' Estella grimaces, pulling it out. 'Felicity's phone is driving me insane!'

She takes out the phone to try and turn off the sound and glances at the screen. Her heart drops to her stomach, because there, on the screen, is a photo of a penis. A large, erect penis.

'Oh my God!' she cries as she scrambles to enter Felicity's passcode ('You'll share your passwords with me until you're eighteen, Felicity Munro!') and clicks on the image. The larger version is no more palatable.

I'm in the library, someone stored as BOY has written underneath. *Come meet me, I'll show u this, and u can show me URs.*

Estella feels the bile rise. She throws the phone like it's a hot potato at Kaya, who catches it and lifts it to her face.

Kaya's eyes widen. 'Is that a . . . *dick*? It is! It's a dick!'

She stares at the phone in her hands, her face frozen in shock.

Estella's own shock has rapidly turned to anger. This is what happens with her emotions: they can change in the blink of an eye, and she has certainly experienced a myriad tonight. She grabs the phone back from Kaya and scrolls through the chat, reading aloud.

Where's the other pic U promised?

U a virgin or something?

Send a pic if you don't want me to share the other 1.

Kaya's mouth is open. 'Oh my God, Estella, this is por-nographic. It's *violent*! Who is sending them?'

'I don't know,' Estella says. 'He's saved as BOY. Give me your phone.'

'What?'

'Your phone!' Estella clicks her fingers and Kaya gets out her phone like a dutiful servant.

'What are you going to do?'

'Call the number, of course!' Estella hears the shrillness in her own voice.

'I wouldn't,' Kaya warns. 'Not while you're angry.'

Estella ignores the call to calm and snatches the handset.

'No,' Kaya says, and grabs it back. 'You're way too emo-tional. I'll do the talking.'

Estella, to her surprise, allows herself to be instructed. Her fingers shake as she clicks on to BOY's contact details. She reads out the number and listens to the beeps of the keys as Kaya keys the number into her own phone, holds it out in the space between them and taps the speaker but-ton. Each ring feels like an eternity, but BOY answers on the third.

'Yep?' The voice is croaky and deep, and the greeting more of a grunt than a word.

'Hi,' Kaya says. 'Is that . . . *Oscar*?'

'Oscar?' mouths Estella with a dramatic shrug.

Kaya flaps her hand at Estella.

'Wrong number,' the voice replies.

'My apologies,' Kaya says, polite and playful. 'Who is this then?'

The voice on the other end of the phone sighs, as if its owner cannot be bothered with the tedium of a middle-aged-sounding woman who can't read a phone number correctly.

'It's Felix,' he says, low and languid. 'Felix Weaver.'

14

Kaya

'Are you OK?' Kaya asks.

Estella's brow knits angrily. 'Of course I'm not. Some teenage pervert is sending dick pictures to my daughter! What do you want? A happy dance?'

And she's back, thinks Kaya. But now they've established themselves as equals, the sharers of a loved one, Kaya no longer feels the need to be subordinate, to appease.

'I'm trying to help you, Estella,' she says evenly. 'There's no need to be rude.'

'I'm . . . I . . .' Estella sighs. 'I apologise. I'm just . . .' She runs her fingers through her hair and Kaya can see that the woman rarely admits she is wrong. 'This has quite thrown me, you understand.'

'Breathe,' Kaya tells her. 'We will work out a plan, OK?'

'A plan? I'll tell you what my plan is,' Estella's breath is shallow, and Kaya can sense the other woman's over-whelm, that her plan is fraught with desperation and not measure. 'I'm going to find Felix's mother and I'm going to show her what is on Felicity's phone.'

'But he's an adult, Estella. He's eighteen. His mother can't tell him what to do.'

'Right, well I'll need to deal with *him* then.' Estella zips up her jacket, which she sees now is much more suited to a teenager than a middle-aged woman, and begins to march forwards, across the oval.

'Estella, wait,' Kaya calls, for the second time in the space of an hour, but Estella doesn't stop.

'I said, wait!' She yells it this time, and this time Estella stops in her tracks like a dog hearing the 'sit' command. 'You are not going to confront him.'

'*Excuse* me?'

Kaya looks Estella directly in the face. 'You're not going to do that because you know it will ruin the twins' chances of getting a place here. Felix is the school captain, remember?'

Estella bites her lip angrily. 'Former.'

'Yes but he is still officially in the role until graduation. You've come this far, Estella. You've committed identity fraud to get your boys a place at Iggy's for God's sake. You know Felix is properly in with Sam Deacon . . .'

Estella blinks, worry flashing over her face.

'And Sam Deacon and his mother make the final call. You cannot get them offside. Do not unravel it now just because of some stupid dick pics. You'll be branded a troublemaker, a difficult parent. They won't want to have to deal with you, trust me. My advice would be to email the photos to yourself and delete them from Flick's . . . I mean Felicity's phone – and I mean the whole message stream – and act normal until you have a place for Jonty and Archie.'

'And let him get away with it?' she snaps.

'I'm not saying that. I'm just suggesting you wait until Felix has officially graduated the school before you act on it formally.'

'What, punish him when he's moved overseas?'

'Just wait a couple of weeks, Estella.'

'But he's threatening to publish his photos. I can't stop that.'

'Then maybe have a gentle word with him if you have to. Tell him you know what he's up to and that he'd better toe the line. But that's as far as I'd go at this stage. You need to do this for Jonty and Archie.'

'Why?'

'To get them a place. Isn't that what you're desperate for, at the end of the day?'

'No, I mean why are you helping me? It certainly isn't because I shopped you to Father Francis.'

'So you *did* tell him my name?' Kaya knows it, she just wants a confession.

'Oh, semantics,' says Estella.

'I *knew* it!' Kaya shakes her head and sighs. 'The reason I'm doing it is firstly because I am a nice person, and secondly because I promised Paul I'd look out for you. Like I said, it was a deathbed thing. He feels he wronged you all those years ago.'

A month before he died, Paul had asked her sit to sit down with him at the kitchen table, where beautiful white lilies in the vase were starting to decompose and he'd told her, 'I want you to promise me some things, for after I'm gone.' They were way past the point of avoiding the 'd' word, although they both knew they were facing it. In some ways, discussing Paul's imminent death had become like chatting about a broken appliance or a visit to her parents' home interstate. Something they dreaded and did

not quite know how to handle, but a necessary evil. Paul
had found acceptance, and so she had to.

He produced a pen and paper. 'Right,' he said. 'I need
you to make me some promises.' He wrote at the top of
the page: *A dying man's last wishes* and then put a number
one in black ink beneath it, which he circled a couple of
times.

'Go ahead,' she said. 'I'm listening.'

Paul cleared his throat. 'First up,' he told her, 'I want
you to move. We always said we wanted a sea change and
since we never got to do it, I want you and Ollie to.' He
wrote *Sea change* and underlined it.

'I mean it, Kaya. Get out of the city, it's way too busy for
you and for Ollie. There's too much pollution, too much
noise. Do what we said we'd always do – make a fresh
start. Spend the money, buy the house on the cliff we saw
that time. Offer them what they asked for it last year.'

'But it's not for sale.'

'They're asking for expressions of interest again,' Paul
said. 'I called the estate agent.'

'But it's not worth that much!' When the owners had
asked for expressions of interest the previous year, it
turned out they had only been looking for unrealistic ones.
And back then, before his diagnosis, Paul hadn't seen the
house as a necessity. But as he prepared for his own death,
it seemed he did.

'We have the money, Ky. I want you to do it.'

She felt uneasy about committing then and there. How
would she know how she would feel after he was gone?
How could she move, when all of the memories of him

were right there, in Klara Bay, in the two-up, two-down terrace with the iron railings?

He read her thoughts, like he always did. Annoying habit. 'You can't languish about in here feeling sorry for yourself,' he said. 'You have permission to be glum for a year, and then you need to start again.'

She had pouted. 'What makes you think that's enough for them?'

He didn't skip a beat. 'Because the agent says they'll take four point three million if we offer it.'

'Four point three *million dollars?*'

Kaya's head had spun at the thought. Paul loved the house – he'd passed it as a boy every day on his way to school, and when he'd taken her to visit the school years later and they'd stumbled on a pre-sale viewing, they'd gone in pretending to be potential buyers. They'd imagined themselves sitting by the firepit in the back garden with a bottle of wine, listening to the roar of the waves against the rocks below. They'd imagined planting bamboo along the side fence to block out the view of the family next door. But *four point three million?* What they had saved wasn't Monopoly money, it was their future. But then again, if he said the money was there, then it was. He was nothing if not organised.

'That was promise one,' Paul said. 'And here's number two.' Paul ran the biro over and over the number in the circle. Then wrote the words *St Ignatius' Boys' Grammar* and underlined them.

'But why, Paul?' she'd asked. 'Why are you so desperate to uproot us?'

'Because there's someone from my past,' was what he said. 'I need you to find her.'

And now Estella is found, and here they are, and Kaya is trying to crack a nut that is so hard she wonders if it is unbreakable. But conversely, she knows what trauma can do to a person and what it can make them become.

'Perhaps I *will* bide my time with Felix,' Estella says contemplatively, as if it is her own idea and not Kaya's. She rubs her hands together as if she is washing them and the sound of skin on skin seems exaggerated in the still of the night. 'Yes, that would be the most sensible thing.'

'Did you just say that you think I am right?' Kaya asks.

Estella glares at her, but Kaya thinks she can see the creases of Estella's eyes crinkle and she feels a stab of euphoria that she has turned a corner with her stubborn neighbour. She wishes Estella had told her the whole story here in the moonlight, but she will in time, Kaya is sure of that. There are questions, things she is desperate to know. Things she forgot to ask of Paul before he ran out of time. But she will swallow them down for his sake. He may have gone, but she will never stop being loyal to him, even though he wasn't always up front with her, even if he *did* leave it to the end of his life to tell her the truth about his past.

She turns towards the main school building. 'I'll see you later, then, neighbour,' she says. 'Good luck to the boys if I don't see you before the letters go out on Saturday.'

Estella nods. 'Yes, you too.'

Kaya is part way across the field when Estella calls after her. 'Kaya?' She looks smaller with some distance between them. 'I appreciate the advice.'

'It's my pleasure.' Kaya turns back towards the main school building with a smile on her face, because she supposes this is as close as she will get to a thank-you from Estella.

Back inside the Great Hall, Kaya realises that not only is she emotionally exhausted, but she is also a little stoned. She knows this because she takes *two* of Bec's individual chocolate tortes from the catering table and eats them in quick succession and each one is like biting into a slice of heaven. It is almost nine o'clock and she will need to take a cab home soon, because she shouldn't really drive after a glass of wine and a toke or five on Estella's spliff – certainly not around that winding bend in the dark and with Ollie in tow. She gets out her phone ready to book a car, but realises she should probably locate Ollie first, in case her ride comes quickly. She knows half of Lawton's Uber drivers will be hovering around St Ignatius' tonight, ready to take home pissed-up Pacific Pines parents who've made the last-minute decision to ditch their cars and get stuck into the free booze.

She drains the last drop of wine in her glass and looks around the hall. She sees Ollie charging towards her dressed in his dirty sports gear again, excitedly weaving in and out of groups of parents and families, saying 'Sorry,' as he passes. He looks like he belongs here, in this hall, just as his father did. Kaya sees it now, how Paul saw it. Ollie *does* belong here in this place, in the lingering presence of his father.

He stops in front of her, breathless. '*Please* Mum, can I get a lift home with Cooper and his dad later?' He puts his hands together in prayer. 'Cooper wants me to play with him and Jonty and Archie outside under the floodlights. Mr Deacon said they're leaving them on until ten o'clock tonight, so anyone who wants to can have a knock-around. Tom says he'll drop me home.' He taps his foot on the floor urgently. 'Please, Mum. It's only another hour!'

Kaya feels a flash of worry – does she feel OK about him being in another person's car on that treacherous road? Has Tom been drinking?

'Please, Mum!'

Kaya sighs. The spliff has chilled her out. And besides, the Lloyds are about as wholesome and trustworthy as a family can get. Didn't Bec say Tom wasn't drinking tonight because he'd had to drop Sage home?

'OK, let me check with Cooper's dad.' She turns to look across the room.

'Yesssss!' Ollie fist pumps.

She locates Tom on the other side of the hall. He has pulled himself up even taller, like a meerkat, waiting for her approval.

'Is that OK?' he mouths and Kaya nods with her thumbs up.

Ollie wraps his arms around her. 'Thanks, Mum!'

He turns to leave and she calls him back. 'I'm so proud of you, Ol,' she says. 'You did so well today. And, you know, whatever happens with Iggy's—'

'Jesus will decide. He makes the decisions,' Ollie chirps.

Kaya doesn't respond because she is a little shocked, so instead she ruffles his hair and smiles down at him (not too far, because he's nearly as tall as her these days), and says, 'You know what, Ollie? Maybe you're right.'

Kaya turns towards the exit and scours for the Deacons so she can thank them before she leaves. Ursula Deacon is nowhere to be found, and Sam is the one on duty thanking parents at the main doorway. She observes the handsome sports master as she nears him – there is something comforting and approachable in his gait.

'Mr Deacon,' she says, clasping the man's outstretched hand. 'Thank you so much for your time with Ollie today.'

'It's a pleasure,' he says. 'Do call me Sam. Ollie played incredibly well. You should be proud of him.'

Kaya feels acute pride that Sam noticed Ollie on the pitch today, that he knows her boy's name.

'I am,' says Kaya. 'I'd love to say thank you to Mrs Deacon as well.' Kaya doesn't say 'your mother' because she wants to keep it professional. 'Is she nearby?'

'Actually,' says Sam Deacon, 'she felt a little unwell, so she's taken her leave and headed back to the principal's cottage. She did ask me to apologise to all of the parents and say goodbye on her behalf.'

'Oh, I'm so sorry,' says Kaya. 'Please pass on my warm wishes. I hope she feels better soon.'

'Thank you, I will,' he says. 'Good night, Mrs Sterling!'

Outside, the air is cool and quiet and the moonlight casts a silvery glow on the gravel. Kaya decides she will do one more lap of the cricket oval before she orders her car, just in case she doesn't get to do it again. She definitely feels Paul's presence here, the closeness of him, and she wants to do it without Estella this time. It may have been their teenage place, but that doesn't mean Estella has the exclusive right to her own memories.

'Are you here, Paul?' she asks as she approaches the ancient oak. She runs her fingers across the bark. 'Can you hear me?'

The branches rustle and she listens hopefully to the silence for a moment, before continuing on. As she walks, she thinks of her moment with Estella under the tree. Of Estella's coldness, which had broken down temporarily in this very spot. She thinks of Bec in contrast, so warm, so *perfect*, so free of the bind of secrets, or of the shackles of grief. Bec who carries herself so gracefully! She tries to imagine herself through other people's eyes, wonders how *she* looks to an outsider. Is *she* cold? Is *she* perfect? She doesn't think she could be described as either. She is the widow, the mother, the overcompensating smile that lights up a room. She is the giver, the self-deprecator, the apologiser, the woman who wants everyone else to feel good. But do not underestimate her. Do not push her. Because there is much more to Kaya than that first layer, so much more. She is steely and capable, she is raw.

She is a volcano bubbling with molten lava of hidden secrets, her dead husband's secrets, simmering ever so gently and just getting ready to erupt.

15

Bec

Bec turns back on herself and walks down the same dark corridor she has just come from after confronting the sports master. It is too stifling in the hall and she needs to think about what she has just learned about Willow. There is also the not-so-small matter of how she will break the news to Tom. Willow has told her it is love and so Tom will need to know. She cannot keep a secret like this from him.

She continues in the darkness in an area that is evidently out of bounds for parents and students alike.

Bec prides herself on being a liberal parent, but this takes the biscuit. *What does he want with an eighteen-year-old girl?*

She passes the library, lit by a sliver of silver light. She feels a sudden urge to be somewhere illicit and quiet, where she is alone with her thoughts and can work through the muddle in her head, and so she turns the doorknob and pushes the heavy wooden door open. The room smells of mould and must and old textbooks that have dampened with time. She can make out walls of bookshelves, neatly stacked, their spines labelled with white, numbered stickers. The large clock on the wall dongs seven times.

She closes the door quietly behind her, something to do with needing to be silent in a library and because Bec is (mostly) a good girl. The yellow light from an adjoining classroom casts a thin triangle on the wooden parquetry flooring, crossed swords with the silver slice of moonlight.

A shadow steps out from behind a shelf.

'Oh my God,' squeals Bec. It's the second time she's come across someone lurking in the dark. What is going on with this school?

'Did I surprise you?' It is a man's voice, and Bec can see when she gets a little closer that it is Felix Weaver, the school captain. He is in the school sports kit, despite no longer technically being a student, and his silhouette is immaculate, aside from what looks like ruffled hair. The screen of an iPhone glows in his hand.

Bec exhales. 'Oh, hello.' She smiles. There is a vague question somewhere in her brain, a question about why this boy is in the library on his own in the dark, lit only by sec-ond-hand light. It is creepy. 'I was just taking a breather.'

'Exploring.' It isn't a question.

'Yes,' she says. 'I'm here for the Gala Day. I mean, that's obvious really, isn't it?' She laughs. 'My son, Cooper, is a prospective student.'

'Cooper Lloyd.' Another statement. The boy is confi-dent, self-assured. At that age Bec would have apologised profusely for her ghostly presence in a dark room and scurried away.

'I'm sorry,' says Bec. 'Were you working?'

'Ha! No.' It isn't quite the level of politeness she was expecting from the school captain!

'Cooper is Willow's brother,' Felix says, his face blank. Bec can't read if it is a good thing or a bad thing that he knows her daughter.

'Yes.' Bec clears her throat. 'Do you know Willow?'

There is a long pause as Felix studies his nail beds. 'Yes,' he says.

'Oh, lovely,' says Bec.

How? How do you know my daughter?

'He's a good player.'

'I'm sorry?'

'Cooper.'

'Oh yes, of course. Thank you. My husband and I certainly believe he has potential.'

'Do you have any other kids?'

He's so strange that Bec wonders if there's something a bit wrong with him. 'Well, yes, Willow, as you know . . .'

'Just Cooper and Willow?'

'Um, no. We have a younger girl, but she's at home with the babysitter. Sage. She's five,' Bec say and her smile slips. She hoists it back up again.

'Ah, Sage.' He nods. 'I'm an only child.'

Figures, Bec thinks. Only children are often oddballs. She doesn't know how she is meant to respond, so she just says, 'I hear you are off to Cambridge University.'

'Yep. I did the International Baccalaureate. Time for me to get out into the big bad world.' He clicks his knuckles and they respond loudly.

'Cambridge, though!' Bec enthuses, the history-lover in her swooning at the idea. 'What an incredible achievement.'

'Yeah, well I aced my exams. My mum's British and I have a passport, so why not? I'm going to St Catharine's College.'

'What will you study?'

'Latin and law.'

Bec is excited momentarily. She knows Latin! 'That's great.' She smiles, forgetting the boy's strange demeanour. She knows Iggy's has produced some Harvard and Yale boys, but she hasn't met a successful Cambridge applicant as yet. Perhaps that intense cleverness is what makes Felix so . . . odd. 'Latin is an incredible language.'

'Yeah well, I'm pretty lucky!' He grins.

'I'm sure it's more than luck,' Bec says generously. 'I actually did a Latin module at university myself.' She doesn't know why she has told him this.

He looks up with dark eyes. 'Do you remember any of it?'

Bec laughs at the insinuation that she is ancient herself and therefore must have memory issues. 'Oh gosh, no,' she says. 'You need to keep it up to remember it!'

She is being modest. She may not *speak* the dead language but she can understand it and even write it still. Sometimes, perhaps once a decade, she will pull out her plump university classics books and read Suetonius' *The Twelve Caesars*, or Virgil's *Aeneid* or Plutarch's *The Makers of Rome* and soak it all up, all that heavenly history. A few years back she wrote Tom's entire Valentine's Day card in Latin, and he'd been forced to consult Google Translate to work out what she had written. He had particularly liked the question, *Estne volume in toga, an solum tibi libet me videre?* (Is that a scroll in your toga, or are you just pleased to see me? and the sign-off line *velim vos manducare sicut placentam delectamentum* (I would like to eat you like a delicious cake). Oh, that had been fun! But Bec is not about to share this snippet of written foreplay with Felix Weaver!

'So no,' she reiterates. 'I don't speak it any more. There isn't much need, really.'

Felix nods as if he's relieved by what she has just told him, because evidently *he* wants to be the only Latin whizz in the room and does not want her revelation to take the sheen off his own hubris (*wasn't this what killed Julius Caesar?*) and share his talent with a middle-aged mother-of-three.

'I came top in the state,' he tells her. 'When I'm at Cambridge I'm going to teach it to high-school kids at private schools to make some money.'

'Most university kids do bar work.' Bec smiles.

Felix laughs, and it is a sharp sound, like an oboe. 'Yeah, perhaps. Or maybe I'll do something really random. You know, like sell my sperm to a donor clinic or something. *Vendere sperma!*'

The hit of the word 'sperm' gives Bec the ick and Felix can tell because he stares at her now with amused eyes. '*Faber est suae quisque fortunae* and everything.'

Bec translates the phrase in her head: 'Every man is the artisan of his own fortune', but she doesn't say it aloud because she doesn't want it to be some kind of 'in joke' between them, to create some absurd sense of camaraderie between herself and this odd boy, because that's all he is, a boy. Barely old enough to drink, barely old enough to drive. Is it appropriate that he talks to her like this, using this kind of banter? She wonders for a split second if this is some kind of test. If her own IQ is being measured by Ursula Deacon and her cronies to assess the family's suitability to be let into the fold? Is she being filmed or something? Is this like some kind of whacked-out integrity test? A version of *The Truman Show*? She imagines Ursula Deacon playing it back for her later, on a laptop, and telling her, 'Gosh, well *done*, Bec. Felix engaged you in some tough and highly inappropriate conversation in the library but you passed the impropriety test. You and your family are a perfect fit for St Ignatius'!'

Is *this* what is happening right now?

But ultimately she finds Felix's manner rude and rather inappropriate. She feels Iggy's school captain should not be speaking to a parent about sperm donation of all things, in the school library.

She pulls her handbag close to her side. 'Well . . .' she says. 'I really must go now.' Is it colder in here all of a sudden? 'It was nice to meet you, Felix.'

'Goodbye, Bec,' he says. 'Good luck.'

'Good luck?'

'With Cooper. Iggy's isn't an easy school to get into.'

Bec does not respond because how can she? What is there to say in the face of such a remark? She turns and walks through the library doors and, when she reaches the far end of the corridor and the doors of the Great Hall, she turns to see Felix Weaver leaning on the doorframe watching her with a half-smile on his face.

16

Estella

Estella usually finds it easy to shut a door on her emotions, but at this precise moment in time it is near impossible. Her overwhelming instinct is to find Felix Weaver and his macramé-making mother and have it out with them both. However, she doubts Martha Weaver with her bumbling manner and her inability to make eye contact will act on the knowledge that her son is sending pornographic photos to teenage girls. She expects Martha is terrified of the boy, and will offer a lame apology and leave it at that. The boy will not be punished in any form she suspects, merely asked pathetically to do the right thing. But boys who send photos of their trigger-happy dicks to young girls are not the kind of boys who have much of a conscience about anything.

Estella is still tempted to take it higher, to Ursula Deacon. But Kaya is absolutely right: if she takes matters further, Estella will paint herself as a troublemaker and jeopardise whatever chances the twins have of admission to Iggy's. And then it won't matter whose knees are dirty and whose knees are mashed up, or who can dissect a John Donne poem and who doesn't understand a single line, because all of her efforts will be for nothing. She considers the police – after all, Felix is an adult who is sending photos to a seventeen-year-old girl! But what would they do,

really? Felicity is almost eighteen and Estella doesn't know
what photos her daughter has sent Felix. Finding out this
information is her current intent as she hurries back to
the Great Hall from the oak tree. She will find Felicity and
establish exactly what has gone on between her and this
vile boy.

Felicity stands by the drinks table with Willow. As soon
as she sees Estella, she puts her prosecco down and picks
up a glass of water, which is laughable. Estella couldn't
give a fuck about a glass of fizz in the midst of cock-gate.

'Hi Estella,' says Willow, her broody eyes fixed on the
floor. She has been crying. Estella could ask her what is
wrong, show some tenderness, but she is not in the mood
to humour her goddaughter and her delicate sensitivities.

She offers a tight smile to Felicity. 'A word please,
Felicity.'

'I can't right now . . .' Felicity's right eyebrow arches.
'I'm *talking.*'

Estella grabs her daughter's wrist, perhaps a little too
tightly. 'Now,' she snaps.

Felicity snatches her wrist away and grabs her prosecco
out of defiance, cradling the bowl of the glass in her palm.
This annoys Estella immensely – everyone knows you
should rest your fingers *lightly* on the base of the stem.
'You can say whatever it is in front of Willow.'

'Fine. There is a photo of Felix Weaver's penis on your
phone.' Estella turns over the phone in the palm of her
hand. 'Would you like me to show it to Willow, too?'

Felicity gasps and makes a grab for the phone, but
Estella pulls her hand back.

'It's really rather small in my opinion. If only I had my reading glasses . . .' Estella studies the screen as Felicity swipes desperately for the phone.

Felicity lets out a low-level growl. 'You . . . you read my *messages?*' She steps forward, places her foot above Estella's eight-hundred-dollar boots and stamps, making another bid for the phone, but Estella holds strong. She has at least twenty kilos on Felicity, unfortunately, not that she would take kindly to anyone else pointing it out.

Willow's eyes are like saucers. She takes a step backwards. 'I'll catch you later,' she mumbles and turns. Felicity ignores her, because her eyes are on the fleshy monstrosity on the screen Estella holds in her hand.

'Frankly, I've seen more appealing visuals on a vivisection documentary . . .'

'How dare you?' Felicity's eyes are narrow, mean. 'Don't I have any privacy?'

'You took *my* jacket,' says Estella through thin lips. 'Your phone wouldn't stop pinging. What was I supposed to do?'

'That explains it,' Felicity spits. 'The incontinence pad in my pocket.'

She pulls out a large Tena Lady pad Estella has stuffed in the inside breast pocket, just in case. Menopause really is playing havoc with her pelvic floor!

Felicity holds the pad aloft. *Game on.*

'You're not in a position to make jokes, Felicity.' Estella looks around the hall and makes a grab for it, but Felicity stands on tiptoes.

'I'm not making jokes, *Estella.*' Felicity waves the pad about above her head.

Estella fixes her with a glare. '*Get. Outside. Now,*' she hisses. She doesn't use this voice often, but when she does, everyone toes the line. She walks towards the door and waits for Felicity to follow her, which she knows she will.

Felicity lets out a loud sigh and stuffs the pad back in the inside pocket of Estella's leather jacket and follows her mother through the doors, past the oval and round the back of the old building, once home to the monks (who would definitely not approve of a mother and daughter tit-for-tat over a sanitary pad and a penis photo).

'Well can I have my phone back or not?' Felicity snaps as they settle beside the door of the chapel. It's her last show of defiance.

'No.'

'Please?' Felicity grits her teeth. 'It's *my* phone.'

'Who pays the bill?'

'Dad!'

Estella presses a few buttons and then tosses the phone at Felicity, watches as the screen illuminates her daughter's face in the dark.

'Where are my messages?'

'Gone.'

'You deleted them?'

Estella shrugs, dusts off her hands.

'Why?' Felicity cries. 'They were for me!'

'They are not appropriate.'

'Well,' whimpers Felicity. 'At least tell me what he said.'

'Who?'

'You know who! Felix!'

'You mean what he said alongside this charming photo of his tiny phallus?'

'Yes!' Felicity looks expectant, and slightly fearful. Estella sees how much this boy means to her daughter in the anguish that's painted on her face. She realises, quite clearly, that she has two choices. She could lie to Felicity, make something up so as to save her daughter's tears, or she could rip the Band-Aid off to make it easier in the long run. She chooses Option B because she is too angry right now to choose otherwise. Felicity needs to know what this boy is really like. Call it the school of hard knocks!

'He said you were a virgin as if it is a bad thing.'

Estella watches Felicity's eyes as they fill up with tears, her chin trembling under the weight of trying to keep her emotions in. She sits down on the bench in front of the chapel steps, so beautifully depicted by Bec in fondant, and Estella follows. There is half a metre between them.

'You can't read my messages,' Felicity says, defeated. 'They're *private*!'

'Have you sent him any photos?'

Felicity begins to cry.

'Oh good God, Felicity!' Estella gets up, begins to pace. 'Well, have you?'

'Just one.'

'Of what?'

'Mum, stop!'

Estella thumps her fist on the bench. 'Tell me now! What has he got a photo of?'

Felicity gestures towards her chest.

'Oh God, no!' sighs Estella.

'I sent it last week,' Felicity whimpers. 'He said he'd deleted it!'

'Well now he's saying he's going to show it to everyone!' Estella sighs again. Was she this naive at seventeen? Who is she kidding? She knows she was! That's how she got into that impossible situation: a life-altering heartbreaker of a situation. She sits down again, closer to Felicity this time. Her voice softens. 'You need to get him to delete it.'

Felicity ignores her. 'Why shouldn't I have sex with him? I'm old enough.' Her eyes are red and desperate.

'Because he doesn't care about you, Felicity! Not like a proper boyfriend should.' She wants to slide along the bench closer to her daughter but something is preventing her, an unknown force, a sort of fear. 'Not if he is telling you you're frigid! I won't allow you to do it, not on these terms.'

'You don't own me!' Felicity cries.

'Well, until you're eighteen, I do! I'm your mother!' She hears her own mother's tone, her lack of empathy, and she hates herself for it. But it's all she knows, isn't it?

'My mother? You mean you gave birth to me? Any stupid whore can do that!'

Estella sees red, lifts her hand, and takes a swipe. Felicity takes the slap, stunned, raises her own hand up to her face and places it over the hot, red mark left.

'Oh . . . God,' Estella says, her hand on her mouth. 'Felicity, I . . .'

Felicity begins to cry, softly at first, and then harder and Estella takes her hand, somehow the ache of maternal love negating her usual coldness, the stiffness of her own upbringing. 'I'm sorry,' she says. 'I'm so sorry.'

'It's Willow he wants,' Felicity sobs. She doesn't care about the slap, only about Felix. Estella gets that, she's been there.

'He's legit in love with her, but she doesn't want him because she likes someone else, so he's settling for me.'

'How do you know this?' Estella asks.

'He told me. He came out with it and said he'd always had a thing for her. Willow says it's gaslighting,' says Felicity. 'Him being awful to me and then watching me come back.'

Estella feels nothing but desperate sadness. Has *she* made Felicity like this? Have her own lack of tenderness as a mother, her impossible standards, made Felicity want to settle for romantic 'love' that is mean and empty and which only *takes*?

It's as though Felicity reads her thoughts. 'Why are you so *tough* on me?' she whimpers.

Estella places her hands in her lap. 'Because I don't want you to make the same mistake I did,' she says, and wonders if Felicity notices the tremor in her voice. She almost tells Felicity everything now. She almost opens up to her. But she cannot because it is not how she was made.

'But I *need* you. Can't you see that? I need my mother! I need *you*, Mum.'

The words are unfamiliar territory. They sting like vinegar on a cut.

'I am sitting beside you, right now,' Estella replies, her shoulders square. 'And I'm telling you to forget about this boy. You are too good for him, Felicity!'

It is true. Felicity is smart and intelligent and clever and far too good for Felix Weaver. Why does she not tell her daughter this more often?

'I can't forget about him,' she says.

'Yes, you can!' Estella is up again, the hardness returned. 'Damn it, Felicity! I will not have him grind you down like this. He is a piece of shit and he will ruin you if that photo gets out. You need to get him to delete it!'

It is the same voice her own mother used twenty-five years before, but this is not the same boy, it is not the same love affair.

'He won't do it! And besides, he knows other stuff about us.'

'What do you mean?' Estella feels the panic rise. 'Besides the photo?'

Felicity begins to cry. 'I told him . . .'

'About what?'

Felicity looks up at her, speechless.

'Felicity?' Estella shakes her daughter's shoulders. 'Tell me now. What did you tell Felix about us?'

'I told him about Jonty and Archie. I told him you swapped them in the rugby matches and the entrance interviews.'

Estella looks up to the heavens. 'What on earth were you *thinking*?'

'I thought he'd find it funny,' Felicity sobs. 'I don't know. I wanted to give him something, to show him I trusted him. I wanted him to want me.'

'Oh good God,' Estella says and runs a hand through her hair and sighs. It's one thing having Kaya know, but quite another having Felix Weaver in on the secret, too.

Felicity begins to rock back and forth, broken. 'Mummy?' Her voice is a whimper.

Estella opens her arms and pulls Felicity in. It is a gesture she has no control over, a gesture borne of instinct. She breathes in the smell of her daughter's skin. Remarkably it smells the same as it did when Felicity was a little girl. That slightly sweet cookie smell. Estella closes her eyes. She thinks of the softness of Felicity's hair as a baby, the silky sparseness of it, and the way she had held her for hours and looked at her tiny, wrinkled face. How she had held her that bit tighter every time the hospital door had opened, frightened that someone was going to make her open up her arms and take Felicity away from her, to deem her unworthy of motherhood, as if she was only a child herself, little more than a pregnant teen, and not an adult worthy of caring for a child.

Remarkably, although she doesn't have time to mull it over too much, Estella doesn't feel the inclination at this precise moment to chastise Felicity for potentially scuppering the chances of acceptance letters arriving on the doormat for the twins in a few days' time. She doesn't feel the need to make a mocking aside about Felicity's hormones getting the better of her. She knows it will not help. What is done is done.

They sit quietly for a moment, save for the soft heave of Felicity's caught breath as she rests against Estella's chest and her tears roll down the shiny black leather of the damn All Saints jacket. Then Felicity looks up, eyes red and snot forming a channel from her nostrils to her mouth.

'Is it going to be OK, Mum?' she asks, like she might have done when she was seven and had spilled paint on the sofa or argued with her best friend. Estella sees that little girl now, in the downturn of her daughter's mouth and in the hot, ruddy cheeks woven with the white salty pathways of evaporated tears. She sees her in the clumping of wet, black eyelashes and the worried knit of her brow. But Estella has had her moment of sentimentality. It is gone as abruptly as it arrived.

What Estella really wants to say to Felicity right now is, 'Thank God, I got to you when I did! Together we will sort it out. He will not get away with it, this sick bottom-feeder who is not worthy of you! I love you and I will make it right.' This is what she *wants* to say. But of course Estella cannot say it.

'Come on,' she says instead, her hand patting Felicity's back. 'Leave it with me'. She needs this moment of drama to be over, despite the burn of emotion in her own throat. She cannot sit about indulging Felicity's teenage angst because she needs to think fast. She needs to stop Felix Weaver before he can overshare anything: photos *or* the news of the Munros' school admissions fraud which has the potential to ruin everything.

She unclasps Felicity's grip from her arm and stands up. 'Come on. Let's find Willow. I'm sure she's looking for you.'

Felicity gets up obediently and Estella feels the adrenalin surge. It has made her almost euphoric, in the idea of confronting the school captain, putting him in his place once and for all. A plan begins to form: a way to salvage her daughter's reputation and ensure the twins are not caught in the crossfire. It is not a pleasant plan, not in the slightest, but it is the boy's just desserts.

17

Bec

It's hard to spot Tom in the packed hall, but Bec finds him by the refreshment table chatting to a woman she doesn't know. He clocks her walking toward him and says a brief goodbye to the stranger.

'There you are, sweetheart,' Tom says, kissing her temple and Bec feels her guts somersault because of Willow and the gym and Sam Deacon. 'Everything OK?'

'Fine,' she chirps. 'Have you seen Cooper?'

'Chucking a ball about with Ollie Sterling,' he says. 'They're keeping the floodlights on, so I said I'd go and join them in a bit and then drop Ollie home.'

Bec looks to the front of the room, to the stage where Sam Deacon stands beside his mother. Perhaps he senses her looking at him because his eyes flick up and meet hers momentarily and Bec turns away with an angry blink. She feels the burning urge to tell Tom, right now, about Willow. She *always* tells him everything, after all, he is her confidant, her co-conspirator. Moreover she needs her husband's advice, his (sometimes nauseating) sense of calm! She knows deep down she should wait until they get home, but Bec feels like this particular secret is burning a hole in her chest, it all feels so . . . wretched. She needs to offload it to her husband, to lighten the load. A problem shared, and all that.

'I need to talk to you about something . . .' She steers him to the side of the hall under a stained-glass window depicting the Virgin Mary cradling baby Jesus.

'What's up?' He bites into a chocolate-chip cookie and shakes his head. 'It's terrible,' he says. 'Inferior. All other confectionery is dead to me.'

'Tom, I'm serious. Promise me you won't say anything to her tonight, but I found out who Willow is seeing.'

'Oh yeah?'

'Well, it's someone a little inappropriate.' *Understatement of the century.*

Tom's smile drops and Bec immediately sees that her decision to tell him here, in the same square feet of space that also houses Sam Deacon, was made in haste. But Tom is nothing if not cool and calm. It takes a lot for him to lose it.

He puts down the half-eaten biscuit on the window ledge. 'Who?'

'Promise me you won't say anything to her yet . . .'

'I promise.' He wears his serious face, brow slightly furrowed, and Bec feels the onset of nerves '*Who?*'

'Never mind. I'll tell you later.'

'For fuck's sake, Bec!' he snaps. 'Tell me now.'

She sighs. 'It's Sam Deacon.'

There is a moment of silence, of comprehension.

'Sam Deacon the sports master?'

'Yes.'

Tom is unnervingly silent for a moment and then he says, 'Are you sure?'

'I caught them together. In the gym. She says she *loves* him, Tom. What are we going to do?'

'What the . . .?' Tom emits a stunned laugh and then his face clouds. He turns to the front of the hall and fixes his gaze on the principal's son. 'You're fucking kidding me!'

'Tom, please. Willow is worried about you knowing, you have to be calm about it.'

'He's in his *twenties*,' he hisses. 'How am I meant to stay calm? Willow's still a kid.'

'Not in the eyes of the law.'

'Well, she is *my* kid.'

Bec sees her husband's shoulders square, the muscles in his jaw clenching. 'No,' he says. 'Not happening.'

'Tom?' She should not have told him! What was she thinking? Here of all places! 'It's OK, I've spoken to her. She's going to be sensible, take it slow . . .'

'Take it slow? It is not happening *at all*.' He clenches his fists, stares down the sports master. 'Not over my dead body!'

Bec watches as Sam Deacon looks up and nods at Tom with a smile which rapidly falters as he assesses Tom's angry expression. Bec sees it in Sam's eyes as the thought runs through the young man's consciousness. *He knows,* he's thinking. *Oh shit, Willow's dad knows!*

Tom takes a step forward.

'Tom!' Bec yanks his forearm hard, but he holds fast, resumes his stare. 'Stay calm, please. Think of Cooper!'

Fuck! This is all she needs. Why on earth didn't she wait until they got home?

Tom pulls away. 'It's OK,' he snaps, his shoulders resuming their normal position. 'It's OK, I'm OK. It's just a shock, that's all. I wasn't expecting it.'

'Neither was I. I said we'd talk to her rationally tomorrow.'

Tom nods. 'Fine,' he says, but Bec is scared of what is going on in Tom's head.

They are silent. What can they possibly talk about now after she has hurled this grenade? Can they go back to discussing the inferiority of the cookie he has just half eaten?

'Where is she now?' he asks.

'With Flick. They're heading to the late movie.'

'Are you serious?'

'Well, we can hardly ground her, can we?'

Tom sighs. 'I need some air,' he says and turns to leave via the emergency exit.

'Tom, please!'

'It's *fine*,' he says and he touches her chin with his fingers. 'I'm all good. I just need a moment to process all of this. Don't worry, I'm not going to do anything stupid.'

'I know,' she says. But does she?

Now she is standing alone with only the stained-glass Virgin Mary and a half-eaten biscuit for company. She casts one last glance disparagingly towards Sam Deacon – a kind of *Look! Look what you've done!* – but he is no longer watching her. Instead he tilts his head and listens earnestly to the fawning parents in front of him, as if he is a sensible and trustworthy young man, and not one who is trying to take advantage of an impressionable teenage girl.

She narrows her eyes as she watches him speak, thinks of his disingenuous lips on Willow's and feels a deep pang of bitterness for the way he has made her world suddenly, and inexplicably, implode.

18

Kaya

Kaya puts her Uber plan on hold temporarily and sits herself under Paul's tree for a little while – she is in no particular rush now that Ollie is staying to play with his friends. People pass: families on their way to the car park on scenic detours of the grounds; older boys of driving age hurling balls to one another across the pristine green grass on their way to the car park; a tall boy with an older woman, using hostile hand gestures. She can't make out any of them, but she sees them all, these shadow people, and she watches them like a voyeur from her vantage point under the tree. From the middle of the oval, in her fawn summer dress, she blends in like a chameleon against the crumbly bark and the thick, exposed roots.

She sees two figures walking towards her and as they get nearer, she realises they are mother and son. She moves herself around the tree trunk so she can't be seen.

'Please, don't say these things,' hisses the woman.

'Stop me!' The male voice is younger. A young adult, Kaya supposes, but she can't quite work out just how old. 'No wonder he did what he did.'

The woman is in tears. 'You were the one who drove him to it!'

'You tell yourself that, Mother.'

Another sob. 'I can't wait for you to leave.'

'You've always wanted me gone.'

'That's not true. You weren't always like . . . this!'

'Don't lie to me.'

'Your father loved you, Felix,' she says, and Kaya starts, realising exactly who the two voices belong to: the school captain and his mother, Martha Weaver. 'Daddy loved you, as complicated as you are.'

'He loved me so much he decided to take off and never come back. Yeah, that's love! You're fucking deluded!'

'Felix, *please* . . .'

'Drop dead.'

The woman pulls at her own hair with her fist. 'Walk home, you little . . . don't think you're coming home with me,' she spits.

'Give a shit?'

Kaya feels bad for Martha. How awful to have your son speak to you like that. Ollie wouldn't dream of it! And to have your husband walk out! Kaya cannot imagine. At least Paul did not choose to leave them.

Once they are a long way past her, Kaya gets up. She dusts off the dried mud on the back of her dress and clicks on to her Uber app, taps in her address and picks a comfort ride – she's going to splash out tonight. The app tells her Richard will arrive in his Audi in four minutes. An Audi? Why on earth is the man an Uber driver if he can afford an Audi? Perhaps he's the kind of man who likes to escape his wife and family at night, to avoid the hellish 'witching' hours between five and eight, when children turn into gremlins and exhausted parents wrangle to get them fed, bathed and into bed.

She heads towards the cricket pavilion because she desperately needs to pee, and she supposes there must be toilets there, just like there are on the adjacent rugby pitch. She doesn't have time to run back to the hall, and besides, she'd probably get chatting to someone again and lose her ride. She isn't in the mood to be all smiley again, not after all the reminiscing she's done under the tree. She's not sad, but she wants to get home. To grab a hot chocolate and surf Netflix until Ollie comes home. Besides, according to her phone, Richard and his Audi are still three minutes away.

Ahead of her, she sees the sports master striding across the green and towards the same building. He looks left and right and lets himself in. Kaya wonders if it would be a bit awkward to go in there for a pee now he is in there in the dark, so she hesitates behind a Moreton Bay fig and waits for him to come out. She clicks on the app. Still three minutes until Richard gets to her, she has time to wait for him to finish whatever it is he is doing – using the bathroom, she presumes.

She looks ahead of her, surveys almost the entire scope of the campus: the Main House with the Great Hall to her left and the new block to the right. She smiles as she sees Willow Lloyd emerge from the new building and creep along the periphery of the sporting field. Then, from the left, comes her father, Tom. Willow glances across and sees her father and his defiant stride and ducks into the bushland that lines the fields. He hasn't noticed her. Is she hiding from him? Or does she just not want him to realise where she is headed? Which seems to be, given her

trajectory, the darkened pavilion where Sam Deacon currently lurks and has not yet switched on the lights.

Kaya watches Willow slink back towards the main
school building and turns her attention to the angry stride
of Tom. It is intriguing to watch – the man had seemed to
her to be so mild-mannered! He reaches the pavilion and
opened the door.

'Deacon?' he calls.

Nothing.

'Deacon? I saw you come in here!'

A light flicks on.

'Oh,' says Sam Deacon. 'Hello Tom! I just came in here
to tidy—'

'Stay the fuck away from her,' snarls Tom.

Kaya puts her hand over her mouth.

'I'm sorry?'

'Stay the fuck away from my daughter, do you understand me?'

'Mr Lloyd. I can assure you my intentions are strictly
honourable. Willow is a beautiful girl . . .'

'Don't you fucking *dare* tell me about my daughter. If
you touch her in any way, I'll report you to the board of
governors. Do you understand?'

There is silence.

'Do you *understand?*'

Kaya exhales a long yoga breath. *Shit,* she thinks. *Willow
Lloyd and Sam Deacon?*

She glances at her phone. Richard is almost at the school
gates. Has she really been standing here, a voyeur, for five
whole minutes? She needs to go now, there is no more

time to stand and listen to see how this argument unfurls. She turns and hurries along the side of the sporting fields, accompanied by the raised voices of Sam Deacon and Tom Lloyd, and rushes through the undergrowth that lines the tennis courts, behind the back of the building that houses the swanky indoor pool and finally towards the wrought-iron gates. There she sees Felix Weaver angrily pushing back the metal bars and stepping out into the orange lamplight of the road.

Kaya is out of breath when she finally stops on the roadside and glances around for her Uber. But she cannot see a single car with lights on. She isn't *that* late, is she? The little icon of the car had showed it was at Iggy's thirty seconds ago, and now the ride seems to have disappeared. Perhaps Richard got the offer of a longer fare. Kaya clicks on to her main phone screen and sees she has three missed calls. She listens to the message: 'Hi Kaya, Richard here, your Uber driver. I'm waiting outside the main gates, a little further to the left.'

The next one, a minute later. 'Kaya? Richard. Everything OK?'

And finally: 'Thanks so much for your thoughtful response, Kaya. Glad to see integrity is alive and kicking amongst the parents at St Ignatius'!'

Kaya is pissed off. She hits the number that's called her and waits.

'Ahh it's Cinderella,' the man's voice says. 'You missed your ride.'

'Well, where are you?'

'I've turned into a pumpkin,' says Richard. 'So if you'll excuse me . . .'

'You can't just go,' Kaya says, incredulous. 'I'm standing in the dark waiting.'

'The fact is, you were eight minutes late and I have to collect my nine-year-old daughter from a roller-disco party before she gets too high on fairy floss. Like her father, she doesn't like to be kept waiting. So my advice, Kaya, would be to go and find yourself somewhere safe to wait and call yourself another cab.'

'Thanks for nothing, *Richard*,' says Kaya.

'That's my name,' says Richard. 'Don't wear it out.'

'Ugh!' Kaya hangs up, annoyed. Eight minutes? Did it really take her that long to get from the oval to the main road? She checks. It did, but she is still angry. She wants to call Richard back and point out tersely that she could get attacked on her way home, and that if she does, it will be his fault. But of course she doesn't do that. She just stands and broods.

She looks around her, into the darkness. Her car is five minutes up the road, in a car park beside the White Lion pub. Her keys jangle in her pocket. Surely she'd be fine to drive, and it's not like she has Ollie with her – because she wouldn't even consider it if he was. But he isn't, so. . . She puts her hand in her pocket, takes out her keys and walks purposefully forwards.

19

Bec

So much for popping out for a minute! Bec berates Tom when he doesn't return and wanders outside in search of Cooper. She shouldn't have opened her big mouth. What part of her thought it would be a good idea to tell Tom about Willow and the sports master tonight of all nights? She has completely misjudged the situation, confused Tom with a placid best friend and not a protective father! *Nice one, Bec!*

She finds Cooper on the rugby pitch with Ollie and the twins, as Tom said he would be, throwing the ball back and forth, back and forth.

'All OK darling?' she calls.

Cooper waves back. 'Yeah, Mum!'

She won't interrupt any further because she wants to encourage the new friendship with Ollie Sterling to flourish, she won't break their flow. Besides, what would she do? Join in? She walks along the side of the old building, its façade almost entirely covered in wild jasmine, and scans the gravel path ahead of her for Tom, but she cannot see him, only the creepy school captain Felix Weaver exiting school property and turning on to the path that lines the cliff edge. He kicks the pavement as he walks, something Bec is sure a school captain is not supposed to do. She thinks back to the library, how strange it had been and how Felix had called her 'Bec' at the end of their conversation. Hadn't she mentioned Willow's name but failed to introduce herself? Had she met him before? She can't put her finger on what it is that feels off-kilter about the encounter, just like she can't put her finger on what it is about Felix Weaver that makes the hairs on her neck stand up. She picks a leaf off the jasmine plant and twists it in between her fingers as she considers what the boy had said to her as he lurked in the shadows of the library: *Only child. Donating my sperm. Latin.* She looks at the Latin words on the gate once more: *felix quia fortis.* Happiness through strength.

I'm lucky. That's what Felix had said. She smiles to herself when the realisation hits her. It's clever really, because Felix Weaver *is* lucky, both figuratively and literally, because that is what his Christian name means when translated to Latin. Yes, the word *felix* means 'happiness', as it does in the St Ignatius' school motto, but it also means 'luck'. He probably thought he was making a little joke that she wouldn't understand when he referred to himself that way. Maybe he had wondered if she would be smart enough to pick it up with what he had assumed to be her rusty gauge of the Latin vernacular, and then been pleased when she hadn't.

She shrugs to herself as she considers this: both of Felix's names have a Latin bent because his surname, Weaver also translates into the ancient language. The Latin word for a weaver – literally a person who weaves – is *textor.* She's pleased she remembers it, actually. She may have forgotten the mandatory French she learned up to HSC level, but the Latin has somehow stuck.

Felix Weaver. Lucky Textor.

Lucki_Texta.

It hits her like a thunderbolt.

She replays the conversation in her head. Thinks of how he asked about Sage. *He knows about me,* she thinks. *He knows my secret and he's threatening me!*

She cannot breathe and bends over, her head to her knees. Her mind begins to flounder as it awakens with realisation. She needs to know exactly what Felix Weaver knows about her, and how he found it out. She picks up her pace, almost falling over herself to catch up with the school captain. He must be a good way along the School Run by now.

She does not notice the other boys, boys she knows, passing her on their way to the main road and muttering polite hellos. She has forgotten about finding Willow, too – she is only after Felix, because she knows for a fact that the 'little' secret of hers he dangles in front of her like a carrot has the capacity to destroy everything she holds dear: her marriage, her family, her life, her relationships with Willow and Cooper and Sage.

Primary colours flash in her brain, and that's when it comes for the third time today: The Rage. Anger at this half-child, half-man who is threatening her and her family, everything she loves. She feels the blood heat up in her veins, her skin bead with sweat. She pulls off her jacket and fumbles desperately in her bag for Willow's spare car keys. Her hand is shaking, her heart thundering. She has to get to Felix, to stop him. She knocks angrily into the wing mirror of a shiny Land Rover and kicks the tyre, clicking Willow's key fob blindly at the road beyond the gates and into the night.

20

Martha

Martha Weaver keeps her head down and pretends not to notice Bec Lloyd searching for her car. They have only met once, in the waiting room of her sister Annabel's kinesiology practice when Martha had gone to pick up Felix, and Annabel had said, 'Bec, this is my sister Martha,' but she doesn't want to say hello. Her eyes are red from the angry crying she's been doing on account of Felix and his caustic tongue.

Besides, she doubts the woman would even recognise her. Bec Lloyd is all perfect highlights and a megawatt smile and a figure that you see in clothing catalogues, and Martha just feels like a mouse in comparison. Hair: greying. Face: pointy. Body: slightly rounded, untoned. She was pretty once – an English rose! But she has wilted through neglect and stress and lack of Vitamin D. She used to surf and sunbathe and find solace in the daylight, but now finds it hard to tolerate too much sun. It's hard to tolerate much of anything.

Martha has visited Bec's Instagram page once or twice, pored over it. She only went there to find a cake recipe but she's been back again since. All those stunning iced creations and the shots of her beautiful kitchen and selfies with Estella Munro, who terrifies the life out of Martha with that steely glare and loud, barking voice which she once brought to her macramé class before pinning Martha down for a reference letter for her twins. Martha wonders if, in a parallel world – if, perhaps, she was a little bit more *glamorous* – she and Bec Lloyd might be friends. Who knows? She often ponders on it when she's lost in those little tiled squares of Bec's, full of cakes and colour and happiness. Perhaps Martha would find it hard to deal with Bec's utopian life, since she suspects the wholesome baker has a beautiful relationship with each of her children (Martha knows she has three because her Insta bio reads: *Baker. Creator. Mum of Three*) – unlike she herself does with Felix.

So Martha ignores Bec Lloyd as she steps into her own trusty Nissan and starts the engine. She rubs her eyes, feels them burning. Let him walk home, dammit! She has half a mind to lock him out, double-bolt the doors so he can't get in. Let him sleep outside. That would serve him right!

Her little boy, once a baby with a beautiful smile. A toddler with corduroy dungarees and a cheesecloth T-shirt and grazed knees from constantly coming off his red tricycle. The boy whose smile turned upside down at the age of ten when his father took his own life in a locked garage with the engine of his silver Audi running and who became suddenly bitter and angry with the whole world and stayed that way, and how Martha wishes she had felt the inclination or the desire in Felix's formative years to marry again so there had been another male role model in his life after Charles had died. A man to show him direction and teach him different ways to channel his escalating aggression:

to fish or to wrestle or to fire an air rifle at the end of the garden. But she hadn't, and so Felix had become the way he had become, her boy, her son. The child she carried in her own belly and loved more than she'd loved any person before him. And it is because of this love, this *history*, that Martha detests herself with every fibre of her being for the thought that dances in her mind morning, noon and night: that she hates Felix so much she wishes him dead.

21

Bec

Bec points the key fob at a row of cars lined up on the grass verge beyond the school gates. She is a little unsteady on her feet, realises she should not be driving, but reasons she has only had a couple of small glasses, and who's going to stop her on the way home when the roads are so clear? She just needs to catch up with Felix, ask him how he found out about Sage and what it is he wants from her. Is it money? Because if it is, she can find it from somewhere, as loath as she is to concede to his blackmail.

Ugh, why can't she find the damn car? Then she remembers Willow has taken it to the cinema.

She hears steps behind her, the heavy tread of a boot. 'Rebecca?'

'Estella . . .'

'What the hell are you doing out here? You're not considering driving, surely?'

'Not any more,' she sighs.

'Thank God for that.'

'What's that supposed to mean?'

'It means I've had a bitch of a night and I don't particularly want to wake up tomorrow morning to find out you've wrapped Willow's shitheap of a car around a lamppost after half a glass of rosé.'

Bec feels affronted. 'Holdens can fetch a lot of money at the moment.'

'Oh, *please*.'

'Well, *you* can't drive! You stink of weed. I can smell it from here.'

'It was only a couple of tokes,' snaps Estella. 'Anyway, where are you going?'

'Home!'

'With a face like that?'

'A face like what?'

Estella sighs. 'I'll take you,' she says. 'My car's up ahead. Besides, do you really want to be seen travelling away from the school in a *Captiva*?'

Bec sighs and stomps forward towards the flashing orange lights of the Munros' primary SUV.

'Right. What's happened?' Estella demands.

'Nothing.'

'You may as well tell me. I know everything else about you.'

Bec climbs in the passenger seat as Estella climbs in the driver's side and they slam their doors shut at the same time.

'Well?' Estella sighs. 'Spit it out.'

Bec pouts. Part of her wants to carry on giving Estella the cold shoulder for being such a bitch about the chapel cake, but the other part acknowledges she could do with Estella's advice right about now.

'Felix Weaver knows about me,' is what she says.

Estella's mouth drops open. 'You mean . . .'

Bec nods. 'He's been sending me spam email, or at least I thought it was spam.'

'Saying what?'

'"I know what you did" and "It's a sage situation".'

Estella twists the key in the ignition. 'Could mean any-thing.'

'No, Estella,' she says. Her chin begins to wobble. 'He *knows*. And I'm not sure what to do about it.'

'OK,' says Estella evenly. 'How did he find out?'

'I don't know! But he's going to tell Tom.'

'That evil shit.' Estella's eyes narrow. 'What's he asking for? Money?'

'Nothing. That's the whole thing. He isn't asking for anything, or at least he hasn't yet. Which must mean he's doing it for the sake of it, for fun. Because he's just plain evil.'

Estella is quiet for a moment and then she says, 'Well, I might know of a reason why he's sending hate mail, aside from the fact he's twisted as fuck.'

Bec looks at her quizzically. What does *Estella* know about why Felix Weaver is threatening her?

'He's in love with Willow,' Estella says. 'He told Flick. Willow rejected him apparently, and quite harshly. He didn't take it very well.'

'So now he's taking it out on me to get back at her?'

'It's possible. He probably knows how close the two of you are, it's obvious to anyone. What better way to get back at Willow than to slander her precious mum?' Is it Bec or does Estella almost sound resentful when she says it?

Bec processes. *Willow rejected Felix Weaver and now he's sending Bec spam emails threatening to unravel her life like a ball of string?*

'Estella, you haven't ever told anyone, have you? About me?'

'Of course not!' Estella is hurt, Bec can tell by the thinning of her lips. 'We might have our ups and downs, but I promised you I would never tell another living soul and I haven't. I *wouldn't*. It's your story to tell.'

Bec had been in a café with Cooper six years ago when she'd made the decision. Cooper was five and eating a gingerbread man with his babyccino. Bec, sipping her latte, had watched a young mother breastfeed her baby and she'd felt the deep-rooted pain of desperation. Not so much an urge but a *need* to carry another child. Biology kicking in in a way she felt all through her body, in her ovaries! She'd been pregnant a year after Cooper but she'd lost that baby at just eight weeks. 'It's not a viable pregnancy,' her obstetrician had told her and she had sobbed all the way home in the car, the road in front of her blurry and cold.

This bone-aching desire, she knew, would not go until she had a baby in her belly again, and so she initiated sex and she was lackadaisical about contraception and she tried to persuade Tom in all the most intimate of moments that maybe they should go again, one more time. And Tom always looked guilty as all hell when he said no, but he still said it.

'I'm sorry, Bec, but we can't risk losing another baby – it almost broke you. It almost broke us!' That was what he said at first. Then it became a case of: 'Are we talking about this again? You *know* my stance.'

She'd started by Googling 'donor sperm', it was as simple as that. She found out that paying for sperm was illegal in Australia so she'd have to go down the clinic route. She found a donor clinic and scrolled through the lists of donors, looking for one that would allow donor insemination and not IVF. Donor D31899Z was Caucasian like Tom – and the babies he had already co-created for previous 'clients' (if that was even the correct term) looked a lot like Cooper and Willow. On paper he was perfect too – he was a lawyer from NSW, blood group O+, and wrote in his bio that he was 'calm and kind and always puts others' needs before his own.' *That*, thought Bec, *is why he's donating his sperm!*

All she needed to do would be to turn up at the clinic when she was ovulating and they would thaw the sperm and insert it into her uterus by intrauterine insemination – nothing more, nothing less. No IVF, just a few drugs here and there. And it was fate, she reasoned. If she made herself forget about the provenance of the sperm then how could it hurt anyone? She knew what an incredible father Tom was, how much he loved his kids. It would be the thing to unify them, to make everything OK again.

'I'm sorry,' Bec says. 'I know you wouldn't. But how does *he* know? I'm screwed, Estella. I'm totally screwed.'

Estella stares ahead, chews on the side of her cheek. 'Did you tell Kaya?'

'Kaya? No, I barely know her . . .'

Estella looks out of the window for a moment and then turns back. 'What about Annabel? In one of your kinesiology sessions?'

'Yes, I did. But she's not allowed to tell anyone. She's a *therapist*. What about client–practitioner confidentiality?'

'Well, that's how he knows, then. Felix works on reception for Annabel after school some nights, doesn't he? She's his aunt, you did know that, didn't you? Maybe he got into your notes.'

Bec now realises it is entirely possible that Felix Weaver knows everything about her, from her vitamin prescription to her anger issues, to her seedy purchased sperm. She imagines him sitting there at the computer beside the sunlit window that lights up Annabel's practice, against a backdrop of vitamin vials and tubs of marine collagen and magnesium and essential oils. All the things that, ironically enough, are on offer to enhance a client's wellbeing, to balance their body with their mind. The very place Bec seeks calm for her rages – which may be hormonal, but may also be due to the weight of the lie she has been carrying – may also be the place that has exposed her! There is no other explanation.

'That's unethical,' she hisses. 'Those notes are private! What am I going to do?'

She lowers her head on to the steering wheel, bangs it up and down a couple of times, fighting to control the anger and the frustration and the anxiety that are simultaneously running through her veins and making her sweat.

'You mean what are *we* going to do?' Estella says, opening her car door. 'I have a bone to pick with that vile little cock-weasel, too. Pull yourself together, Rebecca. We're going to talk to our little friend Felix Weaver.'

Bec feels a pang of fear. She'd been so ready to confront Felix when she got in the car, but now she's afraid, like the mild-mannered version of herself often is. What if he calls her bluff?

'But he's a psychopath,' she tells Estella. 'He'll go public if we corner him.'

'Oh, we're going to do more than that,' says Estella, pulling tight her leather jacket. 'We're going to give him a little fright.'

'We're not the mafia, Estella! What are we going to do? Put a horse head under his Egyptian duck down?'

'Right, well let's just ignore it and see how long it takes the little worm to ruin your life.' Estella gives a self-satisfied sniff and looks out of the window again.

'OK,' says Bec. What other choice does she have? She has heard Estella's brand of verbal warning before, several times. She can be utterly terrifying when she needs to be. Estella knows how to handle adverse situations. It is what she does best. 'Let's do it.'

Estella gives a curt nod and makes to pull out onto the empty road.

'Estella?'

'What?'

'Why are you doing this? For me?' Bec needs to know.

'Oh wake up, Bec! I'm not *just* doing it for you. The little prick has been sending photos of his dick to Felicity, gaslighting her . . .'

'He's *BOY*?'

'Unfortunately,' says Estella. 'Felicity told him I swapped the twins.'

'Swapped?' Bec does not follow. 'I don't understand.'

'For the rugby matches, Bec, give me strength! I *swapped* them. Jonty played both matches and Archie did both interviews.'

'But . . .' Bec can't quite believe what she's hearing. 'That's *fraudulent*!'

'Oh, calm down, Little Miss Prissy. As if you wouldn't have done the same if you were in my situation. Just like I would have made a gaudy sponge cake in the image of Mother Teresa if I could bake.'

Bec thinks back to earlier in the day, Archie's epic catch that ended in a spectacular try. She might have known there was no way Archie could have done that. What Estella has done is nothing short of genius – if she can pull it off.

'I can't believe . . . it's inspired. I mean, considering how terrible Archie is at sport.'

'Yes, well, thank you for your input.'

'Is he threatening you?' Bec asks.

'Not yet, but given what he's doing to you, it's likely. Especially as I've dumped him via text message from Felicity's phone.'

'You didn't!'

'I did.'

Of course she did.

Estella pulls out of the parking space and turns on to the School Run. She glances in her rear-view mirror. 'Kaya Sterling knows about the twins, too.'

'How?'

'Knees, Bec.' She jabs the base of her own femur.

'Whose knees?'

'Jonty's! Keep up! That knee issue I told you about? Osgood–Schlatter disease? She noticed a nodule in his knee which Archie doesn't have. I mean trust her to be a sodding physio.'

'She sussed you out,' Bec says, triumphant, because it's rare for someone to get the better of her friend.

'It seems so. Oh, and for good measure, you should know Kaya Sterling was married to JP. She kept her maiden name when they married and he dropped the J. That's why I couldn't find any record of a Paul Sterling.'

'Your JP?' The images in Bec's head are like the bits of pasta in a minestrone soup, swirling around like lumps. 'Are you serious?'

'No,' snaps Estella. 'I just said it for a joke.'

'But . . .' Bec cannot compute. Kaya's husband was Estella's teenage boyfriend? So that's what they'd been arguing about in the Great Hall. 'But how . . .'

Estella holds up a hand. Conversation closed. 'Not now,' she says.

Bec nods. She has so many questions!

'Now,' says Estella, 'what we're going to do is find Felix, and give him a little warning.'

'He'll be at least halfway to Pacific Pines by now.'

'Splendid.'

Bec looks over at her and sees a look on Estella's face she has seen before. It is a blend of both anger and determination, as lethal together as the components of gunpowder. Bec is the first to admit that Estella has her flaws, by God, does she! But at the forefront of everything she does are her children: Felicity, Jonty, Archie and another child. A baby boy, who was four kilos at birth, wrapped in a tiny blue blanket when he was ripped from her arms. A baby in a faded colour photo tucked inside Estella's designer wallet, far back behind the receipts and the loyalty cards and the identity documents with the perfectly posed pictures. A photo she has shown Bec only once, but which is fiercely guarded by a mother – a lioness whose love knows no bounds and who will stop at nothing to protect her young. And that's when Bec realises it was no coincidence her friend was outside the school gates at the very same moment Bec herself was planning to leave and confront Felix Weaver. It's because Estella had had the exact same idea: to locate the threat and stop it in its tracks.

22

Estella

'What are you going to say to him?' The lights of St Ignatius' fade in the wing mirror as they travel along. 'Felix, I mean.'

'I'm going to tell him to leave my daughter the hell alone.'

'But what if he doesn't listen?'

'Oh,' says Estella with a bitter laugh. 'He will.'

He *will* listen! Who the hell does he think he is doing this to Felicity? Felicity with her puerile menopause jibes and her caustic tongue! Felicity who drives Estella stark-raving bonkers every single day with her rudeness and her sarcastic put-downs and her overbearing sense of self-importance. Felicity who is more like Estella than any other human being on God's green earth and who Estella punishes for having every single one of her own goddamn flaws! Felicity, who she criticises to Conrad on a daily basis, but woe betide anyone else who wrongs her. Estella will take them down. *Felicity.* Her baby, her blood, her girl.

And she loves them all that way, all of her children – all *four* of them – but Felicity is Estella through and through, as if the umbilical cord was never cut and clamped. They are welded to one another, fused like Siamese twins who resent one another's presence almost constantly, but at the same time feed off one another by the osmosis of deep-rooted love: one cannot survive without the other. And this is why Estella plans to make sure, once and for all, that Felix Weaver does not touch her daughter, emotionally or physically. This is not romance in any form, this is coercion, and she has acknowledged over and over that she does not want her daughter to make the same mistakes as her. But at least her mistakes were made out of *love*!

And what of Bec, the only friend she has ever really let in? Can she let this BOY take advantage of her too? Can she let Bec's sometimes nauseatingly sweet nature come under attack for no apparent reason other than bitterness? No, it is all shades of wrong! Estella let the power of meanness, of cruelty, ruin her life once before and she sure as hell isn't about to let it happen again. She pushes her hair off her forehead, roughly, her fingers somehow turgid with anger, and grips the wheel, tight, at ten to two. Then she pushes her foot down on the accelerator, presses into the floor the frustration she feels about the present and the past.

Estella Wickham is about to turn seventeen and she is leaving the cinema with JP. They have just watched *Dangerous Minds*, even though Estella's father says the song 'Gangsta's Paradise' is 'the devil's music' and had forbidden her from watching it. She is due home at nine o'clock. It is eight twenty-two now and Estella and JP decide to walk home along the beach. From there, they will take the ladder up the cliffside and Estella will slip into her house, maybe one or two minutes late, but no one will begrudge her that, not even her parents! And certainly not her younger brother Patrick, who will likely be up in his room playing on his Nintendo.

They walk from Pacific Pines mall down onto the beach, see the stretch of sand arc out in front of them. JP slides his fingers in between Estella's. They have been together for nine months now and Estella knows she loves this boy so much it is inconceivable they will ever be apart.

They sit on the sand and watch the waves creep towards them in the moonlight. The sound is different to the one she hears from her bedroom – that one is angrier as waves meet rock and suck back out again. Here, on the sand with JP, they just glide in and out, leisurely. At ease. JP turns to her.

'I love you, Stella,' he says, squeezing their entwined fingers. 'I can't wait until we're eighteen and we can do whatever we like. We could go somewhere together.'

'What, run away?'

'Yeah. Get married. I'll be a shit-hot surgeon if I get into medical school next year. I could rent us a flat near the hospital. We could go and live there. The rent's cheaper out west.'

'You know I would,' she says and her body feels warm, her heart full. But somewhere deep inside she knows she will never be able to do that. Even when she is eighteen she will be bound by her parents' rules, by their strict moral code. It has been drummed into her since the day she was born: *you will go to hell if you live in sin.*

They walk in silence under the moonlight towards the rocks. JP kicks some spray onto the backs of Estella's legs. She laughs and falls into him. On the rocks, they kiss for a long time, and then Estella pulls JP's T-shirt over his head. It is something she has done before, but they have never really got past this point of their chests touching, skin to skin.

'I want to do it,' she tells him. 'Go the whole way.'

'Shouldn't we wait?' JP asks.

'I don't want to wait.'

'I mean, you know I want to. But Stella, are you sure?'

'I'm sure.'

'What about . . .'

'I got the Pill,' she says. 'I'm almost seventeen. I didn't have to ask my mum.'

It had hurt her, doing that, going against her mother, but she could not compromise on it, nor on JP. That, to her, was only a small misdemeanour, because weren't she and JP in love? They were going to marry one day and make a life together. Wouldn't it be worse not to be careful and to let herself get pregnant? Her parents didn't agree with abortion.

She stands, peels off her jeans. JP does not take his eyes off her face as she does so. She does not blush, because she is not worried about what he might think. She knows him, inside and out, and now she will know him just that little bit better.

'I love you,' he says again.

She bends down to kiss him and he reaches up for her.

Soon, they are moving together on the rocks as sea spray comes up and splashes them. JP moves slowly in case he should hurt her, and she hears herself cry out in ecstasy and emotion, not much pain. And then it is over, her first time and his, and Estella lies in the curve of his arm, breathing in the scent of his skin. He kisses her forehead.

She doesn't know how long they sleep there, on the rocky ledge, but she knows it is late when she wakes up. She sits bolt up. 'What time is it?'

JP looks at his watch. 'Shit,' he says. 'It's eleven.'

'Oh my God!' Estella scoops up her underwear, pulls it on haphazardly, then her jeans, her T-shirt, her shoes. 'Shit!'

Together they scramble up the ladder, JP eager to confront Estella's parents, to take the blame. They heave themselves up over the cliff edge and run across the three gardens that sit side by side, and through the hedge into Estella's family home.

Estella's mother's face is red, her bottom lip trembles. Her father steps out in front of his wife, protecting her from JP, the intruder.

'Where the hell have you been?' he shouts, grabbing at Estella's arm and pulling her in, away from JP who stands, open-mouthed, in the middle of the garden.

'Mr and Mrs Wickham, I'm so sorry . . .' he starts. 'I'm John-Paul Palmer. It's my fault Stella is late, I—'

'*Stella?*' Estella's mother cries. '*Stella?*'

'That's what I like being called, Mum.'

An empty beer bottle chooses that moment to fall out of JP's bag. Estella's mother's eyes widen and a wince escapes her tiny white mouth. 'Have you been *drinking?*'

'We shared a beer at the cinema,' Estella stutters.

Her mother's voice is shrill. 'No. NO!'

'We do *not* allow drinking in this house,' her father yells. 'While you're living under our roof, you will not drink, swear or hang around with . . .' He looks at JP and spits the word. '*Boys.*'

'Mrs Wickham . . .' says JP to Estella's mother, his hands in prayer.

'Don't you speak to me!' says her mother. She will not look at JP. 'I thought my daughter had been raped or killed.'

'Mum, come on,' says Estella. 'I didn't mean to be late. *Please.*'

'Oh, you didn't mean to?' her mother laughs. 'Well, here's something to chew on. You are not to see that boy again, do you hear me?' She points at JP and turns, dragging Estella into the house by her bicep. Her fingers grip tightly and Estella knows there will be a bruise tomorrow. 'A boy like this, who drinks alcohol, will take your virtue. You are not to see him again.'

She turns to JP. 'Get out of my garden,' she snarls and locks the back door.

Estella runs up the stairs and slams her door. She wants to run back downstairs and point in her mother's face and shout at her: 'Did you know JP and I made love this evening? That you're too *late*?' She wants to tell her mother that the feeling of his body inside hers has made her a woman and no longer a girl, that *that boy* has, with that singular, spectacular act of love, given her the intimacy and affection she has ached for from another human being for as long as she can remember. But she doesn't. All she does is cry herself to sleep, and watches her tears drop from her nose onto her pillow in the silvery light of the moon.

'Estella?'

Estella blinks, snaps back to the present, sees the curve of the road up ahead.

'You're going a little fast.' Bec's voice is cut with alarm. 'Isn't the speed limit forty along here?'

'Calm down,' Estella snaps, but she slows to fifty anyway. In the daytime, cars sit bumper-to-bumper on the School Run, and despite her years of living in Pacific Pines, Estella has never really tackled it at speed. Perhaps she should slow down; there could be a boy round that corner, walking, unsuspecting on the thick pathway that hugs the cliffs. A boy with ideas of evil dancing in his head, thoughts of young women and coercion and dirty photos of virginal, never-touched-before flesh.

She puts her foot definitively on the accelerator once more.

'Let's give our friend a little fright, shall we?' she says.

23

Bec

Bec grips the hand rail on the door of the passenger seat as Estella flies along towards the treacherous crook in the road.

'Slow down, please Estella!' she snaps.

Estella, of course, ignores her, and so Bec says no more, simply grips a little tighter and hopes that the years Estella has lived in Pacific Pines have taught her something about tackling the upcoming corner at speed.

She and Tom taught Willow to drive on this road last year, instructing her to slow at the bend, but as it turned out Willow hadn't needed the warning – she is a cautious driver by nature, as she is about many things. She is prone to panic like Bec herself, especially in the car, which is at least one thing Bec does not have to worry about. It will be different, she suspects, when Cooper learns to drive, as addicted to adrenalin and speed and PlayStation games that have racing vehicles as he is.

'Where are you, you little prick?' Estella mutters. 'And I mean that literally and figuratively.'

'Gross,' says Bec. 'I can't believe you have a photo of his penis on your phone.'

'I'm more worried about what he has on his phone,' says Estella. 'Of Felicity.' Bec almost feels the backdraught as Estella speeds up. 'If I have to stand over him while he wipes his entire iCloud, I will . . .'

Estella leans forward as she prepares to navigate the bend and Bec watches as she studies the side of the road. Most of Pacific Pines is at Iggy's tonight and those who are not are likely avoiding the thoroughfare, knowing it is Gala Day and will be jammed later in the night.

'Where are you, Felix?' Estella asks as she scours the road.

'Maybe he took the cliff steps down to the beach?'

'That wouldn't make sense. It's a longer route home.'

'But it's a nicer one,' Bec says. 'Safer, too.'

Estella sighs and hugs the curve of the road at speed. Bec holds on to the hand-rest, her palm filmed with sweat. Yes, she had wanted to wring the boy's neck herself five minutes ago, but there is something about Estella's anger that has levelled hers. Perhaps it's the observation of what this emotion has done to Estella's body and her face. She is rigid at the wheel, lips pursed, eyes like beads. Estella appears to have enough anger for both of them.

'Oh my God,' cries Bec as the car begins to skid. 'Look out! You're going to hit—'

She braces as Estella plunges her foot on the brakes. 'Fuck!' she cries.

The car spins and judders and finally stops by the safety barrier that separates the road from the cliffs.

They are silent, save for the sound of both their breaths, coming thick and fast. Bec feels like she is a statue, scared to move. Eventually she looks down and she sees them. Flecks of blood on her chest beginning to grow. Bright red fresh blood that spools in the centre of her chest. The sight of it makes her feel woozy. She touches it with a shaking hand and looks at her fingers. She touches her finger to her thumb, feels the stickiness of it.

'Oh my God!' Estella pulls at Bec's shirt, searches her chest where the red is splattered all over her, seeping into the fabric of the cream silk, rough at the edges like a snow-flake. 'Where does it hurt?'

Bec cannot feel any pain. Perhaps she is so severely injured she has broken the pain barrier, like those soldiers you hear about in the great wars whose arms are blown off and they pick up their own limbs and walk on with them in their pockets. Their senses have simply blotted it out. Is this what is happening to Bec now?

'Estella?' she pants as the fear sets in, 'Where am I bleeding from?'

Estella looks terrified and this makes Bec panic even more. She throws her leather handbag off her lap and moves about, grabbing at the silky fabric of her shirt. Then she sees a tiny plastic bottle in her lap. She picks it up and looks at the label. 'It's . . . it's red food dye!' She holds up the bottle to Estella and Estella looks at it and lets out a single peal of maniacal laughter before falling deathly silent.

They both stare out of the windscreen, and that's when Bec sees it, to her right – the motionless lump of something on the road ahead. Something covered in dark fabric, and red – red all around. The body lies upwards and the legs are bent the wrong way like a child might bend a pipe-cleaner man.

'Someone's hurt,' she cries.

Estella follows her gaze.

'We need to go and help them,' Bec says.

With a shaking forefinger, she lets herself out of the car and makes her way to the front of the car, studies the mass on the road. The yellow headlights glare ahead, half-blinding her. Behind her, Estella sits in the driver's seat, staring ahead.

'Hello?' she shouts. 'Can you hear me?' She grabs a limp wrist and looks out to sea. 'I can't feel a pulse!'

She studies the face in front of her. A young face, a face of a boy who has only just started shaving.

'Oh my God,' she screams. 'Estella!'

Estella does not move.

'Estella?' It is animalistic, desperate.

Estella gets out of the car, staggers towards Bec. Her skin is clammy, pale.

'It's him,' says Bec. 'It's Felix Weaver.'

Estella looks at the body on the ground, her face impassive, unreadable. In front of her, Felix Weaver lies on his back, his eyes closed, his legs bent unnaturally outwards, his arm upwards, as if in a superman pose.

Bec can barely find enough breath to speak. 'What are we going to do? Estella? He's messed up! Oh my God! We did this! *We did it!*'

Estella's face, which has until that point been devoid of emotion, seems to harden then. The fear has been displaced by determination, a need to be in control. It is her factory setting. Her colour has returned.

'We did not hit him, OK?' says Estella. 'Bec? Listen to me. *We did not hit him!*'

Bec looks at Estella and finally she nods.

We did not hit him, she tells herself. *We did not hit Felix Weaver!*

She does not know what is the truth and what is a lie.

24

Estella

Felix Weaver lies broken on the ground but what really stuns Estella is the silence. It is deathly loud. She blinks as a bat flies overhead, its silky wings black cut-outs against a dimly moonlit sky. She closes her eyes for a moment and almost believes she heard it: the sound of bones breaking, of muscle and sinew twisting out of shape. The sinister thwack of skull meeting concrete.

Her fingers tremble as she navigates the phone in her hand – Felicity's phone. She only has one number to dial, a zero, three times, but her hands shake so violently that she cannot seem to home in on the keypad. The first time she presses the hashtag instead, and then the figure eight, circumnavigating the number she needs, the number that could save a life. Who should she even ask for? Police or ambulance?

Get a grip, Estella! She swallows, flexes her fingers, straightens them and dials triple zero.

'Ambulance,' she says. 'Someone's been hit. A boy. On Pacific Parade, the School Run.'

She waits, hears a voice that is entirely devoid of compassion, almost frighteningly matter-of-fact. A voice that has seen it all, heard it all, can tune out shock and emotion, gore and distress: simply fails to be moved by them.

'No pulse. I mean we don't think there's one. He's not moving . . .' She glances over at Felix, arms and legs at loggerheads, blood pouring from his hip where his Iggy's sports shirt has been ripped by something, speared by it. Eyes closed. A trickle of dried blood running down a pale temple.

'Recovery position? I don't know if we can. It looks as though everything is broken.' Two legs for sure, possibly an arm. Those are the things she can see, but she cannot assess a skull, a back or a spinal cord, hidden things, for damage.

The voice issues instructions.

'Yes,' says Estella. 'We'll stay with him.'

She puts Felicity's phone back in her pocket and then takes it out again, because she thinks she might have forgotten to hang up. She has not. The silence is reinstated once more until Estella hears the sound of Bec's crying.

'Wake up, Felix!' she tells him as she kneels at his side. '*Come on!*' Her hands are covered in blood from where she pressed at the wound in his side.

She turns to Estella. 'This is our fault!' she sobs, her face anguished. 'We wanted it, didn't we?'

'We didn't want to *hurt* him!' Estella tells her. 'Not like this.'

'But we did,' cries Bec. 'We planned it, in the car! He was blackmailing me and Felicity. You yourself said you wanted to teach him a lesson.'

Bec rocks back and forth like she's gone mad. 'It's our *fault*!'

Estella cannot take it, the histrionics. It is not helping the situation one bit. It is just noise – harmful, ugly noise.

'Oh for God's sake, calm down!' she snaps. It is her natural way with Bec, the voice of someone older and with
more authority, the possessor of more common sense. Bec
herself would admit it. 'Don't you dare start telling the
ambulance people we were responsible. Can you see how
that would look? You need to pull yourself together. We
did not do this!'

Bec looks up and realisation seems to dawn. She nods
to indicate she understands what is true – and what is true
is that someone else has hit Felix Weaver and they have
run away from the scene, fled before they can be held
accountable. And now here they are, Bec and Estella, the
first responders.

But Bec should not be surprised, should she? An accident
on the School Run is nothing new. The corner is treacherous, you cannot see if there is a cyclist or a pedestrian on
the other side. Everybody knows it: Pines Council knows it.
That's exactly why they have put up signs warning motorists
to slow to twenty-five km/h. But, signs or not, the School
Run transforms from a hubbub of crawling vehicles to a
veritable freeway as soon as darkness falls. Estella has seen
plenty of P-platers tear around this very corner late at night
on moonless nights, windows down and music blaring,
bodies lined up inside two-door saloons like abattoir-bound
pigs in a cramped truck. She has heard countless stories
and read reports of accidents over the years: the elderly
couple wiped out on the bend of the School Run back in
1989; the woman who pushed her pram so far away from
her as a car rounded the bend that the baby made it, and
she didn't. Two cars colliding at the midpoint of the bend

and mangling one another's bonnets, four people dead. Accidents on this corner are almost the norm and not the exception, and this, tonight, is just another statistic. Felix is yet another victim of the bend. Only this time, the person who put him there has not stayed to help.

Estella doubles the lapels of Felicity's jacket over themselves and allows herself to indulge the thought that has momentarily chilled her. Maybe, just maybe, this was deliberate. Perhaps someone else wanted to teach Felix a lesson, just like she and Bec had wanted to do: a lesson he may not now live to be taught, not looking as messed up as he does.

She is snapped out of this hypothesis by the faint sound of sirens, which seem to switch from a distant lullaby to a deafening screech within the space of mere seconds. The police car is first, and then the ambulance, as if the bulky van cannot quite keep up with the sleek Volkswagen ahead of it.

For the next few minutes, Estella watches as if she is a bystander in a dream, an extra on a movie set: uniformed paramedics hurry towards Felix, affix an oxygen mask to his face, then cry, in turn, 'Felix? Felix? Can you hear me?'

A voice says, 'No pulse. Get the crash cart.'

It is all so quick. Felix's body moves involuntarily as they fire volts into his chest, his broken legs judder as his body bounces up and down on the concrete. Another car stops, a woman's voice. 'Can I help? Is there anything I can do?' A stretcher with a red mesh blanket is being opened and popping up into place, like someone shaking open a sun tent on the beach. Both life-saving items, Estella supposes, in different ways.

But what brings it all home to Estella, the enormity of all of this, is the phone. She only notices it when the ambulance has strapped Felix on to the stretcher and they have closed the doors, and Bec sits in the police car speaking on her mobile to Tom. A phone flashing green at the very edge of the safety barrier that separates the School Run from the perilous cliffs below: the two inches of metal that divide security and devastation.

A phone that cries out in its green flashing, desperate to be answered. No sound but a soft buzz which makes the handset dance the faintest bit closer to the craggy edge. Estella creeps closer and closer still, until she is at the barrier. She glances down and looks at the screen. It reads: MARTHA: MOTHER. She had forgotten in all of this that Felix belongs to somebody, that he is somebody's son. He is Martha Weaver's son – Martha Weaver who's all blustery with her purposeless macramé skills.

Estella watches the phone as it shakes and shudders, but she does not move. It is a mere ten centimetres from the cliff edge.

Behind her, blue and red lights flash, and in front, the waves crash violently against the ragged rocks below.

Estella thinks about the phone, of the images that are on it. The words, typed by her daughter and delivered to the almost-dead boy on the road. The photos of her daughter's virginal chest, illuminated in the pixels of a crudely expensive phone, the implications for Felicity of this vile correspondence, the ramifications of it falling into the wrong hands.

Felicity, like Felix, belongs to somebody: she is Estella's.

Estella sticks out her foot and kicks.

WEDNESDAY

25

Martha

The clock on the wall ticks loudly as the seconds pass, and Martha blinks in time with them as she sits beside her son's hospital bed. It is five in the morning and she has barely slept. How can she sleep sitting in an uncomfortable static chair? They had offered her a camp bed, but she had refused it. She had wanted to be close to Felix, to hold his hand.

She watches the machine that is keeping her son alive as he lies in the gunmetal-grey gurney with stark white sheets (*why can she never get her sheets this white?*) and sometimes she prays, the dutiful mother that she is. Her bare legs itch from the rough edges of the chair and she leans forward periodically, to relieve her back, her head resting on her son's chest. This is what they all expect her to do, the nurses, *everyone*, to sit and cry and lean into her son's body and will him to wake up. They bring her cups of sugary tea and give her sympathetic smiles and ask her if she is OK and if there is anything they can get her and what she wants to say is, 'Please don't pity me! I *like* him like this! When he is like this, he cannot be cruel!'

Felix's face is a mess, the skin peeled off on one half of his face where he hit the hot tarmac and slid across it at sixty kilometres an hour. It looks, Martha thinks, like a plate of carpaccio – all red and bloody and mashed up. His nose broken and his head shaved, a long angry scar across the top of his skull, clamped shut with ugly metal staples. His arm is in a sling, both legs set in casts. He looks almost comical, like a character from a film – a modern reworking of Frankenstein's monster – and when Martha first saw him she had almost been amused by it in that way you are when something is deathly serious.

The medics at Lawton Hospital had taken him into surgery straight away to relieve the pressure on his brain and Martha had sat in the waiting room, dead inside, not knowing if she really wanted him to come back to her and then berating herself for it. But God, how had he become the man he had become? Surely it wasn't all because of his father's ultimate life choice: death. Iggy's was meant to have sorted him out, made him into an honourable man, given him positive male role models and, moreover, made him into one himself! Wasn't that what they promised her from the word go? That they would turn her wayward boy into a community-focused, ambitious and morally upright young man? Isn't that what it said in the prospectus and wasn't that why every mother of boys in Pacific Pines wanted her boy to go there? Then if so, why hadn't it worked with Felix? *Why?* Yes, they had made him excel intellectually – he had a conditional offer from Cambridge University, no less. Yes, he had done all the right things to get himself the coveted position of school captain, but where they had failed had been with his character. They had failed to turn his darkness into light, not even a sliver of it. And she couldn't blame them because she had failed to do it, too.

And the way he had spoken to her last night. She'd watched him walk out of the gates, his bag slung angrily over his shoulder, his face set in a smirk, and she'd hated him. *Hated him.* She'd tried to put the key in the ignition, but her hand had been shaking so violently she hadn't been able to turn it, so she'd sat for a few minutes, staring at the steering wheel and thinking about what he'd said to her outside on the grass.

'You're fucking deluded!'

'Felix, *please . . .*'

'Drop dead.'

She squeezes his hand now, tightly. Tight enough to hurt him, to hurt her boy.

'You just make me so angry, Felix,' she sobs, her head on the bed level with his hips. 'You just push me and push me and push me! I don't know what to do about you any more!'

Under her hand she feels the slight tremor of a finger moving. Of a weak and speechless body trying to make itself heard. She snatches her hand away, spooked.

She thinks back to last night, how she'd followed along angrily after him in her car like some kind of crazed night stalker. She had done it because of the awful things he'd said to her. She'd been so angry, so upset!

She grips the side of the bedsheet, wraps it tight around her knuckles until the skin turns white and she feels the sweet relief of pain, self-flagellation of sorts.

'Oh Felix,' she cries as the clock strikes six a.m. and the chorus of kookaburras begin their maniacal laughing outside the hospital window. 'What have I done?'

26

Bec

Bec enjoys a few seconds of peace before her memory kicks in and her heart begins to thunder as it falls victim to an alarming fight-or-flight response.

She grabs her phone from the dressing table and scours for news. It is ten past six. She sees only a small news story on the *Pacific Pines Observer*'s Instagram page, dated a few minutes prior. There is a stock image of the thirty-five km/h 'slow' sign on the School Run and the caption:

A Pacific Pines boy was seriously injured in a hit-and-run last night. PP Observer *has been told by Pines Command that the victim is Felix Weaver, 18. At the time of posting, Felix is in a critical condition at Lawton General. Stay tuned for updates. Our prayers are with his family.*

Bec closes her eyes and sees the mangled body of Felix on the tarmac, the bone of one thigh sticking up, erect, from ripped skin. A finger bent all the way back, doubled on itself. A gouge in his side, blood pouring like a stabbing. Legs lacerated like scored pork rind.

She jumps up from the bed, runs into the bathroom and kneels on the cold grey tiles. She cannot tell if the desire to vomit stems from the minimal alcohol she drank and is not really used to, or from the vile memory of what she witnessed afterwards. She puts her fingers into her mouth and lets the putrid liquid spill over them. When she sits up and wipes her mouth with the back of her hand, she sees a mass of crumpled fabric on the floor, splattered with bright red food dye.

'Oh God,' she whispers to herself, clinging to the side of the bowl. She cannot get the picture out of her head, Felix Weaver dying on the road like an animal. Why had they taken so long to tend to him while she had worried about the food dye on her chest? What if those extra seconds were the difference between life and death?

'Bec?' It is Tom from the bedroom, his voice sleepy. 'Are you OK in there?'

'I'm . . . fine.' Bec knows she is anything but.

There is a pause as Tom chooses his words. Eventually he settles for, 'Well, I'm just on the other side of the door if you need me . . .'

Bec doesn't reply, and after a few moments she hears the shower being turned on in the children's bathroom next door, and she understands that Tom is giving her space. She uses the thwack, thwack of the water heater to muffle the sounds of her crying. She does not know why, but the tears will not stop.

She had called Tom from the accident scene at about ten o'clock when the emergency services had told her she could go. The police had blocked off the School Run and so Tom had been forced to take the long way back to Pacific Pines with Cooper and Ollie in the car. He'd pan-icked when he couldn't get hold of her, he said, and when she'd eventually spoken to him, he'd been breathless with relief. 'Thank God,' he'd sighed. 'Christ, Bec, I thought it was you who'd been in the accident.' When she'd finally arrived home, Cooper had jumped up and flung his arms around her when she'd walked in through the door ahead of Tom. Willow had just sobbed. 'Oh, Mum,' she'd said over and over. 'Oh, Mum!'

Bec stays in the bathroom for what seems like forever, but it can only be about ten minutes later when Tom pokes his head around the door.

'Are you OK?' he asks.

Bec can see he is now in his suit, ready to go to work. Just a regular day for Tom. A normal Wednesday morning, acting as if nothing happened the night before. The question surprises her. It is obvious, isn't it, how she is?

'No,' she tells him. 'I am not.'

'I'll stay home,' he says.

'No,' she sighs. He has offered, and that is good enough for her. What would be the point in him being here? He can't take away what she saw last night. He cannot erase the image from her brain. 'No, really, I'll be OK. Where are the kids?'

Tom nods behind him towards the bed. 'Sage is waiting for you.' His pleading face is too much for her – as is the idea of Sage in her usual meerkat pose, waiting for Bec to exit the bathroom and deliver her usual morning cuddle.

Bec nods and splashes cold water on her face. Dark circles and a sallow complexion stare back at her from the mirror. She has to get over this. Onwards and upwards.

'Mummy!' Sage sings. 'Daddy said you're poorly in your tummy,' she says. 'Can I cuddle it better?'

Bec opens her arms at the foot of the king bed and pulls Sage in close. 'I'm fine darling,' she says. 'Just a bit sicky, is all.' She puts her chin on Sage's hair, aware of the vomit that's covered her mouth, and rocks with her back and forth, back and forth, soothing herself as much as her little girl. 'I think I must have eaten something funny at the Gala Day.'

I witnessed an accident last night! I saw someone hit by a car, their body a mangled mess on the ground. Bones everywhere! No signs of life! I was part of it all, Sagey! It all stems back to me!

'I'll look after you,' says Sage, snuggling in.

'Oh my baby,' says Bec. 'Thank you.'

At breakfast, Bec goes through the motions of cooking bacon and egg and serving it up on the nice, duck-egg-blue artisan plates (eggs and soldiers for Sage), of stuffing lunchboxes with wholemeal bread sandwiches and healthy treats, of yelling at Cooper to put his socks on, then his shoes. *Have you filled up your water bottle, Cooper?* Telling Willow to get out of bed because she has an interview for a summer job at the organic coffee shop in town at nine so she can earn money for university (because she and Tom won't be offering a free ride). Willow shouting something about almost being ready, she is drying her hair, but Bec suspecting she is really up there on her phone, gossiping with her WhatsApp group about what happened last night to Felix Weaver. *Come on Sagey, please turn the cartoons off now! Willow's going to drop you at preschool on her way into town!* Tom throwing apologetic glances at her as he sips his tea, knowing how much this is killing her, what she has seen.

They all stand at the door, ready to go their separate ways. It is only eight forty-five a.m. but Bec is already exhausted from the mental load, all she is carrying inside her head. She wraps her dressing gown around her and knots the cord tighter. *Chin up, Bec,* she tells herself. *You've got this. The boy will be fine, he will make it. You did what you could to help.* She beats away the other thought that worms its way inside her consciousness: *perhaps he won't be able to expose her now? Maybe her secrets are safe?*

'Mum?' Willow's face, riddled with fear.

'Oh darling, it will be fine,' says Bec. 'Trust me.'

'What's the matter with you?' Cooper asks, gawping at Willow.

'It's her interview,' says Bec. 'Willow's a little nervous.'

'It's only at a café. Why are you worried?'

Willow ignores him and snatches up her keys from the sideboard as Sage tears outside and round the corner towards Willow's car.

'Muuuum?' Her little voice floats across the breeze, over the potted plants and the mosaic tiles on the deck.

Bec sighs as she hands Cooper his school bag. 'Yes, Sage?'

'Where is Willow's car?'

Tom glances at Bec and races around the side of the house towards Sage. A moment later he is back, Sage by his side.

'Did someone move it?' Willow asks. 'Cooper?'

'Me?' Cooper points at himself. 'How would I move it? I can't even drive!'

Willow is panicked and Bec can see she is close to tears. 'Then where is it?' she cries.

'Is it the car thief?' asks Cooper. 'That's so cool!'

'Cooper!'

Willow is sobbing now. 'How am I meant to get to my interview?'

Bec is dumbstruck and can do nothing but stare at the empty space where Willow's car is meant to be. She is not sure she can cope with this on top of everything else. Of all nights for a car to go missing!

Tom, who is the only member of the family who is not overexcited by the disappearance of Willow's Holden, grabs his own car keys and nods towards his car, parked out on the street. 'We'll sort it out later,' he says. 'I'll take you for now.'

Willow follows blindly before turning around to glance, like Bec, at the empty space on the concrete that is usually home to her car – as if she believes the vehicle will suddenly appear out of thin air – and at Sage, who stands in the open doorway of the house singing in full operatic voice, 'Willow's car is gone! Willow's car is gooooone!'

27

Estella

'Well, where is it?'

'Where is what?'

'The car, Bec! Willow's car?'

She'd heard about the theft second-hand from Flick, which was quite often the way with Bec's household matters, since the girls message one another from the crack of dawn. At least Flick had finally stopped the crying, as if Felix Weaver had been the world's most dutiful boyfriend and not a blackmailing sex pest.

'How am I meant to know?' Bec snaps. 'When you had your purse stolen at that restaurant in London, did *you* know where it was?'

'There's no need to be fractious! I was just making conversation.'

'Anyway, where are you? You sound like you're on the car speaker.'

Estella looks up at the road sign that says, *Lawton Sands 3 km*. She overtakes some old duffer driving at the speed limit. 'Lawton, to get the living-room rug repaired. It's rotting a little underneath from the damp, but we got it on our honeymoon, so I'd like to save it.'

'Are you serious? How can you even *think* about a rug after last night?'

'It's called distraction. I'm sure you're baking some twee little birthday cake today to take your mind off it all, aren't you? Anyway, tell me more about Willow's car.'

'What more is there to say?' Bec sighs. 'It was down by the side of the house last night, and now it's not. End of story.'

'And did you call the police?'

'Please will you stop, Estella! I'm not completely useless!'

'Well, *did* you?'

'Of course I didn't . . . Tom did!'

Bec starts to cry and Estella rolls her eyes to herself as she pulls off the freeway and takes the slip road that will take her past the paint shop with the fancy Farrow & Ball collection and the lighting showroom and the Venetian blind specialists. She feels she may be in for a long session of the waterworks because evidently the crash scene has had a bigger impact on Bec's mental health than it has had on hers. *And that*, thinks Estella, *is why it pays not to be too sensitive!*

'It's just all too much,' Bec says. 'I can't cope with the guilt!'

'Guilt?'

'Yes, guilt! We were on our way to have it out with him, weren't we? With Felix?'

'Oh, don't start this again!'

'But I feel guilty about thinking bad things.'

Estella sighs.

'No one knew we were thinking that . . .'

'Well, what if someone *heard* us? Estella, we said we wanted to hunt him down and teach him a lesson!'

'We were inside the car, so unless they can hear through glass and metal, I think we're probably OK.'

'Yes, but we were first on the scene! Isn't that a little suspect?'

'Not really, because my bumper is still pristine and who-ever hit Felix Weaver must have the biggest fuck-off dent in the front of their bonnet. It was hardly a gentle nudge he got, now was it?'

Estella turns in to Divine Rugs, clicks off the car speaker and gets out of the car, Bec in her ear, whinny-ing softly about dislocated fingers and broken bones and brain damage. She waves over a boy of about seventeen inside Divine Rugs, points to the car boot with the back-wards point of her thumb and mouths, 'Rug in there. *Munro!*' and heads to the coffee shop next door to order a latte while her Moroccan handwoven rug is being lugged into the shop by someone she imagines is called Branx-ton or Saxon. As he passes with the rug on his shoulder, his cheeks puffed out with the weight, Estella sees his name is Jayden. *Almost.*

'I mean, we haven't even considered poor Martha in any of this . . .'

'Hmm.' Estella has reached her time limit for Bec's neu-roses. She stirs sugar into her coffee, cradles the phone between her ear and her shoulder and looks out across the industrial estate. Should she pop into the paint shop while she's here? It seems such a waste to drive all this way just for the rug. Does she need new lamps for the bedside tables?

She smiles to herself. This is what Estella does when she is in the middle of a crisis. She distracts herself and tries to pretend it isn't happening. If she is thirty-five kilometres away from Pacific Palms at Lawton Sands tending to her honeymoon rug, then she cannot think about dead ex-lovers and given-away babies and recalcitrant daughters and mashed-up school captains. Now the very act of distracting herself is making her think about her reasons for it. *Gah, stop it, Estella! Don't go there!* She holds out her hand and takes her coffee from a spotty young barista.

Across the road she sees a very attractive middle-aged man in mechanic's overalls at Charlie's Body Shop, bending over a car with a nasty ding in its bonnet. She watches the man as he wipes his hands with an oily rag and speaks to a petite slip of a woman, who is presumably the owner of the car. She is somehow familiar, this woman, but Estella does not know why. She squints and leans forward.

'Anyway, I'm here now, so we'll chat later,' she mumbles into the phone to Bec. She is lost in thought, raking the inside of her brain for something, although she does not know quite what.

Bec ignores her. 'It's not good for Iggy's either, is it?'

Estella watches the way the woman at the panel-beating workshop pushes her hair behind her ear. Short hair, flecked with grey.

'Ursula Deacon will have to put out a statement . . .'

Something twigs as the woman turns around slowly and scans the area around her, lowering her head as if she is trying to stay hidden. Estella quickly turns to face the wall of the coffee shop. Why would *she* be in an out-of-town body shop when there is a garage with a panel-beater at

Pacific Pines? Unless she was trying to repair some ill-gained damage to the front of her car.

'Ursula!' she whispers.

'Yes, that's what I just said,' snaps Bec. 'Are you even *listening*? She'll have to put out a statement. He was the school captain after all, although why he ever got that position is absolutely beyond me. How is Flick by the way? I didn't even ask you how she's taken the whole thing.'

'Fine. Fine.' Estella stares at the shiny silver chrome coffee machine in front of her, sees in its reflection the blurred image of a woman with grey hair hurrying through into the while-you-wait café area to the side of the workshop and hidden from view from the street.

'That's good,' says Bec. There is a pause. 'Perhaps she'll wait until Felix is . . . *you know* . . . before they announce anything.'

'He isn't dead yet!' Estella comes to, her rational brain flicked on. 'Anyway, I must go and get this rug sorted, it's really rather a mess.'

'Yes, well, rot gets into the fibres, doesn't it, and then it destroys everything?'

Estella turns back to the garage, where a mechanic tends to Ursula's car. *Yes*, she thinks. *Yes, it does.*

28

Bec

Estella was right, Bec *is* baking today. She is meant to be creating a Cars cake of all things, but how can she possibly make a red velvet model of Lightning McQueen when she has an actual real-life car drama going on?

The facts are clear: Willow's Holden is no longer parked in the spot to the left of the house where she left it last night. Willow locked up the car, or so she swears 'on Sagey's life', then switched off the lights and came inside at about eleven o'clock. And Bec can corroborate this, because she was in the kitchen unstacking the dishwasher when Willow pulled into the drive and she saw the double-flash of orange as Willow clicked her key fob. Bec was right by the sink washing out a tea mug when Willow came in and threw her keys in the bowl on the hallway table, because they made an awful clang and Bec remembers saying, 'Shhh! You'll wake up Sage,' even though the reality is that a jumbo jet could take off in Sage's bedroom and she wouldn't stir.

Then everyone had gone to bed and in the morning Willow's car was nowhere to be seen, and now here they are, three or so hours after finding out the car is missing and two since Willow returned from her interview (because she couldn't just not turn up: Bec had whispered in her ear something along the lines of 'Keep calm and carry on,' and so off she'd gone into town with Tom). Willow lies curled up on the sofa while Tom, who didn't make it work, flicks through a pile of paperwork for the Holden's insurance information. Cooper sulks on the bottom step of the stairs and says roughly every ten minutes, 'But my soccer boots were on the back seat and they were my favourite Adidas ones!' The first time he said it, Sage followed up with, 'Tough luck. Dad says if you lose something you don't get another one. Isn't that right, Dad?'

And as for Bec? Bec stands in the kitchen cradling her third cup of English Breakfast tea of the morning, and while she is still sick to her stomach from seeing Felix Weaver's legs all twisted out of shape *and* having to deal with Willow and her car, she must turn her attention to the bright-red cake she must make for some entitled five-year-old boy somewhere, without any red food dye, because the bottle got emptied last night in Estella's car.

Tom glances at Willow on the edge of the sofa, her face a picture of anxiety.

'Are you sure you locked it?' he asks, for about the fiftieth time.

'I know I did,' she sniffs.

'I saw the lights flash,' says Bec. 'She definitely locked it.'

'What about my boots?'

Tom glares at him. 'Cooper . . .'

'But they were limited edition!'

'Cooper, *please*!' Bec slams a cake pan down on the kitchen bench and everybody jumps. 'She locked the car, I saw her do it. I was standing *right here* in the kitchen. And even if she didn't, even if my eyes were deceiving me, what difference does it make?'

'Insurance-wise, a whole lot I'd say.'

'As if anyone ever admits their car wasn't locked to the insurance company,' Bec mutters. 'They're hardly going to find out.'

'But that's fraud,' says Cooper.

'Correct.' Tom folds his arms.

'What did the police say?' Willow asks and Bec notices she is shivering with the shock of it all. She takes a throw off the arm of the sofa and wraps it around Willow's shoulders.

'Not much,' says Tom. 'There have been so many stolen cars and car parts over the last few months they can't keep up.'

'Well, did they say they were going to investigate?' Bec asks.

'They took the numberplate and said they'd send an officer round here later on, but I'm going to have to go into work at some point. Willow, make sure you give Mum an inventory of what was inside.'

'My soccer boots for starters.'

Willow jumps up. 'Please will you all shut up? It doesn't matter about the damn car or the soccer boots. What about Felix Weaver? He might have been a dick to Felicity, but he didn't deserve to be smashed to smithereens and left barefoot in the middle of the road, did he? What if he *dies*? You won't all be worried about a stupid missing car then, will you?'

She lets out one long sob, and tears up the staircase, two steps at a time.

Bec gives her a few minutes before she creeps up the stairs behind her and knocks gently on Willow's bedroom door. Inside, Willow lies on her bed in the foetal position, clutching a teddy bear. Bec sits down on the side of the bed.

'Oh Mum!' Willow moves her head from the pillow and rests it on Bec's lap. Sweet, sensitive Willow, who only ever cares about everyone else. 'He could die and we're worried about a *car*!'

'Shhh,' Bec says, stroking her hair. 'It will be OK.'

It may well be a lie. Bec knows it and so does Willow, but it is her job, as mother, to counsel and comfort her beautiful daughter, who feels other people's pain so acutely. She has always been like this, an empath. A feeler of all things to passionate degrees: love, sadness, sympathy, anger. It is in Willow's genetic make-up, a takeaway from Bec herself. The best and worst of Bec's own traits. She had felt that anger last night and aimed it at Felix, the boy who'd discovered her secret and wanted to expose her, and now he was in a hospital bed clinging to life and all she felt was empathy. 'You feel emotions and you feel 'em good,' is what her father once told her. She did, and so does Willow – everything to the extreme.

Willow wipes her nose with the back of her hand and Bec reaches for a tissue from the box on the bedside table and passes it to her, as if Willow was five years old again.

'Felicity is so gutted,' she says. 'What do I even *say* to her?'

Bec recalls Estella had said Flick was OK. But of course she had. Flick does not open up to Estella like Willow does to her. Flick could be in a world of pain and Estella would be blissfully unaware.

'Mum? What should I say to Flick? How can I make it better?'

Bec does not have an answer. 'Just be there for her,' she tells Willow as she pushes away the wet strands of hair that stick to her hot pink cheeks and tucks them behind her ear. 'Comfort her. That's all you can do.'

Willow wipes her nose and nods.

'You're strong, Willow. OK?'

She doesn't answer.

'Willow?'

A feeble nod. 'Yes. I am strong.'

Bec nods and stands up. 'Come on, then. Let's try and get on with things. Don't worry about the car. Things can be replaced. You're safe, we're all safe and that's all that matters.'

She knows Willow is thinking the same as she is: *But Felix is not.* Felix Weaver may well die, or already be dead, for all Bec knows. And whether that happens or not is entirely out of her hands, so all she can do at this point in time is busy herself keeping lines of communication with her precious family open wide and her secrets clutched in close.

29

Estella

Estella is still digesting the news when she gets back to Pacific Pines an hour later. She tries to scroll Instagram for a while and fails. Then she tries to locate a spliff, or at least some weed and a Rizla in Felicity's room while Felicity is brooding about life in the shower, but fails at that task, too. So she settles for sitting at Conrad's desk and staring into the garden, drumming her fingers in thought. She cannot reconcile herself to the idea that the devoutly-religious head teacher of St Ignatius' Boys' Grammar would cover up any kind of crime, but then again, it's not beyond the realms of possibility that the principal has a dark side. Doesn't it happen all over the world? Reverent, God-fearing folk committing heinous, unforgivable crimes? Hadn't Father Francis himself preached the other day: 'If we say we have no sin, we deceive ourselves'?

Estella drums her fingers some more, until she notices the little fingernail-shaped dents in Conrad's leather-bound blotter. She recognises it then, her inertia. She has left it too long, the thing she must do. Like the cleaning of the rug, she has been escaping the realities she must face, and that reality is visiting Ursula Deacon at her cottage in the grounds of St Ignatius'.

She slides on a pair of white trainers belonging to Felicity and scoops up her keys from the hall table. 'I'm just popping out,' she calls to upstairs, forgetting it is only Felicity at home today, despite the fact she dropped the boys to school moments before she'd called Bec on her way to Lawton.

The principal's cottage sits at the end of the driveway next to the Main House. It is tradition for head teachers at St Ignatius' to reside here, or at least it has been since Estella was at Asher's Girls' and sneaking into Iggy's to visit JP. She remembers creeping up the winding pebble drive with three girlfriends one night and diving into the bushes, giggling, as the floodlights burst on. So many years ago, so fewer cares.

She drives slowly across the gravel, and looking up sees Ursula Deacon at the window as she comes to a standstill. Her arms are wrapped around her own waist as if she's providing herself with comfort. The way she looks out is so expectant, as if she's been waiting for Estella to arrive. But how would she have known?

As Estella climbs out of the car, Ursula moves away from the window and it unsettles Estella to see her leave, as if she might be hiding from her – as if she does not want to be called on today – but a moment later Estella hears the scrape and catch of the security chain as it is unhooked from the door.

The woman is dressed in the same pale-blue knee-length skirt and white blouse she wore to the repair shop (of course she is! Why would she have changed?) and a polished gold crucifix hangs from her neck on a delicate gold chain. Up close Estella sees her skin is almost deathly pale, and that she is drawn, sickly. Why had Estella not noticed this before? Had she not seen her just yesterday? Or is this new pallor, this almost-exsanguination, the result of guilt?

'Mrs Munro,' she says with a weak smile.

'Estella, please. Can we talk?'

'Of course. Do come in.'

Ursula leads the way into the kitchen, where she fills the kettle without asking Estella if she would like a hot drink. 'I wondered when you would come,' she says.

Ursula picks up a tea towel with images of the Vatican on it and Estella suddenly wants to laugh at the ridiculous piousness of it. 'How do you take your tea?'

'Just milk,' says Estella. She does not want to drink tea, but nor does she want to be rude to Ursula Deacon, who is the gatekeeper to her boys' futures, as well as the very person who may or not have mowed down her own school captain in her open-topped car.

'It's just me here at the moment,' Ursula says as if to inform Estella that the meeting is private. 'Sam's at the school somewhere. It's inset day for the staff today while we sort out the next intake.'

Estella nods and wonders if Ursula detects her disappointment. She hadn't managed to meet Sam yesterday – the whole Kaya-being-married-to-her-ex situation had put the kibosh on that. But she is desperate to make his acquaintance, *desperate*.

'Do you know if there is any news about Felix? Any update?' the principal asks as she places a delicate china teapot on the kitchen table. 'I know your husband is an oncologist and so it's not technically the right department, but presumably he hears things over at Lawton Hospital.'

'He is still in an induced coma,' says Estella. 'There has been no change at all overnight.'

'They're hoping it might help his organs heal, I expect,' says Ursula, turning away from Estella and towards a red kettle, perched beside a ceramic sink. 'Poor Martha, she'll be beside herself. I cannot imagine how I'd cope in that situation.' She looks Estella in the eye. 'There is nothing a mother wouldn't do for her son.'

'Indeed.' Estella knows the truth behind this statement. There is nothing she wouldn't do for her boys.

'Ursula . . .'

The woman does not look at her. 'Yes?'

'I saw you this morning at the panel-beaters in Lawton, with your car.'

Ursula drops a teaspoon into her teacup with a clang. 'I see.'

Estella straightens her shoulders. 'Ursula, I have to ask you – as a mother, you understand. Was it . . . I mean, it *wasn't* you who hit Felix Weaver, was it?'

Ursula laughs, a loud and high-pitched peal. An exaggerated, fake laugh if Estella were to judge it on its merits.

'Felix Weaver? Me? Oh goodness, no!' she says, blinking wildly.

'Forgive me,' says Estella. 'It's just . . . the dent?'

'A kangaroo,' says Ursula.

'I'm sorry?'

'A kangaroo. On this drive actually. The thing ran right in front of me just as I was moving my car last night. Sam had parked it in the groundsman's spot and I was moving it back. Obviously I wasn't going fast, but he was. He bounced right off the front bonnet. Must have injured him badly. There are plenty of them that live in the bush adjacent to the fields. Pests, really, but obviously it's illegal to cull them. Poor thing must have been startled by my lights – he just ran at me. Made quite a dent . . .'

Estella studies Ursula's face for signs of a lie, but she does not know the woman well enough to ascertain whether or not she is telling the truth. If it was Felicity, for example, or Bec, or even perhaps Kaya now Estella knows her a little better, then she would know in a heartbeat. She would see the flicker of a lower eyelid or the bite of a front incisor on a bottom lip, or an aversion of the eyes and it would tell her all she needed to know. She would have the confidence to say, 'That's utter rubbish! I know it and you know it, so spit it out.' But not here with Ursula, not now.

'My apologies,' Estella says. *Sorry, not sorry.* 'It's just that when I saw you out of town I did wonder if it was you who'd . . . I mean by virtue of being in the workshop, you understand. I wondered if it was you who had hit him.'

'Well, I'm glad to say it wasn't me.'

'Of course not. I should have known that,' Estella says. 'I think I'd rather worked myself up, wondering if it was you or perhaps even . . . Sam?'

'Ah.' Ursula offers up a dry smile. 'Now we get to the reason you're really here.'

I'm sorry. I don't quite understand.'

'You know full well what I mean,' says Ursula. 'You didn't come here because you were concerned I had hit Felix Weaver in my car. You came here because of Sam, didn't you? You came because of your son.'

30

Bec

Bec is forced to rush Cooper to school on account of the car drama and time spent comforting Willow. They are mostly silent as they drive along the School Run. Cooper stares out of the window with a scowl, brooding over his stolen soccer boots, and Bec on account of her busy mind: a mind that replays images of an injured boy, a lost car, a school placement hanging perilously in the balance, and a cake that must be made before day's end. As she makes her first turn on to the bend, a shiver engulfs her, making her shoulders shudder and goose bumps form erect on her bare arms. She glances across Cooper's body and out of the window, notices a small strip of blue-and-white police tape still clinging to the safety barrier along the cliff edge. It dances merrily in the breeze, a sinister remnant of the carnage of just hours before.

'You OK?' she asks, for conversation.

'Uh-huh.'

When they arrive at Pacific Pines Primary, Cooper is in no hurry to get out of the car, despite the fact there are only three minutes until the peal of the school bell. He is almost at the end of Year Six now, and his care factor has faded as keenly as his school hat in the sun.

He turns to Bec, twisting the long ribbon-like strap of his bus pass between his fingers.

'Mum?'

Please don't mention those damn boots!

'Yes, darling?'

'It's about last night.'

Bec turns off the engine.

'Yes?'

'Something Willow said about Felix.'

Bec's eyes snap up. What has Willow told Cooper about Felix? Has she told Cooper about the blackmail? About the photos on Felicity's phone, and the single incriminating photo that Felix has of Felicity on his?

'What did she say?'

'Willow said Felix Weaver was barefoot.'

'Did she?' Bec stares at the hordes of children in various states of disarray in their navy-blue-and-yellow uniforms pushing through the school gates, bags slung over shoulders, laces undone.

'Yeah,' Cooper says. 'She said she felt bad about him because he had no shoes on or something. That he was lying barefoot in the middle of the road dying. Is that right?'

Bec looks straight ahead, and thinks back. *Yes!* she thinks. Felix *was* barefoot, but it is not a detail she had particularly focused on at the accident site. But now she is thinking about it, she sees it. She sees that his trainers were both off, there were no socks. His feet were bloodied and cut, like his face, gashed on the bitumen. Then his legs, scratched and bloody, leading up to the cut on his side, the one from which she'd tried to stem the blood with her palm. A cut with a shard of thick plastic inside it, the tessellated plastic of a headlamp. Bec had touched it with a shaking hand, wondered if it was safe to pull it out, wondering if it was hurting him, embedded as it was in his flesh. But poor Felix, in his state of unconsciousness, clinging on to life, would not have been able to feel anything, let alone the injury to his side or the bloody grating of the skin of his feet. And so Bec had pulled out the reflective plastic with a shaking hand and pressed down hard to stem the flow, let the blood spill between her fingers and down the tender flesh of the inside of her wrist.

'Yes,' she says, out loud now. 'Willow is right, he was barefoot. His trainers had come off. They were on the ground I think. I suppose he hadn't been wearing socks.'

Cooper takes the end of the strap of his school bag and uses the corner to poke under his thumbnail in contemplation.

'But how did she know?' he asks.

'How did who know?'

'Willow. How did she know Felix was barefoot?'

Bec studies Cooper's face. 'I must have mentioned it to her or Daddy last night,' she says. 'When I got home. I can barely remember the conversation if I'm honest, I was still in shock.'

'But I was there and I don't remember you saying that.'

Bec unclips her seatbelt and turns towards him.

'What exactly are you saying, Coops?'

What is this about? Bec wonders. *Is he asking whether or not* Willow *hit Felix? Why would his mind even go there?*

Cooper shrugs. 'I dunno. It's just weird, that's all.'

'Coops,' Bec ventures. 'The accident . . . It's just not nice to think about. Please don't overthink what happened, I don't want you losing sleep imagining the condition Felix was in. All you need to know is that the emergency services arrived fast and he is in good hands at Lawton Hospital. Darling, if any kids start talking about it in the playground today, it would be wise to keep away and not involve yourself. Hearsay is really damaging to people and I don't want you getting all these nasty images in your mind . . .'

Cooper shrugs, dismissive, and Bec is for once relieved he has the attention span of a gnat. Like many children his age, he doesn't sleep well if he's watched a gory movie, let alone hearing the harrowing details of Felix's accident. It is just something his eleven-year-old brain does not need to imagine – or compute. Perhaps that's because he's been brought up in a too-safe environment that is, to all intents and purposes, a case of 'sugar and spice and all things nice'. She has always wanted to protect her boy from gore, from fear, and so she will play down the horror of Felix's accident for Cooper's ears, because the reality is too disturbing to bear. A boy who is clinging to life, his brain likely scrambled and his body entirely broken.

'There's Jonty!' Cooper suddenly exclaims, the gravity of the situation forgotten. He opens the door and yanks his bag out. 'Thanks for the lift, Mum. I'll see you later.'

'OK darling.' Bec kisses his cheek. 'Love you.'

'I know. Love you too.'

And away Cooper trudges, bag slung over his shoulder like the rest of the boys in the pack, leaving Bec feeling unsettled, as if there are questions she should be asking of herself, or Willow. She watches Cooper pass through the gates, just one of many identical pre-teens with too-short shorts and grubby shirts and laces undone, and drums her fingernails on the dashboard in thought.

The truth (and of course she would never have mentioned this to Cooper) is that she doesn't remember mentioning Felix Weaver's feet to anyone in any capacity – barefoot or otherwise.

31

Estella

Estella puts her hand on the back of a teak dining chair to steady herself. The inside of Ursula Deacon's cottage kitchen is suddenly very small and she feels as though she is on the verge of a hot flush. She looks to the window towards an escape, a way back from this emotion that almost suffocates her, and then to Ursula.

'You know, then,' she says. It is not a question.

'That you are Sam's biological mother? Yes, I've known your identity for some time. Well, rather *we* have known your identity . . .'

'We?'

Ursula nods. 'Sam and I.'

'Sam knows about me?'

Dizziness takes hold and the room seems to spin around her. Estella pulls out a chair and sits down, adjusts her shoulders inside her now-sticky shirt.

'Of course. He had been looking for you for quite some time.'

'So you were aware yesterday, at Gala Day?'

'Yes, Estella. That's what I just said. Sam and I have known for some time.'

'But . . . we chatted at the interviews!'

Ursula does not comment, just shrugs, as if the pretence outside her office was nothing. But hadn't she done the same too? Hadn't she played dumb the whole day, trying not to stare at Sam and drink in his features: the beautiful brooding eyes, the familiar tilt of the head, the pronounced Adam's apple, all inherited from his father. Her head feels heavy, a dead weight. It is filled with everything and it is filled with nothing. The knowledge that Sam knew who she was yesterday as she stood nervously on the sidelines, and that he knew he was watching his two identical half-brothers play sport. She cannot compute that Ursula had known at the moment Estella placed a ten-dollar note in the woman's hand at the sausage sizzle. Their eyes had met then, but Estella had seen nothing even though she herself had been acutely aware of the role in her eldest son's life of the woman standing in front of her. What must Ursula have been thinking at that very moment as she did something as banal and unremarkable as putting a sausage in a bun and handing it over?

And now Estella is here, in her love rival's front room (if love rival is what Ursula actually is to Estella), and there are the photos of Sam, everywhere: on the walls, on surfaces, on tiny side tables on top of twee crochet doilies. The place is like a shrine to Ursula's son – to *her* son, the son she was never allowed to know. How the hell did Ursula keep her cool yesterday? Estella simply cannot fathom it. *How?*

So many questions, so much to know! She takes a deep breath. 'How did you find out?' she asks.

'Well, I knew Sam's birth mother was a teenager called Stella Wickham from the Pacific Pines area and that his father was a local who had moved away following the scandal,' Ursula says. 'Because it would have been a scandal back then, wouldn't it? Not like nowadays when teenagers are popping out babies willy-nilly. Anyway, when I saw Jonty and Archie's school applications with the photos on them . . . well! I mean, the similarities are *incredible,* don't you think? The jaw, the eyes, the nose! All three of your sons certainly favour you, don't they?'

'Yes,' says Estella. 'I suppose they do.'

'I didn't all base it on circumstantial evidence, of course! I needed more than that. It was your husband who confirmed it,' says Ursula. 'Although I don't think he realised he had.'

'Conrad?'

'When he was treating me . . . You do know he is my oncologist, don't you?'

Estella nods. She knows, but really she shouldn't.

'I can't remember what we were talking about but I made a very obscure reference to *Pride and Prejudice* and Mr Wickham, and he commented, "Wickham. That's my wife's maiden name."' Ursula pauses, before resuming her story. 'He told me you were Estella Wickham before he married you. Born and raised in Pacific Pines and an old Asher's girl. Most people called you Stella then. I don't know if he realised I'd gone quiet.'

'I see.'

'Of course my active treatment has stopped now . . .'

'I did know that. I saw your name on some of Conrad's notes,' Estella says, and she hopes Ursula does not sense that it is a lie. 'I'm sorry.'

'Yes, well. It's not ideal but I've made peace with it now. I'm ready to meet my maker.'

Estella feels the returns of the flush. What will Ursula's death mean for her and her relationship with Sam? If Sam has been looking for her, then surely he is looking to build some kind of relationship? Why else would he want to know her? Aside from, perhaps, to understand his genetics, to see if he's predisposed to any illnesses or genetic conditions. It's a possibility, of course.

Outside, a crunch of feet on gravel disrupts the silence, and both women look up as the front door opens. Sam stands on the threshold of the house in blue tracksuit pants and a grey T-shirt. His hair is messy, with a side part and the same gentle wave the twins possess. Estella feels the urge to cry. The resemblance to his father is stronger today than it had been yesterday and she feels the presence of JP keenly. The sense of maternal longing feels like a stab wound to the chest, it is a dull ache that radiates across her shoulders and deep into her back. How she would love him to call her 'Mum'.

He glances from Estella to Ursula and back again.

'Hi Estella,' he says and Estella feels the ache deepen. But why would he call her anything else? She was only his mother for forty-one weeks and then for a few hours inside a run-down hospital room in Noosa, and Ursula has had him for twenty-five years. Estella kissed his head and baptised him with her tears for twelve hours, but Ursula bathed him and taught him to ride a bike, bandaged sore knees, held a damp towel over a feverish brow. She fed and nurtured and mollycoddled. She read to him and wiped his tears and listened to his teenage angst. Changed wet bedsheets, replaced outgrown soccer boots, took him for haircuts. She did it all. But Estella wants to be his mother, by God does she want to! She wants it more than anything. This ache inside her is second only to the moment he was taken from against the warmth of her chest, and now her arms want to do what they should have done all those years ago and that is to grab hold of him and not let him go.

She balls her fists beside her hips.

'Hello Sam,' she says, and she hears it in her own voice: a softening, as if the emotion of this moment has stolen the power of her voice, its depth, its force. 'I gather this isn't a surprise for you?'

'No, it's not.' He regards her warily. 'Mum's always been honest with me,' he says, his head to the right, observing her side-on like the twins do. 'I've known since I was little I was adopted, and then when I was eighteen Mum told me you'd been a teenager from Pacific Pines from a devout Catholic family, and that she'd heard you had always stayed close by.

'That's one of the reasons we moved here and Mum took the job at Iggy's,' he says. 'She wanted me to find you.'

Estella looks at Ursula, confused. '*You* wanted Sam to find me?'

The woman nods. 'Sam has been searching for closure for a long time. From what I understand, a good deal of adopted children want it, *need* it, in some capacity. Some do not, of course, but Sam fell into the first category. He has always had a deep longing to find out exactly where he came from, and under what circumstances. I have always said I would help him when the time was right. And that time is now.'

Ursula looks at Sam and smiles a sad smile and Estella sees then just how much she loves him. She only has to glance at any one of the photos on the mantel or the polished sideboard, or at the shiny sporting trophies that glimmer, dust-free, on the bookshelves, engraved with the name Samuel Deacon, to see that.

'It was pretty easy, as it happens,' continues Sam. 'When Mum mentioned the application forms she had from two boys with a mother named Estella, and then her meeting with Dr Munro, I Googled you. All I had to do was enter Estella Munro and Pacific Pines and there you were at some macramé class run by Martha Weaver.'

'I don't typically do macramé,' mumbles Estella.

Sam smiles slightly. 'The resemblance between me, Jonty and Archie is crazy.'

Estella smiles, enthusiastic. 'It is.'

'And Felicity too. I can see myself in her face. It's . . . weird.'

Sam turns away and looks out of the window. 'Yesterday was overwhelming,' he says. 'I had to hide in the gym at one point because I couldn't handle you all being there in the hall, it was too much.'

'Sam, if you'll let me explain . . .'

'When I was younger I looked for you everywhere, in supermarkets, at fairgrounds – *everywhere*. And then suddenly, you were at Iggy's with your kids. It was . . . it happened sort of fast.'

Estella bites her lower lip. 'I've thought about you every single day.' Her throat hurts, it aches. The hot tears are just behind her eyes and she tries to blink them back, but they are supercharged. Tears that have accumulated for twenty-five years, the kind you just cannot stop.

'I was only seventeen,' she says. 'I didn't have anywhere to go. I tried desperately to keep you but I wasn't allowed. In those days . . . I would have been homeless, you see, and I didn't want to bring you up with nothing.'

Sam watches her, the muscles in his jaw working hard to control his emotion.

'The number of times Conrad wanted to move away from Pacific Pines, but I couldn't. I just couldn't do it, even though sometimes I wanted to be somewhere else, anywhere else to shake off the memories. I refused to sell the house after my parents died, just in case you came back looking for me. And I suppose . . . well, eventually you did.'

Sam stands up and steps towards Estella like he might hug her, but then stops. He towers above her. He has JP's broad shoulders and strong forearms: identical forearms. It is strange for Estella to see him, an almost carbon-copy of his biological father, except seven or maybe eight years older than JP had been when Estella last saw him.

He does not hug her. Instead he places his hands on Estella's shoulders, and she reaches up to take his.

'Estella,' he says. 'It's fine. I had an amazing upbringing. I couldn't have been loved any more . . .'

Estella nods. *I would have loved you more.*

They are silent for a moment, taking one another in. Ursula has taken a step back, Estella notices, and she is grateful for it. Then Sam asks, 'How did *you* find *me*? I mean, how did you work it out?'

'I've always known your name was Samuel and when I heard about the new sports master I wondered if it was you, much like I do with any Samuel I come across,' Estella says wistfully. 'Martha Weaver was actually the one who told me you'd been adopted by Ursula. She mentioned it at the damn macramé class.'

Ursula smiles. 'I cannot tell you how glad I am that you have found one another,' she says. There is no bitterness in her face, no *envy*, even though Estella herself burns with jealousy that Ursula has lived a lifetime with Sam and she herself has not. Ursula is a good Catholic, a good Christian. She is everything Estella wishes she was, and perhaps she could be, now she has laid the past to rest.

'The truth is, Estella, you are going to have to take over from me. I only have six months, maybe less, maybe more,' says Ursula. 'I feel well at the moment, apart from this infernal cough I seem to have developed, but I'm stepping down from school once this term is over. It hasn't been announced yet, but I won't be returning to Iggy's next year. I need to put my health first, and truthfully, I'd like to enjoy whatever time I have left without the stress of it. I'm hoping they let me keep the house on compassionate grounds, until the time comes.'

'Mum, don't . . .'

Estella looks to Sam when she hears the word, but he is looking directly at Ursula.

'Please,' he says. 'Don't talk about it.'

'Sam, you're going to be fine,' says Ursula. 'You have a new family to get to know now, and I can't tell you how relieved that makes me.'

Estella thinks of Felicity, of Jonty, of Archie. How will she tell them about Sam? Is she even ready to share him with them yet? After all, she has only just found him herself. Perhaps she can find a way to have him to herself, just for a short while, before her life has to change once more. Yes, that's what she will do. She will wait, and she will hold on to this secret a little while longer.

She watches Sam as he glances out of the window and his eyes land briefly on the shimmering blue metalwork of Ursula's BMW. There is something in the way he looks at it, the way his brow furrows and his eyes narrow. This is what Jonty does when he is panicked about something, when he has a secret to hide. Sam's gaze turns from the car to his mother. His *other* mother, who sits in the armchair beside the mantel, her shrine to him.

Estella has to ask. She *has* to. 'The car. I mean, what you told me about your accident last night . . .'

Sam spins around. 'Mum?'

Ursula opens her mouth. 'Sam,' she says, firm. It is warning for him to bite his tongue. 'I told Estella about the kangaroo. On the drive.' She wrings her hands. 'Bloody pests . . .'

Sam blinks twice. He is Archie now! He is Archie telling a lie. Archie covering for his brother when Jonty has done something he does not want her to know. The time Jonty smashed the window with the cricket ball and Estella asked Archie, 'Do you know anything about this? Well, do you?' And Archie had given her this exact look and he'd said, 'No, Mum.' And technically, Estella may not know this man in front of her from Adam, this man who is in fact her long-lost son, but she knows the look in his eyes better than anyone, because she lives with those same eyes day in and day out – two pairs of them in fact. And what they are expressing right now, right here, is guilt.

32

Martha

Martha studies her son's fingernails. She told him to cut them a week ago and he sneered at her, told her to mind her own business. Now they are long and feminine and rimmed with blood and dirt and scum. She tells herself she will bring in an implement tomorrow to clean under them, and maybe, just maybe, she will push a little too hard when she scrapes the brown gunk from underneath them. Maybe she will dig deep and scratch the red, tender flesh beneath. Felix won't feel it, she knows that – he is unconscious, after all, but it will make her feel better to make him suffer the way he has made her suffer for all these years, since puberty turned him from a beautiful, sweet boy to a vile narcissist who hates her with every (broken) bone in his body.

Martha feels immediate remorse. What kind of mother is she, to feel this way? She begins to cry, at first silently, and then with volume, a sort of hiccupy sob. She places her head on the side of the bed beside her son's hip and she prays to God for forgiveness. And that's when she hears it, a change in the rhythmic pip-pip-pipping from the machine above Felix's head. It seems to slow and then turn louder, into one long, alarming note. Her head flies up to the machine she knows nothing about, where the dancing zigzag peaks and troughs of neon green have now collapsed into a single horizontal line. Flatline.

'Help!' she screams. 'Somebody help me!'

The swing doors fly open and a medic with strong arms ushers her out of the room backwards and into a corridor with green walls and plastic grey flooring. She watches helpless from the latticed windows of the door, her face sweaty against the glass.

A pair of hands hold electrical paddles. 'Crash,' she hears, and 'Stand back!'

'Please let him live!' she cries out loud.

Oh please let him die!

'I shouldn't have left you on the road,' she wails.

She falls to her knees and braces for the words she knows are coming: 'I'm so sorry, Mrs Weaver.'

The clock on the wall inside says five a.m. and still ticks, she can see it with her own eyes; her ears ring from the sound of the singular beep.

And then there is nothing but silence.

THURSDAY

33

Kaya

Kaya hears an ungodly thumping like a hammering heart-beat at Bec's front door as she sips coffee, and glances down the hallway to see Estella's face pressed up to the glass.

Bec is busy picking charred edges off the quiche she has lovingly removed from her state-of-the-art Miele oven and so Kaya gets up off her stool.

'It's Estella,' she says. 'I'll get it.'

Estella continues her impatient knocking when she sees Kaya walking towards her, presumably to denote she does not find Kaya's genial amble pleasing, but Kaya isn't about to sprint down the parquetry floor in her summer sandals on Estella's command.

'For God's sake, Estella,' she snaps as she opens the door. 'You're going to knock the door down.'

'Taking the Lord's name in vain, Kaya? I *am* surprised . . . Anyway, what are you doing here?'

Kaya ignores the pleasantries. 'Having a cup of tea and collecting Ollie's mouthguard. He left it in Tom's car after Gala Day.'

Estella nods and brushes past her towards Bec's open-plan kitchen area, where the faint smell of burnt pastry wafts in the air. Kaya would like her own home to smell like this – burnt or not. Perhaps she needs to start baking more.

'Estella!' Bec leans in and hugs her friend a little more warmly than she'd done to Kaya twenty minutes before and Kaya feels a touch irked. She notes with amusement how Estella's arms hang stiffly as Bec buries herself in her best friend's neck. 'To what do I owe this pleasure?'

Estella pulls away from the embrace. 'I suppose you've heard about Felix Weaver?'

'What?' Bec says, dropping a kitchen knife with a clang on the bench. 'What's happened?'

'Whoa, someone's jittery!' Estella chirps. She takes off her coat. 'Felix died last night. Like properly flatlined. Conrad said they thought he wouldn't make it, but the little shitbag evidently has a rather strong constitution, because he's still with us, more's the pity.'

'Oh, thank God,' sighs Bec, her hand across her chest, fingers splayed. 'That is *great* news.' Kaya notes the colour flooding Bec's cheeks and, just for a moment, she wishes she was the kind of person Bec is – to feel so strongly for a stranger that it manifests in a loss of colour to the skin. The kind of person whose physiology changes because of the empathy they have for others. Bec would mourn and grieve and *feel*. It's not that Kaya doesn't care about Felix, only that she wouldn't have been devastated if he *had* passed away. She'd heard the way he had spoken to his mother, with meanness and cruelty. She isn't sure there is not something seriously wrong with the boy.

'Anyway, I'm not here about Felix,' says Estella. 'I need to discuss something with you.' She glances at the quiche which is burnt on one side. 'Christ,' she says. 'Where did you bake that? Pompeii?'

'I've had a lot on my mind! You know I don't do savoury. Kaya, I swear I'd never burn a cake!'

Kaya holds her hands up. 'Of course,' she says, even though she doesn't actually care in the slightest. 'I'm sure you wouldn't.'

'Yes, best stick to children's cakes,' says Estella.

'Thank you.' There is an underlying 'fuck you' tone to Bec's gratitude. 'Did you say you wanted to discuss something?'

'Yes, and this is not an easy thing for me to broach.' Estella fiddles with the gold disc on the end of her necklace. 'But I'm here because of Ursula Deacon and Sam.'

'What about them?' Kaya asks.

'Well, actually I was hoping to speak to Bec *privately* . . .'

'I invited Kaya here, Estella,' says Bec. 'You're being rude.' Estella rolls her eyes.

'I'm the soul of discretion,' shrugs Kaya. 'Circle of trust and all that.'

'Fine,' sighs Estella. 'I suppose you do have a vested interest in keeping it to yourself, Kaya, given your role in all of this . . .'

Kaya nods solemnly. She does have a role in this. Paul made it that way.

Paul is in his bed, the rust-coloured linen bedspread pulled up to his neck. He is thin now and feels the cold. Kaya gives him his morning morphine and sits with him, reading snippets from the paper, sometimes the classifieds.

'Listen to this,' she laughs. 'John Little has married Catherine Butt. What if they're double-barrelled?'

Paul smirks. She carries on reading, but she hears nothing from him and she looks up. He is staring at her, his face pained.

'Are you hurting?' she asks. 'Do you need more medicine?'

'No,' he says.

'Then what?'

'There's something I need to tell you.'

Kaya nods. 'OK.'

'A child,' he tells her. 'There was a child.'

Kaya thinks he may be hallucinating. Sometimes the morphine does that to him. Sometimes his dreams are confusing – he cannot process make-believe and reality.

She smiles, indulges him. 'What child?' she asks.

'A son,' he says. 'A boy.'

Kaya blinks twice and JP looks her in the eye. Lucid, real.

'Estella,' he says. 'Estella had a baby boy.'

Estella takes a deep, attention-commanding breath. Sucks all the air out of the room. 'Yesterday I happened to be up at Lawton Sands at the industrial estate . . .'

'Quiche?' Bec transfers a slice onto a bone-china plate.

'And who should I see getting a while-you-wait ding out of their car?'

'Ding?' Kaya asks.

'Big slice or small? The egg part isn't burnt.'

'Bec, would you listen?' Estella snaps. 'I'm trying to tell you that Ursula was there, chatting to the mechanic about a dent on the bonnet. So of course I popped over to Iggy's to talk to her about it and she spun me a story

about clipping a kangaroo, but it was obviously rubbish.
I've never seen a marsupial on Iggy's school property, and
believe me, I was up there any chance I got as a teenager
. . .' She glances at Kaya. 'And Ursula was making out it
was like Australia Zoo on the front lawn.'

'You think she hit Felix?' asks Bec.

'I have my suspicions. Anyway, I need to decide what to
do about it.'

'*Do* about it?' Bec wipes her hands on her apron.

'Yes. Whether or not I contact the police and tell them
that I saw the principal of St Ignatius' Boys' Grammar at
a repair shop the morning after Felix Weaver's hit-and-run
getting a bloody great ding out of her bonnet.'

Bec leans in. 'You must do the right thing, Estella. If you
think it's a possibility she hit Felix then the police need to
be informed.'

'What?' Kaya is incredulous. 'You can't dob in the
mother of your own child!'

'Technically *I* am the mother of my own child, Kaya.'

Now Kaya has heard it all! 'OK then,' she snaps. 'You
can't dob in the beloved adopted mother of your biological child.'

'Yes, but if I don't impart this information to the pow-
ers that be, I could be hauled up on charges of aiding and
abetting.'

'Then don't admit to seeing her,' says Kaya. 'It might
not have been her. You know, it was dark . . .'

'It was the middle of the day, Kaya, for crying out loud!
As if I'd be getting my rug cleaned under the cover of
darkness!'

'So just forget you saw her! No one can prove you did, can they? Even if there was CCTV, it can't prove you actually recognised her. Perhaps it wasn't actually her. Maybe the woman just looked like her . . .'

'Yes,' snips Estella. 'Perhaps it was her long-lost twin.'

'Well, you know better than anyone about getting twins mixed up!'

'OK, OK,' shouts Bec. 'Calm down both of you.'

Kaya cuts into the pointy end of her slice of quiche and looks up. 'Right, well before you run to the cops, why don't we address the elephant in the room?'

Estella sighs. 'And do tell us what that elephant is, Kaya?'

'The elephant is the distinct possibility that Ursula could be covering for Sam. Perhaps Sam hit Felix Weaver by accident, or on purpose, or accidentally-on-purpose, and Ursula is helping him hide the evidence? The classic cover-up!'

'That sounds more likely,' says Bec. 'The woman drives so slowly she couldn't dent a marshmallow. And an out-of-town garage? It's a bit suss, isn't it?'

Estella's nostrils flare and Kaya sees a flush of pink travel up her neck.

'I'm sorry, Estella, but don't tell me you haven't considered it?' asks Bec.

'Well of course I bloody have!' snaps Estella. 'Why do you think I'm here trying to work out what to do?'

She puts her head in her hands and then looks up. 'I Googled it, you know, the penalty for hit-and-run. It varies from case-to-case. For a first-time offender it might only be eighteen months' jail time and a three-thousand-dollar fine. But if Felix were to . . . *die*, then the maximum penalty for manslaughter is twenty-five years.'

Kaya feels a pang of pity for Estella, who she now sees is all bravado about wanting Felix Weaver to die, because the facts are clear: if he does, there is a small possibility it was her first-born who's to blame.

She softens her tone. 'Estella, if you need to know on a personal level then you should speak to Sam,' she says. 'Find out the truth.'

'And then what?'

'Then like any good mother would, you keep it to yourself. You make sure Sam and Ursula have their stories watertight and you forget what you saw at Lawton Sands.'

Kaya says this not because she thinks it is what Estella wants to hear but because this is what she would do for Ollie, and what she knows Bec would do for Willow or Cooper. She already feels a strange duty of care to protect Sam, to preserve him for Ollie. To hurt him would be to damage her own boy. She has an allegiance to this stranger she does not know because he is part of Ollie and Paul too. She puts her hand over Estella's. 'It is what any parent would do in the circumstances, isn't it? We do what we have to to protect our children. It is biology, pure and simple.'

Bec does not say a word, instead wipes the work surface with a yellow sponge.

Estella nods. 'Yes, I'll talk to Sam. That sounds very sensible. Thank you, Kaya.'

Kaya feels a pang of satisfaction that not only has she suggested something useful, but that she has also received

praise for it from the woman least likely to dish out plati-
tudes.

'Of course that is what I would have done anyway,'
Estella adds.

'I'm sure it *was* a kangaroo,' lies Kaya. 'Bloody pests.'

Bec, who has remained silent for a couple of minutes,
chews on the side of her cheek as she hangs up her apron
on a row of wooden hooks to the left of her KitchenAid.

'And why have you got a face like a smacked arse?'
Estella demands. 'Please tell me you're not still sulking
about a bloody quiche?'

Bec turns, her arms folded. 'I'm sorry Estella, but it
sounds to me like the truth is staring you in the face,' she
says. 'You'd better hope Sam has his story straight.'

34

Estella

Estella cannot lose her firstborn again, she cannot. Although there is nothing to say it was him and not his mother, if Sam *did* in fact hit Felix – and if Felix were, God forbid, to die – then the consequences do not bear thinking about.

She parks outside Iggy's filigree gates and enters through the side gate. She finds Sam in the cricket pavilion with a group of boys, prepping for a match.

'Boys, finish getting ready and I'll meet you on the pitch,' he says. 'Wallace, bring the balls and Billingham, bring the stumps. I need to have a quick word with Mrs Munro, here . . .'

'Mrs Munro.' He raises a hand to usher Estella ahead of him. 'After you.'

They walk towards the old oak and the irony is not lost on Estella. But now is not the time to tell her son about how his father courted her there, under the great boughs.

'How are you?' she asks.

'Harassed,' says Sam, but he does not smile. 'We're playing Pines Public this afternoon. Organising boys for sport is always hectic.'

She smiles. 'I know. I have two of them, remember!'

They exchange a glance and Estella realises they are thinking the same thing – that she actually has three boys, and not two.

'Anyway, I won't keep you,' she says, although she continues to walk and so does Sam. They fall effortlessly in step. The way he walks is comforting, familiar, although he is not like the twins in this respect. She realises it is JP's gait, his slightly slumped shoulders, yet arched lower back. They stop when they reach the oak and Estella does not realise who led whom there.

'It's OK,' he says. 'I have a few minutes.'

Estella nods. 'Your father and I used to come here,' she says. 'When we were teenagers in love.'

She traces the deep crevices of the oak and sees that Sam is studying her hands – as if he wants to explore her appearance for similarities, just as she does to him.

Sam watches her hand as it moves. 'What was he like?'

'He was wonderful,' Estella says. 'He was kind and sweet and funny – very funny. I loved him very deeply and he loved me. You were conceived out of love, Sam, pure and simple. And then you were taken from me out of bitterness and anger.'

Estella recalls that day so clearly, a stiflingly hot January day. A day made for fun, not pain. But while the girls in her peer group splashed about in saltwater pools and went on bush treks and complained of being saddle-sore from riding country horses, Estella lay in a bed with her legs in stirrups and pushed out a four-kilo baby boy, whose head crowned for a whole two minutes, burning like an iron on flesh. They had stitched her up crudely afterwards, because the birth had split her tender flesh open and she had cried as they did it – tears for her baby son, tears for the agony of it all, both physically and emotionally.

She checked herself out of the hospital two days later with her mother, still feeling the child move inside her like boat legs when you're no longer on a boat. They had not spoken in Aunt Fiona's car to Maroochydore Airport and by the time Estella had taken her seat on the Qantas plane from Noosa back home to Sydney, she was numb, only occasionally feeling the discomfort where the stitches in her perineum burned red beneath her, or with the hot letdown of her milk inside her Myer bra.

'Do not wince, Estella,' her mother said. 'The child is much better off.'

She had at least been able to name him, so she called him Samuel, a good Catholic name, and Estella thought of his soft hair and the ruddy skin on his cheeks and she told him in her head, 'I did it for you, my little one. *I did it for you, Sam!*'

Sam looks at her. 'I thought it would be like that,' he says. 'Or at least I hoped it would be. I did wonder sometimes if you just didn't want me, but Mum always told me you'd been forced to give me up. That was really all she knew.'

'It was the hardest thing I've ever done,' says Estella. 'Giving you up broke me. I have never really healed, so finding you is so . . . so life-altering.'

Sam sits down properly and picks at the grass beside him. 'Thank you for telling me the truth,' he says.

Estella sees her chance, now. To ask him what she needs to know, because if she knows the truth, she can make things better – or at the very least she can prepare herself for what may lie ahead.

'Now I've told you the truth,' she says. 'I'd like you to tell *me* the truth.'

'About what?'

'Did you hit Felix Weaver in your mother's car?'

'Fuck,' Sam whispers it under his breath and Estella closes her eyes.

'Can you just ask me anything else?'

'Please answer me.'

Sam pushes his palms against the tree and then stands back, runs a hand through his hair.

'I did, but I swear to God I didn't leave him like that. I clipped him and that's the God's-honest truth. I was driving towards the bends and I clipped him. It was just a warning really . . .'

'Oh good God! A warning? You mean you *intended* to do it?'

'I didn't mean to hurt him!'

'Then what?'

'I found out from Willow what he was doing to Felicity. Willow and I are . . . we're seeing each other, you see. She told me Felix was threatening Felicity, that he'd made her send him naked photos, and that he was going to send them round the entire school if she didn't have sex with him. It made me sick to my stomach and I flipped. I guess I sort of felt protective over her because of her being . . . my sister.'

She sees him swallow, his eyes wet. She sees he is telling her the truth; she has seen that look in her twins' faces as well as the face of a liar. She feels a deep yearning to hold her son – to comfort him, yes, but mostly to show him how moved she is that he wanted to protect his half-sister (albeit in a misdirected manner) and for doing almost instinctively the one thing she has failed to do for Felicity in seventeen years.

'I was worked up, I guess,' says Sam. 'Tom Lloyd had just confronted me in the cricket pavilion and warned me off Willow, and after that I walked out on to the road a bit fired up and bumped into Felix. I told him he had to delete the photos and he told me to go fuck myself. He said, "You don't teach me any more, mate!" I guess I saw red. I jumped in Mum's car and drove around for a bit and then I went after him.'

'And?'

'I followed him up the road, and when I saw him I slowed right down because I knew the implications of actually hitting him. But the car skidded on some oil or something and the nose clipped him on the thigh – not that hard, but hard enough to dent the car and knock him down.'

Estella closes her eyes.

'But he got up, I promise you. It was just before the bends, where that lorry spillage was with the oil. You can see where I nudged the partition after clipping him. Mum's blue paint is on the railings!'

'And you are sure Felix got up?'

'Totally! He was raging. He gave me the V-sign and shouted, "You dickhead!" or "You fuckwit!" or something like that and then he picked up his bag which had dropped off his shoulder and he stormed off towards the first bend.'

'So he saw you?'

'Yeah. He looked properly pissed off when he realised it was me.'

Sam twists a blade of grass between his forefinger and thumb. 'So there you go, that's the truth.'

Estella feels momentarily concerned that any son of hers would stalk a teenager along the road, until she realises that's exactly what she was attempting to do with Bec, to teach the puffed-up school captain a lesson. Because his morals were – *are, Estella! He's still alive!* – so questionable, so corrupt, that he deserved some retribution.

'Look, I know I did the wrong thing,' Sam says, 'but I was so mad with him. All I could think of when I drove off was, "Fuck, he saw me! What am I going to do?" But I swear on my life, on my mum's life' – *I'm your mother, I am!* – 'that I didn't properly hit him. It must have been someone else.

'Someone must have come along and knocked him down right after me, only that time he didn't get up.'

35

Kaya

Kaya rides her bike to Ursula Deacon's little cottage in the grounds of Iggy's and feels the sun blaze on the back of her neck as she pedals along the School Run. She breathes in the scent of the sea as she pedals, a bunch of tulips and a bottle of elderflower cordial jiggling about in her basket at the front.

She turns in through the school's metal gates and hears her wheels crunch the gravel. She skids slightly as she brakes outside the cottage, where jasmine creeps up the walls and lavender stands up in a row along the outside fence. She takes in the heady scent of both of them — the slightly sour aroma of the jasmine and the relaxing violet of the lavender. She kicks up her bike stand with her foot, straightens the front of her favourite floral dress, empties her Saltwater sandals of stones, takes a deep breath and knocks on the front door. There is no reply, so she places the tulips and cordial on the ground and cups her hands to the window, her breath covering the glass with a white mist.

The house inside is still and she glances left and right before she spots Ursula Deacon on the sofa, sleeping peacefully, her hands clasped together at her navel.

She gives one loud tap on the glass, intended to startle the woman into wakefulness, and then moves to the door

and knocks gently. Kaya can hear her feet padding along
the hall, and her hand fumble with the clasp on the front
door.

'Mrs Sterling,' Ursula Deacon says. 'Apologies – I must
have drifted off.'

'Gosh,' says Kaya. 'I do apologise for waking you. If I'd
have known you were sleeping . . .'

'Not at all. I shouldn't have been indulging myself – far
too much to do!'

Kaya feels her face being studied.

'What can I help you with, Mrs Sterling?'

Ursula Deacon has not invited her in, but Kaya steps
over the threshold anyway. 'These are for you,' she says,
holding aloft the tulips and the elderflower. 'I just wanted
to say thank you for a marvellous day. Ollie had an absolute blast and he was buzzing with adrenalin when he got
home.'

'That's very kind,' says Ursula Deacon. 'Ollie did very
well.' She looks Kaya in the eye. 'Was there something in
particular you wanted?'

Kaya realises she needs to phrase this carefully, to put
it in a way that makes it clear she is not suggesting impropriety of any kind.

'Well,' she begins. 'I've been thinking a lot about what to
do with some of the money Paul, that's my husband, left
in his will . . .'

Ursula Deacon's head tilts to the side.

'You see, he left quite . . . quite a vast sum and since Ollie
has been in the application process for Iggy's and become
very invested in the church, it occurred to me that, as an

old boy, Paul would have wanted me to donate a sizeable sum of money to the school.'

'Go on,' says Ursula Deacon.

'So I'd like to make a donation in his name. I thought perhaps a sum in the region of twenty thousand dollars would be fitting, if you thought it was appropriate, of course. Like I said, it's what Paul would have wanted. Something to help with the ongoing upkeep of the college chapel, perhaps? Or for the tennis courts. I understand you are keen to fundraise for a new surface and net? Of course I would make the cheque payable directly to you, or even to *Sam* if you thought it suitable, him being the sports master and everything?'

Ursula's lower left eyelid flickers.

'You'd be able to distribute it to the school as you saw fit,' continues Kaya. 'I wouldn't care what the funds were spent on, it really wouldn't bother me. I'd be happy to turn a blind eye to where they went, if say you wanted to use them for improvements to the cottage or similar.'

Ursula's eyes narrow. She looks at her wedding rings, twists them on her bony finger.

Then she speaks. 'If Iggy's were to use this money, would it be strictly a donation?' she asks. 'Or are you looking for something in return?'

Kaya's hand flies to her chest.

'Gosh, no!' She holds out a hand. 'I'm not asking for anything, Ursula. Do you mind if I call you that? I just think . . . I just think that as an old boy, this is exactly what Paul would have wanted. He spent his teenage years here, and if I can help in any way to keep that memory alive, I know it would have made him very proud indeed.'

Ursula Deacon squints at Kaya once again, assesses her.
A human lie detector. She must have vast experience at
this, dealing with a school full of pubescent boys.

'I would only hope,' says Kaya, using a cautious tone,
'that you might look on Ollie favourably when you send
out the letters tomorrow morning . . .'

The older woman's eyes snap up. 'I see,' she says. 'Mrs
Sterling, you won't be the first parent to offer me money for
a place at this school and you certainly will not be the last.'

She turns her back on Kaya. 'But credit where credit is
due, you did couch that rather beautifully. I was almost
convinced you were an honest benefactor.'

Kaya stares back at her. 'I am not offering a bribe,' she
says evenly. 'As far as I'm concerned, Ollie deserves a
place and I'm convinced you will offer him one without
the need for anything as base as a bribe, especially given
his outstanding performance on Tuesday. This is merely
a generous offer from a prospective school parent to help
support the school financially, and in particular to support
you as its principal.'

Kaya gets out a cheque from her pocket and unfolds it.
The amount is written as twenty thousand dollars and the
beneficiary has been left blank.

'Like I said, I would have no interest in where the funds
were spent. I mean perhaps you might want to invest in
a new car for school business since yours has been dam-
aged. It *was* you at the panel-beating workshop in Lawton
Sands yesterday, wasn't it?'

Ursula Deacon emits a defeated laugh. Her smile fades
and she looks to her mantel above an ancient-looking

red-brick fireplace, where numerous photos of her son Sam fight for space: Sam as a baby bouncing on her knee, Sam as a toddler in flannelette shorts smiling up from his tricycle, Sam as a pizza-faced teen with silver-grey train tracks on buck teeth, Sam graduating in a black gown and a satin mortarboard, a tassel dangling in front of his eyes.

Tears fill the woman's eyes as she turns back to face Kaya, and Kaya can see in that moment how similar she is to Ursula Deacon. They are both mothers, decades apart but united in one single thing: their unbridled devotion to their sons. Like Kaya with Ollie, the love Ursula has for Sam outweighs everything else in her life. It is deeply anchored in the centre of her heart. Kaya picks up the blue ink pen that lies on top of the newspaper crossword on the principal's kitchen table. She taps the pen on the table and the principal says nothing for a moment. And then she speaks.

'Make it out to Samuel Deacon,' she whispers.

Kaya smiles and scribbles the name quickly. She holds the check aloft but Ursula Deacon does not take it. Instead she stands wringing her hands and so Kaya places the cheque on top of the newspaper and clicks the cap back on the pen, placing it neatly on top. Done and dusted.

'Thank you, Ursula,' she says.

Ursula stares down at the cheque, her face a picture of sorrow, and Kaya feels a momentary pang of sympathy. 'Please don't be upset, Ursula,' she says. 'Think of what you have just given the school. Think of what you have given your son . . .'

Ursula's lips pull up in a sad smile.

'You know, Mrs Sterling? My life will be over soon, much sooner than you know, in fact. And when it does come to the end, I will still face God with a pure heart. Everything I have ever done has been for Him.'

Kaya wonders if the old woman is referring to God, or to Sam.

'I do wish you well, Mrs Sterling, and I hope you find what it is you are looking for, and that you are able to sleep well knowing the decisions you have made and the things you have done.'

Kaya feels a tad irked by this. It feels like criticism, yet Kaya has only done what Ursula has done by accepting the money, and that is putting her son first.

'We are mothers, Ursula, and that is how we are made, and how we will always be,' she says. 'We would both willingly give our lives for our sons, wouldn't we?'

Kaya turns towards the front door and leaves Ursula slumped over the mantel, and as she steps onto the quaint little pathway to the end of the garden where her bike sits shimmering in the noonday sun she hears a muffled sob from inside and then Ursula's voice, loud and pained. 'God forgive me,' she cries.

The bank calls Kaya late in the afternoon and after a few security checks she finds herself chatting to a very sweet woman from Western Australia called Jacinta.

'Thanks for going through security, Mrs Sterling,' says Jacinta. 'May I call you Kaya?'

'Of course,' chirps Kaya.

'The reason for my call today is because someone has attempted to cash a cheque for a large sum against your account. The cheque has been honoured, but we just need to make sure you authorised the transaction.'

Kaya smiles.

'Have you made out any large cheques in the last few days?'

'Yes, this morning, actually.'

'Can you tell me the beneficiary of the money and how much the cheque was for?'

'It was twenty-thousand dollars exactly,' says Kaya. 'And the beneficiary was a Mr Sam Deacon.'

'Wonderful,' says Jacinta. 'You have a great day, Mrs Sterling!'

'Thank you so much, Jacinta. You too.'

SATURDAY: RESULTS DAY

36

Bec

Bec gets up at seven thirty and pads down the stairs in her dressing gown. Cooper is sitting on the front doorstep.

'Why are you waiting here?' she asks. 'The postman's not due for ages.'

'Dunno,' he says. 'It just makes me feel better.'

'Come on inside,' she says. 'Have some breakfast. I'll make pancakes.'

Cooper gets up, shoulders slumped.

'What's up, buddy?'

'What if I don't get in, Mum?'

'We'll still eat pancakes. They make everything better, don't you think?' Bec says it with a smile, even though she knows, in her heart of hearts, that it will take more than a hearty breakfast to console Cooper if he doesn't get a spot at Iggy's. 'Come on, I'll let you flip.'

Cooper is mid-flip of his third pancake (Bec has observed he is perhaps the only child to eat *more* when he is nervous and not less) when Sage runs in from the front garden covered in mud from a series of collapsed cartwheels.

'Mr Postman's been!' she sings. 'Is this Coopie's important letter?'

She holds out a crisp white envelope with the St Ignatius' crest and the familiar motto *felix quia fortis* stamped on the top left in black ink.

'It's so early,' she cries. 'Michael never delivers this early. I'm not ready!'

She dries her hands on a tea towel that says *Keep Calm & Bake Cupcakes* and takes the envelope out of Willow's hands. Cooper throws the pan down on the induction cooktop and snatches the letter from Bec. It's like pass the parcel.

'Open it, then!' Bec squeals, pulling off her apron – as if something of this magnitude should not be done wearing cooking attire – to reveal her dressing gown.

'Yes Coopie, open it!' demands Sage.

'But we need Dad and Willow,' says Cooper.

'Daddy!' screams Sage. 'Willow! Come here now. Coopie's big letter is here!'

'Wait,' Tom calls down the stairs. 'We're coming!'

Then there are thuds on the staircase and suddenly Tom and Willow are in the kitchen, their eyes fixed on Cooper with the letter in his hand. Willow's eyes are hollow as if she hasn't slept, as if she's been under the covers texting all night. Bec wouldn't be surprised.

Tom nods at the envelope in Cooper's right hand. 'Go on then!'

Cooper's nostrils flare as he takes a big intake of breath. Bec wonders if his heart is thundering as much as hers. He looks up at her and she knows it is.

'Here goes nothing,' he says and peels back the flap of the envelope so slowly that Bec wants to grab it out of his hands and rip the damn thing to shreds. It is agony, like the slow peeling of a plaster from soft, downy skin.

'Oh my God, Cooper . . .' Willow snaps. '*Just hurry up already!*'

'I'm bored,' Sage sighs.

Cooper stops in his efforts. His brows knit together. 'What happens if I don't get in?' he asks.

'Nothing will happen, Coops,' says Tom. 'You'll go to Pacific Pines Public School and you'll be a superstar there instead of Iggy's. The fact is, mate, we don't care where you go to high school so long as you're happy. That might sound naff, but that's the absolute truth of it.'

'Daddy's right.' Bec smiles. 'It really doesn't matter to us.'

Two weeks ago this would have been a lie, but Bec realises in this moment that what she has said is unequivocally true. Cooper will be fine. In fact he will be more than fine – he will be excellent! She has wasted so many hours worrying about what will become of him if he does not go to this school, but you just have to look at Felix Weaver to see that it is not the school that makes the character. It is nature, not nurture. Iggy's does not guarantee a better, more well-rounded, more morally sound child. Of course it doesn't. Cooper is proof of that because he is halfway to that beautiful man already. He already has the empathy, the kindness, a wholehearted aversion to cruelty and mean-spiritedness. Isn't that the only thing she and Tom have truly ever wanted for him? Have wanted for any of their children?

Cooper takes a deep breath. He lifts the unripped flap of the envelope and pulls out the letter, which is folded neatly into thirds. He lifts the top flap and then the bottom one and meets Bec's eyes again. She nods and smiles. 'It's OK,' she says.

They all watch Cooper's face as he scans the words. There is no reaction. Nothing. The world seems to stop turning on its axis. The house has never been so deathly quiet. Their family life, at this precise moment, is a Netflix movie on pause.

Then, after what seems like forever, he looks up. His eyes meet Bec's and she searches his face for a clue, anything to give away what is going on in her boy's head.

And then it is there, in his eyes, followed rapidly by a twitch of his top lip: a smile.

'Thank *fuck*!' says Sage.

Tom answers the phone on the third ring.

'Tom Lloyd speaking!' His voice is jovial and it makes Bec smile. Everything is suddenly well in the world. Cooper has a place at Iggy's, Willow finally has a holiday job and here they all are, eating pancakes as the sun streams in through the window and the heady smell of vanilla sponge wafts in the air. They are the family on the postcard! They are the Waltons!

A pause.

'Oh, hello,' says Tom. He looks up at Bec. 'Oh, right, I see. Written off, obviously?'

Willow looks up and mouths at Bec. 'My car?'

Bec shrugs.

'Well, thank you for letting us know.' Tom places his handset on the coffee table.

'That was Pacific Pines police,' he says. 'The good news is, they've found the car.'

Willow sits up.

'The bad news is, it's at the bottom of a cliff.'

37

Kaya

Kaya watches for the postman from the front window, she sees him deliver two white envelopes to the Munros next door and then slip a single white letter through her own postbox. *What's going on?* she wonders. *Why is the postie early today of all days?* Ollie is out on a long walk with Bandit. She kicks herself for letting him go.

Kaya steps out into the sunshine and walks to the end of the drive. She feels a sense of unease. What if Ursula Deacon truly believed the money *was* a gift regardless of Ollie's acceptance? After all, hadn't Kaya laid it on thick about Paul and how he would have wanted Iggy's to have the money regardless? *No,* she tells herself aloud. *Of course Ursula knew what it meant. We had an understanding. And besides, didn't she ask God to forgive her?*

She flicks on the kettle and sits down at the kitchen table, leans the envelope up against the fruit bowl in front of her and stares at it for at least five minutes. Then she gets up, opens the drawer in the kitchen where she dumps her paperwork and puts the letter inside, nestled on top of the Photoshopped photos of Ollie pretending to row, the ones she included in his school application form.

Wait, she tells herself. *Wait until he is home.*

'How important is Iggy's to you?' she asks Paul.

Paul looks across at her. He underlines the words on the paper once again: St Ignatius' Grammar, Pacific Pines. Then he puts the pen down and takes her hand in his, grey and purple thanks to the constant hole-punching of his treatment cannulas.

'Kaya,' he says. 'Iggy's is an exceptional school. I wouldn't have achieved half as much as I did if I hadn't gone there. It opens doors for boys. I want those opportunities for Ollie. But mainly, I want him to get to know his brother.'

'How much will it cost?'

'The current fees are forty-two thousand dollars for Year Seven, and then they go up minimally every year.'

'But we can't afford it!'

'It's not cheap but there's enough in the second savings account. Why do you think I became a surgeon? It's not because I have a knee fetish! We have money, Ky. I cashed in some shares specifically for this and you can live on your earnings. It will work, I promise. We have the funds.'

Kaya drums her fingers on the table in thought. The idea of leaving it all behind, of leaving the home they have made together, is terrifying. She looks into his eyes.

'Promise me,' he says.

Kaya drums her fingers on the table now as she did then. She swore to Ollie she would not open it without him, but what else is a boiled kettle for? She opens the drawer, takes out the envelope and runs the V-shaped flap along the kettle steam. When it is wet enough, she teases it open and unfolds the letter which is scored very precisely into three segments. She skims the words quickly.

> *Dear Prospective Parent,*
> *I regret to inform you that on this occasion your son's application for St Ignatius' Boys' Grammar has been unsuccessful. While we were impressed with his performance at this year's Gala Day, the competition was particularly stiff this year and I have been forced to make some tough decisions regarding placements.*
> *Thank you for your interest in St Ignatius' Boys' Grammar and all the best with your son's continuing education.*
> *Yours sincerely*
> *Ursula Deacon*
> *Principal*

She really only sees the one word: unsuccessful.

No, thinks Kaya. *This cannot happen. She promised Paul! She cannot let Ollie down! She cannot let him know he wasn't good enough for them!*

She feels fury, a fury that clamps around her heart and spurts into her veins. Fury that she has been double-crossed by an elderly woman, a woman of the cloth! Fury her money – Ollie's money – has been stolen from them. And the letter was so cold: *Dear Prospective Parent?* Not even a name, not even personalised. The angry tears brim at the edges of her eyes and she stuffs the letter back in the envelope and puts it in the drawer. Then she scoops up her car keys and gets inside, her body acting on autopilot.

Kaya arrives at the school and brings the car to a stop with a skid. No tulips this time, no sweet elderflower cordial, no soft knocking on the door and a gentle 'Hello?' Again she hears the sound of shuffling and then a cough before the principal opens the door. She seems somehow smaller than she had been that first time in the church with Father Francis, and during Ollie's interview.

'Well?' Kaya demands.

The principal's brow furrows. 'Excuse me?'

'I want to talk to you.'

'It's the weekend, Mrs Sterling. I really must insist . . .'

Kaya puts her foot against the door, her white trainer pushed firm against it. Ursula Deacon looks at her foot and then at her face with a trace of alarm. Kaya lifts up her palms. 'I'm sorry,' she says. 'But I thought we had an agreement!'

Kaya pushes past Ursula Deacon and walks towards the kitchen. Her tulips sit on a vase in the middle of the table. *Her* tulips!

'We *did* have an agreement, didn't we?' Kaya notes the shrill tones in her own voice. 'It was an awful lot of money, which I understand has been cashed.' She runs her hands through her hair.

'Mrs Sterling, now is not the time, not here, not in my home. I'd be happy for you to make an appointment with my secretary . . .'

Kaya breathes in, tries to calm herself. *But you took my bribe in your home, didn't you? Yes, you were happy to do that!*

'Ollie did well in his interview, didn't he?' she demands. 'You said so yourself.'

'He did.'

'And on the sporting field?'

'Yes.'

'Then why did he not get a place?'

'Excuse me, Mrs Sterling, but you cannot come in to my home and . . .'

'I gave you money. I cleaned the chapel. I've done everything I can to show Ollie is good for a place.'

The principal's eyebrows knit. 'Mrs Sterling, I don't quite understand your indignance. In spite of the fact you faked your beliefs to get Ollie a place, I . . .'

'Ollie isn't faking anything,' Kaya spits. She stands up and she is aware then how much taller she is than Ursula Deacon. 'You owe us.'

'Mrs Sterling, please. This behaviour is utterly unacceptable!'

Kaya shakes her head, bites angrily on her bottom lip. 'You cashed the cheque.'

'Which you insisted was a *gift*! Isn't it what your late husband wanted? To gift money to the school, without conditions?'

Ursula Deacon turns and walks into the doorway of her bedroom. 'Now please leave, Mrs Sterling,' she says. 'Or I will call the police.'

'Police?' Kaya takes a step back. 'But I only asked you . . . I'm not *hurting* anyone!'

'This is trespass,' spits the principal. 'You will regret this.'

Kaya looks over the woman's shoulder and sees candles burning, a Bible on the bed and a large bottle of liquid morphine and a syringe on the bedside table. It is a strange combination, as if some kind of ritual is about to take place. Kaya looks at Ursula. Was she about to . . . good God no! Surely not?

'Is everything—' Kaya starts and then stops. 'I mean, can I *help* you with anything?'

Ursula glances at her own bedside table and shuts the door hurriedly. 'I was in the middle of some correspondence when you called,' the older woman snaps. 'Now I'd just like to get on with it.'

'But—'

'I just want some peace!' Ursula cries. 'Don't you understand? I am not long for this world and I don't want to spend the little time I have left dealing with the likes of . . . this. Please, Mrs Sterling, just leave!'

Kaya looks the older woman in the eye and turns away.

38

Estella

'Come on, open one of them, Conny!' Estella thrusts an envelope at Conrad. She has waited months for this, but for some reason the single hour it has taken the boys and Conrad to return from collecting coffees from the centre of town feels like the most agonising wait of her life.

'I can't do it,' says Conrad. 'It's up to the boys to open them.'

'I'd better get in after having to play two matches with a bung knee,' Jonty says.

'Well, I had to do two interviews,' says Archie good-naturedly. 'And trust me, it's not easy making you look smart.'

Flick laughs.

'We don't speak about that any more,' says Estella, her eyes fixed on the envelopes in Conrad's hands. 'As far as we're all concerned, nothing happened and we all played ourselves on Gala Day.'

'But *we* all know about it,' Archie says.

'Yes, but your mother would like to forget, even *inside* the house,' says Conrad. 'She likes to think she's too superior to commit fraud.'

'I don't know what you're talking about. You can't *prove* anything,' Estella sighs.

'Estella, I'm not the FBI,' says Conrad. 'I'm not going to get you arrested, my darling, despite the fact I'd quite like a bit of peace and quiet occasionally.'

'Please, would you just *hurry up!*' growls Felicity.

Conrad looks at the first envelope bearing the stately school crest on it. '"To the parents of Jonty Munro,"' he reads. He hands it over to Jonty. 'Good luck, son,' he says.

Estella cannot breathe. Her palms are so sweaty she is forced to wipe them on the skirt of her Stella McCartney sundress. She grits her teeth, says the first prayer in her head that she's said in years – probably since Felicity got her offer letter from Asher's. But this is even more tense than that. Felicity excelled in everything, and there had been less competition for spaces. Trust Estella to give birth to not just one, but *two* boys in an already boy-heavy birth year.

She grabs the ivory letter knife that Conrad bought in Kenya way before everyone was all woke about animal rights, and hands it to Jonty, but he has already inserted his finger in the corner of the envelope and is ripping the paper roughly.

'Don't tear the letter!' Estella cries, stepping forward. *I might want to frame it!*

'Leave him, darling.' Conrad puts an arm around her and holds her like a human straitjacket.

Jonty scans the words.

'Want me to read it for you, dumbo?' Felicity asks, and Estella shoots her a glare. 'Are the words too small?'

'Well?' Estella clasps her hands together tightly. '*Come on*, Jonty!'

'Chill out, Mum!' says Archie.

Jonty's eyes scan the letter, and then his head shoots up and so does his fist. He pumps at the air and throws the letter at Estella. She flinches and catches it against her decolletage.

'I'm in, Mother dearest!' he says. 'Boo-yah!'

He begins to do the Floss wildly.

'Oh darling!' Estella lets out a whoop and thrusts the letter at Conrad.

'Well done, dickface,' says Felicity. 'Good effort.'

'Good lad.' Conrad grins and ruffles Jonty's hair. 'Good lad! Now I suppose I'd better empty the piggy bank to pay the three grand it costs to secure your place. Let's hope Archie doesn't get in after this, eh, or it'll be baked beans on toast tonight and until you're both eighteen.'

Estella considers the bottle of vintage Dom Perignon she put in the fridge this morning. She's absolutely gagging for a glass.

'Three grand each?' gasps Flick. 'Holy shit. Mum could get a facelift for that. Surely *that's* more of a priority? I mean, those marionette lines are so *extra*!'

'Thank you, *Felicity*,' Estella says with a broad grin, because Jonty has a spot at Iggy's and she is ecstatic and does not give a flying fig about her labial folds. *One down, one to go!*

They all turn to Archie, who is sitting upright on the sofa.

'Arch?' Flick curls up on the floor beside her brother's knee.

Archie grabs the envelope and uses the ivory letter opener to slice it neatly open. He reads the words but his expression gives nothing away. Then he folds it up and places it back in the envelope, turning it to face Estella and Conrad.

'It isn't mine,' he says.

Conrad squints to look at it and holds out a hand. He scans the letter.

'No, it's not,' says Conrad.

Estella is awash with confusion. She grabs the envelope. 'What do you mean it's not yours?'

Archie shrugs. 'That's not my name on the front of the envelope, or inside,' he says as Estella looks at the black printed address label for herself. 'It's addressed to the parents of Ollie Sterling, number eight Ocean View Drive. They've delivered it to the wrong address.'

Estella feels a hot wave of uncontrollable rage.

'That useless fucking postman!' she screams.

39

Kaya

Kaya pulls into the drive and sees Ollie in the front garden waiting for her. He waves. Ollie, her heart!

'Hey Mum,' he says, following her into the house. 'Where have you been?'

'I just popped into Pacific Pines to get a coffee,' Kaya lies. She feels her hands trembling, the aftershock of her angry confrontation with Ursula. 'How was the walk?'

'Good. Did the post come?'

Kaya looks away. 'Yes,' she says. 'It did.'

Ollie's eyes widen and he takes a step forward. 'Did you open it?'

'Of course not!' It scares Kaya how easy it is to lie to Ollie.

'Come on, Mum,' he cries. 'Let's open it!'

Kaya gets up to open the kitchen drawer. She pauses. 'Ollie,' she says. 'Whatever this letter says, you do know it will all be OK, don't you? We will be fine, just you and me? If you don't get in, we'll try again next year, all right? There may be boys who drop out and spaces will become available . . .'

Ollie looks at her quizzically. 'I know,' he says.

Kaya takes out the envelope with a sunken heart. How *dare* that woman do this to him?

Ollie opens it and sits at the table, his head in his hands.

'Oh, my darling,' she says and she feels the pain of it, his disappointment. 'I'm so sorry.'

She could cry for him. The pain, the anger, the sorrow.

There is a loud rasp at the door. Kaya ruffles Ollie's hair and heads along the hallway.

It is Estella. Estella with the colour drained from her skin and with wild eyes. *Uh oh*, she thinks. *Estella got the same letter as Ollie. One of the twins, or perhaps both of them, didn't get in.*

Estella barges past Kaya and through into the kitchen. 'Did you get a letter?' she demands. 'From Iggy's?'

Kaya nods. 'Now is not the time . . .'

'Show it to me!'

'Estella, no!'

'We got each other's letters! The boys did!'

'I don't understand . . .'

'I have yours, and you have mine!' Estella shrieks. She waves an envelope in the air like she's possessed. 'That bloody useless postman mixed them up. I have Ollie's and you have Archie's!'

She thrusts the envelope into Kaya's hand and Kaya stares at the printed addressee on the front. She hadn't thought to look at the name on the envelope! An overwhelming sense of nausea takes up residence in her stomach. She opens up the letter and begins to read:

Dear Mrs Sterling

I am delighted to inform you that Ollie's application for a place at St Ignatius' Boys' Grammar has been successful. We were thoroughly impressed by his performance at Gala Day and as such believe he would be a perfect fit for St Ignatius' Boys' Grammar.

*If you would like to accept this placement, please pay
the sum of $3000 by Friday April 30. Details of our
payment portal are attached to this letter.*

*We wish to welcome you to St Ignatius' Boys' Gram-
mar and wish your son Ollie a happy and fruitful
education at St Ignatius' Boys' Grammar.*

Yours Sincerely
Ursula Deacon
Principal

She stares at the letter, open-mouthed, the implications
of her ugly showdown with Ursula Deacon beginning to
take shape like a dark cloud. She hands the letter to Ollie
in a trance. He only reads the word 'delighted' and begins
to cry.

'I did it, Mum!' he laughs.

'Well?' says Estella, clicking her fingers repeatedly.
'Don't keep me waiting. Where is Archie's?'

Kaya feels a pang of dread. She holds out the envelope
and Estella grabs it, unfolding it with a manicured index
finger. She scans the words, row upon row of black print
that Kaya already knows intimately having now read them
twice, and lets the paper flutter to the floor. Kaya bends and
picks it up,

Dear Prospective Parent, it reads, as Kaya already
knows it does. *I regret to inform you that on this
occasion your son's application for St Ignatius' Boys'
Grammar has been unsuccessful.*

Kaya looks at Ollie, and Ollie looks at Kaya, and it is only once Estella has fled through the front door and they hear their gate slam shut with the fury of a snubbed woman that they fall into one another's arms. Kaya closes her eyes as she holds her boy, drinks in his smell. It is the smell of a birth, a childhood, a lost husband and a lost father. It is home, this smell, this boy. Kaya has never known a love like it and she never will.

Ollie pulls away. 'What will happen now?' he asks.

'Now,' says Kaya, 'we start prepping you to start at Iggy's in twelve weeks.'

Ollie grins. 'I can't believe the postman mixed them up.'

'I know.'

Ollie looks up to the kitchen ceiling. 'Thank you, Jesus!' he says, and Kaya feels a little awkward.

'You know what?' she says.

'What?'

'Your dad would be so proud of you.'

'Thanks, Mum.'

'You can have an hour of Fortnite to celebrate if you like, and then we'll get pizza.'

'Yesss!' Ollie grins and runs upstairs.

Kaya sits down on the sofa, her head in her hands. She thinks of Ursula Deacon and the exchange they just had in the tiny cottage, how Ursula had looked and sounded unhinged, like a woman on the edge. How Ursula had told Kaya she would regret her actions. Why on earth hadn't the principal told her she was mistaken and that the school *had* offered Ollie a place? Did Ursula in fact say it and Kaya just hadn't listened? Kaya leans over the sink and takes a deep breath. She hopes she will be able to laugh about it by the time Ollie starts at Iggy's. It wasn't her finest moment, to challenge a sickly woman – the school principal no less – but Ursula had seemed so *confrontational*.

'It's OK,' she tells herself as she leans against the ceramic sink. 'It will all be OK.'

She sits down at the kitchen table, picks up her phone and scrolls for a moment, then opens up her emails and does what she always does, works from the bottom of the list, up. She deletes a bit of spam (*This German doctor will show you how you can stay UP all night*), opens a couple of messages from the old crew back in Perth, a round-robin from a bookshop offering a three-for-two deal. Then she sees it, an email from Iggy's. The subject is: *In God's Hands*.

Kaya scans the words:

Dear Parents & Friends of St Ignatius' Boys' Grammar,
Few of you know that I am dying of cancer, and I have decided to take my fate into my own hands before my right to choose is taken from me. By the time this email is delivered, I will have ended my life and I would like it to be known that this was my choice. I would also like it to be known that I was the one responsible for the terrible accident on the School Run three days ago. I can no longer live with myself knowing Felix Weaver is critical and may not live a normal life again. My heart is with his mother Martha, and may she, and God Almighty, forgive me for what I have done.
May God bless you all.
Ursula Deacon

Kaya blinks twice and skim-reads the email once more
before placing her phone down on the table and staring,
open-mouthed, ahead. The first thought that goes through
her mind is that she cannot quite believe Ursula Deacon
is dead, that she is gone from this world and will never see
another day. The second is not altogether altruistic: *I was
only with her an hour ago,* she thinks. *I might have been the
last person to see her alive. What if people think I pushed her
to it?*

40

Bec

'She wrote *what*?' Bec's neck twists round violently and she feels the hot spasm of a pulled muscle. 'Show me!'

She has not yet checked her emails today, not with all the results excitement. It's ironic that she checks her inbox every single morning without fail just in case there's a cake order, and then today, when there is major news afoot, she has neglected to do it.

She snatches the phone from Kaya, who loiters at the fence in running gear, and scans the words. '"I have decided to take my fate into my own hands",' she reads. 'Holy shit!'

Bec feels the strange impulse to laugh at what she has just read, a giggle at a funeral, but she holds it back.

'Can you believe it?' Kaya asks Bec. 'That she confessed to hitting Felix Weaver? I hope you don't mind me coming over but I had to talk to someone about it. It's pretty shocking.'

'I don't know what's *more* shocking,' says Bec. 'The fact Ursula Deacon killed herself or the fact she hit Felix. The whole thing is just bizarre.'

'And to write an email to the entire school database,' says Kaya. 'I don't understand it. I wonder how she did it?'

'On her phone, I presume . . .'

'No, I mean . . .' Kaya's voice lowers to a whisper. 'How she *killed* herself. I don't want to be gory, but there are so many possibilities. I'm kind of curious to know.'

'I don't really want to think about it.' Bec grimaces. 'I wonder why she confessed to hitting him? There are no cameras on that bend. It's not like she would have been found out.'

'I suppose lying wasn't her thing. You know, being a woman of God.'

Bec sighs. 'You're shivering. Come in for a cup of tea.'

Kaya follows Bec inside. 'Thank you, I'd like that.'

'Gosh,' says Bec. 'I didn't even ask! Did Ollie get his letter?'

Kaya smiles and sits down at the kitchen bench. 'He did! I'm assuming from the party streamers that Cooper got an offer, too?'

Bec nods. 'We're so proud,' she says and then she remembers about Ursula. 'But I feel terrible being happy about it now that this awful news has come through.'

They are both silent for a moment.

'Imagine being that unhappy . . .'

'She was dying anyway,' says Kaya. 'I suppose it was a way of taking control of her own destiny. I don't think it's an altogether negative thing, for her to have been the master of her own fate, even if it's against her religion.'

Bec nods. 'Well, I suppose when you put it like that . . .'

Kaya looks over her shoulder towards the staircase. 'Where are Tom and the kids?'

'Willow's working today at Pine Street Café – she got the job she went for on Thursday and they asked her to start straight away. It's a good distraction for her what with the car and everything. The police called this morning. They found the Holden at the bottom of Dahlia Point.'

'Like the others?'

'Uh-huh.' Bec pours boiling water into two mugs. 'Excuse me not making a pot.'

'You don't need to stand on ceremony for me.'

'So what else did the police say?'

'Not a lot. Just that it looks like it's the same kids who've been stealing Holdens for parts. The front and back light casings were missing, along with the hubcaps, which would make perfect sense. They reckon the same kids are coming in from Lawton or Shivers Beach or somewhere just to cause trouble.'

'Shivers Beach? That's miles away.'

'I suppose it could be anywhere. The police just think it's out-of-towners.'

'Shouldn't you push them to investigate some more?'

Bec looks up. 'What's the point? The car's a write-off. As long as the insurance pays out, it doesn't really bother me who did it. It's terrible, isn't it? Still, Willow doesn't seem to mind. She's hoping to get a new car with the insurance money. Milk?'

'Just a dash, thanks.'

'Anyway, to answer your original question, Tom's taken Cooper and Sage to the organic markets to get some ingredients for dinner. We're having a celebratory dinner for Cooper here at home. I would invite you and Ollie to join us, but I must be mindful of Estella at the moment. I don't think she'll be in the mood for celebrating given Archie didn't get a place.'

'You heard from her?'

'Conrad called Tom after the letters were delivered. I'm going to let Estella have a couple of hours to digest it all and then I'll pop over to see her. She'll be fine, I'm sure.'

'Will she? From what I can see, Iggy's is all she really wanted for the boys.'

'No,' says Bec. 'Finding Sam is all she ever really wanted – anything else is just smoke and mirrors. Estella will be fine.'

'What about Archie?'

'Archie is so smart he will thrive wherever he goes. Besides, can you really picture him at a sporting high school? The poor kid – the pressure would have been enormous if he'd got a place at Iggy's.'

'I suppose,' says Kaya. She sets down her mug. 'Anyway, I'd better get back to Ollie. I told him we'd go for a celebratory cycle ride and then get ice cream. Thanks for the tea and the chat.'

'It's a pleasure, any time!'

When Kaya has gone, Bec decides to give half of Cooper's celebratory cupcakes to Estella – with a less cheery buttercream, of course. She opts for red, which could denote sympathy or celebration. This is Bec's love language, a kind thing to do for a friend, but also her time to think, her meditation. Her time to mull and muse. She switches on the food processor and listens to the hum as the eggs meet the sugar and the butter inside the bowl. Watches as the egg is obliterated and consumed by the folds of the sugary mixture. She picks up the bottle of red food dye and empties five drops into the bowl and observes as the contents of the bowl turn blood-red.

She thinks of Felix, the sticky blood at his head, like maple syrup.

There is a car, Willow's Holden Captiva, at the bottom of a cliff collecting rust.

'Shouldn't you push to investigate some more?' Kaya had said.

There is red food dye on Bec's hands, now, like blood. She will have to scrub hard to get it off: this blood on her hands. Willow had seen it there, on her shirt, when she came home from the scene of the accident on Gala Day.

Bec returns from the scene of the accident, tearily embraces Tom and then goes upstairs to change out of the silk blouse that is stained with food dye. She hears it as she walks past Willow's door, the gentle sound of sobbing.

'Willow?' She knocks gently. 'Darling?'

She does not wait for a reply, but opens the door a crack. Willow turns, her face red and her eyes swollen. 'Mum? Your shirt!'

'Food dye,' says Bec, shrugging. 'I'm not hurt.'

Willow nods, stares into her lap.

'Why are you crying?' she asks. 'What's wrong?' But Bec already knows the answer because of what she has in her back pocket. She fingers it there, before pulling it out – the oval corner of a car light. It is a small, sharp triangular shard of clear plastic, and on the side of it is half a sticker, a sticker that says YOLO, in neon pink. Bec had recognised it as soon as she'd seen it sticking out of Felix Weaver's pelvis, the pink sticker Willow got somewhere in Europe on holiday the month she started learning to drive. *YOLO:You Only Live Once.* A sliver of prismed plastic standing like a tombstone in the mulch of Felix's flesh. She had acted on instinct as she pulled it out fast and put her hand over the wound, treacly blood oozing from the cut and spilling between her fingers.

Before she'd gone inside the house, Bec had gone straight to the car. Willow had driven in front-first instead of reversing in as she usually did, and Bec had been forced to creep along the side of the house to get to the front of the car. She had turned on her phone torch as she held up the plastic to what remained of the front light, knowing even before she did it that they would fit together like the two halves of a locket.

Bec holds it out to Willow as she sits beside her on the bed.

Willow begins to sob again. 'I didn't mean . . . I was just so . . . angry,' she cries.

'Angry?' Bec's heart thunders. 'Are you saying you did this on purpose? Oh my God, Willow. No! Why?'

'He threatened me. And he said that you . . .'

'What did he say? Willow?' Bec takes a deep breath. 'Start from the beginning.'

Willow nods. 'It was after you saw me with Sam in the gym. I was on my way to the cricket pavilion to talk to him about it. I know I said I was going to the cinema but I needed to talk to Sam. But then when I was on my way over there, I saw Dad going to confront Sam, so I waited a while. I saw Sam leave the pavilion and walk towards the car park and I was just about to run after him when I felt my phone ring in my pocket and it was Felix. He was walking home along the School Run and he was mad as hell. He said he was going to send me some photos of Flick and that once I'd had a good look he'd send them round the whole school if I didn't go and meet him in Pacific Pines.

'I said I didn't want to meet him. I said, "I've got a boy-friend and you're dating Flick," and he said, "You're such a fucking tease, Willow Lloyd," and I was like, "What? When did I ever lead you on?"

'He said I'd been making eyes at him when he was with Flick and that I'd been looking at him all through Gala Day, so I told him I'd been looking at Sam standing next to him and that we were together. Mum, he lost his shit!'

'Go on.'

'He told me I was a slut and that he was going to make me pay. And then he said to me, "Your mother's a slut too and I can prove it. I've got something on your family that's so big it will blow your mind." Then he said, "Watch your email, Willow, and wait for your pretty little life to implode."

'I asked him what it was and he said, "Your sister's not your full sister. Ask your mum."'

Bec feels her face flush red. *He said what?*

'I was so angry, Mum. I got in the car and I sat there for ages and then I went after him. He was on the bend when I saw him. I don't know why I did it, but I pressed my foot on the accelerator. Before I knew it I'd hit him. Mum, I panicked. I didn't know what to do so I drove home. You know you said you'd do anything to protect me? Well, it goes both ways.'

She begins to sob, proper heaving sobs. Sobs that denote sorrow, regret, fear.

'Oh Willow!' Bec wraps her in her arms, rocks her gently.

'It wasn't . . .' Willow begins. 'It was a lie, wasn't it? What Felix said.'

Bec must think carefully. Would confessing the truth merely be a measure to appease her own conscience?

'Willow,' says Bec. 'Look at your baby sister. She is Daddy's girl through and through, isn't she?'

It is not a lie. Sage is Tom's girl. Perhaps it might be classified as a white lie, lying via omission, but it is the kindest cut. Why should Willow know anything more than this: Tom is Sage's beloved daddy and he always will be.

Willow sniffs, wipes her nose on the back of her hand. 'What am I going to do?' she asks. Her voice has lost its confidence, it is the voice of a child.

Bec pulls Willow in close, her brain ticking over furiously. 'It's OK,' she says, even though she does not know this, not at all. 'It's all going to be OK.'

Bec sets her alarm for one in the morning and creeps out of the house. She is not worried about the children waking up because her kids sleep like the dead. She jumps inside Willow's car and she turns on the engine, reversing slowly. She drives to the vacant lot on the cliff edge at Oakland Drive, where a house will soon be built and a fence erected to safeguard the owners from the deadly perils of the rocks below. The locals have been up in arms about safety after some kids were caught playing perilously close to the sheer drop, but Pacific Pines Council, luckily for Bec, is yet to react. It is usually the case that something will be done *after* an accident, and not before. Could what Bec is about do to be the catalyst?

Bec steers the car carefully across the empty rectangle of soft earth to the cliff edge and climbs out of the driver's door. Brake off, she stands with her arms out in front of her, ready to push with all her might, and as her hands hover on the back bumper she does not give a second thought to what she is about to do. All that matters – all that has ever mattered to Bec – is Cooper, Willow and Sage. There is nothing she would not do for any single one of them, no mistake she would not try to fix.

When she wakes up the next morning she is blissfully unaware for a cool few seconds until the memory hits her like a hot flush. She jumps up and runs to the bathroom and vomits, while Tom tries to soothe her from the bedroom.

'Bec?' he calls to her. 'Are you OK in there?'

'I'm . . . fine,' she replies.

'Well, I'm just on the other side of the door if you need me.'

She makes breakfast on autopilot, prepares to send Willow off to her job interview at the café with no advice except these words whispered in solidarity in her daughter's ear: 'Forget about it. *It never happened.* Do you hear me, Willow?' and preps Cooper for school. Then Sage announces from the front garden, like the town crier: 'Willow's car is GONE!' and Bec feigns shock and confusion. *She* feigns it, but so does Tom, and he does it very well. Because after all, it was Tom's strong hands that ultimately pushed Willow's faithful Holden Captiva over the edge of the cliff at the vacant lot at Oakland Drive in

the dead of night. It was Tom's hands – hands that cradled all three of their babies right after birth, hands that
play her own body like a violin – that sent the car into the
black ocean abyss below along with Bec's deepest secret,
securing its destiny as just another stolen car and not the
very vehicle that smashed Felix Weaver to smithereens.

SUNDAY

41

Estella

Estella and Flick sit on the stone bench at the end of the garden in silence.

'What do you want to talk to me about? Am I about to get another bollocking for something? Did I borrow Jonty's pencil sharpener without asking?'

'Felicity . . .' Estella's tone is soft.

Felicity sits up, unused to the smooth edge to Estella's voice. 'What's wrong? Is someone dying?'

'No!'

'What then?' She sits up straight.

Estella rummages in her pocket and pulls out a spliff. She holds it between her thumb and forefinger and looks at Felicity.

Felicity's face drains of colour. 'Oh shit, Mum. It's not mine, I promise! I mean, it *is* technically mine but I haven't smoked it.'

'Well evidently,' Estella sighs. 'Because it's only just rolled. Anyway, I'm not here to lecture you about smoking weed. I was going to ask if I could light it.'

Felicity gives her a sideways glance. 'Is this a trick? Are you going to ground me if I say yes?'

'No! I am inviting you to smoke it with me. You know, "Pass the dutchie on the left-hand side," and all that.'

'Pass the . . . *dutchie*? What the fuck, Mum? Are you OK?'

'I'm perfectly fine. Are you going to join me, or have you suddenly developed a conscience?'

Felicity shrugs. 'If I smoke it with you, it doesn't mean I'm admitting I've smoked one before,' she says. 'This is totally my first time, OK?'

'Of course it is,' Estella says.

Felicity tilts her head to the side like a confused dog. 'What's happening here, Estella? Have you been secretly taking night classes in woke parenting? Or have you simply taken a few lessons from Bec? I thought your stance on drugs was "Just say no!"'

'Oh, do stop being such a smart arse, Felicity! I want to tell you something important. It's something you really need to know, and it will come as a shock.'

She takes out a lighter and holds the flame to the twisted end of the joint, and then she takes a deep drag. Felicity watches her, impressed, and Estella notes a slight look of fear, too. As if Felicity is thinking, 'Where is my mother, and who is this imposter?' But it is about time Estella gives her daughter some credit. It is about time she started behaving like a parent.

'There was a child when I was a little younger than you,' says Estella. She hands the spliff to Felicity, who takes it wordlessly and puts it to her own lips. 'A baby that I had to give up.'

Felicity is confused. 'What do you mean?'

Estella's mouth is dry. She does not know how Felicity will take the news, but she has to let her know, it is time.

It has been time for a while, but there was never the right moment in between the arguing and in between . . . life.

'I got pregnant when I was sixteen,' she says. 'By a boy I loved very much, and my mother, your grandmother, forced me to give the baby up for adoption.' She looks out to sea. 'I didn't realise I was pregnant for fourteen weeks, although looking back, the signs were there. I was tired. I was hungry but also completely off my food. I was nauseous first thing in the morning but fine by eleven o'clock. Then my mother found out. We wanted to get married, but . . .'

'I don't understand.' Estella hears the catch in Felicity's voice. 'Is this a joke?'

'No, Felicity. It isn't a joke. I'd gone on the Pill, you see. I didn't need my mother's consent to get it after I was sixteen, and I'd taken it religiously, so I didn't think a baby was possible. But it turns out it was.'

Estella is sixteen. There are sanitary products on the end of her bed – a box of thick towels. All the other girls at school use Tampax tampons with cardboard applicators, but Estella is not allowed those ones, because her mum says they are filthy. *Inserting something inside yourself? Disgusting!* She doesn't want Estella inserting anything inside her until she's a suitable age. But little does she know that Estella has had something inside her, or rather someone she loves with the whole of her heart.

It is a week later when she comes home from school that she knows something is wrong. Her mother sits on the sofa and watches her as she hops in through the front door after a long day at Asher's.

'Hi Mama,' Estella says, placing her schoolbag neatly beside the piano.

Her mother does not answer.

'Mama?'

Her mother stands up, grabs something from the coffee table on her left and hurls it across the room. The packet of Libra pads hits Estella in the belly and she bends down and picks them up. 'What's wrong . . .'

Her mother flies at her, rips up her school jumper and the blouse underneath it, studies Estella's belly and breasts.

'How could you?' she snarls. 'How could you? This will kill your father, kill him!'

Estella ducks as her mother lifts her hand to swipe her, catching her awkwardly on the back of the head.

'We're going to get this sorted,' her mother says and later, Estella will recall that all the way to the doctor's in the car, her hand was on her own belly, protecting the growing baby inside.'

'Oh, Mum!' Estella feels the warmth of Felicity's hand on hers, but she doesn't dare look at her daughter's face. *Don't crumble*, she tells herself. *Don't give in to it. You are the parent and she is the child! You are the strong one. Lead by example!* She takes another deep drag on the spliff.

'What happened next?' Felicity asks.

'They sent me away. As you know my parents were very religious and the idea of abortion abhorred them, although my mother had double standards. I'd seen a contraceptive packet stuck with Blu Tack to the top of the bathroom cabinet. She hated being a mother. But abortion was too much, a step *too* far, and I was, at least, relieved about that. The deal was that I was to hide my pregnancy under my school uniform until January and then I was sent on a "summer camp" to Aunt Fiona's in Noosa Heads where I had the baby.'

'Aunt Fiona's?'

'Yes, your great-aunt. Your grandmother's sister. That's where I had the baby. Fiona was wonderful – she was a true Catholic, kind and understanding. A real Christian. She tried to persuade my mother to let me keep my baby. She even said she would bring it up in Noosa, keep him in the family, but my mother wouldn't have it. She wanted a clean slate so it couldn't bring shame on the Wickham family.'

'Him?'

'Yes. I had a little boy.'

Felicity's eyes fill and Estella swallows against the ache in her throat. 'What happened when you got back to Pacific Pines?'

'When I got home, the baby's father, JP, had gone. His family had moved away, left the area, with no forwarding address. Life carried on as normal for everyone else but me. I felt like I'd lost two people I loved.'

'Oh, Mum!' A single tear runs down Felicity's cheek, leaving a streak of black. 'I had no idea you went through this. No wonder you—' She stops. 'I mean, no wonder you sometimes get a little . . .'

'So now you know. You have no idea how like me you are, Felicity, how similar you are to the way I was as a teenager,' Estella says. 'That's exactly why we clash. I see my myself in you and I want to better you. And when

I say that, I mean I want to better myself. I want you to make wiser decisions as a young woman than I did. Not that I'll ever regret having my son, because how could I?'

'But you're so hard on me! That's why I push back, Mum. That's why I'm so rude and hateful. It's because I resent it so much. I just want you to go easy on me.'

'This is precisely *why* I'm hard on you, Felicity, don't you see that? Because you're *too* good. Too good for a little prick like Felix Weaver, too good to feel you have to play second fiddle to Willow Lloyd. Too damn good to mess it all up like I did when I was your age. I'm not going to accept that for you. Not for my baby girl.'

Felicity takes a deep drag on the spliff. 'Why are you telling me this now?'

She looks at Felicity, really looks at her. 'Because I've found him, Felicity. I've found the boy I was forced to give away.'

'Found him?'

'Yes. Daddy helped me track him down.'

'Dad knows?'

'Your father has always known, from the very beginning.'

'And he kept it secret all this time? You both did?'

Estella nods and takes the spliff. 'It was hardly dinner-table conversation, was it? We decided we would only tell you if we found him.'

'So where is he?'

'He's closer to home than I ever thought possible.'

'What do you mean? How close?'

'Oh God, I just have to spit it out . . .' Estella lets out a deep exhale. 'Felicity, you know him. It's Sam Deacon. Sam Deacon is the son I gave up, your half-brother.'

Felicity's face contorts in confusion. 'As in Sam Deacon from Iggy's? The *teacher* Sam Deacon?'

'Yes.'

Estella watches the expressions that flash across Felicity's face like on a cine-screen, one after the other: the confused furrowing of the brow, the twitch of the right eyelid, the turn-up of the top lip in . . . a smile? *Yes, it is a smile.* Estella watches as the grin spreads across Felicity's face and is followed by single burst of laughter.

'Felicity?'

'Oh my God,' she says, trying to catch a breath. 'It's just so messed up. It's so messed up, it's funny. Sam *the sports master* Deacon?'

And for some reason, quite possibly the large spliff they have almost finished smoking, Estella joins in, and they sit on the bench and laugh until there are rivers of mascara streaming down both their cheeks. And when they came up for air, and her smile finally drops to absolute seriousness, Felicity says, 'He looks like Archie.'

'Not Jonty too?'

'No,' says Flick, who can tell the twins apart even better than Estella can. 'Just Archie.'

Estella nods.

'Does he know about us?'

'He does.'

'Does he want to meet us? You know, like properly?'

Estella smiles. 'He does.'

'Is that . . . Is that why Ursula Deacon did what she did? You know, killed herself. Because he'd found you?'

'Good Lord, Felicity, no! She was a very sick woman. Daddy was treating her, and she was very close to death anyway. I think she couldn't live with herself for hitting Felix in the car. I think she couldn't live with the guilt.'

'That's so sad,' says Flick.

'We will need to be there for him, for Sam, while he gets over it. Will you be all right if he joins us for some dinners, perhaps? I will need to tell the boys all of this, of course.'

'Why did you tell me first?'

'Because I owe it to you, darling, and because above all, you are my friend as well as my daughter.'

Felicity sniffs and nods, stubs out the spliff under the heel of her trainer.

'Mum?'

'Yes?'

'I'm sorry. You know, about the arguing and stuff. I mean some of the things I've said. I mean, well, you look pretty hot for forty-four.'

Estella's eyebrow arches. 'Forty-two thank you very much, Felicity. And I'm sorry too. I know I am hard on you, but contrary to what you believe, I do love you very much,' she says. 'Everything I do is an attempt, in whatever way it manifests itself, to prevent you making some giant fuck-off mistake in life, like I did. Do you see that, Felicity?'

'It's Flick.' Flick drops her head onto Estella's shoulder, and Estella rests hers lightly on top of her daughter's in a motion that feels as natural to them both as breathing. 'And I love you too.'

A YEAR LATER

WEDNESDAY

42

Bec

Bec stands over a wire rack on which fifty mini lemon meringue tarts are lined up in rows of ten. She'd set the alarm on her phone and switched off the oven at five o'clock in the morning, and now, at eight o'clock, she has only just taken them out. Bec knows full well that meringues should not be removed from the heat too abruptly, but rather allowed to cool in time with the oven, otherwise they will be covered in unsightly cracks, and she cannot have that. She has a reputation to uphold.

Sometimes (and she knows this is strange), she feels like she sees Ursula Deacon's face in the strangest of places. A few weeks ago it was on a painting that Sage had done of a tree of all things, and now, here it is on the surface of a single shiny meringue, a curve at the top like the curl of white hair that left a calligraphic C on Ursula's forehead, a double ridge like the thin, pursed lips of the late woman's mouth, two dips like the hollows of her cheeks.

Poor Ursula, so fearful for her son's future, for his reputation, that she had taken her own life, swapped it for his freedom, confessed to something that her son had not actually done. The email she had sent had been so poignant, so poetic. She sighs and wipes her hands on her apron. She will not be dragged into the mire of considering Willow's role in what happened to the tragic former principal. As far as she is concerned, much like the sperm donor, Willow's little misdemeanour will be filed to the annals of history, ancient history. She cannot dwell on the past, because then she might realise the implications of everything Willow did – hitting a boy and then leaving him for dead – things which are not in her daughter's character. No, Bec prefers to believe that Ursula was dying anyway, so she took the easy way out, although why the school principal admitted guilt for the hit-and-run still utterly flummoxes her.

'It's tragic really, isn't it?' she says to Tom. 'Ursula.'

'At least she got the acceptance letters out first,' Tom says with a shrug and Bec shoots him a good-humoured glare.

'I can't believe it's Gala Day again tomorrow. Life has changed so much, hasn't it?'

'You're not wrong. How about a bite?' Tom reaches towards a plate of her now-famous chocolate tortes, which are lined up beside the meringues.

'No.' She slaps his hand. 'They're for the parents!'

And it's the least she can do – after all, hadn't she promised Ursula Deacon she would be there for Iggy's for all of the school's cake needs? She will make good on that promise in light of what Ursula ultimately did for Willow, whether the old woman knew it or not. Tomorrow she and Cooper will deliver the goodies ahead of Gala Day and Bec knows she will look with pity upon the harried parents who are desperate to get their boys a place at Iggy's for the coming year. She will remember how she felt, that sense of longing, of desperation.

'What's this one for?' Tom nods his head towards a chocolate sponge on the kitchen bench. 'Ollie. I'm making something for his birthday party.'

'I thought you were having a clampdown on making free cakes?'

'Yes, but it's *Ollie* . . .' she says, aware she is a complete pushover where her friends and their offspring are concerned.

Sage wanders into the kitchen, her hair ruffled and her eyes sleepy.

'Looking forward to school today, kiddo?' Tom asks.

'Nah,' says Sage. 'Kindy is boring!'

Bec knows that come seven thirty in the evening, just as she's being tucked in, Sage will want to talk about nothing but school and how much she loves it, despite closing off the subject for the entire day. It is always the way, a child's way, a kind of fight against sleep.

Having Sage at school has been bittersweet. Bitter because she misses her little buddy, but sweet because it has freed up her time to bake – and to focus on her new friendships with Kaya and Martha Weaver.

Shortly after the incident with Felix, Bec had offered to stop by and help Martha, because as it happened, when Felix woke up two weeks after Gala Day, he could only speak in Latin. Bec had provided her services as a translator, helping him converse with his mother ('"*Ego sum famelicus,*" you say, Felix? That literally translates as "I'm famished," Martha. Have you got a snack for him?'). She'd done it out of guilt to start with, because she felt so bad about what Willow had done and how she had covered it up, but as it happened, everything seemed to work out for the best.

Martha and Bec have become good friends and Bec is grateful for it. They catch up at least once a week and Bec always asks about Felix, who is out of hospital and living at home – his place at Cambridge deferred until next year – to find out if he has remembered anything of the accident and the weeks leading up to it. At this stage he only remembers his life a month beforehand and, for obvious reasons, this is absolutely fine with Bec. It means her secret is still safe.

Tom looks at her now, and she smiles back. He winks, she blushes. Nothing has changed. Nothing will. He is hers and she is his. They do not, and never will, talk about the secret they are aware they both know. The fact is, Bec knows full well why Tom didn't want to try for a baby. It was because he couldn't make one any more, it was impossible. And it was impossible because Tom had gone for a vasectomy shortly after Cooper was born and he'd kept it from her. Bec had found out when the clinic called the landline (stupid, stupid Tom!) and asked her if her husband could return Dr Gary Backman's call regarding his recent procedure. *Procedure? She hadn't known he was having a procedure!* It only took a quick internet search to realise what procedures Dr Backman specialised in! And she had brooded and cried and felt so cheated, until she realised that if she kept it to herself, if she kept it hidden away in her back pocket, she might be able to use it to her advantage.

Tom will never tell her he had a secret vasectomy before Sage was born, and she will never admit that she used donor sperm to make their baby girl. Here's the thing: Tom was meant to return to the clinic after the procedure to have his sperm tested, to check he was firing blanks so to speak, but he never did it and Bec knows this because Bec saw the specimen pot with the pathology request form buried deep in the same bin in which she had buried her positive pregnancy test. Bec would never cheat on Tom, and Tom knows this – and so as far as he is concerned, Sage is his, and any cursing of Dr Backman he may have done at the time would have been immediately regretted once he held Sage. Nobody who sees the two of them together could fail to see their bond, their likeness.

Perhaps one day when they are sitting in their large embroidered chairs in their retirement home, holding one another's veiny hands, Bec and Tom may talk about what they both did, but there is no point now. They are better than ever and Bec, of course, pretends she is on the Pill.

Bec's mobile phone rings now and Sage snatches it up. 'It's Willow,' she cries and presses the green button. 'Willow!'

'Sagey!' Bec hears Willow's tinny voice reply.

'Put it on speaker', says Bec. She waits for Willow to press the button. 'Hello, darling!'

'Hi guys,' Willow says. 'What's up?'

'Well, Daddy's drinking coffee before work, Cooper's in the shower, Sagey's eating breakfast and I'm baking for Gala Day tomorrow!'

There is silence on the end of the line and Bec knows what Willow is thinking. It is what she is thinking too – how Gala Day ended up last year, what almost happened. The reprieve mother and daughter were awarded when they found out Felix would live.

'So,' chirps Bec. 'To what do we owe the pleasure?'

'I wondered if you guys are around this weekend? At home, I mean?'

'Of course we are!'

'Great, well I thought I'd leave campus for the weekend and come home to Pines. And I wondered if I could bring someone with me?'

'Who?' Bec feels a flush of excitement. She glances at Tom and grins. Willow hasn't mentioned a boyfriend since she broke up with Sam, and that had been back around the time Cooper was accepted into Iggy's. The breakup had been Willow's call as it happened – she knew the relationship couldn't go anywhere once she was at university, and there had been all this talk of Sam moving to London. It had been a hard time for her, but she'd been so mature in her decision-making and she'd thrown herself wholeheartedly into university life without so much as a glance back.

'His name is Stefan.'

'Stefan!' coos Bec. 'Lovely!'

'He's not your professor, is he?' Tom asks.

Willow laughs. 'No, Dad. Don't be ridiculous! He's in my halls of residence. He's studying engineering. He is super-clever and he's German.'

'Ahh, *wunderbar*,' says Tom.

'Willow's got a *boyfriend*,' giggles Sage.

'We would love to meet him,' says Bec. 'Come on, tell us! What's he like?'

Willow pauses for a moment and Bec can hear the smile in her voice. 'He's a hot and incredibly sweet apple strudel.'

43

Estella

'Which box do you want brought down, exactly?'

Conrad is in the attic and Estella stands at the top of the ladder with her head poking through the hole. 'The plastic tub with the blue lid,' she says. 'At the back.'

She watches Conrad lift boxes and stack them on top of others. 'Here we are,' he says. 'I've got it.'

'Wonderful.' She feels a flash of anticipation, the speeding of her pulse. Her hands are a little clammy.

He passes Estella the box and she hands it down to Archie.

'What's in here, anyway?' Archie asks.

'Memorabilia,' she says. 'Of your older brother's. I just felt like looking at it.'

'Cool.' He nods. 'Can I go now? I'm going to be late for school.'

'OK, Arch. Thank you. Have a great day.'

'See ya, guys,' he says over his shoulder.

'Archie?'

'Yes?'

'Can you remind Jonty to grab his water bottle?'

'Affirmative.'

Estella smiles as Archie heads off down the stairs. This year has been the making of him. A year ago, she'd been livid about him being denied a place at Iggy's. She'd raged about it and written to the board of governors, and she'd done it all because she feared for Archie, floundering in the dreaded state system. But then the *Good Schools Guide* had been published and she'd been surprised to see that Pacific Pines High School had achieved even better academic results than St Ignatius' Grammar! Estella had been forced to eat her hat! Of course Iggy's still led the pack for sport, but Pacific Pines High had produced some HSC results that were utterly outstanding; the ATAR scores were averaging in the early nineties.

Moreover, Archie had *wanted* to go to Pines High. 'The maths programme is out of this world, Mum,' he told her in his first week. 'It's all about academia and less about sport. Mum, I really love it.'

And Estella knows it is the right fit. Archie has already been selected for the Opportunity Class for gifted students and his first parents' evening a couple of months back was incredible. His teachers (all high-achieving graduates themselves) reported his natural talent and his amazing ability to address logical questions – he is top of the class in all of the sciences, too. And Estella has been pleasantly surprised to see that the other parents are a group of intelligent and interesting people. Dare she admit she had been something of a *snob* in the past?

'Christ, Conny,' she'd said on the way home from parents' evening. 'Why the bloody hell are we paying for Iggy's?'

And Conrad had joked, 'Because Jonty isn't smart enough for Pines High!'

But Jonty *is* trailblazing on the field. In a school that is all about sport, Estella is thrilled that he has already been tipped as team captain for the rugby First XV in Year Eight, and he was recently lauded in the school magazine as 'One to Watch'. The new sports master who was appointed when Sam moved back to London, Craig Miller, is brilliantly popular with the boys. Cooper, Ollie and Jonty all report how much of a laugh he is, how motivational on the sporting field.

So yes, Estella believes the whole Iggy's admission thing has worked out for the best, and she thanks Archie when they're alone for doing his brother's interview so well. She suspects, although she hasn't actually asked, that Archie may have bungled his own interview on purpose so he ended up in the right high school for him.

Estella holds the ladder and waits for Conrad to descend. At the bottom he turns and smiles. 'Right-o. Would you like me to leave you to it?'

Estella reaches up and touches his face. 'No,' she says. 'I'd love to show you these things if you have the time.'

'I don't have to be at the hospital until eleven today, my darling. I have plenty of time.'

Felicity appears from her bedroom, with bed-head. She looks a mess. It's reading week for her at university so she has come home, although she has done sod-all reading since she's been back.

'Is this Sam's baby stuff?' she asks.

Estella nods. 'Come and look,' she says. 'And then for pity's sake, brush your hair.'

Conrad picks up the box and carries it to the spare room. Estella lifts the lid. The first thing she sees is the blanket – a little blue-and-white-and-pink thing, hospital regulation. Estella smiles and pulls it out, putting the fabric instinctively to her cheek.

'Well,' she says. 'Exhibit One. This is what they wrapped him in.'

'It's tiny,' Flick coos.

'Babies are. This is why you don't want one until you're at least thirty.'

Flick rolls her eyes. 'Will you show it to him when he's back from London next?'

'That's why I'm getting it down. I'll show him at Easter.'

Felicity pulls out a cream-coloured rabbit. 'This is cute!'

'That was his little rabbit, but he only had it when he was in the hospital with me,' Estella says. 'They wouldn't let me pack it in his bag.'

Conrad takes it from her and smiles. 'Felicity had one like this . . .'

'I still have green rabbit,' she says. 'I took her to uni.'

'What did the boys have?'

'Blue rabbit,' say Estella and Flick in unison.

'Did you get us all the same rabbit because Sam had one?' Estella nods.

'You never told me that,' Conrad says.

'Too hard to say it,' she says.

She digs deeper into the box and brings out a tiny plastic wristband. 'Ahh look,' she says. 'It says "Baby Wickham" on it.' She puts her fingers to her lips.

Conrad pulls her in close. 'Are you all right?'

'I really am,' she says. 'Thanks to Sam. He might be fifteen thousand miles away, but I still have him, don't I?'

'You do.'

'It's funny,' she says. 'He just feels like one of my boys.'

'Yes.' Conrad smiles. 'He does.'

She rests her head on his shoulder. 'Thank you, Conny.'

'What for?'

'For being here for me. For understanding why I needed Iggy's so much. For wanting me to find Sam.'

'We're a team, darling, aren't we? I simply do not work without you.'

Estella looks up at him. 'I do *love* you, Conny,' she says.

'Eww, get a room, would you?' says Flick, and she retreats back into her bedroom and closes the door with a grin.

'Now what else do we have in here?' Conrad puts his hand in the box and pulls out some clothes, a couple of photos and . . . a mobile phone? 'I'm sure they weren't around when Sam was born, were they?'

It takes Estella a moment to realise who the phone belongs to, and then it hits her. The phone, damn it!

'Why are you housing strange phones in Sam's baby box?'

Estella sighs. 'It's Felix Weaver's phone. I stole it from the roadside because it had those foul photos of Felicity on it. I went to kick it off the cliffside but I changed my mind and put it in my pocket. I suppose I wanted to have something on Felix, to be able to prove he'd been threatening her if it ever came to it. You know, leverage.'

'Oh Estella,' he says. 'You should have told me.'

'I know,' she tells him. 'But I wasn't particularly proud of stealing a dying boy's phone.'

Conrad holds out his hand. 'Time to let it go. Give it to me.' He slips the perfectly preserved device in his pocket. 'I know exactly what to do with it.'

Estella looks him in the eye and realises he is going to do with it what she herself should have done on the night of the Gala Day.

'Does it involve a clifftop and an open car window?'

'You know me so well.'

44

Kaya

Kaya stands outside the gates at Iggy's and waits. Ollie usually gets the bus home, but today it is his birthday and so they're going for dinner at his favourite pizza restaurant in Pacific Pines.

Iggy's hasn't changed a jot since last year's Gala Day, except for the Principal's Cottage. The lavender planted in pots that flourished a year ago have lost their mint-green hue and sit, almost brown, under the window ledges. Elsie Dixon doesn't have Ursula's green-fingered touch, but she is an exceptional principal, everybody says it. Long may she reign.

Jonty flies through the gate first. He has grown like a weed, this boy!

'Hi Kaya!' he calls over his shoulder, his voice bearing the tell-tale squeak of puberty. 'I'll see you soon! I'm meeting Archie on the bus!' Kaya watches him fly down the street towards the bus stop. 'Bye!'

'Bye Jonty!' Kaya calls after him. She smiles to herself. Who'd have thought it? The Munro twins voluntarily hanging out together. Apparently they get on famously now they're at different schools. Estella often arrives on Kaya's doorstep with a bottle of wine to brag about Jonty's sporting achievements ('Have I told you he's in the first team for rugby *and* cricket?'), or Felicity's degree course ('She'll be a barrister, Kaya, you mark my words') or Archie who is 'top of maths, top of science. *Top, Kaya! Top!*' She never forgets to include Sam, who video-calls a couple of times a week from London where he's teaching at some posh private school. Westminster School, Kaya thinks Estella said.

Kaya looks ahead and sees Ollie crossing the quad at the far end of the school campus and she thinks how similar his posture is to Paul's. Tall and almost bent over at the top, as if trying to disguise his height. Perhaps it was just a genetic thing after all, because Ollie isn't ashamed of his height; he says it's what God gave him. And God's word is *everything* to Ollie. He recently told her he wanted to get confirmed, and Kaya seriously wouldn't be surprised if he asked to be ordained at some point in the future. Perhaps this is the price she must pay for pretending he was Catholic. At least, as Bec says, she won't have to worry about drugs or vaping or whatever it is teenagers get up to these days, because her boy is a serious man of the cloth.

'Mum!' He throws himself into Kaya's arms. She breathes in the smell of his hair – there is nothing like it, nothing like the scalpy scent of her boy, the very presence of his head resting on her shoulder. This human being right here is who she would die for, who she would *kill* for. She stares over Ollie's shoulder as she holds him and she is back there, at Iggy's on that day in October last year.

The day she killed for him.

'Leave now, or I'll call the police.' Ursula Deacon had been angry, her previous politeness turned sour. She regarded

Kaya through narrow eyes, a quiver of her top lip. Kaya
had caught a glimpse of it then, the paraphernalia in the
bedroom behind Ursula's shrunken figure in the doorway
– the lit candles with their flickering orange flames sending
black twirls of smoke upwards, the leather-bound Bible
and the open bottle of liquid morphine. An almost imposing brown glass bottle, just like the one that had stayed on
Paul's bedside in his final days. 'They give you that right
at the end,' a woman in the hospital had told Kaya. 'When
there's nothing but the pain.'

But it was the candles that had thrown her, and the
Bible, and the smart blouse and shirt, as if Ursula was
about to conduct some kind of ritual.

'Is everything—' offered Kaya. 'I mean, can I *help* you
with anything?'

'Can *you* help *me*?' Ursula laughed then. 'I'm as good
as dead, Mrs Sterling. Nothing fazes me, including your
threats and your bribes. They mean nothing.'

Kaya bit on her cheek. 'I didn't bribe you.'

'You and I both know that is a lie.'

'Then give me my money,' Kaya spat back. 'Or I'll tell
everyone about the dent in your car. The one Sam made.'

'It would be my word against yours.'

'But they'd investigate, wouldn't they? They'd go to the
garage and find out you'd been there. So why don't you do
your son, and mine, a favour.'

Ursula shakes her head slowly, and Kaya sees her lip
quiver with anger.

'I have completely underestimated you, Mrs Sterling,'
the older woman says. 'I knew you were faking your

interest in the church, but I didn't take you for a criminal. I feel sorry for your son.'

The words had stung and Kaya had seen red. She a criminal, she wasn't dishonest. *She was a mother!* She had taken a single step forward and it was enough to make Ursula stumble back through the bedroom door. Kaya lifted up her hands. She wasn't a violent person, she was a peacekeeper, but this woman had committed an act of violence against Ollie. She had cheated him, denied him, stolen from him – because that money was an investment in him, in his education.

'Are you going to hurt me, Mrs Sterling?' Ursula had smiled then. 'I would advise against it. It wouldn't help your son's cause one bit, would it?'

Don't you mention Ollie, Kaya had thought. *Don't you mention him!*

But the woman wouldn't shut up. 'What kind of a mother are you?' she asked. 'Faking your beliefs and encouraging your son to do the same? He is as bad as you. A liar!'

'Stop!' Kaya had said. 'Please!'

But she didn't. She didn't stop, and so Kaya stopped her speaking.

She'd been on autopilot, in a sort of trance. She hadn't thought about what she was doing. It was as if it was someone else's hands raised up, fingers erect and pushed the woman back onto the neat double bed. As if it was someone else who straddled her small body and forced the tiny woman's mouth open and poured the open bottle of morphine in, who had held tight as Ursula coughed and spluttered and thrashed around until she became resigned to her fate and merely stared up at Kaya with cold eyes and swallowed the bitter liquid – *just a spoonful of sugar*! And then Kaya had put a pillow over her head just like she had done with Paul and the kicking had started up again, just for a few pathetic seconds, until it had stopped for good.

And like she had done with Paul, Kaya remained resolute the whole time, even though she heard herself say, 'I'm sorry, I'm so sorry,' as she carried on. And when it was done, she sat back almost in child's pose, like she would do at the end of a gym class, and she'd told Ursula's lifeless body like she'd told Paul's, 'I did it for Ollie, don't you see? I did it for my boy!' Because he, like Ursula, had wronged their son.

In his dying days, Paul had decided to change his will to offer a lump sum to Sam, his long-lost son, and Kaya could not let that happen. She could not let Ollie be snubbed like that, to have his beloved father give what was rightfully Ollie's to a man he had never met simply because of guilt, simply because he had impregnated someone as a teenager and left her. Nor could she allow Ursula Deacon to brand Ollie a liar. Ollie had chosen a path to God – a path Kaya herself would never choose – and he was no liar, he would never be.

And Kaya told herself, as she sat astride Ursula, that she had merely done what needed to be done, and that in fact it had been the kindest thing for Ursula, as it had been for Paul. That these two human beings – one she had loved beyond measure and one she had not – had both been suffering. Wasn't Kaya's act a selfless one when all was said

and done? Wasn't she merely helping them avoid the inevi-
tability of what was to come? Wasn't she simply being cruel
to be kind?

Afterwards, she had smoothed down the dead woman's
blouse and grey A-line skirt as a sort of apology. She
placed one small hand on top of the other. Tiny, pale
hands with tissue-paper skin that would not have been
able to fight back even if they had tried a little harder.
She picked up Ursula's mobile phone from the bedside
table with a shaking hand and held it in front of Ursula's
face, waiting for the screen to come alive. It did, instan-
taneously, and Kaya clicked on the mailbox icon and
then, once inside, selected 'Compose'. She called the
message *In God's Hands* and wrote it in the way she
thought Ursula would: an explanation, an apology, a
sign-off begging forgiveness from her omnipotent God.
Then she clicked send and felt a rush of something like
adrenalin or relief.

She closed the front door behind her on her way out
and cycled along the School Run as fast as she could, her
heart hammering, back home to Ollie and to the envelope she did not know had been incorrectly delivered by
Michael the postman.

Ollie pulls away from the hug. 'Sorry I'm late, Mum,'
he says as they stand together at the gates of Iggy's, and
Kaya blinks her gaze away from the cottage. He hands
her his schoolbag – it is something he has done since his
kindergarten days, a force of habit. Kaya takes it without
question and slings it over her shoulder. 'Sam facetimed

from London when I was emptying my locker to say "Happy birthday",' he tells her with a wide grin.

'That's good of him.' Kaya smiles.

Ollie often asks Kaya why Sam doesn't just live here, and Kaya explains that people have their reasons for wanting to keep their distance from their homes, for keeping their families at arm's length. It suits her, Sam's absence. It means she does not have to share Ollie with anyone else – blood relatives at least. He is hers and hers entirely, and she will relish it as long as it lasts. She dreads the day he comes and says he is in love because Kaya knows she will not be able to share him, she never has been able to. She can share him with God – she thinks – but not another woman. That would never work.

'How was your first Iggy's birthday?' Kaya asks.

'Great. They gave me the bumps in the playground!'

'That's sweet. I think!' Kaya can't help seeing the image of a banged head and concussion.

Ollie slides his arm round her waist and they walk arm in arm to the edge of the road. Richard sits in his car across the road and he waves at them as they approach.

'Hello, you two,' he says as they get in the car. 'Uber for Kaya?' It's their usual joke.

'Good day at school today Ollie, mate?' asks Richard.

'Yeah, it was awesome.'

'Did they sing you a song and give you a cake?'

'Yep. We baked cupcakes in home economics. They weren't as good as one of Bec's though.'

Kaya smiles, because she knows Bec is bringing a cake in the shape of a labrador, just like Bandit, especially for

Ollie. Somehow she has managed to get herself and Ollie on Bec's special list of birthday freebies and she doesn't intend to move from it. Not now she has put down firm roots in Pacific Pines. They drive along the School Run and around the turn where Sam Deacon – or Ursula, who even knows? – hit Felix Weaver. Richard and Ollie chat about science stuff and Kaya listens contentedly until they reach the centre of town and climb out and head for Ray's Pizzeria.

As Richard and Ollie walk ahead, Kaya observes as her son laughs and falls against Richard. She feels it immediately, a small pang of jealousy towards her boyfriend. *Kaya, stop!* She must have a word with herself about this. She *can* do it, she tells herself. She can bear to share a little of Ollie with Richard, providing it is not too much.

Richard holds the door for them and Ollie and Kaya walk through the restaurant towards the back where old-school jukeboxes and pinball machines line the walls, alive with dancing and tunes and prosperity. That's when the crowded table ahead of them begins to whoop: Estella, Conrad, Jonty, Archie, Felicity, Bec, Tom, Sage and Cooper.

Ollie looks up.

'SURPRISE!' they all shout.

Ollie laughs and dances his way through the chairs, enjoying the high-fives, the hugs, the ruffled hair, and Kaya smiles. He is her boy and hers alone. He is her everything.

When he reaches the end of the table he turns back and searches for her through the crowd.

'Thanks Mum,' he mouths.

Kaya smiles back. 'Of course,' she says.

But what she really means is 'anything'. Because that is what she would do for Ollie: anything. Because that is the strength of a mother's love.

Epilogue

Felix Weaver sits at his desk at home and tries to remember his email password. He tries a few Latin phrases because he's been told that when he first woke up, he spoke almost entirely in the ancient language. Apparently Bec Lloyd spent ages at the house translating it all for his mother.

Felix thinks it's a bit weird that she took such an interest in his recovery, always asking if he remembers anything of Gala Day and the weeks that came before it. He'd much rather Willow came – he remembers her, of course. Sexy Willow! She's gone to university now, his mum says, reading Psychology at UNSW. Stupid cow turned him down, ended up getting it on with the sports master . . . what was his name? Ugh, he can't remember!

There's loads he can't remember, like social media handles and passwords and stuff. If he knew all of his codes, if he knew how to get into his email for example, he could go through his sent items, build up an idea of what he was doing in the days running up to his accident, but he can't, however much he tries. He can't even look at his camera roll because his phone went over the side of the cliff, they said, and he hadn't backed it up in the cloud!

Felix gets up from his desk and goes to the toilet. While he sits and waits for nature, he notices a spider on the top right-hand corner of the bathroom attempting to trap a fly in its web. He watches it for a while, intrigued as the fly escapes and the spider resumes her spinning. He has an urge to trap it, to pull each and every leg off slowly just to see if it does anything when it is just a torso unable to move. He'd like to watch it try to build a home then!

He picks up an ancient copy of the Daily Telegraph *that's stuffed between the toilet bowl and the 1960s blue-tiled wall and turns to the back, to the classifieds. He reads about the hookers looking for fun, looks at the tiny photos of women with plunging necklines holding up mobile phones as if to entice him to call. There is an ad asking for someone who's reliable to mow the lawn at a retirement village. He skims the pages and sees another advertisement that catches his eye. It reads:*

SPERM DONORS WANTED FOR REPUTABLE NSW CLINIC. CALL THE SYDNEY WEST SPERM DONOR CLINIC ON 1800 893997 TODAY AND FIND OUT HOW YOU CAN HELP SOMEONE MAKE A FAMILY!

Felix feels something stir in his brain, a memory of some sort. He hears the doorbell ring downstairs and Bec Lloyd's saccharine voice reverberate along the hall. 'Hello Martha, how are you? You look wonderful. I brought you some flowers. Shall I pop them in a vase?' His mother coos something back. Felix hears a cupboard open and close, a tap running.

'How's Felix doing today?' Bec asks. 'Good?'

'Great,' his mother says. 'I'm pleased to say he is doing very well indeed. Every day he seems to take a step in the right direction. Tea?'

'Yes please.'

Felix looks at the advert in the paper spread across his lap and reads it again. He pictures Bec's smiling face in his mind's eye: the glisten in her eye, the fine lines that concertina as she smiles, the dimple in her right cheek. There is something about this woman and the words 'sperm donor' that are achingly familiar. What is it? He almost has it, almost! It is hovering there at the very tip of his consciousness! But like the fly in the silken web above his head, the thought evades capture and flees to some other distant corner of his brain to tease him another time. Felix stares intently at the spider, furiously weaving her intricate trap.

He will figure it all out eventually.

Este omne tempus in mondo.

He has all the time in the world.

Acknowledgements

The idea for this book came, as many ideas do, from a chat with friends about the high-school selection process. One friend confessed she knew someone who'd baked a giant cake for the admissions team at a boys' school (yes, her boys did get places) and this was what sparked the idea for Bec, Estella and Kaya, and the rigorous vetting procedure at St Ignatius' Boys' Grammar. It's important to point out that Iggy's is a completely fictional school, and certainly not based on one I know of, or have ever been to. That's what made this story so much fun to write. I loved the idea of mothers quite literally competing to the death for their sons and it was a joy to dream up a plotline that incorporated parents behaving badly again.

I owe a massive debt of thanks to Kimberley Atkins for trusting me to run with this story – thank you so much, Kim! *The School Run* is infinitely better with your magic touch. Olivia Robertshaw, thank you for completely 'getting' this book and helping me work it into the best possible shape – I'm so grateful to you for all of your input and suggestions. Amy Batley, I'm so excited for the next adventure.

To the Hachette ANZ team, in particular Louise Stark, Nicky Luckie, Melissa Wilson and Alexa Roberts, thank you so much for everything you do for me here in Australia. I love being part of the Hachette ANZ gang and am forever telling everyone how fantastic you are.

Marina de Pass, you handle everything with such efficiency and a cracking sense of humour – I love being one of your authors and I thoroughly enjoy our cross-hemisphere check-ins and your always-enthusiastic WhatsApp messages. Thank you.

A shout-out to my amazing writing friends, in particular my 'work wife' Vanessa McCausland. Vanessa, I am so grateful for your support and encouragement in all things bookish *and* non-bookish – your friendship means the world to me.

I am incredibly lucky to be part of a gang of Australian writers who support one another at launches and festivals, on social media and coffee dates. There are too many of these brilliant folk to name, but you know who you all are, and you are all wonderful. This camaraderie has become such a valued part of my life. A special shout-out to the Faber gang who were there from the very start.

Books don't get sold without the enthusiasm of booksellers, Bookstagrammers, TikTokers, podcasters and bloggers. To all of the incredibly generous folk who have embraced *The Trivia Night* and *The Running Club* and picked up this book too, please accept my boundless thanks. I am truly grateful for, and always overwhelmed by (in the best possible way), your ongoing support.

Joey, thanks as always for being my best friend as well as my big sister – I love you. Alice Ierace, Fiona Pogson, Debbie Wise, Leonie Lincoln, Jayne Murphy, Pip Prentice, Georgina Blaskey – my best girls – here's to a hat-trick of acknowledgements. Thanks for supporting me always, for embracing the dad-jokes and putting up with my pathetic inability to stay out past nine o'clock at night. Tanya Andrews and Alice Ierace please don't stop the daily British humour/cat memes, they feed my strange inspiration. Heidi Earl, thanks for the airport photos.

The name of Bec's character was offered up as an auction prize at a school fundraiser on Sydney's northern beaches and was bought by Michael Rudnev in memory of his late wife Bec Lloyd. Here's to the memory of beautiful Bec and thank you, Michael, for entrusting me with her name.

Rob, thank you for putting up with me when I'm in the zone and for being my biggest supporter. To Raff, Sav and Bug, who inspired this book and continue to inspire me every single day in multiple ways: I love you. I promise I will never kill someone in the school community or bake an embarrassing cake of any kind to further your education (or will I . . . who knows?). Just know you are everything to me. This book is for you.